THE ENCHANTED MOMENT

CW01336003

Barbara Cartland

Barbara Cartland Ebooks Ltd

This edition © 2024

ISBNs

9781788677653   EPUB

9781788677684   PAPERBACK

Book design by M-Y Books
m-ybooks.co.uk

THE BARBARA CARTLAND ETERNAL COLLECTION

The Barbara Cartland Eternal Collection is the unique opportunity to collect all five hundred of the timeless beautiful romantic novels written by the world's most celebrated and enduring romantic author.

Named the Eternal Collection because Barbara's inspiring stories of pure love, just the same as love itself, the books will be published on the internet at the rate of four titles per month until all five hundred are available.

The Eternal Collection, classic pure romance available worldwide for all time .

THE LATE DAME BARBARA CARTLAND

Barbara Cartland, who sadly died in May 2000 at the grand age of ninety eight, remains one of the world's most famous romantic novelists. With worldwide sales of over one billion, her outstanding 723 books have been translated into thirty six different languages, to be enjoyed by readers of romance globally.

Writing her first book 'Jigsaw' at the age of 21, Barbara became an immediate bestseller. Building upon this initial success, she wrote continuously throughout her life, producing bestsellers for an astonishing 76 years. In addition to Barbara Cartland's legion of fans in the UK and across Europe, her books have always been immensely popular in the USA. In 1976 she achieved the unprecedented feat of having books at numbers 1 & 2 in the prestigious B. Dalton Bookseller bestsellers list.

Although she is often referred to as the 'Queen of Romance', Barbara Cartland also wrote several historical biographies, six autobiographies and numerous theatrical plays as well as books on life, love, health and cookery. Becoming one of Britain's most popular media personalities and dressed in her trademark pink, Barbara spoke on radio and television about social and political issues, as well as making many public appearances.

In 1991 she became a Dame of the Order of the British Empire for her contribution to literature and her work for humanitarian and charitable causes.

Known for her glamour, style, and vitality Barbara Cartland became a legend in her own lifetime. Best remembered for her wonderful romantic novels and loved by millions of readers worldwide, her books remain treasured for their heroic heroes, plucky heroines and traditional values. But above all, it was Barbara Cartland's overriding belief in the positive power of love to help, heal and improve the quality of life for everyone that made her truly unique.

1

The train slowed down at the station. The large man on the seat opposite collected his luggage and with many wheezings and puffings descended from the carriage, slamming the door behind him.

Sally was alone. She jumped up, stretched her arms above her head and eased the stiffness of her legs, then she knelt on the seat and looked at herself in the narrow mirror fixed to the carriage wall.

"I wonder what Lynn will think of me," she asked aloud and then began to reflect how long it was since she had last considered her appearance seriously and critically. There never seemed time for anything at the farm. She would wake at dawn and come running downstairs after a hasty wash to help prepare the breakfasts. After that there was the washing up, the cleaning of the rooms, bed-making and fire-laying to be done, the animals to be seen to, new visitors coaxed or cajoled into coming out into the fresh air, eggs to be collected, luncheon planned, vegetables to be fetched into the house and a thousand and one other small jobs to be begun or finished while all the time she must be cheerful, bright and sympathetic with the guests who made constant and continual demands upon her time and interest.

Aunt Amy had believed that animals and the countryside were the best cure for war-shattered nerves and she had proved herself right not once but hundreds of times since she had opened Mythrodd Farm as a rest home and a shelter for those who had suffered in the war. Always a woman of determination, she had let nothing stand in her way when first the idea had come to her, shortly after the Battle of Britain, and she had bought Mythrodd Farm after a few weeks' search, declaring it perfect for the uses to which she intended to put it.

It lay in lovely, unspoilt country amid the mountains of Wales, about five miles from the sea, and the farm house, large and rambling, had been partly modernised so that there were bathrooms, basins in the bedrooms and an excellent hot-water system, though there was no electricity or gas for lighting. One of Sally's jobs was to trim the old-fashioned oil lamps as the evenings drew in.

Sally had been half afraid that her aunt would send her away to school when her project was first started, but luckily in the village there was a retired teacher with a lifetime of educational experience and Sally learned from her. Her education was also considerably widened by contact with the many and diverse people who came to the farm – women who had been bereaved both of their husbands and of their children, men who, after a bad operation, had nowhere to go but to the overcrowded homes of their sons or daughters, children tragically orphaned or nervous wrecks after their experience of terror raining from the skies.

Aunt Amy had got in touch with various organisations who recommended people as guests, but she never took one without a personal interview with the individual concerned and the final selection lay entirely in her hands. Sally wondered sometimes, when she saw the letters that were written to her aunt, how she was able to refuse many of the more pathetic cases, but Aunt Amy, methodical in all she did, had a certain plan in her selection from which she never deviated. Women were always in the majority but never more than eight at a time, three or four old men to keep one another company and the same number of children, usually boys, who were thrilled by the farm and worked themselves back to health and strength.

But however much the guests helped on the farm or in the house there was always an immense amount to do, and when Sally went to bed, she was often so tired that it was with the greatest difficulty she must force herself to finish undressing before she went to sleep, and when at last her head touched the pillow she had no time to think but was lost immediately in a dreamless slumber from which she would wake in astonishment to find that it was already morning.

No, she had had no time to think about clothes or indeed her personal appearance, save she must look neat and clean or Aunt Amy would be annoyed.

"Your hair is loose, Sally" she would say sharply at times, or "You had better change your blouse before tea and wash that one out when the meal is over."

Sometimes when Sally went down to the village for her lessons she would see other girls of her own age wearing well-cut tweeds or pretty bright-coloured winter coats and so wish Aunt Amy would buy her something of the same sort. But she knew exactly what she would be given year after year – for this winter a plain tweed coat and skirt and a Jaeger overcoat, all in the same nondescript beige colour, and for the summer, a few simple cotton dresses and perhaps a brown cardigan to wear over them which would tone with her jumpers for the winter.

She had not really minded this nondescript uniformity for there had been so much else to think about but now, staring at her own reflection, she was worried. What would Lynn say?

Sally recalled Lynn's lovely and expressive face, the exquisite clothes she always wore, the fragrant perfume that scented the very air in which she moved. The last time she had seen her, Lynn had put her fingers under her chin and turned her face up to her.

"You are pretty, darling," she said, "and one day you will be prettier still. I am glad, terribly glad for you."

Then Lynn laughed, that entrancing silvery laugh that made one want to laugh too and take nothing that she said very seriously.

But Sally's heart had beaten quickly. Was she really pretty? She had never thought so. Now Lynn was pretty – no, beautiful – with her heart-shaped face and dark, mysterious eyes. Sally had looked at her own rounded cheeks, blue eyes and fair hair and felt how banal and ordinary she was. Yet if Lynn said she was pretty, it must be the truth. But that was five years ago. What would Lynn think of her now?

Sally stared and stared in the little mirror and then suddenly she pulled her felt hat from her head and threw it down on the carriage seat. That was what was wrong – the conventional, uninteresting, old-fashioned brown felt hat pulled low over her forehead. Now she could see her hair, pulled back tightly from her forehead and caught in a knot at the base of her neck.

Aunt Amy had disapproved of short hair.

"Why should girls want to copy men?" she had said in a tone of voice that made it clear that she considered men were inferior creatures anyway. And so Sally had never been allowed to have her hair cut short, but she had felt that perhaps it was also because, if Aunt Amy had a vanity of any sort, which was doubtful, it was for her hair. Although dark and uninteresting in colour and turning grey at the temples, it was still long enough at sixty for her to be able to sit on it. When she was in a good mood, Aunt Amy would mention this with pride, though what advantage this was to her, it was difficult to say, as she plaited it in a tight plait and wound it neatly round her head where it constituted itself a self-imposed halo.

More than once, Sally had suggested tentatively that her own hair, which refused obstinately to grow more than an inch below her shoulders, might be cut really short, but Aunt Amy had refused to allow it and insisted that she pin it back into a neat coil.

But now Sally, pulling out the pins, shook her hair free. It fluffed itself out as if, tired of being imprisoned, it welcomed a new freedom. It was naturally wavy and from the outdoor life she had led was bleached almost silver from the sun.

She climbed up on the seat to reach for her suitcase and unlatching it, sought with her hand until she found a comb. Bracing herself against the movement of the train, she parted her hair a little lower on the side and combed it until the electricity in it crackled with the motion of the comb. It certainly looked better, although her intuition told her that Lynn would think it dreadful until it had been cut and shaped.

Of her coat and skirt in the inevitable beige tweed she dared not think, but surely Lynn, knowing Aunt Amy, would expect her to be dressed like a frump?

Sally sighed. What else could she do to improve her appearance? Looking over her shoulder as if she half expected to see someone watching her in disapproval, she opened her bag and drew out a lipstick. It was not a new one, yet she stared at it as if half afraid and then very tentatively she applied a little to her lips. She remembered Mrs. Bronson giving it to her.

She was a portly, good-natured woman whom Aunt Amy had always considered to be one of her mistakes. She had arrived at the farm a shivering, inarticulate bag of nerves, having been in Coventry on the night it was smashed into ruins, but after a fortnight her nerves recovered and she became a garrulous, good-humoured woman who, until her marriage, had lived a genial, companionable existence as the barmaid of a well-known public house. Aunt Amy had disliked her and had been glad to see her go, but she had fascinated Sally. More than once she crept into her room for what Mrs. Benson called a 'cosy pow-wow' and it was on the evening before she left that she said to Sally,

"You won't be so bad-looking, dearie, when you grow up and when you do you take a chance and get away from all this and see life. The old girl won't let you if she can help it. I can see that but don't you tie yourself down to good works. There's plenty of time for them when you are her age. You see a bit of life, and don't forget I told you to. And here, when you go out on your own, stick some of this on your lips and a dab of powder on your nose. Men like a bit of colour, I can tell you. 'Penny Plain and Twopence Coloured', as the saying goes, and there's not one of them as will not go for the 'Twopence Coloured' whether he can afford it or not."

Sally had not liked to refuse her gift of the used lipstick and a half-empty box of face powder. Had she behaved as Aunt Amy would have expected her to do, she knew that as soon as Mrs. Bronson had gone she should have deposited both her presents in the waste-paper basket, but somehow she had felt that one day they might come in useful and so she had hidden them in her room behind some books, where Aunt Amy was most unlikely to find them. They had lain there ever since, although once or twice in a dare-devil mood she had taken them out and experimented with them.

When she left the farm this morning, she had brought them with her and yet now when she had put on the lipstick, she rubbed her lips until it was nearly invisible. She looked at herself in the mirror, remembered Lynn and put on some more. How frightening it all was – this moment of being uprooted from an old life and journeying towards a new one! Here in this railway carriage it was like being in No Man's Land between the past and the future.

She could hardly believe it possible that Aunt Amy was dead. She had died so suddenly and unexpectedly. Why only last week she had been talking of what she meant to do to the farm in five years' time. She had no thought of dying then, nor had Sally any thought of living anywhere else but at Mythrodd. But now Aunt Amy was dead and the farm had been taken over by Miss Mawson.

From the very moment she had come to the farm to help Aunt Amy, Sally had felt that Miss Mawson disliked her. She was an ugly, big-boned woman of forty with a gruff way of speaking and she had suspicious eyes which, seemed ready to believe the worst of everybody with whom she came in contact.

And yet her life had been one of constant service to others. She had been a missionary in Japan, had suffered incredible privations and hardships when the war started and eventually had come home to work in a Dockland Settlement. After four years of attending to the bombed-out and homeless, a threatened nervous breakdown had brought her into Aunt Amy's life and, having come to the farm as a guest, she stayed on as an assistant,

Sally had not liked her from the very first because more than once, she fancied that Miss Mawson had gone out of her way to be unpleasant to her. But she had paid no particular attention to this, thinking it was in reality, just her manner. She was used to encountering all kinds of nerves and neurasthenia, which made people disagreeable without any real reason. But when Aunt Amy had said to her one evening, "Sally, I have asked Miss Mawson to stay on as an assistant here," she had quite involuntarily let out a little cry of protest,

"Oh, no, surely not. Aunt Amy."

"No?" Aunt Amy queried. "Don't you like her?"

Sally, thus challenged, had felt that she was being unjust and unkind.

"I don't dislike her," she said, "it is just that she seems difficult – a rather prickly sort of person – and – aren't we happy as we are?"

For a moment Aunt Amy's face had softened.

"I am glad you are happy, child, but I am getting on in years. I was sixty on my last birthday and lately I've found some of our guests rather a strain. We are doing good work, Sally, really good work, and there are so many people who want to come here. I would like to build a new wing and perhaps we shall be able to now that the war is over. But this was never meant to be only a temporary war relief home, I want it to be a permanent rest home. There are always people who will need building back to health both in mind and body. I want this farm to go on even after I am dead, Sally, and that is why I have asked Miss Mawson, who is a comparatively young woman, to stay here and help me."

"I understand," Sally said, "and of course, if you feel she will fit in, Aunt Amy."

"She is a fine woman," Aunt Amy said, "and she has great principles and unswerving integrity. That is all I should ask of my successor."

Sally had said no more, but it seemed to her that from the moment that she had a definite position in the house. Miss Mawson did her best to oust her from her former place in Aunt Amy's affections. No longer was she consulted as to where people should be put or what was to be planned for them, or about all the innumerable little things that go into running a home of that sort.

It was Miss Mawson who was consulted. Miss Mawson who discussed matters with Aunt Amy, Miss Mawson who took instructions but, far from finding her work lighter, Sally found it getting heavier. There were now two people calling after her.

"Sally, cut some cabbages for lunch."

"Sally, there's no wood for the fire."

"Sally, tell the cook I want to speak to her."

"Sally, light the lamps, it's getting dark."

She seemed to be on her feet from morning to night. More than once she suspected that Miss Mawson chose her for all the more unattractive tasks and then she rebuked herself for being uncharitable because she did not like the woman. But after Aunt Amy's death Sally learnt that her suspicions had not been unjustified.

Sally had loved her aunt, who had in fact acted as father, mother and guardian to her ever since she was a baby and though she was a severe, strict and undemonstrative woman she had been so much part of Sally's life that she could hardly imagine an existence without her. She had died after only three days' illness and the shock of it left Sally bewildered and uncertain, wondering pathetically to whom she was to turn.

It was after the will had been read and both Sally and Miss Mawson learned that everything Aunt Amy possessed had been left in trust to carry on the work of the farm, that Miss Mawson struck. When the lawyer had gone, saying that he would be round in the morning to confer with Miss Mawson as to how much could be advanced for their work, until probate was approved, Miss Mawson said to Sally,

"You will, of course, be finding yourself other accommodation as soon as possible."

Sally stared at her. Her eyes, dark-ringed from weeping, were wide with astonishment.

"Other accommodation," she repeated stupidly. "Do you want me to go?"

"Yes, of course," Miss Mawson replied, "I prefer to remain here in entire charge and there is nothing you do that could not easily be taken on by one of the other maids."

Sally gasped and felt the blood rise to her, face at the insult, then she said quietly,

"You think my aunt meant me to leave the place that she and I built up together?"

Miss Mawson's lips twisted in an unpleasant, smile.

"I think you flatter yourself," she said, "you are only eighteen and most of the time you have been here, I understand you were having lessons."

"All the same I have worked hard," Sally said and then could have bitten back the words as soon as she said them.

Why should she justify herself to this woman? Why indeed should she explain that Aunt Amy had made that will soon after the farm was started? She had told Sally all about it, adding,

"I am making a will just in case we get bombed, even here, I might be killed, who knows? but supposing that happened I still want the farm to go on," and then she had added, "I have made no provision for you, dear, because you are already provided for under your father's will, He wanted you to live with me until you married or until you were twenty-five. That is a long way off and when you get to that age, we can talk about it again."

"Oh, don't talk of dying," Sally cried with a child's instinctive horror of death.

Aunt Amy smiled.

"There is no reason to think about it yet, Sally. But it is a difficult world at this moment with wars and pestilence all around and we must always be prepared for death, even in the midst of life."

"Yes, but…" Sally had started, to be interrupted by her aunt. "There are no buts dear. If I die – and I expect I shall some day – I wish the farm to continue with its good work. You will know how I want it run and I daresay, like all things once started, you would manage very well without me."

"You know that is not true," Sally protested.

Her aunt had smiled at the conviction in the girl's tone, but there was nothing in writing to say that Aunt Amy had wanted her to continue at Mythrodd, there was only the money left in hands of executors, whom Sally had never seen and of whom she knew nothing.

Some deep-set pride within her told her that she should not plead for what might well have been her own inheritance.

"Very well, Miss Mawson," she said quietly, "I will leave as soon as possible."

She had gone from the room very quietly, feeling in some way that she gained not only a victory over Miss Mawson, but over herself. And yet now she was afraid, afraid of all she had left behind, afraid too, because there had come no word from Lynn in response to her letter. She had expected a telegram – for telegrams were like Lynn, quick, impulsive and there almost before you were expecting them – but while she would have liked to wait until she heard, Sally, having said that she would leave, would not go back on her word.

She packed all her belongings, her books and more personal possessions and took them down in the farm cart to the Vicarage to ask the old Vicar, whom she had known for many years, to store them for her.

"Can't you leave them at the farm, child?" he asked, vaguely sensing there was something wrong.

"I would rather not, and they will be no trouble to you in your old attic."

"No, of course not," he said, "I will be glad to help you, but if there were anything wrong, you would tell me, wouldn't you?"

"There is nothing wrong – but I am going away to stay with friends," she had added, lying because she felt that he would be hurt unless she gave him some acceptable explanation.

His anxiety had been soothed, as she had known it would be.

"With friends! That is all right then – but you will be coming back?"

"I expect so," Sally answered, lying once again, because he was old and incapable of helping her and there was no point in leaving him worried as he would be if he knew the truth about her departure.

But that morning, as she turned away from the farm and took her last look at Miss Mawson, standing in a proprietary attitude in the doorway, she knew that she would never come back. Mythrodd was no longer her home. She was alone, alone in the world except for Lynn – and Lynn had not answered her letter.

Standing there in the railway carriage Sally thought that being alone was the most terrifying experience she had ever encountered in her life. Better be persecuted by Miss Mawson than be alone without the least conception of what the future held in store for her.

For a moment her lips, newly painted with the lipstick, trembled and there were tears in her eyes. Then suddenly she rubbed her mouth almost savagely with the handkerchief and turned away from the mirror. What was the point of trying to alter herself? She would go to Lynn just as she was. She could only pray that Lynn was in London. How awful it would be if she was away and that was the reason she had not replied to her letter!

Sally opened her bag. She had very little money left, for her ticket had been expensive. There were only two pounds in notes and about six shillings in silver. She wondered how much it would cost her to stay at an hotel.

At this juncture in her thoughts the train drew up with a jerk. The afternoon sun was sinking and the sky was red. They were right out in the countryside and there was no sign of a station. Sally wondered why they had stopped and got up to open the window so that she could look out, but at that moment the door into the corridor was pulled open and the ticket collector put his head into the carriage.

"You for London, miss?"

"Yes, London!" Sally answered.

"That's all right. But I'm 'fraid we shall be very late in."

"Shall we?" Sally exclaimed. "Why?"

"Floods on the line, miss. There's a bridge damaged ahead and the line's shifted. They've had a cloudburst or something in this part of the country. There's a repair gang at work and we hope they won't be long, but it will be some hours, at any rate, before we get through and there's no alternative route. The restaurant car is on in front so you'll be able to get a meal."

"I am glad to hear that, Sally said, "but how awful about the line."

"Oh, it often happens nowadays," the collector replied. "Can't help thinking, myself that the atomic bomb has got something to do with the strange behaviour of the weather. Never know what to expect from one day to the other. Well, they've had a deluge down here all right. We are going to pull into a little wayside station in a few seconds and you'll be able to stretch your legs and look around you."

"That will be nice," Sally said, "and thank you for telling me."

"Didn't want you to worry," he said cheerily and shut the door.

When he had gone, Sally jumped up and opened the window. Yes, she could see now that the country round about was flooded, some of the lower fields being completely under water. She was used to great torrents of rain in Wales when the tiny streams down the mountainsides would become cascades, lovely to look at but terrifying to the sheep and lambs who would often be caught in them and drowned,

She wondered if these floods in the broader, less isolated country were responsible for many deaths. She hated to see animals hurt or even cold and bedraggled by the storms.

They would be late into London. She supposed there would be no chance that Lynn might come to meet her and yet she had sent her that telegram before she left. She wished now that she had not done so. Perhaps Lynn would be worried. Then Sally smiled. No, Lynn would not be worried. Lynn worried about very few things and how ridiculous it was to think that she would meet her! She might send Mary. Darling Mary Studd, who was never flustered and never put out about anything. No, it would be all right and she would explain when she got there.

The train stopped and Sally, looking out, saw that they had drawn, into a very small and attractive station. There were just a couple of waiting rooms and the Station Master's office, but somebody had been enterprising enough to plant beds of flowers all along the platform, and though now many of the flowers had drooping heads and broken stems, evidence of the recent rains, they were still bright with colour.

Passengers were alighting, one by one, looking about them, staring up the line, talking loudly and concernedly about the delay.

"The damage is half a mile further on," Sally heard one person remark and then as she opened the door of her carriage and got out, she took a deep breath of the warm and sweet-scented country air and felt that delays did not matter when the calm and the peace of the countryside was all around her.

She stood looking out to where in the far distance she could still see the mountains of Wales, purple against the vivid gold and crimson of the sunset. They looked lovely and remote, and once again she had the feeling of being suspended between yesterday and tomorrow.

Suddenly she felt something cold against her leg and looking down she saw it was the nose of a friendly spaniel. Sally bent down and patted it. It was a nice-looking dog, with the spaniel's inevitable trusting brown eyes and the wistful expression of one that is always anxious to please.

"Are you bored with travelling too?" Sally asked him, feeling that the dog was as thrilled to be in the fresh, clear air, as she was. The spaniel wagged his tail and then a voice called him.

"Bracken! Come on, old boy."

She looked up and saw further down the platform a man, standing with another, who also had a dog with him. His was a big retriever, which he held on a lead. The spaniel gave Sally a last affectionate lick and then turned to obey his master.

Sally watched him go. The man spoke to the dog again and, though Sally could not hear what he said, she had a full view of his face. It was a thin, sunburnt face, good-looking in a clear-cut, rather sharp manner. Deep lines running from his nose to his mouth gave a somewhat cynical twist to his lips. The man turned away and yet Sally had the idea that she had seen him before. Where or how she had no notion, but the idea persisted.

The two men and their dogs walked down the platform and disappeared from view until Sally saw them a few minutes later, wending their way down a road towards a small village half-hidden by the turn of the road. She had a sudden urge to go to the village herself and then she thought it might look strange if she followed the men and their dogs so, after walking up and down the platform for some time, she went back to her carriage.

She must have been there for nearly half an hour thinking, letting her thoughts run backwards and forwards over the events of the past few days in anticipation of what lay ahead of her, when she looked up and saw the two men pass the window. She had another glimpse of the spaniel's master and once again she had that strange sense of having seen him before.

He had taken off his hat and his head was silhouetted against the sky which had already changed from crimson to the translucent blue of dusk. Sally suddenly thought of him as a knight in armour with a sword and with a plumed helmet.

'Is that what he looks like?' Sally asked herself, 'a Knight of olden times?'

But there was no reply to her imaginings.

Drawn by some impulse she could not fathom, she leaned out of the window and watched the two men go down the platform. She saw them reach their carriage and one of them get in. The master of the spaniel was left standing on the platform.

Once again Sally found herself thinking of armour and a Knight resplendent with a plumed helmet. It was only an impression. She could not quite grasp the thought itself and make it tangible – and yet it was there.

Then she saw that the two men were taking out their luggage. There were suitcases, four of them, a heap of overcoats or mackintoshes and several long brown cases, which obviously contained fishing rods. They had been fishing in Wales, Sally thought to herself and wondered what they had caught.

A porter came hurrying up with a barrow, loaded on the suitcases and threw the coats over them.

"I will carry the rods," Sally heard one man say and then they came walking down the platform, the dogs at their masters' heels.

"We're certain to get there sooner," Sally heard one man say and then the other replied,

"I doubt it, but it is better than hanging about here anyway."

With the porter leading the way they disappeared down the platform.

'They are going by car', Sally thought to herself and as she watched them disappear, she had a sudden sense of loss.

It grew darker. She thought of the two men driving on in the darkness as she sat in the immobile train, waiting, waiting, waiting.

Presently the dining car attendant came along to say that there would be a meal served immediately and a second service later. He, too, seemed friendly.

"Better get along for the first service, miss. There's none too much food to go round. We were not expecting a crowd."

"Thank you," Sally said, as she held out her hand for the ticket. "I think it is wonderful the way you manage."

"We do our best," the man said, "and no one can ask more, can they?"

"They can't," Sally agreed, but his eyes twinkled at her.

"Oh, but they will! You listen to them," he said and with that he departed to the next carriage.

When Sally went along to dinner, she found he was right.

"I call it perfectly disgraceful that delays like this can happen on a main line," one woman was saying in tired, well-bred tones which, however, carried from one end of the dining-car to the other. "And besides being put out in this manner there seems to be nothing one can really eat on the menu."

Sally, luckily, was not so particular and after enjoying a plain but wholesome and well-cooked meal, she went back to her carriage. She sat staring out into the darkness, watching the distant hills deepen from purple to sable and then vanish into the night sky. Soon she could see only her own reflection in the carriage window and her thoughts turned to Mythrodd.

At last, when from the sound of impatient and querulous voices everyone had become utterly tired of the delay, the guard came hurrying down the platform to tell the passengers to take their seats.

"Is it all right now?" a woman asked him.

"I hope so, ma'am."

"So do I," the woman retorted tartly as she got into a first-class carriage.

Then, with a jerk of the carriages, slowly, very slowly they started to move. Down the line at the bridge the breakdown gang were standing sweating and crimson-faced in the light of the flares as they slowly passed them. There were cheers from some of the passengers and the men waved back, conscious of having done a good job in record time.

There was almost an audible sigh of relief as the train moved on slowly and without mishap over the new track, then the engine gathered speed and they were on their way again to London.

Sally looked at her watch and found that by this time it was eleven o'clock and after enquiring where they were she worked out that it was unlikely that they would be in London until about five o'clock in the morning.

She decided that she had better make herself as comfortable as she could in the carriage, lying full length on the seat and covering herself with her overcoat. She did not expect to sleep much as hen thoughts were too busy, but habit was strong. Almost at once she was asleep, wakening only once as they drew into a station but falling asleep again as soon as the train went on its way.

She was properly awakened by her friend, the guard, opening the door and saying,

"We'll be pulling in, miss, in five minutes."

Sally sat up with a jerk.

"In five minutes!" she exclaimed. "How marvellous! What is the time?"

"Two minutes off quarter to five and you look as if you've had a good night."

"I have," Sally answered.

She jumped from the seat, pulled down her creased skirt and looked at her untidy hair in the mirror. Almost instinctively she started to gather it back from her face into the way she had always worn it and then she remembered, letting it loose again and combing it as neatly as she could. She took up her coat, decided not to wear her hat, and pulled down her suitcase from the rack.

Five o'clock! What a time to arrive! Would anyone be likely to expect her?

The dark sky was beginning to grow pale, the last evening star was disappearing into oblivion, then they seemed to be shrouded in darkness once more as the train drew into the station There were few porters about so Sally took up her own suitcase and stepped out on to the platform.

People, unwashed, dishevelled and very cross, were collecting their luggage from the van. There seemed to be very few taxis and Sally quickly came to the conclusion that it would be unlikely that she would get one.

"I had better put my suitcase in the left-luggage office," she thought, "and come back for it later."

She went to the office, where a sleepy attendant gave her a ticket, and then she turned back towards the platform. As she walked across the station she noticed that another train had just come in and that men were unloading great crates of fruit and vegetables. Vans were waiting to receive them, and one of them bore the name *Gregor & Sons, Covent Garden*. Sally decided that, having arrived in London so early, she would go to see the one friend she knew she had in London. Daringly, because she was shy, she walked up to the driver of the van.

"Excuse me," she said, "are you going to Covent Garden?"

"When I'm loaded."

"I suppose," Sally said hesitatingly, "you would not be very kind and give me a lift there? You see, I have only just got off the train and there are no taxis. I particularly want to see someone who is working there."

"Well, it's against rules and regulations, but I don't suppose anyone is going to worry about them at this time of morning. Hop in."

Sally did as she was told and climbed into the front seat. A moment later one of the men who was loading at the back came along and said,

"O.K., Bert." He saw Sally, grinned and asked, "Where d'you find the lady friend?"

"She found me," the driver replied. "Hop in, we're off."

They set off at a good pace through the empty streets.

"It is kind of you," Sally said, "but I never expected to arrive at this hour, so I don't think that the people I am going to will be expecting me so early."

"Most folks are tucked up nice and comfy until the earth has warmed up a bit," the driver answered. "Can't say I blame them, though it isn't so bad this morning. But you should try it in the winter. Coo, it's cold then and is it a job to start this 'ere bus I'll tell you it is."

He looked at Sally curiously as if he was unable to place her.

"Who's your friend at the Garden?" he asked.

"It's a boy called Tommy Mathews," Sally said,

"Expecting you?"

Sally shook her head.

"No, he will be surprised to see me, but I have got a message for him from his mother who made me promise that if ever I got a chance I would go and see him in London. This seems to be the chance, thanks to you."

"Know who he works for?"

"Yes, I think the name is Fraser," Sally answered.

"Oh, old Joe's place. I can show you where that is. It's not far from where we unloads ourselves."

It was not long before they were running into Covent Garden. Already fruit and boxes of vegetables were being unloaded and arranged ready for the buyers. There was, bustling to and fro and a merry sound of whistling as the men unloaded their vans and there were cheerful shouts of one to another as they greeted friends whom they had not seen since the morning before.

"Well, here we are," the driver said, drawing up before a great warehouse, "and you'll find your friend straight down there and the first turning on the left. Don't miss it. It's the first turning, mind, and I thinks I'm right in saying it's the second warehouse."

"Thank you so much," Sally said.

She did not think of tipping him. Instead, she held out her hand and he shook it warmly.

"It's been a pleasure," the driver said, "and here's luck."

"The same to you," Sally smiled and set off to look for Tommy Mathews.

Tommy had come to the farm four years ago after his leg had been broken by a doodle-bug bomb. He had loved every moment of his time there and two months ago he had written pleading that his mother, who had had a severe abdominal operation, might be allowed to come to the farm to convalesce. Aunt Amy agreed, and Mrs. Mathews had proved as nice as her son.

Sally had been half afraid that she might not recognise Tommy, but there he was, looking just the same, only a little bigger. His blue eyes were still alight with mischief, and his nose powdered more thickly than ever with brown freckles.

Being intent on his work he did not see her until she was standing right beside him.

"Tommy," she said.

He looked up at her and let out a whoop of surprise.

"Miss Sally! Well, you could knock me down. I wasn't expecting to see you, not half I wasn't."

"I was not expecting to come," Sally said. "Tommy, it's good to see you and how well you are looking!"

"I'm fine, miss, never felt better in my life. And how's mother?"

"She is getting on splendidly. She asked me to tell you that she hoped she would be coming back to you in another fortnight but you were to let her know where you were staying, as in your last letter you said that you were uncomfortable and were thinking of leaving your lodgings."

Yes, I've moved," Tom said. "Funnily enough I was not certain until two days ago where I was going to. I'll write tonight, I promise you, miss."

"You know she worries about you."

"I know she does, but I can look after myself, miss."

"And her, too, from what I hear,"

"That's right! But what are you doing in London, Miss Sally?"

"My aunt, Miss St. Vincent, is dead, Tom."

"Oh, miss, I'm sorry to hear that. It must have been a bit of a shock."

"It was."

"And what about the farm, miss?"

"Oh, that will go oh just the same and your mother is to stay until she is quite well, but I think she's longing to be back with you."

"I bet it's 'cause she wants to see what I'm after," Tommy said. "Doesn't trust me out of her sight since that trouble with the doodle."

"She misses you very much," Sally said softly and she felt suddenly envious of Tommy with his broad grin and his crop of red hair.

"And I'll be that glad to see her again. If you're writing, miss, tell Mum she's not to worry about me. I'm in comfort now, real comfort, "cause my aunt has taken me in."

"Oh, I am glad," Sally said.

"Ran across her quite unexpected like. Mum hasn't seen her for ages, they dropped out of touch with each other during the war, but she's been as kind as kind. Mum herself couldn't do more. Tell her that when you're writing and tell her not to worry about me."

"Yes, Tommy, I will, but don't you think you had better give me your address just in case you forget to write?"

"Not trusting me far, are you? Right-oh, then, just in case. If Mum hears it twice she'll know it's O.K." He put his hand into his pocket. "Here's a pencil, miss."

"Oh, thank you. Now what is it?" Sally asked.

"C/O Mrs. Bird, 263, Hill Street, London, W.l. That's a posh address, isn't it! Tell Mum, too, that it's her sister Ellen."

"Ellen Bird!" Sally repeated and then stared at Tommy. "It couldn't be – could there be two? Was your aunt ever a child's nurse?"

"Yes, miss, I believe she was before she married. Funny enough, now I think of it, when I was telling her where Mum was, she said she once knew some St. Vincents. Worked with them, she did, only it was down in Devonshire."

"But it's Nanny – my own Nanny Bird! Oh, Tommy, what a coincidence! I must see her! Will you tell her that I am in London? She looked after me for years, in fact until she married."

"Well, miss, fancy that. Isn't the world strange!"

"Oh, I'm so delighted at the idea of seeing Nanny again. Is she usually in or does she go out to work?"

"No, you'll find her at home right enough, she and her husband are caretakers at some flats, and she'll be right glad to see you. Why don't you pop along there now, miss, and see her? You could have a bite of breakfast."

"Oh, but it is too early," Sally interrupted.

"Not on your life it ain't. Aunt Ellen was up at four o'clock giving me mine and I know she doesn't go back to bed again. You get along there, Miss Sally, and tell Aunt Ellen I sent you."

"Thank you, I will."

"It's been fine seeing you, miss, but I must be getting busy or the boss'll be after me."

"Goodbye then, Tommy, and thank you. I think I shall take your advice and go and see Nanny Bird right away."

"That'll be okeydoke, miss, you see if it ain't."

Tommy shook Sally by the hand and added,

"If you're taking a taxi, Miss Sally, I should go down the Strand, there's always a chance of nabbing one there around Charing Cross."

He pointed the way. Sally walked along the street and sure enough she saw an empty taxi coming from the station. She hailed it and got in. It was still only a few minutes after a quarter past five, and she thought that the idea of going to breakfast with Nanny Bird was an inspiration, as it would enable her to pass the time before she dared ring the front-door bell of Lynn's house.

It was not long before they reached Hill Street. The street was empty and the windows of the tall houses shuttered or shrouded with drawn blinds at this early hour, seemed to look down disapprovingly, so much so that Sally paid off the taxi and thanked the driver in a low voice, feeling quite guilty that they should disturb the silence.

With a sense of relief she remembered that Berkeley Square was just next door and she could easily walk to Lynn's house when she left Nanny. Then she looked up at the house to which she had just come. It was an imposing mansion of red brick with wide, white marble steps. Sally was about to mount the steps when she remembered that Tommy had said that Nanny Bird was caretaking, so changing her mind she pulled open the basement gate and went carefully down the iron steps. There was an electric bell on the door and she was half startled by the noise it made in response to her touch. There was a few seconds' wait and then she heard some footsteps approaching.

The door opened slowly and there in the doorway stood a short, plump woman with greying hair. She and Sally stared at each other, then Sally spoke first.

"Nanny, don't you remember me?"

Mrs, Bird gave a cry.

"If it isn't Miss Sally! Oh, my dearie, what a surprise! I couldn't believe my eyes. I thought I must be dreaming for the moment. 'That's my baby', something told me, but I thought as I must be imagining things. Come in dearie. But what are you doing, here? You're the last person I expected to see in a month of Sundays."

Still talking, she drew Sally into the house, shut the door and led her down a stone-floored passage into the rather dark living room where, however, Sally recognised many of Nanny's personal things. There were the two cushions embroidered with steel beads that had always been her most treasured possessions, there was the little padded velvet box ornamented, with seashells and the china pig labelled, 'A present from Brighton', with which Sally had been allowed to play as a treat on special occasions, and then on the mantelpiece was a photograph of herself as a baby and by the armchair the big wicker work-basket, that had stood at Nanny's elbow as long as she could remember.

Impulsively Sally put her arms around Nanny, kissed her and gave her a hug.

"Oh, Nanny, it is good to see you."

Nanny wiped her eyes.

"There, child, I'm that excited at seeing you I don't know where to put myself. How you've grown and what a pretty girl you've turned out to be! But first of all tell me why you're here and how you found me."

"It's a long story," Sally said and started to tell of Aunt Amy's death and how she had started for London but there had been a breakdown on the line, how she had gone to Covent, Garden to give Tommy a message from his mother and from him had learned where he was staying and where Nanny lived.

"Well, if that doesn't beat everything," Nanny said, "I always said the world was a small place."

"That's what Tommy said."

"And fancy my sister being with you and Miss Amy. I never dreamt that you had gone to Wales."

"We moved at the beginning of the war, in 1940. My father died you know." Sally explained.

"I heard as how the poor gentleman was dead. I meant to write, but I was having such trouble myself at the time. We were bombed out of our little house in Stepney and I went North to my sister-in-law in Yorkshire. Couldn't get on with her, I couldn't, and there wasn't any work for my man, so back we came again. Then we were bombed again, not badly, but the roof was blown off and so we moved to Surrey. Just temporary like, sharing a house with some other people whom I couldn't abide. As soon as the war ended, back we both came. We've had several caretakers' jobs – it is the one way of getting a house – and we only moved to this place recently. A nice place it is too. I did write you once, at Christmas, but I got no answer."

"I expect it got lost in the post," Sally said, "and, Nanny, I ought to have written to you, but somehow we never had a moment at the farm. You have heard all about it from Tommy, I expect?"

"Yes, dear, and what a wonderful place it must be. Fancy Miss Amy thinking of anything as fine as that to help people. I wish I had known about it. I could have done with a week or two there myself."

"Oh, I wish you had come, Nanny, it would have been lovely. But I shan't go back there again, Nanny, now that Aunt Amy is dead,"

"No, dear, I can understand that and you'll miss her too, I'll be bound, after all blood is thicker than water any day."

At the kindly words Sally's eyes filled with tears. She seemed to have been through so much that the kindness, coming quite unexpectedly, was almost more than she could bear. Nanny's attitude turned at once from sympathy to command.

"Now, sit you down, dearie, you're tired and stupid creature that I am, to keep you talking without even a cup of tea to cheer you up, I expect you could do with one and a nice piece of bacon."

"Oh, but I feel it is too early…" Sally began, but Nanny interrupted her.

"Too early! That's a joke, I've been up since four o'clock with that Tommy of mine. It's no trouble either. I never was much of a sleeper, you know, too used to listening for a child to cry out. Not that Tommy, young limb that he is, would thank me for calling him a child. Thinks himself a man now, he does."

Sally laughed, even though her laugh was slightly shaky. Nanny bustled to the door, but Sally got up to follow her,

"I am coming to eat in the kitchen, Nanny. I am used to eating in kitchens and I much prefer them."

"Well, come along, my dearie."

~27~

Talking all the time, Nanny prepared tea, hot toast and a slice of bacon with some fried bread.

"Now, eat it all up," she said and Sally heard that tone echoing down the ages and wondered if she ought to say her Grace, just as she had done in the nursery.

"And who have you come to stay with in London?" Nanny asked.

"Some – some friends, Nanny."

"And where do they live?"

"In Berkeley Square," Sally answered.

"That's nice and convenient," Nanny said with satisfaction. "You are just round the corner, so when you have nothing to do, you can drop in and see me. What are you going to do with yourself now – get a job?"

"I don't know," Sally answered. "I don't know, Nanny. It has all happened so quickly. Aunt Amy's death, coming here…"

"Now, don't you worry and if you want me, here I am, my dear,"

"Oh, Nanny, it's wonderful of you to say that."

"You are looking a bit peaked," Nanny said critically, "but I expect it is all you have been through this past week."

Sally smiled.

"You are longing to feed me up. Don't I remember of old how much you enjoyed looking after me when I was ill and wanted picking up?"

"Nonsense, get along with you," Nanny said, but Sally could see that she was not annoyed.

"Tell me about yourself," Sally said. "You say you like being here?"

"Well, it's a cosy little place as basements go," Nanny said. "The people who own this house have turned it into three flats – and very nice and convenient they are. There's two gentlemen, one has the ground-floor flat and the other the top-floor flat. They are brothers. Then there's a married couple as has the first and second floor. A lovely maisonette they have made of it, too. He's something – oh, I never can remember what – at the Italian Embassy. But they are in Italy just now and won't be back for two months. So, I only have my two gentlemen to look after. When they are here, I do for them. They only have breakfast and go out for the other meals."

"It sounds perfect and I expect you mother them all just like you used to mother me."

Nanny's eyes twinkled.

"They need it sometimes," she said, "not that the elder brother isn't a perfect gentleman, but the other – he's a wild lad. Yet one can't help liking them. He's got a way with him too, I can promise you."

At that moment the door opened and an elderly man, wearing shirt and trousers, came into the kitchen. Nanny went towards him.

"Oh, here you are, Fred. I thought it was about time you were getting up. We've got a visitor. This is Miss Sally St. Vincent, whom you remember I looked after when she was a baby. It's often I've talked about her and to show that's no lie there's her picture on the mantelpiece as large as life."

"How do you do?" Sally said, getting up and holding out her hand. "I hope you don't mind my coming in to see Nanny at this early hour of the morning."

"No, miss, pleased to see you, I'm sure," Mr. Bird murmured in a hoarse voice.

All the same Sally could see that he was uncomfortable. He put his hand up to his neck as if conscious of his collarless state. He hitched up his trousers and looked at his wife as if for guidance. Sally got to her feet.

"I think I will be running along now. I will be around to see you again, Nanny, as soon as I'm settled, you can be sure of that."

Nanny made no attempt to stop her going and Sally guessed that she too sensed that Mr. Bird was embarrassed at having visitors to breakfast.

"Well, goodbye, Nanny," Sally said, moving towards the back door.

"Now, wait a minute," Nanny said, "this way."

"Don't I go through that door?"

"Indeed you do not," Mrs. Bird replied firmly. "You go out through the front door. Whoever heard of such a thing as a St. Vincent using the basement!

"Oh, Nanny, these ideas went out with the war."

"Not with me they didn't," Nanny said stoutly. "Now just run up these stairs. I won't come with you, if you don't mind, but you'll find the street door just in front of you. Mr. Bird will be waiting for his breakfast."

"Yes, of course, Nanny. Goodbye, darling, and thank you so very, very much for the breakfast."

Sally waved her hand and ran upstairs. She went through a small doorway into a large marble hall with an imposing-looking stairway wending its way upwards. Part of the hall had however been partitioned off, and there was a smart-looking door with a silver knocker in the centre of the new wall – obviously the entrance to a flat.

She walked towards the street door through the glazed glass of which, the early sun was shining. She put her hand on the latch and as she did so, she was aware that someone was standing outside. She pulled the door towards her and found herself facing a man who was in the very act of inserting a latchkey into the yale lock. Behind him a chauffeur was lifting a suitcase out of a car and, beside him, looking up at her and wagging his tail in welcome, was a golden spaniel.

Involuntarily Sally let out a surprised, "Oh!" as she recognised the man who had been on the train. It was the man with the spaniel. He stood aside to let her pass. As she did so, she looked up at him and because she recognised him again, she smiled up into his face. But there was no response. He looked at her coldly, almost with contempt it seemed to her – her smile died on her lips and she turned away in embarrassment. As she ran down the steps he turned with an almost imperceptible shrug of his shoulders and walked into the hall.

Sally walked down Hill Street towards Berkeley Square. There was sunshine everywhere – the pale golden sunshine of the early morning, but she felt suddenly cold and utterly alone.

Would Lynn be pleased to see her?

2

Lynn stared at her reflection in-the carved and gilt mirror. She was very lovely. Her tiny oval face was beautiful in its contour, her grey-green eyes held shadowed secrets and the curves of her red lips were inviting. She narrowed her eyes, remembering that a critic had said that when she did so, she was 'desire personified'.

"Thirty-eight next month," she said out loud, "and I swear that no-one but you could guess it."

"Of course not," her companion answered quietly with a hint of amusement in her voice. "I can't think why you don't forget it yourself, Lynn. You will give yourself wrinkles if you worry so much."

Lynn Lystell turned from the dressing table and swung herself round to face her secretary.

"I don't know which is the more irritating – worrying or having you tell me not to."

Mary Studd laughed. She was a pleasant-faced woman with no pretensions to beauty, but she had a quiet charm of her own and she was at her very best when she smiled.

"You don't look a day over twenty-five, Lynn dear," she said. "That is what you want me to say, isn't it And though that may not be exactly true, I will tell you something that is. You are far more attractive now than you have been at any time in your whole career. There, I really, am telling you the truth – so listen attentively."

"Listen! Of course I am listening," Lynn retorted. "It is the sort of thing I like to hear. Go on, Mary."

Mary shut her shorthand notebook with a snap.

"There is nothing more to say," she said. "Besides you have heard it so often from millions of people. You are a lovely woman Lynn, and if I were you, I should forget my age."

"How can I, when you are always with me?" Lynn asked, almost pettishly.

"Well, I am in actual, fact two years older than you," Mary said, "and I have always looked it. Do you remember when we first met and I thought you were seventeen?"

"Don't remind me of our first meeting at that awful audition," Lynn pleaded. "How frightened I was."

"Yet how sweet you looked," Mary said reflectively, "but you have grown lovelier year by year. Personally, I would not change you now for what you were at twenty-five, nor for that matter would your *public*."

She said the last two words with a faint accent of mockery, but Lynn obviously took them seriously.

"My public," she repeated, "they frighten me, Mary, for the first time in my life."

"Nonsense!" Mary said briskly.

"It is not nonsense!" Lynn, insisted. "They may mind my marrying a South American."

"Well…"

Mary paused for a moment after the word and gave an almost imperceptible shrug of her shoulders. She continued,

"To be honest, that is a question I have asked myself. But Erico da Silva is a rather exceptional South American. You might almost say that he is an international figure. Besides, he is an extremely glamorous person, with his Racehorses, his private jet-propelled aeroplane, the success of his polo team, all those things have given him a popularity in England that will make it easier for them to accept him as your husband."

"I hope so," Lynn said, "but I've had so much publicity lately as England's foremost actress that I feel as if the Union Jack were branded on my chest."

"We are all very proud of you."

There was a hint of mockery in Mary's voice.

"Oh, don't let us talk about it," Lynn exclaimed. "It is done now! The announcements will be out in two days' time and pray Heaven no nosy reporter finds out my real age."

"It is very unlikely," Mary said, "we have managed to keep it dark all these years. The last guess the press made was – let me see, I have got it filed away somewhere."

"Thirty-two!" Lynn said tersely, "and that, I may remind you, is exactly Erico's age."

"How very suitable."

"Very!" Lynn replied drily, but it was obvious that she still worried as she rose from the dressing table and walked across the soft hyacinth-blue carpet to the window. Pulling aside the heavy peach silk curtains, she stood looking out into Berkeley Square.

It was typical of Lynn that she should have a house in Berkeley Square, and typical of her too, was the long grey and silver Rolls Royce which stood outside the front door. Lynn Lystell was not only glamorous but she had all the trappings of glamour. One of the great theatrical producers had recently described her as the only actress on the English stage who had that quality. It was hard to explain what it was, and yet it was so undeniably there – in her merest gesture, in the manner in which she entered a room, in her deeply-fringed eyes and the way in which her clothes clung to her lithe figure.

People who wished to be nasty said that Lynn had taken lessons in the very art of seduction, and it might have been true, for every word she uttered and every movement she made were perfectly timed and were infected with that same indefinable allurement that is called 'glamour' for want of a better word.

However banal the line, however bad the plot in the play in which she was acting, Lynn managed to infuse it with something magnetic – a personal charm that reacted immediately on the box-office receipts and ensured that every evening a 'House Full' board should be propped outside the theatre where she was playing.

Mary Stubbs had been with Lynn for nearly fifteen years, in fact from the beginning of her stage career. She and she alone was Lynn's confidante, and she combined the role of secretary, friend, adviser and nanny to Lynn, guiding and protecting her as though she were a child, and a very beloved child at that.

Sometimes, when she was not too intent on considering herself, Lynn would wonder what she would do without Mary, but the question always went unanswered, for she could not imagine life without her. It was by no means an easy post, for Mary not only had to manage Lynn's personal affairs, and keep at bay her more importunate admirers, she had also to try to guide Lynn herself. Child-like in many ways and impulsive, Lynn could easily be swept off her feet, could get herself into situations from which it took all Mary's brains and ingenuity to extract her.

Yet her career had been meteoric. She had broken all the rules, confounded all the prophets who have averred for generations that an actor or actress must be a trouper before achieving success on the West End stage.

Lynn had been far older than anyone imagined when she first appeared in a theatre, but somehow that strange quality of hers, though by no means so developed as it was now, had from the very first moment of her appearance before an audience reached out over the footlights and gripped their hearts, carrying her swiftly to success.

It had not been easy, of course. She had had to work hard, she had to study each of those tiny but important gestures that now occurred so naturally and which were so much a part of the Lynn Lystell tradition. She had relearned to walk, to talk, to carry her head, to enter and leave a room, to sit on a chair and to rise from it – nothing that had been natural in ordinary life was right for the stage. And yet in doing these things some individuality of her own gave them a unique quality – a difference from other people that was obvious from the very first, even before she became the mature and finished product that was to make her a national figure.

Lynn Lystell! There were few people now who had not heard of her, few who had not seen her name in glaring lights outside a theatre or seen her on the screen.

She had been terrified of failing on the films but she need not have worried – and it seemed that nothing except the hand of old age could impede her progress.

"I wish I did not have to go to South America," Lynn said from the window.

Mary sighed.

"It is only for six months," she said, "and it was fixed before you got engaged. What is more, you certainly won't be having a quiet honeymoon. Let me see. You play in six tours and you have innumerable personal appearances to make, besides attending a formidable number of banquet receptions and I don't know what else which me to be given in your honour."

"Yes, yes, know, I have read all about it," Lynn said, 'An Ambassadress from England', they have called me. Will they feel that I am as English as all that when I produce a South American husband? Erico says he is a hero out there but, of course, I have got to take his word for it."

Mary sighed more deeply.

"Oh, Lynn, we have gone over this so often. You know that you want to marry Erico – in fact you insist on marrying him – so why worry? Everything else will sort itself out when the time comes."

Lynn's expression lightened. She smiled and made an exquisite gesture with her hands as though she threw away her troubles.

"I love Erico and he loves me," she said softly, "I have never, never loved anybody else like this before and he can give me so much."

"Then don't worry," Mary said.

"I won't. As you say, our plans are made and I promise you that I won't go over them once again."

She looked at the diamond watch on her wrist.

"I had better get ready. It is after half past six and I am going to that cocktail party at Lady Marling's."

"Yes, I know," Mary said, "and Mr. Thorne is waiting for you downstairs."

"Dear Tony! He said he would take me," Lynn said, "and I have got to break the news to him of my engagement. I cannot let him wake up and see it in the headlines, can I?"

"No, of course not," Mary agreed. "Do you want your hat? Shall I ring for Rose?"

She had already stretched out her finger towards the rose-quartz bell by Lynn's bed, when there came a knock at the door.

"Come in," Mary said.

The door opened and a small plump woman with greying hair stood in the doorway.

"Oh, Rose, I was just going to ring for you," Mary said.

"Madam wants her hat for the cocktail party."

"I will get it," Rose replied. "There is a telegram for you, Madam."

She walked across the room to Lynn with the telegram on a silver salver.

"I wonder who it is from," Lynn exclaimed, "I hope Erico has not been delayed in Paris. His aeroplane is due here at 9.30 and I was looking forward to seeing him."

"Worrying again," Mary teased. "Here, give it to me if you are frightened to open it yourself."

"Of course I am not frightened," Lynn answered. "It is just that I've had a presentiment all day – or is it a hangover from last night? We were late."

"Probably a hangover," Mary said unimaginatively. "Here, give me the telegram."

She took it from Lynn's hands and opened it, then as she read she looked startled.

"What is it?" Lynn asked.

"I don't understand," Mary answered, "but perhaps you will. It says,

Arriving 9.30 this evening. Hope that all right. Had expected to hear from you. Sally.

"Sally!" Lynn exclaimed.

She snatched the telegram from Mary's hands and read it herself.

"Arriving tonight. But, Mary, what does this mean? Why is she coming here? But it is impossible! *She cannot!*"

"Why had she hoped to hear from you?" Mary asked. "Have you had a letter from her lately?"

"No, not for ages," Lynn answered. Then she put her hand up to her face. "Oh, Mary, I believe there was one a few days ago and I have never read it."

"Where is it?" Mary asked.

"Now let me think," Lynn said. "I saw the writing on the envelope and knew it was from Sally. I meant to read it, I did really, and then I had an engagement – or something – I thought I would open it when I got back but I forgot – it must be lying on my desk."

"I have always said," Mary remarked with a sigh, "that it would be better if I read all your letters."

"And I am beginning to think you are right," Lynn said humbly.

"I will go and get it," Mary replied, and she hurried from the room. Lynn heard her running downstairs.

She stood staring at the telegram. Rose's voice recalled her thoughts.

"I thought you would wear the hat with the ospreys, Madam."

"What for?" Lynn asked absentmindedly. "Oh, for the cocktail party. Of course, Rose, and the sable tie."

"Very good, Madam."

Moving quietly and efficiently, Rose took the things from the cupboards and laid them on a small chair covered in peach brocade ready for Lynn to put on.

"Is there anything else, Madam?"

Lynn shook her head.

"No. But Rose, I will wear my new white and silver dress tonight with the diamond necklace."

"Very good, Madam, but you did tell me this morning."

"Oh, did I? I am getting so forgetful."

"That is true enough," Mary said from the doorway, "because here is the letter, unopened and lying in the blotter on your desk."

"Oh, dear," Lynn sighed.

"It is marked 'Private', you see," Mary said, "and you have always said I was never to open any letter marked 'Private'."

"Yes, yes, I know," Lynn exclaimed. "I am not saying it is your fault, silly. I ought never to have told Sally to put 'Private' on her letters, but she has done so for years."

"Yes, years," Mary said. "Let me see, she must be nearly nineteen now."

Lynn looked at Mary, and the same thought was in both their minds although they did not speak it aloud. Then without a further word Lynn opened the letter.

It was written on cheap paper in large, clear handwriting. There were two pages of it and Lynn read them straight through without comment until she came to the end. Then with a gesture that was more theatrical than any she used on the stage she handed the letter to Mary and sat down in the chair.

"I knew from the moment I got up this morning that something was wrong. I told you I had a presentiment. Well, it couldn't be worse. Aunt Amy has died, the funeral is over and Sally, having nowhere else to go, is coming home to … her mother. It couldn't be worse, or could it?"

Mary did not answer for a moment, as she was reading the letter for herself. Then when she had finished, she automatically folded the pages tidily together.

"This letter came six days ago," she said accusingly.

"Yes, darling, I know, and I did not open it," Lynn said testily. "It is no use saying I ought to have. As the telegram tells us, Sally is on her way here and is arriving at 9.30. We can't stop her.

"No, we can't stop her." Mary said, "and even if it were possible I don't see that you could do so."

"Why ever not? Lynn asked.

"Surely this letter explains it. She has nowhere else to go. She has lived with her aunt all these years and now that Miss St. Vincent is dead Sally has no home. After all, the girl is only eighteen."

"Only eighteen!" Lynn exclaimed. "Isn't that old enough to look after herself? Oh, Mary, what on earth am I to do? How can I produce a grown-up daughter at this moment? Heavens, why was I ever fool enough to have a child?"

"It is rather late for regrets of that sort," Mary said drily, "and in the meantime Sally will be arriving."

Lynn got to her feet.

"You must take her away. Suppose Erico finds out who she is!"

"Wait a minute," Mary said and walked across the room to shut the door, which she had left open when she returned with the letter.

"Now listen, Lynn, you have got to think this over sensibly. I agree with you that it is quite impossible for you at this moment to produce a daughter of eighteen, but you have got to be careful. You can't just leave Sally lying about the place as if she were an unwanted parcel. If you just palm her off anywhere, who is she to say she is? As far as we know, she has never told anyone she is your daughter, but we have got to make sure that she doesn't do so in the future."

"Old Amy has kept it quiet enough all these years,"

"Yes, I know because she was ashamed of you. But Sally has never been ashamed of you. She is proud of you and she loves you, and if I know anything of human nature she will want to proclaim your relationship from the roof-tops."

"Well then, if she loves me, she must keep her mouth shut. I will send her to Brighton, Paris, anywhere – it does not matter."

"It isn't exactly a question of location, is it? A girl of eighteen cannot go to Paris unchaperoned."

"Yes, yes, I see that," Lynn said frantically. "But what can I do?"

"Well, at least it can't be done in three hours, which is all the time you have got at the moment. You have got to see Sally and you have got to be nice to her. You have got to persuade her to keep the truth a secret."

"Why, *why* did Aunt Amy have to die now?"

"She died of pneumonia."

"I don't care what she actually died of," Lynn replied sharply. "She always disliked me and I always hated her. If it had not been for her interference, my first marriage might have been a success."

"Oh, Lynn, that is not the story you have told me before," Mary said.

"Well, she made things as beastly as she could," Lynn replied. "I was very nearly in love with Arthur, and he loved me – when he could remember that I was there. But I could not compete with the lure of medieval architecture or whatever it was he was writing a book on at the time and what with Amy nagging at me, and the boredom of that ghastly house in Devonshire, was it surprising that I ran away?"

Lynn spoke defiantly as if she were defending once again that impulsive action that made her throw overboard security and respectability and elope with the suave but very unreliable financier who held her affections for less than three years. And yet, however difficult things had been, she had never really regretted the decision, which had taken her to London and brought her into contact with all sorts of very different people, eventually propelling her into a stage career.

Even so, it was extraordinary that after all those years and after she had met so many other people, Amy could remain so vividly in her mind and appear much more real than the majority of the people she had known since. She could see her now – flat-bosomed and disapproving, and yet she had been an intelligent woman, a woman with strong interests and an undeniable personality.

Lynn had hated her because from their very first acquaintance. Amy had so obviously disapproved of her. Deeply religious, Miss St. Vincent based her judgment of other people on a kind of religious clairvoyance, which seemed invariably to seek out the weak spot in those she scrutinised and judged. Lynn felt that every weak and foolish thing she had ever done was written on her face for her sister-in-law to see. She felt, too, that Amy could see deep into her heart and know that the love she had for

Arthur St. Vincent was a very childish, unstable affection born principally from an anxiety to escape from her own home where she was unhappy.

Once Amy had said scathingly to Lynn,

"You don't know what love means!"

Lynn had been all the more furious because she felt that this older woman did have more conception of real love than she herself could conjure up with her youthful desire.

Arthur, interested only in his research into medieval times, in the books that he wrote laboriously and without pecuniary advantage, should never have married, but he had been swept off his feet by Lynn's beauty, by the encouragement she gave him and by the intoxicating joy of feeling her mouth beneath his and her soft young body pressed against him.

Only Lynn knew how much of the courting she had done. Arthur was too bemused and astonished to grasp the fact that this child, who was hardly out of the schoolroom, had sought him out and deliberately enticed him into proposing to her. Ignorant where women were concerned, he did not realise that it was not by chance when he met her so often as he went for his long solitary walks over the countryside, that it was not by chance when Lynn's hand, young and eager, touched his as though accidentally. It was not without intention, either, that she asked to borrow books from him and would listen wide-eyed and with parted lips to the stories he could tell her of medieval times.

He was an extraordinarily good-looking man, but he had been brought up to have an unusual modesty. His mother had died when he was a child and his only sister, older than himself, had very strait-laced ideas about vanity.

He did not tell Amy that he was going to marry Lynn until the engagement ring was actually on her finger and then Amy realised that it was too late for anything she could say to alter his decision. Lynn had suffered for this but looking back now she was honest enough to admit that Amy had had a certain amount of justification for disliking her.

Marriage had been a new experience, an excitement and an escape from home. She had not wanted it to mean anything else and she had not been interested in Arthur's house. It seemed to her only a bigger edition of her own home where she had been unhappy. She had thought that a wedding ring would bring her freedom from stupid restrictions, would mean being able to go to parties when asked, buying lots of clothes and having a man so much in her power that she could make him unhappy by a frown, or bring him happiness by a smile.

Lynn had not wanted a husband but, as it were, toys and dolls to play with in a new nursery, and it had taken her less than a year to find that she had only exchanged one authority for another and that having a baby was quite a serious business. She had not wanted Sally. She had believed, not without reason, that she was far too young to have a baby and she had been angry with Arthur but still angrier with her own ignorance.

She had hated the months when she must go carefully and could not rush about the place like a streak of lightning or race her horses over the parkland. She loathed the suggestions that Amy made that she should sew and knit for the child that was to come and she even grudged the money that must be expended on the nurseries, feeling that she might have had it to spend on herself and her own ornamentation.

Yet when Sally was born, she was quick to realise that here was an instrument in her hand that she could wield with a quite considerable power. She had taken an almost savage delight in ignoring Amy's suggestion that the child should be given a family name. The St. Vincents had always been called Charlotte or Melloney. For six generations the eldest daughter had borne one of those names, and for four generations the second one had been called Amy.

There were names, too, for the eldest son, the second son and even the third son, but Lynn would have none of them. It was pure perversity which made her choose the most commonplace name she could think of at the moment and stick to her choice determinedly.

"She shall be called Sally."

"Sally Charlotte, then," Amy said desperately, feeling that she was fighting a losing battle.

"Sally! Just plain Sally!" Lynn repeated and because Arthur was still in love with her and grateful beyond all words that she had not died in childbirth, as he had feared for one long sleepless night, he agreed and for the first time the eldest daughter of a St. Vincent ignored tradition.

How trivial it all seemed now and yet at the time it had mattered so tremendously! Then gradually Lynn had begun to realise there was nothing else to fight about. Arthur had resumed his researching into medieval history. He had taken up once more the pen which he had temporarily laid aside when he had gone over to her father's house for dinner and seen her sitting opposite him, so young, fresh and lovely in the black velvet dinner frock that had been her mother's but which had been cut down for her when she was old enough to go down to dinner.

Lynn had been sensible and honest enough with herself to realise that she was just an episode in Arthur's life. He did not live in the present, he lived in the past, and though she might have been able to fight another woman for his affections, she could not fight the lure and the thrill of the forgotten days of bygone centuries.

She had looked round for something with which to amuse herself and found, it. Amy had not realised at first what was happening. She was too busy making arrangements for the baby to be looked after, running the house and doing all the things in the village that Lynn found too incredibly boring to give them even a thought.

"Don't you understand," Amy had said once, "that the more important one is, the more are one's responsibilities to other people. It is your duty as Mrs. St. Vincent and a member of our family to look after those who live on our estate, to lead and guide those who, in poorer circumstances than ourselves, live in our immediate environment."

Lynn had not argued. She had learned that much the best way to circumvent Amy was to agree and then do nothing about it. She had smiled that bewilderingly lovely smile, which Amy thought was false, but which, later on, millions of people were to acclaim.

"You are quite right, Amy," she said seriously, "and I know that you are actually asking me to go and visit old Mrs. Hunter. But I cannot, really I cannot. She smells, and besides I loathe people who are ill."

She had run out of the room before Amy had time to answer and she had heard her running down to the stables whistling for the dogs.

It was useless to try to alter her. Amy realised that, but she knew her duty and she went on trying. Every corrective word, however, every sentence of well-meant advice widened the gulf between them until the two women hated each other with a bitter, deadly hatred.

It was not long before Lynn discovered that riding was not only enjoyable and an escape from home – it also had more practical uses. A horse could carry her quite easily, for instance, to the nearest town, which was only four miles away. She could not only shop but she could also put up her horse at the old coaching inn and spend an amusing time in the bar having a cocktail and making the acquaintance of the people who habitually frequented the place.

Most of them were well-to-do farmers whom she had not met in all the years she had lived in the neighbourhood because they were not considered 'county'. But one day a car broke down and a stranger stopped for luncheon while it was being repaired. In this way Leslie Hampton met Lynn. It was one of those quick, passionate affairs that happen like a summer storm and are over just as swiftly.

It was impossible for Lynn, reckless, bored and hungry for experience, to resist something so infinitely exciting. Years later she used to laugh when she thought of Leslie Hampton, and at the same time she would be slightly ashamed of herself because she had not realised that he was not only a bounder, but also a bombastic, self-opinionated man who cared for nobody but himself.

Like Arthur he had been infatuated with Lynn, too infatuated to count the cost of anything save the desire to possess her and they had run away in the most traditional manner. Lynn even put a note for Arthur on her dressing table and left beside it the small pieces of jewellery that he had given her since their marriage.

How funny and childish it seemed now! And yet she could still recall the quick beating of her heart, the feeling almost of suffocation, the fear of being discovered, which had spurred her to walk quicker and quicker as site hurried down the drive at midnight, carrying two suitcases and leaving behind her both her husband and her child.

Leslie's kisses, fierce and demanding, had seemed then to be the answer to everything. Leslie's arms round her, his hands touching her, his mouth against her neck – could she ask more of life?

How quickly the ecstasy faded! No sooner, it seemed to her, had the divorce gone through and they were married, than they parted and Lynn was searching once again for something more exciting, more thrilling and more satisfying. Of her marriage with Leslie Hampton there was nothing left, only a few rather misty, besmirched memories that seldom raised their heads. He had been killed in the war and she had been almost glad, instead of sorry, when the news of his death came to her because now she could behave – even to herself – as if that marriage had never been.

Of her marriage to Arthur there remained Sally. Arthur had never been unkind or disagreeable about her seeing the child. It would indeed have been foreign to his nature to have been really unkind to anyone and whenever Lynn wrote to him saying she would like to see her daughter, Sally had been brought by her aunt to London to spend the day or night, whichever was more convenient, alone with Lynn.

Sally as a baby had not particularly interested Lynn, but as a small child she had found her rather attractive and when she was a little older it had been amusing to hear the news of Arthur and Amy and of all the people in Devonshire whom she had known ever since she was a child. Sally learned to regale her with gossip, delighted because her mother smiled and laughed at the stories she told her. She was eager to do anything that would amuse and entertain this lovely creature who flashed into her small life like a bountiful fairy but disappeared as quickly, leaving behind only memories of loveliness and expensive presents that made Aunt Amy purse her lips in disapproval.

Later Sally went to school, but she spent all her holidays with her father and her aunt, until unexpectedly Arthur died. He also was a war casualty, but not in the same way as Leslie. Leslie had been killed in action, but Arthur, getting wet one Sunday on a Home Guard parade, had caught a very bad chill. Amy was away at the time or he would not have been allowed to ignore it. He went on taking his duty guards, working at his book and struggling to keep the garden in fairly good trim because all the gardeners had been called up and he considered it part of his war work.

By the time Amy returned he had collapsed with a really bad attack of pneumonia and despite everything that his sister and the local doctor could do, he died the following Sunday. Sally wrote and told her mother, but Lynn was not particularly interested save that his death raised several personal problems.

Sally was one of them. The house had to be sold – Arthur had left that in his will. That was the first thing that surprised Lynn, for somehow she had never imagined that he would want a stranger to possess the place that had been part of the St Vincent family for so long. But Arthur at his death had proved more practical and indeed more astonishing than she had ever anticipated.

Firstly, the house was to be sold, secondly, half of his fortune was to be Amy's for her lifetime, the other half was to be in trust for Sally until she married. Not one penny was she to be allowed to anticipate until then. Sally, if unmarried, was to live with Amy until she was twenty-five.

Lynn's first reaction to reading Arthur's will was surprise and secondly anger.

"He does not trust me," she stormed at Mary. "He thinks I will be a bad influence on my child and far worse, he thinks I might steal my daughter's money. Can you imagine anything so degrading? Of course it is Amy who has put him up to it, but that Arthur should stoop to make such a despicable will really hurts me."

Mary had said something consoling, but in reality she was not surprised. She knew that both Arthur and Amy were suspicious of how Lynn lived so luxuriously, although she was by now firmly established on the stage. She knew too, that from the very moment that Lynn had left Arthur they had been shocked by the expensive presents she had given Sally while making no effort whatsoever to contribute towards her upkeep. Never once had Lynn given her child useful presents or offered to pay for her clothes or education – instead she had sent her expensively dressed dolls, pearl bracelets, aquamarine and diamond pendants, little evening bags set with brilliants for which she could have no possible use and mechanical toys that cost a fortune but which were not really the type of thing to appeal to a girl. It was unlikely, Mary thought, that they would be impressed by Lynn's expensive presents or think, when they saw them, that she would be the right sort of person to bring up and educate a child.

As the years went on, Lynn earned more and more money, but she was incapable of saving, and in fact the more she earned, the more she owed. Clothes had always fascinated her, the orchids and jewels she wore were not always contributed by adoring young men and the big cars in which she drove about with their uniformed chauffeurs, her flats and houses, which must always be in the most fashionable part of London – all cost an enormous amount of money every year,

In her own way Lynn was generous and those who worked with her on the stage knew they could always rely on her to give them a cheque if they were down and out. Charities, where a donation was rewarded with publicity, were never turned away empty-handed. But in consequence as the years passed Lynn's bank balance grew more erratic instead of more stable.

That Lynn had decided to marry for the third time was, as Mary knew, an economic as well as an emotional necessity. It was easy for Lynn to talk of sending Sally to Paris or elsewhere with a chaperone, but money would have to be found for these flights of fancy if they were to become facts and Lynn was at the moment, heavily in debt and being pressed by her creditors.

"Will Sally have any money of her own?" Mary asked.

"You remember the will," Lynn retorted sharply.

"Yes, of course," Mary said, annoyed with herself , for not having recalled it sooner. "And Sally is not yet married therefore… "

"Therefore, to put it bluntly," Lynn said, "unless Amy has left her money, she won't have a single penny until the day she marries."

"I am sure Miss St. Vincent…" Mary began.

"You need not be sure of anything where Amy is concerned," Lynn interrupted. "She hates me, and if she wanted to be spiteful she would think that Sally would have plenty when she marries and so she would give her nothing now. Besides, you know what these old maids are with their good works. That rest home, or whatever it was she was running in Wales, will get the lot, you see if I am not right."

Somehow, Mary thought, that was more than likely.

Lynn knew little about the farm except from Sally's letters. Sally wrote regularly to her mother, invariably once a month a letter came from her, but usually Mary answered them. After having reminded Lynn countless times without results that she ought to reply to Sally, it seemed easier to write the letter herself, sending Lynn's love and apologies for being too busy to put pen to paper.

Mary, staring at Sally's letter with its round, almost childish writing, thought suddenly that neither of them had for a very long time worried about Sally as a person.

"Do you know how long it is since you have seen Sally?" she asked.

"Oh, not very long," Lynn answered, and then she looked at Mary and an expression of surprise came into her eyes. "Mary, it's years – yes, years! She was a pretty child, rather plump but definitely pretty because I remember thinking…"

Mary interrupted her.

"The last time you saw Sally was over five years ago!"

"It can't be!" Lynn exclaimed. "Oh, Mary! Is it as long as that? I suppose she will have altered."

"She will have grown five years older," Mary said and almost instinctively Lynn turned towards the dressing table.

"Don't torture me, Mary."

"I am sorry, "Mary said, "I am as worried as you are. We have got to do something."

"One thing," Lynn said, "there has obviously been nothing in the papers about Amy's death. That is one blessing. We should have seen it if there, had been. But still there is no reason why it could ever be connected with me. I have never mentioned to anyone that I was a St. Vincent. When I went on the stage, as you know, I pretended I was seventeen. I conveniently forgot my two marriages and no-one, as far as I know, has discovered about them. My family were too annoyed with me to contradict the stories I told of stepping straight from the schoolroom to fame, their only consolation being that I had changed my name. We have got to stick to my story, Mary, whatever happens."

"Yes, of course," Mary said, "don't worry. When Sally arrives, I will see her and then we will make some sort of plan. As you say perhaps she will go to Paris – or…"

"If Amy has not left her any money, it is not going to be easy," Lynn said.

"I have been thinking of that," Mary replied.

"Well, she is eighteen," Lynn said, "it is time she got married. Perhaps she will have found somebody."

Then she shrugged her shoulders.

"But there is not much chance of that, not with Amy about. She always hated anything to do with youth or love. She would make quite certain that Sally would never meet an eligible man. But the best thing that can possibly happen is for the child to get married and quickly. When she marries, she will come into two thousand a year or more, for the money Arthur left will have accumulated by now."

"Poor Sally," Mary said quietly, "she may not want to be pushed into marriage with the first man who comes along."

"Who is pushing her?" Lynn said. "You will see, the girl will fall in love! She is my daughter, isn't she?"

She smiled at Mary suddenly, who, in spite of all her worries, smiled back.

"Yes she is your daughter," Mary said, "but she will never be as pretty as you."

"She will be pretty enough if I remember rightly," Lynn said. "What we have got to do is to make her meet the right people. After all, a girl with two thousand a year is not to be sneezed at."

The little clock on the mantelpiece suddenly struck the hour.

"Goodness," Lynn said, "it is seven o'clock! I shall be frightfully late for the cocktail party. Give me my hat at once, Mary, I must go."

"Yes, you must – and poor Mr. Thorne has been waiting over half an hour."

"Oh, Tony won't mind waiting," Lynn said and then suddenly she gave an exclamation. "Tony Thorne!"

She put her hand down suddenly on the dressing table and knocked her gold hand-glass against the array of scent bottles, which made them jingle.

"Tony!" she repeated. "There, Mary, is the answer to all our problems."

"What do you mean?" Mary asked.

"Leave it to me," Lynn said. "I have thought of something absolutely perfect."

She took up her hat and put it on her head, the ospreys dark against the pale loveliness of her skin. Then she hung her sables round her neck and picking up a great bunch of mauve orchids from her dressing-table pinned them on her shoulder.

"What do you mean?" Mary repeated. "Tell me."

Lynn turned from the dressing table. Her eyes were sparkling and she was shilling.

"Don't worry, Mary darling! I have got it all settled in my own mind. There is nothing to worry about."

With that she swept from the room, leaving Mary staring after her, the fragrance of her perfume heavy on the air. Mary heard her run down the stairs and then her voice, soft and sweet, yet with that intrinsic carrying quality of the theatre, calling,

"Tony! Tony, I want you.!"

3

"A little to the left, *s'il vous plaît, Mademoiselle?*"

Sally did as she was told and stifled a yawn. She had often felt tired at the farm, but she had never imagined it. was possible to feel tired from being fitted for beautiful clothes, yet she found standing hour after hour was very tiring.

She was thrilled to have the clothes and she told herself that she was being very ungrateful indeed to her wonderful Lynn in not feeling more excited and more elated about the things that were being made for her. Nevertheless, she knew that deep in her heart she found fitting clothes a bore. It was fun to choose them and even more fun to wear them when they were finally ready, and it was the most, thrilling thing she had ever known to hear Lynn exclaim with delight at her appearance.

Never, never, would she forget the humiliation of the morning of her arrival when she had gone into Lynn's bedroom and heard her say,

"Sally! How pretty you have grown!" and then add in tones of horror, "But, my goodness, where *did* you get those clothes?"

She had known Lynn would dislike her appearance, but she had not been prepared for the scathing remarks and the laughter that her suit evoked.

"Did you ever see such a thing, Mary?" Lynn asked. "Look at the colour and the awful, way the coat is out of proportion to the skirt. Oh, poor, poor Sally! It is so typical of Amy, isn't it? Why do good people always have to make everything about them so monstrously ugly?"

It seemed to Sally that Lynn would never stop criticising her clothes and begin to pay some attention to her personally. But Lynn, sitting up in bed, was soon absorbing every detail.

"You have got lovely eyes, Sally. They are the same blue as your father's. And those eyelashes! When they are darkened, they will shatter the heart of every young man with whom you come in contact. And your hair is a good colour. Of course, it wants trimming and shaping. Thank goodness you don't wear it pinned back. I was half-afraid Amy would persuade you to drag it off your face as if you were a washerwoman. She always affected that style herself."

Sally coloured a little, but she said nothing and after a moment Lynn nodded to herself as if with satisfaction.

"We will make something of you, Sally, don't worry, and it will give me the most intense satisfaction to burn that garment you are wearing with my own hands."

"But not before I have got something else to wear," Sally protested.

Lynn laughed.

"No, darling, I will find you something. My clothes would be much too small for you, but Mary, like the good angel she always is, will no doubt lend you something of hers."

"Yes, of course," Mary said. "We are about the same size, aren't we, Sally? And it isn't so big, Lynn, I will have you know. You talk as though we were giantesses. The truth is you are much too tiny – or should we say a pocket Venus?"

Sally looked envious of the way Mary was able to tease Lynn, for though she adored her she felt that she was in the presence of a Goddess and would never dare to be so familiar with this lovely, fascinating, unexpected mother of hers.

"And now, darling," Lynn said, "I have got to have a long talk with you. We have got to plan your future. You must listen to me very attentively because I have a lot of things to tell you. Sally sat herself down at the side of the bed.

"Oh, Lynn," she exclaimed, "it is so wonderful to see you again!"

"Darling! You always were the sweetest child."

"Please, Lynn," Sally went on, "please can we be together for a little while? You see, I have seen so little of you and I do hope you will let me live with you now that Aunt Amy is dead."

"Well, darling…" Lynn began, and then Mary almost brusquely, because she felt she could not bear to see the dawning disappointment on the child's face, interrupted.

"You don't want me, Lynn, do you? I have got a lot to do." Lynn raised her eyebrows a little at Mary's tone before she said,

"Of course, if you don't want to stop."

"You have only got to touch the bell if you want me," Mary said and she went from the room.

Lynn set herself more comfortably against her lace pillows. Her bed-head of pale blue satin ornamented with gilt carving was, Sally thought, the perfect setting for her exquisite beauty. The bedspread of antique lace lined with peach satin to match the curtains was littered with Lynn's morning post. On it there were newspapers, piles of letters, tickets, magazines and a pink leather box lying open, which contained a big wide bracelet of glittering diamonds and huge pigeon-egg rubies. It glittered and gleamed so insistently, that almost against her will, Sally found herself staring at it.

Lynn bent forward and picked tip the bracelet.

"It is a present," she said, and her voice almost purred with pleasure. "An engagement present, Sally, and that is one of the things I want to tell you about."

"An engagement present?" Sally faltered.

Lynn nodded.

"Yes darling, I am going to be married."

"Oh, Lynn."

Sally could not keep the disappointment out of her voice and Lynn, looking at her, exclaimed.

"Oh, darling, it is annoying, isn't it, just when you, have come to stay with me? But how was I to know that Aunt Amy was going to die. She might have lived for ages and you know that your father had arranged that you were to stay with her until you married."

"Are you going to be married soon?" Sally asked in a rather small voice.

"Yes, darling, I am afraid I am. Because I have got to go on a tour in South America and the man I am going to marry, Erico da Silva – you will love him, he is such a charming person – is a South American, so obviously it will be perfect for him to come out with me and not only introduce me to the right people but see that I don't make mistakes over all the customs and conventions which are always strange in a new country."

Lynn looked down at the bracelet she held in her hand, then she put it against her wrist and smiled a little half smile to herself as if she thought of the great happiness that was in store for her.

"There is a ring to match this," she said after a moment. "Erico is bringing it for me this afternoon. He gave it to me last night, but it was a little too big for my finger. It is the most wonderful ruby you have ever seen, Sally. It must have cost a king's ransom."

"How nice…" Sally began, and then almost as though she words burst from her, she asked, "Oh, Lynn, what about me?"

"You! Oh, darling, of course I have thought of you. I have planned everything, but I don't want to tell you too much yet because it is just to be my secret. What I want you to do is to enjoy yourself while we are together. That will be fun, won't it?"

"Oh, yes, of course," Sally said enthusiastically, her eyes shining.

"We will see lots of each other," Lynn went on, "and I want you to meet Erico, but, Sally there is something I must make quite clear first, it is about our relationship. You see, darling," she went on quickly, as if she were half afraid that Sally would say something, "no one knows that I have ever been married before. Your Aunt Amy was so ashamed of me that she made me promise years ago that no one should ever know that I was your mother. When you used to come and see me, if you remember, Amy used to bring you to London so that even the servants at home had no idea that I was still in existence. I often felt that Amy must have told them I had died after I had run away, except that I cannot imagine her telling a lie."

Sally smiled.

"I think she inferred it indirectly, but after we left Devon, of course, there was no one to ask about you."

"I suppose that is why she went and buried you in the wilds of Wales. Oh, well, perhaps it was all for the best, darling, because, you see, it would have done me no good if people knew that I had been married and had a big grown-up daughter. When I went on the stage, I took a new name and because I looked very young and inexperienced people thought I was much younger that I was. As I wanted to forget all those miserable unhappy years, I didn't contradict them. You don't blame me for it, do you, darling?"

"No, of course not," Sally said.

"So there we are, darling, you see why I cannot possibly produce a grown-up daughter now. It would be too surprising, and everyone has thought I was wedded to my art, as indeed I have been,"

"Well, what are we to say?" Sally asked, and it seemed to her that in her throat there was a little hard lump which she had difficulty in swallowing.

"I have thought it over very carefully," Lynn said, "and you know, Sally, we don't want to lie any more than we need. I hate lying, and I am sure you must have been brought up to hate it too. I shall just say that you are the daughter of Arthur St. Vincent, an old friend of mine who was very kind to me and who, unfortunately, died during the war. You see all that is the truth. And as you don't look the slightest bit like me, no-one need ever suspect that there is any closer relationship between us."

Lynn smiled triumphantly and Sally made a great effort to smile back. She did not know that it was Mary who had said, 'If you are going to tell a lie, make it as near the truth as possible, otherwise you are certain to be found out. A good lie should be at least nine-tenths of the truth anyway'.

Looking at her daughter, Lynn wondered if it was possible that she had in fact given birth to this pretty, fair-haired creature. How long ago it all seemed and somehow she had never felt very maternal. But it was obvious that something had to be done about the girl and as far as she could see, her plans — and she had made them with the greatest care — should, unless something very unforeseen happened, be fool proof.

"Now, darling," she said brightly, ignoring the cloud in Sally's eyes and the faint droop of her mouth, "I want you to tell me lots about yourself. What you have done, whom you have met, and don't tell me that with eyes like that you haven't got a young man?"

Sally laughed.

"No, of course I haven't. I don't think I have ever met one — at least not what you would call a young man. There were boys who worked on the farm and the old men who used to come to stay and get well again, but the man I loved best was the Vicar. He was so sweet to me, but he was over seventy and I don't think you would call him a young man."

Lynn nodded her head. It was as she had expected.

"Well, all that has got to be changed," she said. "The first thing I am going to do is to give you some lovely clothes and then I am going to introduce you to some charming young men of the right age. Youth will go to youth, and you need someone to tell you how pretty you are, just as I have always needed it."

"Oh, Lynn, oughtn't I to think about getting a job and earning my own living?"

"There is plenty of time for that," Lynn said. "We will think about it in a week or so. In the meantime, I want you to have a good time but promise me that it will be as the daughter of my old friend, Arthur St. Vincent. Swear on your honour that you will never, never reveal to anyone our real relationship?"

"Of course, I swear it," Sally said, and her voice was solemn.

"Then everything is arranged," Lynn said, "and now run along to Mary and ask her to find you something presentable to be seen in, and tell her, if she hasn't already done so, to make an appointment for you to go to the hairdresser's as soon as possible. I am going to ring up my young man and thank him for this bracelet."

Sally got to her feet.

"Oh, thank you," she said, "thank you, thank you for being so wonderful to me. Oh, Lynn, I do love you so."

She needed only the slightest encouragement to fling her arms round her mother's neck and kiss her, but Lynn blew her a light kiss across the bed and turned to pick up the telephone.

Sally knew she was dismissed and went from the room in search of Mary.

Mary was ready for her and by the time she had changed into one of Mary's slim, well-cut dresses and been hurried away to one of the most famous coiffeurs in the West End, Sally began to feel that she was a different person. The past had receded so far, and it was almost hard to remember that the farm and its ailing guests were still a reality.

A few days later the fittings had begun, hour after hour of them.

Madame Marguerite's voice recalled her to the present.

"Please stand straight, *Mademoiselle*, I must get this hem even."

"I am sorry," Sally said, pulling herself up almost to attention.

At that moment, the door opened and Mary came in.

"Have you nearly finished" she asked.

"In two minutes," Madame Marguerite replied.

"Oh, thank goodness," Sally breathed. "It is such a lovely day. I want to go for a walk. May I?"

Mary looked at her watch.

"I don't think you will have time," she said. "Lynn wants you to have luncheon with her, and you are to wear that new blue dress, which was finished yesterday, and the big hat."

"Are we going out for luncheon then?" Sally asked.

Mary nodded.

"Yes, you are motoring down to Bray with Mr. Thorne and going to have luncheon there. He will be calling almost at once."

"Oh!"

Sally's voice was interested and Mary gave her a look, then turned away, but she had not missed the expression on her face.

However much she disapproved of Lynn's plans and very often she did disapprove, she had to admit that Lynn was a good judge of human nature. It was perhaps her theatrical training and her sensitiveness to an audience that enabled, her to know almost instinctively the way people would react to certain situations. She had wanted Sally to be interested in Anthony Thorne and she was stage-managing the whole thing with a cleverness and an intelligence that were gaining exactly the right result, without Sally having the slightest idea that she was being manipulated.

Last night she had sent a message to Sally to tell her to put on a new evening dress that had just been finished. Sally had been only too pleased to obey, for the previous nights she and Mary had dined alone while Lynn had gone from the house, glittering with diamonds and rubies and wearing great sprays of orchids on her ermine wrap, to dine with Erico.

"Is Lynn going to be here for dinner tonight?" Sally had asked eagerly.

Mary nodded.

"Yes, there's to be a little party. There will be you and Lynn for the women and Erico and another young man whom Lynn wants you to meet."

"What is his name?"

"Anthony Thorne," Mary replied, "but most people call him Tony."

And then Sally had asked the one question that Mary had dreaded.

"Is he in love with Lynn too?"

Mary gave a little laugh.

"Oh, he is much younger than Lynn," she prevaricated, "he admires her, of course – who doesn't? but they have been friends for a long time. And, as you know, she is not interested in anyone except Erico."

Sally had seemed satisfied with the somewhat makeshift reply and Mary, with a sigh of relief, had talked of other things.

But Lynn had had a great deal more to say, when surprisingly and unexpectedly she came into Sally's room before dinner.

"I want you to be very kind to Tony Thorne tonight," she said to Sally. "He has had a great disappointment recently. He was very anxious to get a certain post in Paris, but the head of the firm has taken a dislike to him and has refused to take him on. He has worked so hard, poor boy, to perfect his French, and he is feeling rather fed up with life altogether. You must try to cheer him up, Sally, and after all, that is something at which you should excel – cheering up people who are miserable or ill."

"Yes, but not 'London' people like Mr. Thorne," Sally said in a rather frightened voice. "I won't know what to talk to him about, Lynn. Oh, dear, if only I were not so ignorant. I feel out of place here."

Lynn smiled.

"Nonsense, darling! It makes you all the more attractive because you are not like all the other girls. Besides, let me give you a tip. If you have not got anything to say to a man – listen. Look at him with those big eyes of yours and ask him to tell you about himself. It works like a charm with every man I have known and has never yet failed. And by the way, Sally, darken your eyelashes a little. I told Rose to show you how to do it. Has she done so?"

"Yes, Lynn," Sally said, "but it makes me so different somehow."

And then her sense of humour bubbled to the surface.

"Oh, Lynn, what would Aunt Amy say?"

Lynn, put her hands up to her ears.

"Don't tell me. I can guess."

She moved towards the doorway and when she had reached it she turned with that graceful, perfect timing which every audience expected from her.

"By the way, darling, don't come downstairs until exactly one minute past half past eight, will you? I want to have Erico to myself for a few moments."

"Of course, Lynn," Sally said, "I understand."

She did not, of course, nor was she any wiser later when she made, what Lynn termed to herself an almost perfect entrance into the long, pearl-grey drawing room, at exactly one minute after half past eight.

Both Erico and Tony had been surprised to find their hostess waiting for them when they arrived. They were used to waiting for Lynn, who was well aware that a little anticipation sweetened the moment of realisation.

Now she gave both men a cocktail and allowed Erico to bury his lips in the palm of her hand.

"I have got a treat for you tonight, Tony," she said, "I want you to meet a very sweet girl. I don't think I have told you about her before. Her father was an old friend of mine who was very kind to me when I was about Sally's age. He died in the war and the poor child has been living with an aunt in the wilds of Wales. Now the aunt has died and for the first time she has come to London to see a bit of life. She is a dear child and one day she will be very rich. In fact you ought to be very grateful to me for bringing you together."

"How sweet of you, Lynn," Tony Thorne said, but there was something mocking in his voice and in his eyes as he took the cocktail she offered him.

"I met Sally today at luncheon," Erico said. "She is a very charming English girl."

"If you admire her too much, darling, I shall be jealous," Lynn smiled.

"You need not be that," he said, and his dark eyes were on her mouth as though he kissed her. "There is no other woman in the world as far as I am concerned."

Lynn narrowed her eyes a little, and it seemed as if something electric passed between them lighting a flame in the secret depths of their dark eyes. Then with an effort Lynn turned again to Tony. He was watching them both and the half smile of his lips was still mocking.

He was tall and extremely attractive and he wore his clothes with an Englishman's ease and grace, which somehow made Erico, beautifully dressed though he was, seem slightly ornate. Both men were handsome types and yet Tony Thorne's good looks were somehow unimportant beside his air of breeding, while Erico was obviously conscious of his as a weapon and a power to be used to his own advantage.

It was at that moment that the door opened and Sally came in. Her dress of soft white chiffon moulded her young breasts, then fell in heavy folds to the carpet. She wore no jewellery and her hair, dressed by a master hand, framed the lovely, rounded curves of her face, just touching the whiteness of her shoulders. Her eyes were very wide and her lips were slightly parted as if she were half afraid of what lay in front of her, yet at the same time savouring it deliciously because of its very excitement.

She hesitated for a moment as she came into the room. There was something infinitely young and somewhat appealing to her indecision. Tony Thorne stared at her and then quietly, like the opening bars of a prelude played by a master hand, Lynn glided forward.

"Here you are, darling," she said, and, taking Sally by the hand, she drew her into the room. "You have met Erico. He has been saying very flattering things about you and now I want you to meet a very great friend of mine, Tony Thorne."

"How do you do?"

Such conventional words with which to greet anyone, but Sally, raising her eyes to Tony's, thought how nice he was and how extremely good-looking. Her shyness began to disappear as Lynn, with an experienced master hand, managed to have them all talking at once and to make their little party in the white and gold dining room an intimate, cosy affair despite the formality of being waited on by a butler and footman.

There were silver dishes and big lighted candelabra and the table was decorated with orchids. No wonder Sally felt as if she was dreaming and when Lynn made her have just half a glass of champagne and Tony lifted his glass to her in, a silent toast, she felt indeed that a fairy must have waved her wand and she was in a transformation scene that had wafted her into an incredible wonderland.

After dinner they went on to a night club, the first Sally had ever been to. The lights were low on the table, which divided them into two couples – Erico and Lynn speaking together in quiet voices and she and Tony being left, isolated as it were, to get to know each other. They talked of many things and somehow she lost her shyness of him and she went to bed that night thinking about him until she slept, to awake still thinking of him the next morning.

And now she was to meet him at luncheon! How exciting it was! No wonder Lynn had said it was amusing to know young men. Somehow she had always imagined men as frightening creatures, with whom one had little in common. Now she knew she had been mistaken. Tony was easy to talk to and easier still to listen to. He had lots to say, he chattered naturally, and she guessed that it amused him to tell her things when he discovered how unsophisticated she was.

"Do you mean to say you have never seen that?" he exclaimed not once but a hundred times during the evening and when she begged him with shining eyes to tell her about it, she knew that Lynn was pleased with her for she caught her glance of approval across the table.

"I will be seeing you soon," Tony had said when she was saying good sight.

And now, joy of joys, 'soon' meant at luncheon today. What fun to be going into the country with Tony and Lynn! Could she ask more of life?

"This dress will be ready for you tomorrow, *Mademoiselle*," Madame Marguerite said.

"Oh, will it? Thank you very much. You have been so kind."

"If it was not to please Miss Lystell, so many dresses would not have been made in six months," Madame Marguerite said, "but she has been so kind to me and has recommended me to many people in her profession. Next month I am to dress the entire cast of a new play. It is all due to Miss Lystell and I show my gratitude by doing what she wants when she wants something.

"And I am the gainer," Sally said. "Well, thank you very much indeed."

She let Madame Marguerite take the pinned garment off her, thankful to be free and able to move about again. She had been standing for nearly two hours.

"I will go and get ready straight away," she said to Mary, who was still waiting in the room.

"All right," Mary answered, "I just want a word with Marguerite."

Sally sped from the room and as she went she heard Mary say,

"Now, about the account, Marguerite."

She heard no more and it suddenly struck her that she had not been sufficiently grateful to Lynn for all the lovely things she had given her. Impulsively, though she had already guessed that it was an understood thing that no one went to her room unless sent for, Sally went to Lynn's bedroom and knocked on the door.

"Come in." Lynn was at the dressing table, half dressed, and Rose was arranging her hair.

"Oh, it's you, Sally," she said.

Now that she was in Lynn's presence, Sally felt the impulsive words of gratitude difficult to say, especially with Rose present, nevertheless she knew that Lynn was waiting for her to explain why she was there, and going across the room she said,

"I have just finished my fitting, Lynn, and I want to tell you how grateful I am and how kind it is of you to give me all those marvellous clothes. They must be costing an awful lot of money. Words are such inadequate things in which to say thank you." Lynn smiled, but her voice was sharp.,

"They are certainly expensive enough, but never mind that, you will be able to repay me."

"Repay you?" For a moment Sally was astonished, "Oh, I hope so, but it will not be for a terribly long time, not until I earn some money of my own."

"It will take more than a week's salary to pay for these dresses," Lynn said , "but don't worry, child, you will have plenty of money when you are married."

"And that means you will have to wait years and years. Oh, Lynn, ought I to have them?"

"Most certainly," Lynn said in an amused way, putting a drop of varnish on the tip of one of her long fingernails, "besides, who said anything about it being years and years before you are married? You are eighteen, Sally, and you will find that there will be plenty of people wanting to marry you. Take my advice and marry soon. It is all very well to want a career, but the right place for a woman is in a home of her own."

"It sounds lovely," Sally said, "but all the same, Lynn, I have got to think about a career, whether I like it or not. Erico was talking last night about your trip to South

America, it is not so very far away and by then I must have a job – I simply must."

Lynn seemed to stiffen.

"I can't be bothered with that at the moment, Sally. Run along and get dressed."

There was a rebuke in her voice to which Sally reacted immediately. Abashed, she slipped from the room wondering why Lynn was annoyed when she talked of getting a job.

During the short time that she had been in the house Sally knew that money was not so easily come by as it appeared on the surface. She had overheard Mary telling the cook that there must be economy in the housekeeping bills, and she had heard her, too, dealing with someone on the telephone who was obviously pressing for the payment of a bill, while Mary was promising that payment should be made in as short a time as possible, but not immediately.

"Perhaps Lynn is waiting until she gets married," Sally thought innocently. "Of course, she could not ask Erico for money now."

But at the same time she was vaguely perturbed, feeling that there was something she did not understand about the finance of the house, a feeling that she had never had at the farm where they lived frugally, but where everything was paid for immediately it was purchased.

But she forgot money and Lynn's rebuke when she was dressing for luncheon. The dress Mary had told her to wear was lovely. It was in the very softest, pale-blue wool, so light that it might almost have been silk, with white collars and cuffs and a little white belt with a blue buckle. If echoed the colour of her eyes and was a perfect background for the pale gold in her hair. Holding her hat in her hand and a white bag to match the trimmings of her dress, she ran downstairs about twenty minutes later to find Tony waiting in the drawing room.

"I hear we are going into the country," she said, when he had taken her hand in greeting. "I am so excited. It is such a lovely day and though it is wrong of me to find fault with London, I do feel that it is rather stifling."

"I feel like that sometimes," Tony agreed. "In fact just today I've moved from my flat to a house a friend has lent me on the river at Bray. I like the river in the hot weather, but I gather you like the country at all times and in all seasons."

Sally nodded.

"I have never lived in a town before, so perhaps I am not much of a judge, but to me the country is beautiful at any season of the year. Don't you love the winter when there is snow, when the trees without their, leaves look like etchings silhouetted against the sky?"

"I have never thought of that," Tony said, "but I suppose they are rather like etchings. But though I like the country, I find one has the best time in towns, or should I say cities - London, Paris and New York, I have had a jolly good time in all three of them and so will you before you are much older."

"I wonder," Sally said. "You see, I shall have to think about getting a job soon and I don't think I have any qualifications that would enable me to get a job in a city. I shall have to go back and work on a farm. I am good with animals."

Tony was just about to make some reply when Lynn came into the room. To Sally's surprise she was dressed very elaborately in a dress of dark red silk, a hat with feathers and a big spray of white orchids spotted with red on her shoulder.

"Darlings," she said, "I have got the most terrible confession to make to you both. When I arranged for us to go to the country today, I completely forgot that Erico was expecting me to have luncheon with him. I have got to go.

It is a most important luncheon given by the Brazilian Ambassador, so you'll just have to forgive and forget me and go off on your own. You can take the car because Erico is sending his for me. I won't expect you back until I see you."

"Oh, Lynn," Sally said, genuinely disappointed.

Lynn laughed at her.

"Don't pretend you will miss me," she said, "and quite frankly it makes me feel old to be chaperoning you both."

"That is one role I cannot imagine you playing," Tony said.

Lynn raised her eyebrows.

"Can't you?" she said. "Well, I may have to do it yet. Run along, Tony, and look after the child. Remember I want her to enjoy her stay with me very, very much. It is important."

"I won't forget that," Tony said, and there was a note of bitterness in his voice. Sally thought that he and Lynn looked at each other for a second as though they were antagonists. Then she dismissed the idea as absurd.

Often, she had strange fancies about people. Ever since she was a little girl, she had made up stories by herself and somehow the creatures of her imagination had become interwoven with her daily life. Sometimes the real people she met fitted in with the stories that were going on in her head and sometimes she saw them in different surroundings like the man she had seen in the railway station who had reminded her so vividly of a knight in armour.

She had thought of him once or twice, and wondered if, when she went to see Nanny Bird again, she would meet him and his nice cocker spaniel. Now she had the impression that Lynn and Tony were almost enemies of each other, then the moment passed and she told herself that once again she was imagining things.

The day was so glorious, she felt as if she were wakening up for the first time in her life, wakening up to a consciousness of her own strength, her own youth and the possibilities of happiness there were in a world so lovely and so easy.

Lynn's Rolls Royce, grey and silver, was waiting for them. Tony dismissed the chauffeur, saying that he would drive himself. And then they were speeding out of London, leaving the houses and the crowded streets behind, and finding green fields, country lanes and great open stretches of unspoilt land.

"What do you think of the view?" Tony asked suddenly as he stopped at the top of a hill. Below them lay a valley in a great stretch of open country.

"It is lovely," Sally said, "but where are we?"

"In Surrey," Tony replied. "I know this part of the world well."

"But I thought we were going to Bray."

"Not on your life. That is Lynn's place, not yours."

"What do you mean?"

"Never mind," he said, "there is a little pub down here where we can get something to eat. It will not be an elaborate luncheon written out in French, but an honest-to-God English meal which we can augment with a pint of draught ale."

There was some inner meaning in this that Sally did not quite understand, but she was content to do what he wished and soon she found herself in a small, oak-beamed room with a large portion of steak and kidney pie in front of her.

"This is good," Sally exclaimed. "I am awfully glad we came here."

"I thought you would be," Tony said, watching her, "and now tell me about yourself."

"There is nothing to tell," Sally replied, "you know all about me. I have had such a dull life. I want to hear all about you."

"I can't condense my life into two or three hundred words," Tony said evasively, "but I don't want to know about your experiences or what you have done. I want to know what you think about or what you feel. Tell me, what are your reactions to Lynn?"

"You mean what do I think of her? I think she is the most wonderful and beautiful person I could ever imagine. I love her more than anybody else in the whole world."

There was a passion of sincerity in her voice that quite startled Tony for a moment.

"And she seems very fond of you," he said after a moment. "She says your father was kind to her many years ago. He must have been very kind indeed for Lynn to take so much interest in a woman and an attractive one at that." There was a hint of criticism in his voice, which Sally resented.

"Lynn's life is full of kindness," she said quickly. "I know that, even though I have not seen much of her during the past few years."

"You used to see her then, in the past?" Tony asked.

Sally sensed there was danger ahead.

"Yes, sometimes," she answered.

"Well, she must owe a great debt of gratitude to your father to do so much for his pretty daughter."

"Thank you for the compliment," Sally said, hoping that in some way she would be able to turn the conversation to another subject.

"But you know you are pretty, don't you?" Tony asked,

"Shall I be honest with you and tell you that this is the first time anyone but Lynn has ever told me so"

Tony was genuinely astonished.

"Good Lord! Where have you been living?

"In Wales."

"I never did think much of the Welsh as a nation," Tony said, "and now I am certain that all the worst libels I have ever heard about them are not exaggerated."

Sally laughed.

"You are funny!"

"I am not trying to be," Tony said, "but tell me, aren't there any men in Wales? Hasn't anyone made love to you in a nice singsong voice or tried to kiss you up in the lonely mountains?"

"No to both those questions," Sally replied. "The only men I met on lonely mountains were old shepherds and they were far too taken up in looking for lost lambs to have time for young women."

"Would you like to be made love to, Sally?" Tony asked, and there was something in his eyes that made her look down at the table.

"I don't think so," she answered. "I-I don't know."

"You seem rather undecided about it," Tony said and suddenly he bent across the table and took her hand in his.

They were alone in the room, for there were no other guests and the waitress, having bought them two large cups of coffee, had disappeared. Tony held her hand and at the touch of his fingers Sally was seized with a sudden shyness that made her tremble,. She had no idea whether she should take her hand away or leave it in his – she was conscious only of the quick beating of her heart and that her cheeks were burning.

"Such a little hand," Tony said quietly and turned it over in his until it lay palm-upwards.

"You have got nice artistic fingers, Sally," he continued, "but you have worked hard." He touched two little blisters beneath the second and third fingers of her hand.

"Yes, very hard," Sally murmured, for something to say.

"And now let me tell your fortune. You will have a long life and a healthy one, you will be loved not once but many times and by many men. In a few years you will be a very beautiful woman. Are you glad about that?"

"I think you are talking nonsense," Sally said, and her voice was breathless as if she had been running for a long way.

"You wait and see if I am not right," Tony smiled.

He held her hand even tighter in his and she felt that he was drawing her towards him.

With a sudden panic she got quickly to her feet, pulling her hand from his and picking up her handbag which lay on the floor beside her.

"It is getting late. I feel sure we ought to be getting back. Lynn might want me."

Tony leant back in his chair and looked at her, then he gave a little laugh.

"All right, Sally, you can always run away from experience, you know."

Sally pretended not to hear him. She left him to pay the bill while she walked out of the dining room, through the little hall and outside to where the car was waiting. She wished that her heart did not beat so quickly, yet now some of her fear was gone. She was conscious only of almost intoxicating excitement.

Was this what people meant when they talked about people making love to you? She was not sure, she only knew that the sunshine was suddenly brilliantly golden as Tony came out through the porch to join her.

They drove back to London almost in silence, yet it was not an embarrassing silence. It seemed to her that there was no need for words. It was friendly and nice to be beside someone like Tony, driving through sunlit countryside and what was there to say when one's whole being was singing a song of joy

Only when they reached Berkeley Square did Tony, pulling up the car, turn and face her.

"Have you enjoyed yourself, little Sally?" he asked.

"So very much," she answered, "and thank you."

He looked at her for a moment almost as if he hated her.

"Don't thank me, thank Lynn."

"But of course we must," Sally said. "She thought of it, and she lent us this lovely car."

"Yes, she thought of it." Tony said and he leant across Sally to open the door for her. As he did so she was conscious of the warmth and strength of his arm against hers and of the faint fragrance of his hair oil.

Once again, because he had touched her, her heart beat faster and half afraid of her own emotions, Sally jumped out.

"Are you coming in?" she asked.

"Most certainly. I must report to Lynn that I have returned you safe and sound."

"I wonder if she is back." Sally said, but the butler on opening the door told them that Lynn had not returned.

"Very well, I will come in and smoke a cigar," Tony said. "You deprived me of the one I promised myself after luncheon by being in such a hurry to get away."

"Oh, I'm sorry," Sally apologised. "I didn't know men smoked after luncheon."

"Invariably, when they have had a good meal with a delectable companion."

"I shall remember another time," Sally said, then blushed because it sounded as if she expected him to invite her out again.

He saw the blush.

"So you will come and have luncheon with me again?"

"Of course," Sally replied, "if you ask me."

"Then you have forgiven me?" Tony insisted.

"But what for?"

Tony had taken his cigar out of a leather case which he now replaced in his pocket. But he made no attempt to light the cigar and after a moment he put it down on the mantelpiece.

"I am suggesting," he said gently, "that you might be annoyed at my making love to you."

"Oh!"

Somehow Sally had not anticipated this remark and the colour flamed once again to her cheeks.

Tony stood looking down at her, and suddenly in a voice that was half a groan, said,

"You are so young, so pitifully young."

Sally said nothing, uncertain of what to answer to this remark and still embarrassed by his previous one. Then suddenly, as if he made up his mind to do something, Tony stepped forward and putting his arm round her, put his hand under her chin and tipped her head back against his shoulder.

"You are very lovely," he said and before she could move or cry out his mouth was on hers.

She was conscious of a sudden fear and there was a sense of shock as if her heart suddenly stopped beating. It seemed to her at that moment that the world held nothing but the warmth and magnetism of Tony's lips. She had a sense of suffocation, of being overwhelmed, of being taken by storm because she had not the will to resist. Then as swiftly as he had taken her in his arms, she was free.

She stood for a moment facing him, before she gave a little cry that she would have found hard to interpret even to herself. It was all too chaotic for her to know what she thought or what she was feeling. She only knew that everything was beyond her understanding and that she must find sanctuary. She turned, and like an animal that has been startled rushed from the room.

As she crossed the hall, she was aware that the front door was opening and that someone was coming into the house, but she did not wait to see who it was. She tore upstairs to her room and flung herself, face downwards, on the bed, hearing only the drumming of her own heart and the swift intake of her breath.

In the drawing room below Tony was lighting a cigar as Lynn came gliding into the room. She stood just inside the doorway, pulling off her long suede gloves and looking at him from under her long eyelashes.

"Well?" she said at length, and it was a question.

Tony stared at her across the room, drawing at his cigar three or four times until the end flamed red, then he flung the burnt match into the fireplace.

"I have been wondering to myself," he said at length, "whether you are a bad woman, Lynn, or only an utterly selfish one."

4

Lynn walked into the drawing room and pulling her cape of platinum fox from her shoulders threw it over the back of a chair.

"A lovely evening, Erico," she said softly to the man behind her. "But I must go to bed, I have a rehearsal tomorrow morning."

"The night is still young," he replied, and reaching out he took her hand in his, kissing it gently, his lips lingering on each soft white finger until they came to rest in the centre of her palm.

"I love you," he said and his voice was low.

Lynn made no answer. She was standing very still almost in the centre of the room and her dress of grey tulle made her seem ethereal, almost ghost-like, as though she might vanish at any moment.

Erico's lips were on her wrist and then in the little blue-veined hollow where her arm bent. He murmured something in Spanish and fiercely, possessively drew her close to him. His kisses, burning and passionate, rained on her neck and white shoulders until he possessed himself of her mouth. Lynn lay limp in his arms, her whole being surrendered utterly to the tempest of his love, until slowly and insidiously she felt a fire kindle within herself. Suddenly she raised her arms, clasped them around his neck and gave him back kiss for kiss.

"Lynn! Lynn! *Querida mia*! I want you!"

There was no mistaking the fire within Erico's eyes and the passion in his voice. He would have lifted her up off her feet at that moment, but quickly Lynn escaped from his arms and moved away. Her eyes were shining and her breath came quickly through her parted lips, but she spoke quickly,

"No, wait, Erico. I am tired. I have told you I must go to bed."

"Then I will take you there."

She shook her head, because for the moment she dare not trust her voice. His virile masculinity aroused her as she had never been aroused before, and every time they were alone she found it more and more difficult not only to control him but to control herself. Lynn had been married twice and had known many men in her triumphant and successful career, but there had never been one who had quite the same effect on her as Erico. There was something about him that drew her like a magnet so that for the first time in her life her mind was subservient to her heart and it frightened her more than anything else that had ever happened.

She put up her bare arms now to smooth her hair and Erico, seeing the lovely lines of breast and hip, cried out,

"But you are beautiful! I adore you. Let me show you what love means. What are we waiting for? What difference can a priest, bell and book make to us? You are mine and I want you."

But some age-old wisdom in Lynn made her refuse not only his desire, but her own. When she had lost Leslie, her second husband, she had sworn to herself that she would never marry again. There would always be men in her life, she was quite sure of that, but not with any legal hold over her. Her two marriages had both been failures – she would never attempt a third.

But from the first moment that she saw Erico she had been aware that here was a man who was going to mean to her something different from all the other men who had loved and courted her. She had known instinctively and with a sure judgment based on long experience of his sex that he approached her with a swashbuckling confidence, certain that she was his for the taking.

He had been overwhelmed by her beauty, that was very evident, and he had first denied her and then grown to love her with a savage, almost barbaric intensity.

It was not only his wealth and great possessions which attracted her – although she was honest enough with herself to admit that she would not have contemplated marriage with Erico had he been a poor man – it was something much more, something that even now she could not express to herself. He fired her, he made her vibrate as if she were an instrument over which he had complete control. And yet there was still something else, something to which she could not put a name.

She looked at him now and the expression in her eyes was very soft. How handsome he was and how very much a man! Unexpectedly the memory of Arthur came to her and she remembered his perplexed gentleness and thought how lucky he was to have held, even for a short a time, a woman like herself.

Erico was the man to whom she would be proud to admit mastery and feel no shame in her confession. She walked across to him now, moving with that exquisite grace which was so much a part of her stage training.

"I must go, Erico, my darling," she said. "If you stay any longer, we shall both of us be sorry."

"You do not know what you are saying," he retorted. "It is not prudery that makes you send me away. You are like all English women, cold as an icicle. Well, I will melt you, show you what love means. *Ven aqui, querido mio.* Come here!"

He put both his hands against her naked shoulders and drew her towards him, but swiftly, before his lips could touch hers, she laid her fingers against his mouth.

"No, no, Erico, I cannot bear it."

He bit her fingers at first softly and then a little more sharply, making her cry out in pain.

"You are cruel," she said, pretending to pout a little, then, turning away from him, she stood looking down into the embers of the dying fire. He came up behind her, standing so near that she could feel his strength emanating from him and despite her every resolution it made her tremble.

"You will drive me mad," he said and his voice was deep and hoarse. "Sometimes I feel that I could kill you because only that way will I find any peace."

"Kill me," she smiled, "and I shall no longer be yours."

"Yes, but it would also be impossible for you to belong to anyone else. I am jealous, I tell you, jealous of everyone you see and everyone to whom you speak. I am jealous of the audiences who watch you move and speak upon the stage, jealous of the men with whom you play, jealous of the very flowers you touch. Yes, I am even jealous of this pretty child you invite here, and who can be with you alone in this house, while I am shut outside."

Lynn sighed.

"Poor Erico!" she said softly.

"Is that all you have to say to me?" he asked, the fierceness fading from his voice to be replaced by a soft, insistent, almost mesmeric tone.

"There is not so long to wait now," Lynn whispered consolingly.

"To me it seems like a long-drawn-out century, a lifetime of frustrated longings and dark nights when I must lie sleepless without you. When you are alone in that beautiful bed, do you not sometimes think of me?"

Lynn did not answer his question in words, her eyes gave him the answer before she turned away. A second later she felt his lips touch the base of her neck and move lower against the firm beauty of her white back. She felt a delicious tremor run through her and quickly, because once again she feared that rising flame of desire within herself, she turned round.

"Go, Erico," she pleaded. "Please go."

He knew now that she meant it and, taking both her hands in his, smothered them in kisses and turned towards the door. Lynn followed him, picking up her wrap from the chair, ready to go upstairs to bed, but as Erico opened the drawing room door, they heard a key turn in the latch. Instinctively Lynn reached out her hand and turned out the lights. They stood in the darkness as the street door opened and they heard Sally say,

"Thank you ever so much for taking me out, and – goodnight."

"I shall be seeing you tomorrow."

Tony's voice was low and deep.

"Oh, I suppose so," Sally answered, "but…"

"There is no but about it," Tony interrupted. "I am coming round to see you, and then you must give me your answer."

"I won't know what to say," Sally replied quickly, "besides, Lynn…"

"Lynn will be delighted." There was a hint of amusement in Tony's voice.

"But will she? How do you know?"

"You ask her and see" Tony said, "and don't look so worried, Sally. You mustn't be frightened of me."

"Oh, I'm not – I mean – it is not that. Oh, I don't know what I do mean. I think I will go upstairs. Goodnight, Tony."

There was a hint of tears in Sally's voice and she pushed the street door to with a slam, then quite oblivious of the two people standing in the drawing room, she ran up the broad carpeted stairs and disappeared into the darkness of the landing.

Erico turned to Lynn and would have spoken, but she put her fingers against his lips.

"Hush," she said, "she must not know we have been listening. The child is upset, having obviously received her first proposal."

"The man is a fool," Erico answered. "He does not know how to make love."

But Lynn shushed him into silence and leading the way across the hall she opened the door into the street. He kissed her hand once again.

"Goodnight, Lynn darling, my lovely one. May our dreams soon be forgotten in reality."

Lynn heard his footsteps fade away into silence before she went slowly up the stairs. Sally's room was on the other side of the corridor from her own. She hesitated a moment, then knocked on the door and as she did so turned the handle.

Sally was sitting in front of her dressing table, her head bowed in her hands. There was something pathetic and very young in her attitude. She was not crying, she was just crumpled up as if she felt too small to face the decisions which confronted her.

"I looked in to see if you were back," Lynn said softly as Sally got a little awkwardly to her feet.

"Are you tired?" she continued as if she noticed nothing untoward in Sally's appearance. "If not, come along to my room and talk to me while I am undressing."

"Oh, I would love to," Sally exclaimed, and Lynn led the way across the corridor.

The lights, low and shaded, were lit beside the bed and there was a fire burning in the grate, for however warm it was Lynn always felt chilly at night. It seemed as if both in her acting and in her contacts with other people she depleted her vitality, so that gradually as the day wore on she needed more artificial heat than the average person. To

Sally the room seemed unbearably hot, but Lynn shivered a little as she took off her dress, threw it over a chair and drew on a wrap of satin and lace with bands of white ermine on the wide sleeves.

"Sit down, child," she said as Sally stood watching, and walking across to the dressing table she took off her star-shaped diamond earrings.

"Did you have a nice evening?" she asked.

"Yes." Sally's reply was hardly audible.

"Aren't you going to tell me about it?"

There was silence until Sally, clasping her hands together and looking as guilty as a child who has been caught put in some misdemeanour, burst out,

"Oh, Lynn, Tony wants me to marry him."

"Darling!" Lynn's little exclamation of surprise was perfect theatre. "But how wonderful! I couldn't be more thrilled. Aren't you glad Aren't you happy"

Sally's eyes were tragic.

"Oh, Lynn, I don't know what to say. You see I am not certain if am in love with him."

"But, darling, of course you are. How could anyone help being in love with Tony. He is so attractive. I have known him for years and I promise you he is one of the most attractive young men I have ever known."

Sally seemed to relax a little.

"Then – then y-you are pleased?"

"But of course! I am. Doesn't every mother want to see her daughter married? And though we have to pretend, you and I, Sally, I am still your mother. I want to see you married, settled and happy."

"You think…" Sally paused. "You think Tony is the right person for me?"

"But of course! I would not have introduced him if I had not known that he would be a good friend to my little girl and now that he has had the sense to suggest that you be his wife, I like him more than ever."

"I-it is only that I…"

"You have got doubts, of course. One always feels like that the first time one falls in love."

"But do you really think I am in love?" Sally asked. "You see I have never known a man. I have – I have never been kissed before."

"You liked it?" Lynn asked.

"I don't think I did," Sally answered. "It was so strange and rather frightening."

Lynn laughed.

"Darling baby, of course it is frightening the first time. But you will get used to it and like it very much indeed, I promise you. Now don't worry your silly head with doubts and worries. Everything will smooth itself out. I will see Tony tomorrow and tell him that he must be very gentle and very kind to my unsophisticated Sally."

"But he is, Lynn. He couldn't be nicer or kinder. It is just that I have a feeling inside me that…"

"Listen, darling," Lynn said impatiently, "you are being a little bit ridiculous and you are trying to make difficulties where there are none. I expect you have been reading too many fairy stories when you were young or dreaming too many dreams alone by yourself on the farm. Love is never quite what one expects it to be, but when you are as old as I am you will find it is a very marvellous thing all the same. You don't want to refuse love, Sally. You don't want to grow old and unwanted and uncared-for like poor old Amy. You are pretty – we should be very grateful for that – and you have had the good fortune within a few days of your coming to London to find someone as charming as Tony who wants to marry you."

Sally sat back in her chair.

"Oh, Lynn, if you think it is all right? It was only because I was so frightened."

"Silly girl, you must not be frightened of Tony or anyone else. I expect, if the truth were known, he is very frightened of you. Women are always very superior to men when it comes to making love, don't forget that."

"I don't feel very superior," Sally said.

"But you will. Think how proud you will feel of a husband all your own, of a lovely house, and perhaps, later on, children." Sally's face softened at the word and then suddenly she laughed.

"Oh, Lynn, you are funny! You have got it all planned out. I feel as if my whole life is there for me to see, stretching out into the future without any difficulties attached to it,"

"Why should there be any?" Lynn answered. "And I will tell you something else I have planned. It has just come into my head at this moment and it is the best plan I have ever made."

"What is it?" Sally asked.

"That you shall be married before I go to South America and then I shall be able to be at your wedding."

"Oh, no, Lynn!" Sally's cry was one of horror. "I couldn't marry as quickly as that. I couldn't really."

"But, darling, how unkind of you! Don't you want me to be there? After all, Tony won't wait for you all the many months I shall be away, and it would make me so terribly happy to be at my only daughter's wedding."

Lynn's voice, reproachful and a little plaintive, vibrated across the room. Sally's reaction to it was instantaneous.

"Oh, but, Lynn, I didn't mean to be unkind. Of course I want you at my wedding. I couldn't bear to be married if you weren't there. It is only that I thought I would just like to wait a little. Six months is not a long time anyway, and then – you will be back."

"But, darling, don't you see, I shall be worrying all the time as to what will happen to you. Mary will tell you that it has been constantly on my mind as to what we could do with you while I am away. I have been lying awake at night worrying and that is why I have not talked to you about a job or anything like that. I was just worrying and worrying, and perhaps praying a little that something would turn up. And it has! The nicest thing in all the world has happened – that Tony is in love with you and you are in love with him."

"You are quite sure?" Sally asked.

"Quite, quite sure," Lynn said. "You must allow me to judge for you in this, Sally. I am much older and I have had so much more experience. I can promise you, darling, that you are doing the right thing and that Tony will make you very, very happy. Now don't think about it any more tonight. Go to bed so that you will look your very best and loveliest for Tony. I will do all the planning and all the worrying."

Almost automatically Sally got to her feet. She stood by Lynn, who reached out her arms, drew the child's face down to hers, and kissed her cheek.

"Goodnight, my sweet, I am so happy about this. It really has taken a great load off my mind."

"If you are happy, Lynn, that is all that matters," Sally said quickly.

"Not a bit of it," Lynn retorted with a smile. "It is your happiness we are talking about and I promise you that you are going to be very happy indeed. Now off you go to bed."

Sally bent down and kissed her mother once again.

"Oh, thank you, *thank you,*" she said, "you are so wonderful to me."

Back in her room Sally undressed slowly. She had thought that Lynn's room was hot, but now she was conscious of feeling cold, although her cheeks were burning.

She thought of the evening she had spent with Tony. It was all rather hazy and incoherent. They had dined, but Sally had no idea of what they had eaten. They had been to a theatre, but even during the thrill of seeing all the play and of being absorbed in the plot she had been conscious all the time of Tony's nearness. Then they had gone somewhere to dance and sit at a little corner table with a pink, shaded lamp on it.

She had known that Tony was looking at her strangely, not once but many times. It made her feel queer and embarrassed so that she clasped her hands together and made what sounded to her very stupid remarks about the room and the people who were dancing. Instinctively she felt that the evening was only a prelude to something else, something that was approaching her almost as if she stood on a railway track and could hear the screech of an express train but was unable to move out of its way.

Something was coming nearer to her and, while she was afraid, she was yet fascinated by it. Was this living? Was this love? She asked herself the question more than once and thought of how quiet and peaceful and uneventful things had been on the farm. Could she really be the same girl who had found untold delight in the birth of a new lamb or joy in scrambling up the mountainside with only a small dog as companion? So many people had come to the farm and needed attention and care that once she had thought herself experienced in the knowledge of others.

Yet nothing she had ever done had prepared her for this – for the man who watched her and of whose nearness she was acutely conscious, so that she could not escape from him even for a moment.

Sally got into bed and turned out the light. As she lay down, she knew that she could not sleep. Over and over again snatches of conversation, incidents of the evening came crowding into her mind. Over and over again she could hear Tony's voice saying,

"Why don't we get married, Sally?"

Then her own half hysterical reply.

"Why do you ask me that? Is it a joke?"

"You know as well as I do, it is not a joke."

He was driving Lynn's car, which he had borrowed for the evening and now he turned off Piccadilly and driving swiftly through St. James's Park, came to the Embankment. The lights of the bridges were reflected in the water. It was very quiet. Occasionally a lorry rumbled towards them, a steamer hooted or there were the footsteps of a policeman going on his beat, Otherwise there was to Sally, only the thumping of her own heart to break the silence.

Tony turned round in his seat to look at her.

"Aren't you going to answer me?" he asked.

When she did not reply he insisted,

"Don't you want to marry me, Sally?"

"I-I don't know," she stammered. "I have known you such a short time. Somehow I have never thought of marriage."

"I am sure that is not the truth," Tony smiled. "All girls think of marriage."

"Do they? I don't think I have thought of it except as a romantic dream, never as a reality."

"Well, I am real enough."

"Yes, I know," Sally whispered miserably.

"Well, what is worrying you?" Tony asked. "What do you think about in that funny little head of yours?"

"Everything seems so muddled," Sally confessed. "You see, until now my life has been very simple. There have been things to be done and I have known exactly what they were and how I should do them. And when I was by myself, I have thought about the other things – those that matter –

living and being good and all that and they, too, seemed quite simple and uncomplicated. I just knew what was right. It was there inside me, but now my life, my thoughts, everything is in a fearful tangle and I don't know what I want or what I ought to do."

It was a cry for help, but Tony did not seem to realise it. Instead he laughed and put his arm round Sally's shoulder, drawing her close to him with an almost brotherly affection.

"What a funny child you are!" he said. "Now don't worry! I will marry you and look after you and that, will be that."

There was silence for a moment, a silence that seemed to Sally vast and empty. Something within her was crying out that there was an answer to all her questions if only she could find it. It was just that it was eluding her. Then she felt Tony's hand tip her chin back and his mouth was on hers. He kissed her and looked down into her eyes.

"You are a sweet person, Sally," he said. "There are not many of them in the world, but you are genuine enough."

She neither moved nor responded to his touch, but almost piteously she asked,

"Why do you want to marry me, Tony?"

For a moment he did not reply but kissed her again and took his arm from behind her shoulders.

"Isn't that answer enough?" he asked as his hand went out towards the starting switch. "And now I am going to take you home. Lynn will be wondering what has happened to you."

Did she like being kissed? Sally wondered in the darkness. Lynn had asked her the same question and she was not sure of the answer. Somehow right at the back of her mind was the feeling that she was vaguely disappointed. In books kisses seemed to mean so much, but Tony's kisses either frightened her or made her feel that they were vaguely disappointing. He had kissed her again when the car reached the house and then he had taken her hand in his.

"I shall have to get you an engagement ring," he said. "What is your favourite stone?"

There was something in his matter-of-fact attitude and the quiet casual tone of his voice that had thrown Sally into a panic. He was speaking as if everything were arranged and everything settled. It was all too quick, all too overwhelming and in terror she longed for the security of the house and to be alone in her own bedroom.

And yet now that she was alone, alone in the darkness, she felt even less secure.

Lynn was pleased, Lynn was happy about it all. Sally wished she could feel more elated. How good-looking Tony was! Any woman would be proud of him and grateful for his love. She loved him – of course she loved him. She must be mad to think of anything else.

She wondered if Aunt Amy would have liked him and somehow convinced herself that she would. This, at least, was the solution to all the problems that had beset her day after day. Now she need not worry about a job or earning money or repaying Lynn. Now all these lovely clothes that Lynn had given her would come in useful, where before she had wondered if perhaps they were not a terrible waste of money. One could hardly go lambing in pale blue wool with white collars and cuffs, or clean out the pigsties in leaf-green crepe fastened with jewelled buttons.

Also to be Tony's wife would give her a standing in life that she had never known before. No longer would Miss Mawson be able to turn her away and fling her out into the world with nowhere to lay her head. She would be safe because there would always be Tony with his good-natured smile and strong, long-limbed body to stand between her and the world.

"I am lucky, terribly lucky," Sally told herself, speaking aloud in the darkness.

And now at last she began to grow drowsy. Dreams mingled with her thoughts. She was driving along the road with Tony, it was a long road which wound alongside a silver river, and there on the other side, almost out of sight and yet she could still see him, was a Knight in armour...

*

When Sally had left her, Lynn sat for a long time at her dressing table, staring at her own reflection, and when at last she had finished arranging her hair and creamed her face for the night, she walked across the room to the fire, crouching down to hold out her hands to the flames. She remembered how cold it had been on the night when Sally was born. It had been winter and the snow was thick on the ground. She had walked up and down the big, old-fashioned bedroom where she and Arthur had slept since their marriage. She remembered hating the pain that was beginning to grip her, loathing the brisk efficiency of the maternity nurse who was arranging the room, her starched apron rustling as she moved.

'I never wanted a child,' Lynn thought, 'I was too young, only a child myself for all I knew of the world.'

Some voice within her told her that Sally was even younger at the same age, too young to be whisked into marriage before she was sure of her heart or knew what she wanted from life.

'Nonsense,' Lynn argued with herself, 'marriage is the only thing for her. She has no money and, Heaven knows, I cannot give her any at the moment.'

The thought of money brought Erico to her mind. For the first time in her whole life Lynn had refused money when it had been offered to her. From other men she had taken with both hands, greedily, without a thought save for her own ends, but with Erico she was too clever for that. Almost instinctively, or because of something Mary had said inadvertently, he had guessed that she was hard up and there were heavy bills to be paid. But when he had offered to settle them, she had shaken her head.

"I won't allow you to keep me before we are married."

"I am only offering you a present."

"I won't accept money," she said, and he had realised the subtle difference even as she had.

Jewellery and flowers were gifts on which she imposed no limit, but money was a different thing. Erico's successes in the Social world and that of sport had not been attained without a great deal of gossip. Lynn knew of many beautiful women with whom he had been connected one way or another. On all of them he had been prepared to pour out his wealth, but she was determined to be different. Never, Erico had assured her, in the whole of his life before had he ever proposed marriage to any woman, therefore as Erico's intended wife she would not behave as other women had behaved, whom he had not honoured in such a manner.

Her shrewdness had the result she had anticipated. Every time she said, 'No' to Erico he grew more and more infatuated and she had refused to worry about anything, although Mary went about the house with a long face and said that if they were not careful the day of reckoning would come quicker than she anticipated.

"Once I am married it will be different," she replied and she had known by the look that Mary gave her that her secretary was half afraid that the marriage would never materialise.

She was well aware that for all her attraction, for all her power of beguilement, Erico was notoriously elusive. Many women had tried to capture him and all of them had failed.

Now that the announcement was in the papers, Lynn felt happier and more at ease, but at the same time she knew that she would never really breathe freely until the moment when the ring was on her finger and she could sigh her name on a cheque as Erico's wife.

Only a few weeks more! Well, he would not grow tired of her in that time!

Lynn stretched her hands above her head and as she did so the thought of Erico's insistent kisses that evening. It excited her. She wanted him as she had never wanted a man in the whole of her life before. Everyone thought that love was different when it came to them. In this case it was true. Never had she been so near to losing that steel-like control, which she had always exercised over her body, never before had she known herself tremble because a man merely touched her hand or because she could sense his nearness without even looking at him.

She shut her eyes for a moment, feeling Erico's lips again on hers. Then with a little shiver, half of cold and half of ecstasy, Lynn got into bed.

"I shan't sleep tonight," she told herself and reached out her hand for the box of sleeping tablets.

But even as she did so, the telephone by her bed trilled sharply. It was a private line and only a very favoured few were entrusted with the number. It would be no one but Erico. Eagerly Lynn put the receiver to her ear.

"Hullo!"

Her tone was low and expectant. But it was Tony's voice that answered her.

"Are you alone?"

"Of course! What do you want?"

"To talk to you, of course."

"Why the 'of course' Tony, it is late and I'm tired."

"All the same I have got to talk to you. Lynn, I can't do this.

"Can't do what?"

"Marry that poor child!"

"Why not?"

"Because it is not fair. She is too young. She knows no more about life than a kitten that hasn't got its eyes open. It isn't right and you know it isn't."

"I don't know what you are talking about," Lynn said. "Sally has just left me. She is very happy and very thrilled at the idea of marrying you."

There was a moment's pause.

"I wonder if that is the truth."

"Of course it is," Lynn said sharply. "After all, as you say yourself, the child is not sophisticated. It is all rather strange and exciting to her, so you have got to be very gentle and not rush your fences."

"You think that we shall be happy like that?"

"Of course you will – why not?"

"Lynn, you are not a fool," Tony said, "but neither am I a knave. I tell you here and now that I can't go on with it."

"But you have got to Tony, you gave me your promise. Besides, this squeamishness is ridiculous. You are not hurting anybody – in fact you will make Sally very happy. If she is not head-over-heels in love with you now, she soon will be. Who wouldn't fall in love with an attractive man like you?"

"You wouldn't for one Lynn. You know that I love you. I have loved you for years, and I shall always love you. What is the point of making for myself – and for Sally – a living hell on earth?"

"Poor little Sally couldn't make a hell for anyone and, Tony, you promised to do this for my sake. If you love me, you will not back out."

"If I love you! Do I have to tell you again and yet again that I do love you? Do you know what it is like seeing you with that man you have promised to marry, when you belong to me?"

"Tony, what is the point of going over all this again? You know that we could not go on as we were. You are in debt, I am desperately and *damnably* in debt. Do you know how much I owe? I won't tell you for it frightens me even to think of it. We have had our happiness together, let us be grateful for that. Sally is a sweet person, you say so yourself."

"Of course she is! That is what makes it all the more *damnable*. I am not the least in love with her – I never could be in love with her – and *you* know why."

"All the same, Tony, you will marry her. Don't forget, dear, that you can be very comfortable on two to three thousand a year, which is what Sally will have. Besides, she has nowhere else to go and I couldn't think what to do with her when I go off to South America."

"Hasn't the child any relations Who was this father to whom you are so grateful?"

"Oh, Tony, how suspicious you are! Can't I do a kindly action without your suspecting an ulterior motive behind it? I am thinking simply and solely of Sally and her future. Poor little thing, what job is she fitted for? And she will love you very deeply. She is already in love with you, although she isn't yet quite certain of it."

"It is no use, Lynn, you are using all your usual wiles, which make it so hard for me to resist you, but I cannot and will not do it."

There was a moment's pause. Lynn sighed and her lips tightened, then she said slowly,

"I still hold a little piece of paper with your name on it, Tony."

"Good God, Lynn!" he exclaimed, "do you have to blackmail me after all we have been to each other? Tear up the *damned* cheque and forget about it. I was drunk when I did it and I should never have thought of doing it if you hadn't gone on and on about that ring you wanted. I thought I would win the money back the next night and that you would love me all the more because I had given you something for which your greedy little soul craved,"

"A pretty explanation," Lynn said, "but in a Court of Law would it be an excuse for forgery?"

"Oh, *damn it all*, Lynn. I believe many things of you but not that you would use that against me now."

"I might ask your brother for the money," Lynn suggested. "It would keep Sally until somebody else came along and was prepared to marry her both for her face and for the fortune which she will inherit on her wedding day."

"*Damn you*, Lynn, you are a devil, aren't you?"

"Am I? You have called me an angel often enough."

"Thank God you remember that! Listen to me, darling, I love you, I adore you. Get rid of this *damned* man you are going to marry."

"Oh, Tony, you are incorrigible! I wonder how many times in the past year we have had this conversation. Now listen to me. I am tired, I want to go to sleep. I have a long day in front of me tomorrow. Let us make it quite clear once and for all that you are going to marry Sally. And if I must make it clearer, you will marry her for two reasons – first because you love me and because you want to help me and secondly for the reason which we won't mention again but which is still locked up in my safe,"

"I wish to God I could hate you," Tony cried. "I have plenty of excuse for it."

"But you don't hate me and so what is the point of talking about it? You love me, Tony, and because you love me, you are going to do what I want you to do."

"Lynn, do you ever think of that little hotel by the sea?"

"Is there any point in remembering it?" Lynn parried.

"I think I was nearer heaven then than any man has a right to be on this earth. How beautiful you were, Lynn! Won't you come there once again with me before it is too late? Won't you let me hold you close, so close that neither of us can breathe, and let me tell you that I love you, let me hear you whisper, as you whispered that first night long ago, that you love me? Come away with me, Lynn!"

"No, *no*, Tony, and that is final. We have grown older, you and I, and what has happened in the past can never be revived. Besides – and I am going to be brutal now – I don't want to." There was a long silence. At last Lynn asked,

"You will marry Sally, won't you, Tony?"

He did not answer and so she went on,

"But why do I ask you? I know you will. You have always done what I wanted and I know you won't fail me now. Goodnight, Tony, and bless you."

She took the receiver from her ear, heard his voice call out, "Lynn", and again, "Lynn!" then there was only a click as she replaced the receiver.

5

"You look lovely!" Mary exclaimed to Sally as Rose fixed the wreath of orange blossom over her lace veil.

She was not exaggerating. There was something exquisite this morning in Sally's face lifted to the mirror and something, too, so young and fresh and untouched that Mary, unsentimental though she was, felt a sudden moisture about her eyes and a lump in her throat as she looked at her.

"Do you think Lynn will be pleased?" Sally asked a little anxiously.

"Of course she will," Mary answered reassuringly.

"Then that will make me happier than ever," Sally said, "not that I could be much happier, Mary." And turning from the mirror to look up into the older woman's face, she added, "I am lucky, aren't I?"

It seemed to her that a shadow passed across Mary's eyes and there was a seconds hesitation before she answered,

"I think your future husband is lucky, too."

Sally smiled.

"Don't tell him so," she begged. "Nothing is more irritating than for people to keep telling you how fortunate you are in having some particular thing. It always makes one want to find faults with it – at least it does me."

She paused a moment, wondering vaguely to herself why Mary looked sad, before she continued,

"It is so lovely to think that I am being married properly. I mean with orange blossom and in a white dress. Despite all this haste, dear, kind Madame Marguerite has managed it, I have promised to write to her on my honeymoon and tell her exactly what a success all my dresses are. She will be at the church to see this one, and it is lovely, isn't it, Mary?"

"Lovely," Mary repeated.

She did not add, as she might have done, that the idea of Sally's wearing white and being married in church had been entirely hers.

Lynn in her anxiety to have the wedding over before she went abroad, had been all for a quick ceremony at the Caxton Hall Register Office and only Mary's sane common-sense had dissuaded her.

"If you want the child talked about and reporters suspicious, you can go no better way about it," Mary said. "A hole-in-the-corner wedding is always suspect, especially when neither of the parties are divorced and there is no ostensible reason for it. Make everything dull and conventional and I assure you that no single newspaper will give it a passing thought. They will have to have a special licence, for there will not be time to read the banns, but no-one need know about that except the Vicar who marries them. Arrange the ceremony at some unfashionable but respectable church nearby and have a small reception of friends here and who will ask questions? Nobody, because it will just be uninteresting. There is no news in the commonplace and well you know that, Lynn."

Lynn thought it over and said,

"You are right, of course you are right, Mary. You always are about things like that."

"There is no need to put the engagement or the marriage in *The Times*," Mary went on, "there may be St. Vincent relatives whom you know nothing about and it might revive their memories and make things awkward for you. Just arrange things quietly while making it clear that there is no secrecy about them. No-one in London knows Sally, and Tony Thorne, as far as I can make out, is quite prepared to leave it to you to have things done as easily and as quietly as possible."

Lynn gave a sharp glance as though she wondered just how much she knew or guessed about Tony's feelings, but she made no comment, only giving Mary full permission to go ahead with the arrangements for Sally's wedding, which included a conventional white wedding dress, a choir and a three-tiered wedding cake.

Now as Mary looked at Sally's radiant face framed in the lovely lace veil that Lynn had surprisingly dug out from an old box where it had lain since her marriage to Arthur St. Vincent, she felt as if Sally's excitement and gratitude were almost more than she could bear. Yet what could she say, for what indeed, she asked herself, was the alternative to what had been planned?

"There, I'm ready," Sally exclaimed, "and of course I shall have hours to wait. I am told one is either too early for one's wedding or too late. One never achieves a happy medium."

"I will go and see if Lynn is dressed yet," Mary said, "and if Dr. Harden has arrived,"

"Yes, do," Sally said, "and I must not forget to go up the aisle on his right arm, must I? Somehow it always seems easier to walk on someone's left."

It was Mary again who had suggested that Dr. Harden, who was an old friend of Lynn's and a devoted admirer, should give Sally away. He was only too honoured at being asked and any protegee of Lynn's was sure of his kindness and courtesy. He and Sally had met two or three times before the wedding, because Lynn was always having treatment for something or other. They liked each other and Sally was delighted that he should play an important part in her wedding ceremony.

"There, Miss Sally, you are ready" Rose said, standing back to admire the way she had fitted the veil under the simple wreath. "Oh, thank you, Rose. Can I stand up?"

"Yes, miss, but be careful. If you do, you must not sit down again until you get into the car."

"Very well," Sally smiled. "I would not crease this dress for anything and I want to do you credit. You are coming to the church, aren't you?"

"Oh, yes, miss, I am going now. I am leaving the moment after Madam."

"Well, get a good seat," Sally said, "not that there is any likelihood of there being a crowd. I don't suppose there will be more than half a dozen people in the church."

"Oh, you'll be surprised, miss," Rose said, "and if the rumour gets round that Madam is going, there will be a crowd all right."

"I'm sure there will," Sally said, "but she isn't to take all my limelight, Rose."

"I won't let her," Rose promised with a smile, "but you know what Madam is."

"Yes, she's the most beautiful person in the world," Sally said impulsively, "and I should want to go and see her whatever she was doing and wherever she was, not just to look at some ordinary unknown country bride, however pretty she thought herself."

Rose laughed.

"Oh, Miss Sally, how you do run on! At times you remind me of Madam, you do really. That is just the way she often talks, mocking at herself."

"That is the nicest compliment I have ever had, Rose," Sally smiled.

But at the same time she felt a little apprehensive fear clutch hold of her. It would be awful if she ever did remind people of Lynn, for what would Lynn say?

But why worry? All would be well after today. She would have a husband and another name and why should anyone ever connect Mrs. Anthony Thorne with the glamorous, sensational Lynn Lystell?

"Mrs. Anthony Thorne!" Sally whispered the name aloud.

Rose had gone from the room and she was alone and now she moved across to the window to stand looking out yet seeing not the trees and the dusty garden of Berkeley Square, but rather the strange, exciting future lying ahead of her. Tony's wife! How lucky she was. How very, very lucky that someone like Tony loved her.

He had been so sweet and so gentle with her lately and never since that first night when he proposed had he frightened her again or left her bewildered and startled by his actions. In fact it had seemed to Sally at times as though he was determined to make her feel at ease with him. When he kissed her, it was very gently and as often as not on the cheek and when he put his arms round her, it was in a friendly, undemanding manner – more brotherly than lover-like.

And yet Sally knew that she was very conscious of him as a man. It was such fun to dine, to dance and spend long lazy afternoons in the country with a man who was as good-looking and as interesting as Tony. She had been half afraid at first that she might bore him, but it seemed as if there was plenty to talk about, and even if conversation failed, she was happy enough to sit in silence with him, not feeling, embarrassed when their tongues were silent, but calm and contented and at peace.

Never before in her whole life had she known what it was to have someone to look after her, helping her in and out of her coat, putting a firm arm under hers to lead her across the road, handing her into a car, as though she were not capable of scrambling into it by herself and consulting her on every occasion as to what they should do or where they should go. It was all so exciting and unusual and it was completely thrilling, too, to have flowers brought to her with Tony's card attached to them or to look down at the small sapphire and diamond ring on the third finger of her left hand.

She had been prepared to panic somewhat at the speed with which they must be engaged, married and away on their honeymoon, all to suit Lynn, who was leaving for South America in two days' time. But somehow when she thought that it was Tony whom she was marrying, Tony who was so kind and considerate, Tony who had become undoubtedly the greatest friend she had ever had in her life, she was no longer afraid.

She was, however, bitterly disappointed that she would not be able to be present at Lynn's wedding. Lynn's engagement had been splashed across most of the newspapers in headlines, but she was curiously reticent about her marriage.

"I don't know when it will take place," she told reporters. "My future husband has many things to arrange before we can make any announcement."

Lynn's public had to be content with this ambiguous statement, but Lynn had confided to Sally,

"It will have to be a secret marriage, you will understand why. They will ask all sorts of tiresome questions as to where I was born and if I have been married before. I think, and so does Mary, that the quickest and best way will be to find a Consul as soon as we set foot in South America or maybe the Captain of the ship will be obliging, that is if we don't fly. Anyway, I can't be married in England and so you can't be there, darling."

"Oh, Lynn," Sally said reproachfully, but Lynn said sharply,

"Don't be stupid, Sally. I believe you have some idea of being my bridesmaid. I can't imagine anything more unsuitable."

"No, of course I wasn't hoping for that," Sally protested, "but I would have liked to be present, Lynn. You are certain to look lovely, and, well, I suppose it was just a silly idea of mine, but I wish I could have seen you."

"Ridiculous child," Lynn said, but her voice was no longer sharp. She could always be moved, however cross she was, Sally discovered, by a reference to her beauty. Mary would have said in her usual, far-seeing way that it was because Lynn was beginning to. question how long that same beauty would last, but there was no reason for her to worry yet. She had never looked lovelier than during the weeks which followed the announcement of her engagement to Erico and at the many festivities that were given in her honour. Love appeared to have brought to her a new bloom and a new radiance that she had never possessed before.

Sally found herself wishing not once, but many times, that she had inherited not her father's more conventional English looks but Lynn's passionate loveliness with dark, seductive eyes and a full, beguiling mouth. But what was the point of wishing? Apparently Tony liked her enough as she was.

Dear Tony! Often when she was alone she repeated his name to herself as if it was a kind of talisman. Not only had no-one ever made love to her in her life before, but she had never had a real friend. It seemed to her that Tony combined the two so perfectly. He was always ready to listen to her and when she did not talk he could tell her things that she had always wanted to hear. Things about people and places and to Sally there seemed nothing he did not know. Day by day she realised how narrow her life at Aunt Amy's had been. It had been an isolated, concentrated existence with all their interests pinpointed on the farm while the world outside had gone forgotten for weeks, if not months on end.

Tell me more, tell me more, she would beg Tony, just like a child.

Usually he would laugh and oblige but once he looked at her seriously and said,

"What a funny little thing you are, Sally! I am so fond of you and I would hate to hurt you or make you unhappy."

"But you make me very happy," Sally answered, rubbing her head softly against his shoulder as if she were an affectionate pet animal.

"I hope I shall always be able to do that," Tony answered and then abruptly he got to his feet and, moving away from Sally, walked across the room to stand looking up at Lynn's, picture over the mantelpiece.

They had been sitting in Lynn's *boudoir*, a small room, which in actual fact was seldom used, for Lynn was either in bed or receiving in the big silver and grey drawing room downstairs. Decorated in pale blue with skilful touches of coral silk, the *boudoir* was dominated entirely by a picture of Lynn that had been painted three years earlier by one of the most eminent artists of the day. The picture was outstanding in that there was no colour in it at all save the crimson of Lynn's lips. But every tone of black and grey could yet contrive to be so sensational that one had only to enter the room where it was to find it impossible to ignore the picture or to forget it afterwards.

Sally, as she followed the direction of Tony's eyes, had the strangest feeling that Lynn was listening to their conversation. Tony was standing very still, his head was thrown back and his shoulders squared, yet there was something in his silence as he looked up at Lynn's pictured face that made Sally ask,

"What are you thinking about, Tony?"

"Lynn!"

"It is a wonderful likeness, isn't it?" Sally said warmly. "How lovely she is!"

"Yes, how lovely," Tony agreed.

He spoke easily, but there was something raw in his voice, something that Sally heard and did not understand,

"She has been such a wonderful…" Sally hesitated, and then found the word she sought, "friend to me."

"Has she?"

Still Tony did not turn round from his contemplation of the. picture.

"I shall always be grateful to her," Sally went on, "and I must always do what she wants of me, whatever it is, Tony, you understand that?" Tony turned suddenly.

"Yes, we must always do what Lynn wants," he said, and there was an unexpected note of mockery in his voice as though he jeered at himself.

He walked across to the sofa and took Sally's hand in his.

"Come on," he said, pulling her to her feet. "We are going out. I hate this room. Let us take a walk in the fresh air. I need some exercise."

"But, Tony," Sally protested. "I thought…"

"Well, don't," Tony said. "Don't think, don't argue. Go and get your hat or whatever it is you want. I will be waiting for you in the hall."

He held the door open for her, and as she went to her room he ran downstairs as if he were escaping from something. But when Sally joined him again, she had forgotten to be surprised at his sudden change of plans.

Now, thinking of Tony, she wondered if he was really as fond of Lynn as he should be. Sometimes when he spoke of her, she had heard again that strange note of mockery in his voice. She hoped that when they were married he would not make any difficulties about her seeing Lynn, but the thought was there only for her to laugh at. She could not imagine Tony making difficulties of any sort. He was so kind and good-natured, so ready to be obliging. At the same time there was just that faint uneasiness at the back of Sally's mind because, she told herself, however much she loved

Tony she could never, never love anyone more than she did Lynn. She must come first, yes, always first, in her life.

It was almost a vow that Sally made to herself, standing there, a vow of utter subservience to Lynn, whatever her demands might be and then as she made it she heard Lynn's voice almost before the door opened to admit her.

"Darling, are you ready?"

Lynn, looking breathtakingly lovely, was standing in the doorway. She was wearing a dress of deep sapphire blue with a hat to match and there was a necklace of diamonds and sapphires round her neck and a bracelet of the same stones glittering on her wrist.

"Oh, Lynn!" Sally exclaimed.

"And I might say the same," Lynn replied. "Oh, Sally! You look sweet, my darling, very sweet and very young. Tony is the luckiest man in all the world and I'll see that he doesn't forget it."

"And I was just thinking how lucky I am," Sally said, "because I have you."

"Silly child," Lynn smiled. "I hope you will always think so. I am going now, and Dr. Harden has orders to bring you along in exactly four minutes' time. Your bouquet is waiting for you in the hall, so don't leave without it."

"I won't," Sally promised, "and, Lynn, in case I don't get a moment with you again, I want to say thank you."

"Darling Sally, as though I wanted you to say anything of the sort," Lynn expostulated.

"I know you don't," Sally said, "and that is what makes it all the more wonderful. You have done this for me at a moment when it was highly inconvenient. I am grateful, terribly grateful, Lynn, and I shall never forget it, never."

There was a break in Sally's voice, but Lynn merely put out her hand and touched her check.

"You are sweet," she said and turned towards the door. "I'll see you in the church, darling, and good luck."

"Thank you," Sally whispered.

Alone again, she fought against the emotion that threatened for the moment to overwhelm her when she tried to thank Lynn.

'I am being sentimental,' she told herself, 'and Lynn was right to pass it off lightly.'

Yet somehow deep in her heart she wished that Lynn had said something more, somehow, ridiculous though it was, Sally had a great longing that she might once – only once – call Lynn, 'Mother'. How wonderful it would have been if, when they were alone just now, Lynn had let the pretence drop and allowed Sally to kiss her and in return had held her close as an ordinary mother might hold her only daughter on her wedding day.

But Lynn was quite right, Sally told herself loyally, and chided herself for being over-sentimental. She took a last look in the mirror and then slowly walked downstairs to where she knew Dr. Harden would be waiting.

Lynn, driving to the church alone, for Erico was coming to the reception and not to the ceremony, was thinking about Sally with nearly as much affection as Sally herself might have wished. After all, Lynn thought, she had done well by her daughter. Anthony Thorne might not have any money, but he was of a good family, well-bred and well-brought-up. He was good-looking and charming and nearly everyone with whom he came in contact liked him. He had a fine war record, above all he was a kindly person who would never be cruel to Sally and he would doubtless, Lynn told herself, settle down and make her an excellent husband.

What more could any girl want? Besides, when Sally grew older she would be wise enough to realise that she held the purse-strings and that the woman who paid the piper could call the tune.

Yes, Lynn thought as she settled herself a little more comfortably in the back of the Rolls-Royce, she had done well for Sally. One day she would be very grateful to her mother. And in the meantime, her immediate future was settled and she would not have to drift about penniless, seeking a job, as had so many other girls of her age.

The thought of money was always unpleasant and Lynn, thinking of the great pile of bills that had got to be met somehow, wondered whether she would dare to show them to Erico immediately after her wedding, or whether it would be wise to wait a little while and let him down gently. Somehow they would have to be paid, and some of them would not wait much longer. However, she was well aware that on the announcement of her engagement her creditors, who had been getting more and more unpleasant as the months went by, had breathed again and felt fairly certain that a settlement would be made once Lynn got her hands on the much-vaunted wealth of the South American millionaire.

'What a nuisance money is,' Lynn thought and hardly noticed the glitter of her bracelets as she adjusted the short cape of wild mink that she had thrown over her shoulders to keep herself warm in the car.

The church was only a short distance from Berkeley Square and Lynn was pleased to see that there were only half a dozen women of uncertain age hanging about near the red and white striped awning to note who entered the church. It was about the first time in her life that Lynn had not been anxious for an admiring crowd to watch her arrival or departure and she got out of the car quite hurriedly, walking quickly up the steps into the porch, but not before she had heard one of the women whisper inquisitively,

"Now who is that, dearie? I'm certain sure I know her face."

As Sally had predicted, there were very few people in the church. Most of them indeed were people who, having dressed Lynn for years, had been cajoled into making things for Sally in a phenomenally quick time. There were Madame Marguerite and two of her assistants, two girls who always made Lynn's hats and who had worked late the whole of the week finishing Sally's, Lynn's hairdresser and her manicurist with a few of their friends who had come to look at Lynn rather than at Sally. Besides these, to swell the attendance on the bride's side of the church, there were Mary Stubbs, looking unusually smart in a new hat trimmed with a brown feather and Dr. Harden's wife and daughter.

On Tony's side there were even fewer people, two or three old women who might be merely curious onlookers and in the front pew, a tall, rather good-looking man whom Lynn had never seen before. She guessed that he was Tony's brother, of whom he had seldom spoken because, as she had taunted him more than once, he was afraid of him.

Smiling and lovely, Lynn swept into the front pew and then glanced across the aisle, expecting that Tony's brother would be looking at her. Instead, he was looking ahead, his features set sternly in an expression that Lynn sensed quite correctly was one of disapproval.

'He ought to be pleased,' she told herself angrily. 'After all, it is time Tony settled down. He has sown enough wild oats in all conscience and not only with me. I was not the first woman in his life and I don't imagine for a moment that I have been his last.'

She looked across the aisle again, but still Tony's brother made no sign that he was aware of her presence. Mary bent towards her from the pew behind.

"Is everything all right?" she asked.

"Everything," Lynn replied. "I told Sally and Dr, Harden to follow me in exactly four minutes."

At that moment the choir, consisting mostly of very small boys with untidy hair, came shuffling into their places and as the congregation rose Lynn was suddenly aware that a youth in messenger's uniform was standing beside her.

"Miss Lystell?" he asked in a hoarse whisper.

"Yes," Lynn replied.

"This is for you, then," he answered. "I took it to the house, but they said you had come on to the church. It is urgent, so I brought it right away."

Lynn looked down at the note that he held out to her and only her years of training prevented her from giving an audible exclamation of astonishment as she recognised the writing on the envelope.

"Sign here, please, miss," the messenger requested, but Lynn made a gesture as if to dismiss him, and Mary, bending forward, took his book and signed in the allotted space.

Lynn, sitting down in her seat, tore open the note.

"What is it?" Mary asked, sensing only too clearly that something was wrong.

"Wait a minute," Lynn whispered.

She drew the two sheets of paper out of the envelope. Sentences seemed to jump from the page to confront her.

...unfair, cruel and unforgivable – She's too young, too trusting – I love you and only you – heading for Paris – leaving immediately by air – well rid of me – "

She finished reading and sat there rigid, staring at the note, then she drew a deep breath.

"What it is, Lynn?" Mary asked again.

There was a pause when it seemed as if for a second Lynn was unable to find her voice. When she did speak, her tone was hardly recognisable.

"He isn't coming."

There was no need to ask whom she meant.

"Why not?" Mary asked.

Lynn folded the note over in her hands.

"For no reason I can possibly say."

Mary was very still. As always when Lynn ran into difficulties it was up to her to find a way out. Only for a moment did it seem to her as if her mind was too chaotic

~114~

for sensible thought, then quickly, so that as she spoke her words almost tumbled over one another, she said,

"The bridegroom has been taken ill, go to the vestry and tell the Vicar. I will stop Sally at the door and send her home."

"Ill?" Lynn questioned.

"Yes, ill," Mary said quickly. "Go, Lynn, there is no time to be lost."

Lynn turned then and her face was very white.

"I will never forgive him for this," she murmured.

Her lips tightened and there was such an expression of hatred in her dark eyes that Mary almost instinctively recoiled. Then her usual common-sense made her reply.

"That can wait until later. We don't want a scene now or anything in the papers."

It was as if the mere mention of the newspapers was all that was required to galvanise Lynn into action. She got up from the pew, walked into the aisle and went towards the vestry as Mary hurried towards the West Door.

It only took Lynn a moment to tell the Vicar, surpliced and waiting, that the wedding must be cancelled owing to the sudden illness of the bridegroom. He expressed his regret and said that he would make an announcement from the chancel.

As Lynn came from the vestry back to her seat, she found herself looking straight at Tony's brother. She stopped in front of him,

"The Vicar is about to make an announcement that Tony is ill," she said. "I wish to see you immediately. Will you kindly come back with me to my house?"

"Most certainly."

He spoke courteously, but now Lynn was certain that her first impression had been correct. He disapproved of her and if anything could have famed the mounting fury of her anger it was that.

She went to her place in the front pew. A second later the Vicar made the announcement that the bridegroom was ill and the service was therefore most regrettably cancelled. He added that their thoughts and prayers would be with him for a speedy and complete recovery and with the bride in her anxiety.

There was an audible whispering amongst the sparse congregation as the choir shuffled out again and then, determined not to speak with anyone, Lynn swept down the aisle with her head held high, aware that Tony's brother was following closely behind her. Her car was waiting and she was thankful to see that there were no signs of Sally and Mary and that they must already have driven away. She got in and was not too hurried to notice that there were no press photographers about and no-one who looked in the least like a reporter.

"Shall I come with you?" a voice asked, and she impatiently beckoned Tony's brother into the seat beside her, telling the chauffeur to take them home.

As they moved off, stared at only by the curious, middle-aged women, whose mouths were wide open with astonishment, Lynn said,

"You are Sir Guy Thorne, I believe?"

"I am," was the reply. "Is my brother really ill?"

"He is not," Lynn answered, "he has ratted at the last moment."

"Surely that is rather unexpected?" Sir Guy said quietly.

"I saw Tony two days ago when he told me he was about to be married. He gave me very few details except that the wedding was to be a quiet one and that he did not wish Mother told until after the ceremony had taken place. He invited me to be present and I agreed, though I was extremely against a hurried wedding of this sort, which seemed to me quite unnecessary."

His tone was very cool and dignified and Lynn, feeling angrier than ever but controlling herself with admirable restraint, said,

"I have a great deal to say about this and perhaps, as we are nearly at my house, it would be wise to wait until we get there."

"As you wish," Sir Guy said courteously and sat back in his seat apparently quite at his ease until the car drew up at Lynn's house in Berkeley Square.

There was no sign of Sally, but Mary was waiting in the hall, Lynn waved her on one side.

"I wish to speak with Sir Guy," she said, "please see that we are not disturbed.

She led the way into the drawing room and Sir Guy followed her, closing the door behind him, Lynn, facing him with her back to the mantelpiece, was conscious of his calm, unhurried manner and that in contrast her own hands were trembling with sheer unbridled rage.

"Now," she said, "we can talk. I want to tell you exactly what I think of your brother and what I intend to do about him."

"Before we go too far, Miss Lystell," Sir Guy said, "perhaps you will be kind enough to enlighten me as to what exactly is your position in this matter. My brother informed me that he was marrying a Miss St. Vincent. He told me that her parents were dead. I was not aware that my brother's future wife had anything to do with you or that you were likely even to be acquainted. It was only on our way here that I connected the address at which the reception was to be held with your residence. May I therefore ask your relationship with the bride?"

His words had the effect of pulling Lynn up sharply.

"I am no relation to Sally," she said quickly, "but she has, as you might put it, been under my guardianship. Her father, Arthur St. Vincent, a member of a well-known County family, was an old friend of mine and I also knew Sally's mother. I have taken an interest in the child ever since she was born and when recently, through the unfortunate and unexpected death of her aunt with whom she was living, she was rendered homeless, I had her to stay with me. They met here and she became engaged to your brother."

"Oh, I see," Sir Guy said, "she is in the nature of being a *protégée* of yours?"

"Or ward, if you prefer the word," Lynn said. "Anyway, Tony proposed to the child under my roof. He asked my secretary to make all the arrangements for their marriage and for a reception here. He has now in this eleventh hour gone back on his word. He tells me in this note," she drew it from her bag "that he has received a letter this morning offering him the post in Paris that he was so anxious to obtain. He has decided to accept the position and cancel his marriage."

Lynn paused for a moment and her eyes, looking at Tony's letter, were obviously choosing what parts of it she should read to Sir Guy and what parts she should keep to herself.

"Am I to understand," Sir Guy said, "that the choice was one or the other? The position in Paris or marriage with your – ward?"

"No, it was not," Lynn said sharply. "I will be frank with you, Sir Guy. I was anxious for Sally to be married and settled before I went abroad. She will, on her marriage, come into a considerable income. Tony is completely and absolutely broke, as I imagine you are well aware."

"And being so, he was prepared to nibble at the bait you so skilfully offered him," Sir Guy said sarcastically.

"Tony was only too delighted to have a chance of paying his debts," Lynn said savagely.

"Indeed! I was aware that my brother owed certain sums of money, but not that he was being pressed so hard as all that."

"He shall pay for this," Lynn said angrily. "When I think of all I have done for Tony, when I think of what he owes me and of the harm I could do him, I am astonished that he dare behave in such a manner."

"What he owes you?" Sir Guy interrupted quietly. "You said that, didn't you? Tony is in debt to you? May I know to what extent?"

"Yes, you may," Lynn said, too angry now to be cautious. "Over a year ago your brother forged a cheque in my name. It was honoured by the bank and then later queried. I have that cheque and up till now I have taken no steps in the matter. It was for a thousand pounds,"

Sir Guy said nothing, and because his silence angered her more than words, Lynn went on,

"He was always afraid of your knowing. Well, now that you do know the truth, perhaps you would like to deal with him."

"I am surprised and shocked, as I think my brother anticipated," Sir Guy said. "I will, of course, send you my own cheque for the amount, Miss Lystell, immediately on my return home. There is only one question I would like to ask, perhaps it is not entirely an impertinent one – why was it so necessary a year ago for my brother to have a thousand pounds? Have you any idea how the money was spent?"

His eyes never left her face and for the first time Lynn was conscious of Sir Guy Thorne's personality. Here was a man who was neither bemused nor excited by her beauty, here was a man who disapproved of her and who was not carried away, as almost any man of her acquaintance would have been, by the idea that she personally had been injured and hurt by Tony's reprehensible behaviour.

Sir Guy's words showed her all too late the pit yawning at her feet into which, if she were not careful, she would fall. Swiftly she realised that he was aware not only that Tony's life had been entangled with hers for many years, but also that his debts, or a considerable portion of them, had been accumulated for her and by her. Finally she knew that his dislike and disapproval of Tony's behaviour were equalled or even exceeded by his dislike and disapproval of her personally.

She stared at him, trying hard to find an answer to his question and when she did not speak, he went on,

"You have been frank, Miss Lystell, let me also be frank. I have been distressed for many years by the affection my brother has shown for you. It has done Tony no good and, as you well know, the sole reason why he did not get the job in Paris upon which he had set his heart was that rumours of his attachment to you had reached the ears of his future employer. That he has now been offered the post is, I imagine, because your engagement has been publicly announced to another man. That in the meantime Tony could have been so foolish as to involve himself, whether under pressure of blackmail or not, with a ward of yours is, in my opinion, extremely reprehensible. But the girl will very probably find other young men anxious to share her fortune with her, or if she is unable to find them for herself, doubtless you will be there to advise and, help her."

His words were like a whip and for once Lynn forgot to act, forgot to pretend, and spoke only the truth.

"But you don't understand," Lynn said, "Sally loves Tony. She is only eighteen. She had no idea of all this. She loved him for himself. Surely even you can see the tragedy in that?"

Sir Guy obviously did not miss the ring of sincerity in Lynn's voice.

"I am sorry about that," he said quietly.

"Besides, what is the child to do?" Lynn went on, seeing for the first time a faint chance of gaining an advantage. "I am leaving for South America in two days' time. My fiancé is going with me and there is every possibility that we shall be married as soon as we land. It will not be practical or in any way possible to take Sally with me. She has nowhere else to go for – as I have already told you – she has no father or mother, and incidentally until the day she marries, she has no money – not a single penny."

"This is all extremely unfortunate, Sir Guy said. "I am sorry for Miss St. Vincent, very sorry, but no doubt, as you have already stage-managed her life to date, you will go a little further and find something else for her to do."

"I could, but why should I?" Lynn asked passionately. "It is your brother who has let her down. I consider it is up to you to do something for her now. I have done my best or…" Lynn added with a sudden flash of humour that was wont to make her almost irresistible even when people disliked her most, "my worst."

She smiled as she said it, but there was no answering smile on Sir Guy's face. After a moment he said gravely,

"Perhaps I should see Miss St. Vincent."

"You shall see her now," Lynn replied. "But may I remind you that she is suffering quite enough as it is and there is no reason for you to tell her that Tony was marrying her for her money. She had no idea of it."

"I shall certainly not injure her more than she has already been injured," Sir Guy said in. a voice that condemned Lynn as clearly as if he had said so outright.

Lynn went to the drawing room door and opened it. Outside, as she expected, Mary was waiting in the hall.

"Where is Sally?" she asked.

"She is in your boudoir," Mary replied.

"Is she alone?"

"Yes. Dr. Harden was with her, but he left just a few moments ago."

"Sir Guy Thorne wishes to speak to Sally," Lynn said. "Will you take him up to her?"

"Of course," Mary answered. "Will you come this way, Sir Guy?"

The door of the dining room was open and Sir Guy, as he turned towards the stairs, could see a table bearing the big white cake and rows of empty glasses waiting for the unopened bottles of champagne.

Without a word he followed Mary to the first floor. At the door of the boudoir Mary paused for a moment.

"Sally has not yet been told that your brother is not in reality ill," she said, "I left that to Lynn, but as you are seeing her first, perhaps you will tell her the truth."

If Sir Guy resented the job allotted to him, he did not say so. Instead, he made a gesture as of assent and Mary opened the door and went in.

"Sally, here is Tony's brother, Sir Guy Thorne, come to see you," she said and then without another word slipped past Sir Guy and closed the door behind her.

Sally was sitting on an upright chair by the writing table. She had evidently not moved since she first came into the room, for her bouquet was just beside her and her head was lowered a little as she stared with unseeing eyes at a lace-edged handkerchief she held in her hands. As Sir Guy entered, she jumped to her feet and walked towards him.

"Oh, what is wrong with Tony?" she asked. "No one will tell me. Mary is so mysterious about it and Lynn has not yet come upstairs to speak to, me. Please tell me what is wrong."

She paused for a moment and then, as he did not answer her, she cried in a voice in which he could hear the far beating of her heart,

"He isn't dead, is he?"

"No, he is not dead," Sir Guy said quickly and was silent once again as Sally put her hands up to her face and a shudder of relief ran through her whole body.

"Thank God!" she murmured. "I was afraid of that, afraid from the moment Mary brought me back from the church and would not say what had happened,"

She stood very still for a long moment as though she forced her self-control and when she raised her face there were no tears in her eyes, only her lips trembled to show what an effort it had been.

"I am sorry to have been so silly," she said quietly "and now, please, will you tell me what is wrong with Tony."

As she spoke, she looked up into Sir Guy's face for the first time since he came into the room. She recognised him instantly. He was the man on the train – the owner of the friendly spaniel.

6.

For the moment Sally thought of nothing and nobody except Tony. Vaguely she was aware that this man whom she had seen twice before in her life was looking at her with a set, grave face and that there was something about him which seemed antagonistic. But her anxiety and her distress for Tony transcended all else and it was only afterwards that she was aware that there had been an undercurrent of other thoughts and feelings of which she was not entirely conscious at the time.

"Tell me about him," she begged, "please, please tell me about him."

Sir Guy walked across to the hearth to stand looking down into her eyes, dark with anxiety, her face almost as pale as the lace veil that framed it.

"I am afraid you must be prepared for a shock, Miss St. Vincent," he said slowly. "My brother is not ill, nor, as far as I know, is there anything the matter with him physically."

Sally looked utterly bewildered.

"Then why…?" she began.

"Please allow me to finish," Sir Guy interrupted. "I think you would rather that I should be completely frank with you and so I will tell you the truth as far as I know it. My brother, Anthony, has decided not to get married."

For a moment Sally stared at him as if the meaning of his words did not penetrate her mind, then she went, if possible, even paler and, her hands raised themselves with a little convulsive gesture towards her breasts.

"You mean…" she asked, and her voice was hardly above a whisper, "you mean that – Tony d-does not want to marry me?"

"That, I believe, is the truth," Sir Guy said. "As I have already said, this will be a shock to you Miss St. Vincent, and I must express my regret for my brother's behaviour in this matter."

"But I don't understand," Sally cried piteously. "Yesterday he seemed happy. He was so kind to me, so understanding about everything. What has happened?"

"I am as much at a loss in some ways as you are," Sir Guy replied. "All I know is that my brother has written to Miss Lystell saying that he has decided not to go on with his marriage to you, that he has been offered a position in Paris and has already left this country."

"The job in Paris," Sally said brokenly. "He wanted it so much."

Suddenly, as if her legs could no longer hold her, she sat down in the chair. She bowed her head a little, staring at her hands. But she did not cry. She was in fact very far from tears for there was a sense of utter desolation within her, a feeling of loneliness so great that tears would have been too petty an expression of the darkness that overwhelmed her. Tony had been her friend. She had grown to rely on him, learnt to trust him, and now he had gone without a word, without even an explanation of his change of plans.

She had been so sure that he loved her, sure because his very kindness had been something she had never known before in her whole life and she had reached out towards his strength and warmth with the simplicity and trust of a child. Then as she sat there searching inwardly for some point of contact with the outer world, another thought struck her. She looked up at Sir Guy.

"Is Lynn angry?" she asked, and there was a note almost of horror in her voice.

Sir Guy's lips twisted a little.

"I think Miss Lystell is extremely annoyed with my brother."

"And with me?"

"I am afraid I have no idea what Miss Lystell's feelings could be towards you," Sir Guy replied. "But I see no reason why you should be implicated."

"But she had planned everything, the wedding, our honeymoon and she had even offered to lend us her car. Oh, I am sure Lynn will be terribly upset, especially as she herself is going away. What shall I do?"

Sally spoke more to herself than the man who was listening and again his lips twisted.

"Miss Lystell has made it very clear that my brother's actions have made things most inconvenient where she is concerned, in fact that is why she asked me to speak to you. As I have already said, I can only apologise on behalf of my family and myself for my brother's behaviour. It is in many ways inexcusable – although perhaps he had in his own eyes adequate reasons for such an action."

"I wish I knew what they were," Sally murmured.

"Perhaps Miss Lystell can help you there," Sir Guy replied drily.

"Lynn told me that Tony was in love with me – she told me how much he wanted to marry me. You see," Sally said confidentially, "I know very little about men. I have not had any experience except, with Tony."

"But surely your own better instincts…" Sir Guy began, but he stopped abruptly as if he was afraid of being involved in an argument that he did not wish to pursue.

Sally waited and it seemed to her as if he stiffened and became even more formal and antagonistic than he had been before.

"I think," he said at length, "that it is useless for us to continue this discussion. I have thought things over, Miss St. Vincent, and in one way I do agree that you have been – how shall we put it? – harshly treated by my brother in that this sudden flight of his has left you, for the moment at any rate, homeless. Therefore, I think it only right and just that, until you can find some employment or some other place of residence, I should offer you the hospitality of my home. It is in Yorkshire and I shall be going there myself first thing tomorrow morning. May I suggest that you accompany me? In the meantime, I will notify my mother that you will be coming with me."

Sally drew in a deep breath. Then, after a moment's hesitation, she replied,

"It is very kind of you to ask me, for I know that neither you nor your mother will want me in the least, but I feel that Lynn would wish me to accept, wouldn't she?"

"Undoubtedly," Sir Guy answered.

"Then – then thank you very much and I promise you that I will try to make other arrangements as soon as I possibly can."

Sally's little effort at dignity was almost heart-breaking, her hands were trembling and her lips quivered as she spoke. At last the numbed sense of darkness was passing from her and now she knew herself very near to tears. She forced herself to stare up at Sir Guy, thinking how unlike he was to Tony and how remote and unsympathetic he seemed at this moment when her whole being cried out for kindness and comfort.

"That is settled then," Sir Guy said, "I will call for you at ten o'clock, if you will be ready."

"You will ask Lynn first, won't you?" Sally pleaded.

"I am sure we shall have Miss Lystell's complete approval," Sir Guy replied and his voice was bitterly sarcastic, but Sally seemed not to hear it.

He walked towards the door.

"Goodbye, Miss St. Vincent."

"Goodbye," Sally answered and now she had the utmost difficulty in speaking, yet she held the tempest within her in check for one more moment until the door was shut. Then she buried her face in her hands.

It seemed to her a long time later that she felt Mary's arms round her shoulders.

"Come to your room, dear," Mary advised, "and don't cry like that. Don't, Sally, no man in the world is worth it."

"But I don't understand. That is what is so – so awful," Sally stammered, "Oh, Mary, what did I do wrong? What made him hate me – suddenly – and at the last minute?"

"He doesn't hate you. You have got it all wrong, dear," Mary said and wished that she could tell Sally the truth and take that stricken look from her face.

But what indeed was there to say She laid aside the lace veil and unfastened Sally's white wedding dress. She cursed herself that she had ever been inveigled into taking part in this cruel tragedy.

Seated before her dressing table in her flimsy white chiffon underclothes, her fair hair falling on to her shoulders, Sally looked little more than a child and Mary searched her brain for any explanation that could bring her comfort and reassurance. What had happened had struck at her very spirit, it had annihilated with one blow that newly found, self-assurance and pride in herself which had developed like a lovely spring flower during the past weeks. If in the past Sally had been unsure of herself, she was now a thousand times more so, if in the past she had doubted her own attractions she was now utterly certain that she had none – in fact, Mary realised that deep in her heart Sally believed that it was some repulsive quality within herself that had driven Tony from her side.

But what could she say? What could she do? She could not tell Sally the truth, could not reveal the deception that had been practised on her from the very moment of her arrival in Berkeley Square.

"Forget him, just forget him," Mary urged the broken girl. "There are other men in the world and he is not worth your tears nor indeed one seconds unhappiness. We have all got to take knocks in our lives at some time or another. This is a terribly hard one, I know, and all the harder because you don't understand it. But Lynn is deeply distressed too and you don't want to make it worse for her, do you?"

Mary had struck the right chord. She had made the only appeal that could penetrate at the moment. Lynn must not be upset, whatever happened. Sally's love for her mother was such a real, vital thing that she was capable of making any sacrifice for her. Mary noticed how she had straightened her shoulders, how after a moment her tears stopped and she made an effort to wipe her eyes and wet cheeks.

Mary thought that it was essential, whatever happened, not to destroy Sally's faith in her mother. That at least must remain inviolate, for without that last sanctuary for her faith, she would indeed be lost.

When Sally came downstairs sometime later, every trace of the wedding had been cleared away. Morbidly, because she had in some way a desire to hurt herself, she looked into the dining room to see if the cake was there, but it had gone and so were the bottles of champagne and the rows of glasses. Even the white flowers that Mary had ordered to decorate the sideboard and the fireplace had been taken away. All trace of the wedding had vanished from the house, and it only remained for Sally to dismiss it from her heart.

But how impossible that was! She had only to go into the drawing room to see Tony as she had seen him that first evening, standing by the cocktail table, a glass in his hand, his eyes meeting hers with something youthful and challenging in his face. She had only to advance a little across the room to stand again on the very place on the grey carpet where he had first taken her in his arms and kissed her. She had only to listen to hear his voice, teasing her. She could hear his laugh with its note of deep amusement ringing out in the empty room. He had been so vital, that somehow it was difficult to think of him without a smile on his face. And now – now he was in Paris, taking up the job he had wanted more than he wanted her.

Why? Why? *Why?* Sally asked herself the question again and again within her heart and fatalistically she knew, even as she asked the question, that she was never to receive an answer.

Lynn came in late that evening and allowed herself only a short while to change for dinner. She was dining out – an engagement that had been arranged before Sally's wedding. She came quickly into the drawing room, pulling off her long suede gloves as she did so, and Sally awaited her with a shrinking heart, a little pulse of fear beating at the base of her throat. But Lynn was deliberately casual.

"Hullo, darling," she exclaimed. "I hope Mary has remembered to order you something for dinner. I am going to be late for mine if I don't hurry. Are there any telephone messages?"

"They are on your desk," Sally said. She forced the words from between her lips, feeling even as she did so that they might choke her.

Lynn picked up the little pieces of pink paper on which Mary always wrote her messages.

"There's nothing that can't wait until the morning," she said a moment later and put them down again. "Now I must hurry."

She flashed Sally an unreal, theatrical smile and moving across the room, opened the door and went upstairs.

For a moment Sally had a wild desire to run after her, to fling her arms round her mother, to cry against her shoulder and then even as the impulse was there, she mocked at herself for having thought of it. She knew only too well that

Lynn hated scenes that were not of her own making. Disturbances or people's unhappiness were not allowed to upset her if it could possibly be avoided. She might be temperamental, but those around her must remain calm, she might rush tempestuously about, but those around her must take things quietly and unflurried in their stride.

It was all too obvious to Sally that Lynn had raised a barrier between them where this matter of her broken marriage was concerned. It was a barrier that must not be broken down, and indeed, as Sally told herself piteously, there was nothing to say.

After dinner with Mary, at which neither of them could eat very much, Sally went upstairs to pack. Before she began, she said quietly to Mary,

"Does Lynn wish me to take away the clothes she gave me for my marriage?"

"But of course," Mary replied quickly,

"I shall not now be able to pay for them, for a long time,"

Mary's mouth tightened.

"You are not to think about repayment," she said sharply. "They are Lynn's present to you, and there is no question of your ever paying for them."

"I will pay for them one day," Sally answered, "otherwise I shall always feel that I have obtained them under false pretences. But for the moment that is impossible, as you know. I suppose we could sell them?"

"You will sell those clothes over my dead body," Mary cried and then, because she saw that Sally was about to argue, she added, "Lynn would be very hurt if you suggested such a thing to her."

Sally capitulated at once, as Mary knew she would.

"Oh, if Lynn wants me to have them…"

"She does," Mary answered, telling herself firmly that in this if in nothing else, she would have her own way.

There was not much packing to be done for most of Sally's things had been ready for her to take away on her honeymoon. A few dresses that were to have been stored at Berkeley Square until her return were added to the suitcases, she took out a coat and skirt to wear the following day and replaced it with the silk dress and matching cloth overcoat in which she was to have left for her honeymoon. Mary sat on the bed and watched her, trying to talk lightly and brightly, but somehow there was so little to say that she heard her own voice dying away and was conscious only of Sally kneeling on the door, her head bent as she folded the clothes that had been bought to delight Tony.

"I am writing down my address for you and my telephone number and if there is anything you want, Sally, you are to get in touch with me," Mary said. "I am not going to South America, as you know, but I won't be here because this house is going to be shut up."

"All I want is a job," Sally replied, her back turned to Mary.

"I know, dear, but they are not easy to find at the moment. You are more likely to pick up something in the country if, as you say, you want something to do with animals."

"It is the only thing I can do," Sally said and her voice was forlorn.

"Something will turn up," Mary remarked, trying to appear more convincing than she felt "If only you could type or do shorthand that would have been a help."

"I can't do anything really useful," Sally sighed,, "except cook or clean out a room, and somehow I don't think Lynn would approve of my taking a job as a kitchen maid or a daily help."

"I am quite certain she wouldn't," Mary said, "you mustn't do anything crazy or anything that would bring you unwelcome publicity."

"I don't think you need worry," Sally said. "There is only one thing for me to do and that is to get on a farm. There must be farms in Yorkshire. Perhaps Sir Guy will give me a reference."

For a moment the bleakness of the future caught at her throat, then she tried to smile with a bravery she was far from feeling.

"He can at least say I'm willing…"

"People will only have to look at you…" Mary began and then realised that any reference to Sally's appearance was rubbing salt into the wound of her shattered self-esteem. "Why not get into bed?" she suggested. "You must be tired."

"Yes, I am," Sally answered despondently and obediently began to undress.

"Do you want a book, or have you got something to read?" Mary asked, talking because she was afraid of the silence that lay between them.

She was conscious of so much that was being left unsaid. The big suitcases seemed to be crying out that they should not be here, but in the hotel where Lynn had decided that Sally and Tony should spend the first night. Sally's face, white and drawn, was the face of a widow rather than of a bride and so far, she and Mary had both tactfully ignored the little sapphire and diamond engagement ring that lay on the dressing table. At last, with an effort Sally picked it up.

"Do you think you could send this to Tony?" she asked. "I expect Lynn will know his address as he wrote to her."

"I will see to it," Mary said abruptly.

She thrust the ring deep into the pocket of her dress as if the contact of it with her hand burnt her. Sally got into bed.

"Goodnight, Mary."

"Goodnight, Sally dear," Mary replied.

She longed to add some words of comfort but could think of nothing.

"Goodnight," she repeated and went to her own bedroom.

*

Sally was up very early in the morning for she had not slept the whole night through. She lay awake, listening to the chimes of a distant clock and watching first the moonlight and then the pale fingers of the dawn creep through the open windows of her room. She took a great deal of care with her appearance, for one look at her haggard face in the looking glass told her that Lynn must not be confronted by such dark-eyed misery. Lynn liked people to be smart and pretty and Sally knew there was nothing she would dislike more than that she should appear crushed and defeated by the adversities of Fate.

She made up her face with great care, even putting a touch of colour on her cheeks. Somehow the result was not as successful as she would have wished, but at least she looked less like the ghost of her own self. Her coat and skirt of deep green tweed were beautifully cut, and there was a little hat trimmed with a soft bunch of feathers of the same colour to wear on the back of her head.

At eight o'clock Sally left her room and went downstairs. Mary usually breakfasted at 8.30 for she had a lot of work to get through before Lynn was called.

Lynn always had her breakfast in her own room, usually at about a quarter to ten. This morning when Sally reached the hall, she saw a message in Lynn's handwriting lying on the table. She read it almost before she was aware that she had done so and her heart seemed to stand still, for in Lynn's big, curly, characteristic writing she read the words,

I am not to be disturbed under any circumstances until ten-thirty.

And Sir Guy was to fetch her at ten o'clock, so she would not be able to say goodbye to Lynn. For a moment Sally could hardly believe it was true that she was to leave the house, to go away with a stranger, to a strange place without even a word of farewell to the person she loved best in the whole world.

Lynn could not have known the time she was leaving, she told herself hurriedly, but some small inner voice whispered the truth. Lynn knew and she had no intention of inflicting upon herself any signs of Sally's unhappiness.

Sally was still standing staring at the paper when Mary came downstairs. She read the note over Sally's shoulder and she too knew that Lynn had deliberately chosen to be called later so as to avoid her daughter. She slipped her arm through Sally's.

"Come to breakfast," she said quietly, "and Sally, as someone who has lived much longer than you have, may I give you some advice?"

"Yes, what is it?" Sally questioned dully.

"Never expect from people more than they are capable of giving," Mary replied. "Love people as they are, not for what you expect them to be. The root of so much heartbreak and so much unhappiness, is that we are always trying to credit the people we love with so much higher standards than they can in reality attain. Everybody has a definite individual horizon. We can't receive other people's and they can't see beyond it, any more than we can see beyond ours. Once accept that, once force yourself to see and act on that irrefutable fact and you will be a much happier person."

"I will try to remember what you have said," Sally said humbly, but Mary saw the hurt was still in her eyes and heard the pain of it in her voice."

"Sometimes," Mary went on, "in fact often in life, people do behave with a greatness and fineness that is better than

~135~

our highest expectations of them. Perhaps those moments come to all of us, enchanted moments when even the smallest person becomes great through sacrifice of self for an ideal."

"It is not easy to sacrifice self," Sally said quickly.

"Yes, I know," Mary replied, "that is why it is so infinitely worthwhile."

Sally's smile suddenly flashed out across the breakfast table.

"You are putting it very nicely, Mary, I know I am only thinking of myself and – and I will try not to, I will try."

"Bless you," Mary replied, and the two women's eyes met in a moment of perfect understanding.

Sally was waiting in the hall when a taxi drew up outside the front door and Sir Guy Thorne got out. She caught sight of his face, grave and rather cynical and in a moment of panic she put out her hand towards Mary.

"Must I go?" she asked, and then answered her own question. "There is nothing else for me to do, is there?"

"No, dear," Mary answered sadly.

"You won't forget to give Lynn the little note I have written her?" Sally begged. "I have thanked her so much for everything. And you will write and tell me all the things that you hear of her in South America, won't you? She is not a very good letter writer."

"No, I know she isn't," Mary said, "and I will let you know everything that I possibly can."

"Oh, thank you, *thank you,*" Sally whispered, kissing Mary as the door was opened by the butler and Sir Guy stood on the threshold. She clung to Mary for just a moment longer than was necessary and then, with her head held a little higher than usual, she turned towards Sir Guy, her hand outstretched in greeting.

"You are ready," he asked. "Good! We have got plenty of time, but sometimes this train is very crowded."

Sally's suitcases were put on the taxi and she got in. Sitting on the seat and wagging his tail in welcome was the golden spaniel she had seen before.

"Get down, Bracken," Sir Guy commanded, but Sally put her arm round him and held him close.

"There is plenty of room," she said. "Do let him stay where he is."

There was something comforting in the warm, furry body and she held Bracken beside her as the taxi drove off. She did not look back at the house, she did not even wave to Mary standing in the doorway. For a moment everything was blurred and obscured in a mist of unshed tears.

On the way to the station they exchanged a few commonplace remarks about the weather. The porter found them two corner seats in a first-class carriage and their luggage was put on the rack. Sir Guy's fears were unfounded and the train was not crowded. Another man got into their carriage just before the train started, and Sally was glad because she felt it precluded any chance of conversation. She sat back, looking out of the train window and watching the countryside flash past.

Soon her thoughts encroached upon her and she was seeing nothing but incidents in the past, going over and over conversations that had taken place, recalling a gesture or a movement that would start a long train of thought involving inevitably Tony and, when not him, Lynn.

Tony and Lynn. For the past weeks they had filled her life to the exclusion of all else and now once again a train was carrying her away into an unknown future and all that she had known intimately, was left behind.

Sally thought of the last journey she had taken by train and how lonely and lost she had felt, and she told herself that her loneliness then was nothing compared with the agonising sense of being utterly abandoned, which she was experiencing now. But she would not indulge for long in self-pity. She tried to think of other things and even to force herself to read the morning papers, which Sir Guy had bought at the station.

She looked down the list of employment vacancies in *The Times,* but nobody seemed to want a girl of eighteen with few capabilities and less ambition.

At twelve o'clock Sir Guy suggested that they go along for the first luncheon service, leaving Bracken to guard the luggage. Here once again they exchanged a few commonplace remarks and it was almost with relief that Sally realised that Sir Guy was as anxious to avoid any intimate conversation as she was herself. Once or twice when she looked up unexpectedly, she found his eyes upon her and realised there was once again a look of disapproval in his expression. She felt uncomfortable and wondered miserably what was wrong with her. that first Tony should desert her, and then his brother find her so unpalatable. Yet was his disapproval a personal thing – concerning her appearance or her character?

For the first time she began to think of Sir Guy's reactions towards what had occurred. After all there was no reason why he should have been pleased at his brother's intended marriage to an unknown girl whom none of the family had met. Vaguely, too, hardly as yet formulated in her mind, she had the idea that Sir Guy did not like Lynn or perhaps, like Aunt Amy, he had an antipathy to anyone who was on the stage. Sally began to wonder rather ruefully what sort of time she would have in Sir Guy's home. Perhaps his mother would be even more disapproving than he was.

She remembered the time when she had opened the front door of the house in Hill Street to find him on the doorstep. She had smiled at him and her smile had frozen on her lips. Until this moment she had not really grasped the fact that Sir Guy and Tony were the two young men

Nanny Bird had spoken to her about. She could remember her very words.

"The elder brother is a perfect gentleman, but the other, he's a wild lad. Yet you can't help liking him. He's got a-way with him."

Sally's heart cried out that Tony had indeed got a-way with him. How right Nanny had been and how strange a coincidence that her 'two young men' were Tony and Sir Guy. If only she had seen Nanny Bird again, there was so much she might have learnt.

But she had told Mary about Nanny and she had been horrified at the idea of anyone who had known Sally in the past, making contact with her while she was staying with Lynn.

"Don't mention it to Lynn," Mary had advised. "She would be frightened that your Nanny might guess who she is."

"I'm sure she wouldn't," Sally replied.

But obedient to any wish of Lynn's, expressed or unexpressed, she had not gone to see Nanny again nor written to tell her of her intended wedding.

Tony had arranged that on their return from their honeymoon, they should stay at the house in Bray, which had been lent him by some friends. He had talked of their returning to his London flat for the winter, but it had all been rather vague and in the rush and flurry of the wedding, Sally had been content to know only their immediate plans and she had not worried as to what lay ahead. Now she regretted her own lack of curiosity, the secrecy and her smothered sense of disloyalty to Nanny. How easily one subterfuge or lie led to another, she thought, and she wished miserably that she was back with Aunt Amy and her unfailing sense of right and wrong.

After luncheon they returned to their compartment and on an impulse Sally went along to the lavatory and there, in

~139~

the small glass over the wash basin, she cleaned the rouge from her cheeks and much of the lipstick from her lips. Somehow she felt more like herself and less like the glamorous, exciting person Lynn had wished her to be for Tony's sake. She washed her hands, felt cooler and cleaner and came back into the corridor.

She went towards their carriage. The train was passing through a particularly lovely part of the country, so she stopped in the corridor to look out of the window. As she did so she heard a carriage door open and a small, frightened voice beside her said,

"Please, can you help?"

She looked down to see a small boy. He was very thin with large, beautiful eyes and an exquisitely shaped face of such delicacy and beauty that Sally instinctively thought of a painting by an old master.

"Please, can you help?" he repeated.

"Yes, of course, what is the matter?" Sally replied.

"Mummy is ill," he said. "I don't know what to do."

"Where is she?" Sally asked, then as if he had run out of words and must rely instead on actions, the child put his hand into hers and pulled her quickly through the open door of a compartment.

Sitting on the seat was a young woman, bent almost double as though in great pain, and standing beside her was a little girl, smaller than the boy but with the same beautiful features and a white, frightened face.

"Let me help you," Sally said, going forward. "What is the matter?"

The woman raised her face, gave an audible groan and Sally saw there were beads of perspiration running down her face.

"I – am – sorry," she panted, "terribly sorry – to be a – nuisance – but I am – afraid – it is my – my appendix."

She said the words with the greatest difficulty and then put out her hand to Sally as if in desperation. Sally took it and the woman clung to her fiercely for a moment as if the human contact might in some way assuage the pain.

"Wouldn't you be more comfortable," Sally asked, "if I lifted your feet on to the seat? Then I will get help. There may be a doctor on the train."

The woman said nothing and Sally, taking silence for assent, bent down, lifted her legs and moved them gently on to the seat. The woman gave a groan and for a moment her head fell back against Sally's shoulder. She was quite young, very pretty, but her face was ashen with pain and there were drops of perspiration on her forehead and others on her upper lip.

"I will get someone at once," Sally said soothingly, and turning to the little boy she said, "Hold your mother's hand. It helps a bit."

He seemed to understand and Sally went out into the corridor. She looked up and down and to her relief she saw a ticket collector coming towards her. She ran towards him.

"Can you find out if there is a doctor on the train?" she said, "there is a woman in the carriage here with an inflamed appendix. She is in extreme agony and her life may easily be in danger."

The ticket collector followed Sally to the compartment, took one look at the woman and then looked at his watch.

"We are running through a station within three minutes," he said in a low voice. "We do not stop but shall be in York in a quarter of an hour. If I get them to telegraph, they can have an ambulance waiting."

"That will be splendid," Sally said.

"I will see to that, miss, if you will stay with the lady, and then I'll find out if there is a doctor or nurse on the train. I don't see that there is anything else we can do."

"No, I am sure that is best, "Sally answered. "I'll do what I can in the meantime."

She turned back to the woman, who was lying with closed eyes, white and exhausted. It seemed as if for a moment the extreme agony of her pain had passed. The children were standing beside her, both of them holding on tightly to one of her hands, their little faces strained and anxious.

"Suppose you both sit down," Sally said quietly and when they obeyed her, she said to their mother, "We shall be at York in a quarter of an hour and an ambulance will be waiting for you."

The woman opened her eyes but shut them again as if she were afraid to move any portion of her tortured body. Sally took out her handkerchief and wiped the sweat from her forehead and upper lip. Again the woman opened her eyes for a fleeting second but made no effort to speak. The children sat silent. Sally, however, was acutely conscious of them behind her, so she turned and smiled at them.

"Don't worry," she said, "your mother will be all right. Where were you going to?"

"To York," the boy answered.

"Is anyone meeting you there?"

He shook his head.

"We don't know anyone in England."

Sally looked at him in astonishment.

"No one?" she questioned.

He shook his head again.

"But where were you going to in York?"

"We were going to find a hotel," the little girl piped up, "it was my turn to choose one. Mummy said so."

It sounded such a strange story that Sally instinctively looked towards their mother for confirmation. But the woman was still lying with closed eyes. Suddenly Sally felt her fingers tighten on hers, and by the sudden contraction of the muscles on her body, she knew that the pain was starting again.

"Try to relax," she said quietly, "don't fight against it. It only makes it worse."

She saw the woman bite her lips and knew that she was trying to fight against crying out. Then to Sally's utter relief the corridor door opened to admit the collector and behind him was a woman in the uniform of the St. John Ambulance Brigade.

"I am so glad to see you," Sally said, "I am afraid the pain is very bad. The lady says it is her appendix."

The nurse nodded and without wasting words took command of the situation and the patient.

"I got the wire off, miss," the collector said to Sally. "With any luck the ambulance should be waiting."

"That is splendid," Sally answered.

"We will get this luggage down and at the door," the collector went on, starting to take the suitcases from the rack. He carried them along the corridor, the children watching with wide eyes.

The woman gave a deep groan.

"You will be all right in a few moments," the St. John nurse said gently. "Try and hold on."

"I am…trying."

It was obviously difficult for her to speak, her eyes opened again and she looked up at Sally.

"Please – look after the children," she said, each word uttered laboriously.

"Yes, of course I will," Sally replied, "don't worry. I promise you they will be all right."

She spoke impulsively without thinking and then even as she said the words, she knew that somehow, however difficult, she would fulfil her promise. She turned to the two children.

"I shall be back in a moment or two. I have got to get my things from the next carriage."

"You will come back?" the little boy asked, and it seemed to Sally that already he trusted her and feared to lose her. Once again she said,

"I promise you."

Hurrying down the corridor she found her own carriage. Sir Guy was sitting looking out of the window, the newspapers on his lap. He looked up as Sally entered and made a polite gesture as if to rise. Sally sat down opposite him.

"Listen, Sir Guy," she said, "there is a woman a few carriages along with peritonitis. She is in agony. Her little boy came to ask me to help and the collector has thrown a note out of the station we have just passed through asking the stationmaster to wire for an ambulance to be waiting at York. There is a nurse with her now. The trouble is that she was taking her two children to a hotel and they tell me that they know nobody in York, nor for that matter in England. I've – I've promised to look after them."

The last words came out in a rush. For a moment Sir Guy stared at Sally as if he did not quite understand.

"Oh, you have?" he said at length. "And how do you propose to do that?"

"I don't know," Sally replied, "but I promised her, and I must keep my promise. They are awfully sweet children. But I don't know whether they have any money. They are travelling third class and they don't look very rich."

Sir Guy slowly and rather deliberately took the newspapers off his knee and put them on the seat beside him.

"Suppose I come and see them," he suggested.

Gratefully Sally looked up at him.

"Oh, thank you," she said. "I felt sure you would understand."

His lips moved as if he was about to contradict her, and then he changed his mind and followed her down the corridor.

The children were sitting as she had left them, but their faces lit up as they saw her return. The St. John nurse straightened herself and leaving the woman's side came across to Sally.

"She is very bad," she said so quietly that only Sir Guy besides Sally could hear her words and they were inaudible to the children. "There is nothing else I can do, but we shall be in York in a few minutes. If you like I will go with her to the hospital."

"Oh, would you?" Sally exclaimed, "that will be very kind of you."

"We can only hope that the ambulance will not be delayed for long. It is obvious to me that it is a case for an emergency operation," the nurse said. "We may be in time – or we may not."

She hardly breathed the last three words, but Sally heard them and she looked first at the children and then up at Sir Guy.

To her surprise he spoke gently and in a far kinder voice than she had ever heard him use.

"We must hope for the best, Nurse." he said. "In the meantime, if you will see to your patient, this lady and I will see what can be done about the children."

"We must not forget them, must we?" the nurse answered.

There was a slight groan from the woman on the seat, and she turned and went back to her. Sally, looking up at the rack, saw two small coats. She pulled them down and handed them to the children.

"Perhaps you had better put these on," she said. "It is easier than carrying them."

As she touched the coats, she was quite certain that she had been right in thinking that the family were not rich. They were of cheap material with poor linings.

A few seconds later the train slowed down as it approached the station.

"I will get Bracken and our luggage out," Sir Guy said to Sally, "and meet you on the platform."

"Very well."

She lowered the window and looking down the train saw the collector looking anxiously along the line of taxis and cars drawn up alongside the platform. A moment later she saw him wave his arm and spied two ambulance men with a stretcher hurrying down the platform.

"It's all right," she said to the nurse. "The ambulance is here."

"Thank goodness for that," she muttered, and then in calm, professional tones she said to the woman, "The ambulance is here. We shall have you into hospital in no time now and all your troubles will be over."

It was obvious from the woman's face that it was going to hurt her to be moved and Sally, picking up a few parcels from the seat, said to the children,

"Let us leave this carriage to Mummy, we will get out next door."

"Does Mummy mind going to hospital?" the little girl asked.

"No, of course not," Sally answered. "They will make her well there."

"They won't hurt her?" the boy exclaimed.

"Oh, no," Sally said reassuringly.

He seemed to accept her word and got up to follow her into the other carriage. Then the little girl put out her hand and touched Sally's.

"Please, can't I kiss Mummy goodbye?"

"Yes, of course," Sally replied.

The children moved swiftly to their mother's side and bending down touched her cheek with their lips. She opened her eyes immediately and Sally saw anxiety as well as pain in her expression.

"Don't worry," she said clearly. "I'll look after them. I promise you."

Once again the woman looked reassured and then, followed by the children, Sally led the way into the next carriage.

There was the usual noise and flurry as the train drew up in the station. A stentorian voice was talking through a loudspeaker, there were a dozen cries of, 'Porter', and the rattle of barrows and milk-cans. For a moment Sally felt bewildered as she stepped down on to the platform. Passengers boarding the train pushed past her and she felt as if she breasted a tide. She held the little girl's hand tightly in hers and after a moment she saw the boy's fingers on the crook of her arm.

"Mind yer backs, please!" came a sharp voice as an electric truck was driven past. There was a sea of faces, all strange, and then at last Sally saw Sir Guy coming quietly and reassuringly towards them, seeming to tower above the other passengers as he walked with unhurried deliberation. Bracken moving beside him on his lead.

For the first time Sally felt that he was someone on whom she could rely in a fantastic and utterly chaotic world.

"Come on, children," she said and went towards him with a smile.

7

The children were tired after they had been driving for over an hour and sitting one on each side of Sally, they began to droop towards her, first one head and then the other nodding against her shoulders. Sir Guy had warned them that there was a long drive ahead of them.

"It is quicker than going by the branch line," he explained briefly, and he helped them into the low but comfortable seat of the car, while he sat in front beside the driver. There was no division between the front and the back of the car and Sally wondered more than once whether he was paying any attention to the conversation going on behind him.

But his back was uncompromisingly straight and he appeared to be watching the road ahead and taking no interest in his passengers. It was, of course, inevitable that Sally had to subject the children to some sort of catechism about themselves. First of all, she asked their names.

"I'm Nicholas," the small boy told her, "and I don't like being called Nick 'cos that is what they call the devil."

"But the real Nicholas was a saint and that's more than you are," his sister said pertly.

"I know," he answered gravely, "but it takes time to be a saint and I may be one by the time I've grown up."

Sally laughed. She could not help it. He was so sweet in his seriousness.

"I think it is a very nice thing to want to be and I promise you I will always call you Nicholas."

"Thank you," he said, accepting her promise as if it were something that might be expected in common courtesy.

"And what is your name?" Sally asked his sister.

"I was christened Prudence," she said, "but I like to be called Prue. Prudence is such a terrible mouthful."

"It certainly is," Sally said, "and now will you tell me your Mummy's and Daddy's names?"

"Redford," Nicholas told her, "and my Daddy is a major because he was made it in the war."

"And where is he now?" Sally asked.

"He's in India," Nicholas answered, "at least I think so, but he has promised to come to us just as quickly as he possibly can, so he may be getting on a ship at this very moment."

"Yes," Prudence chimed in, "he may be on the sea in a big, big ship like we were."

"You have come from India then?" Sally suggested, thinking that this explained the delicate appearance of the children, and the way both of them seemed to have outgrown their strength.

It was not long before she pieced together the little story. Major Redford had apparently worked in India before the war. When the war came, he had joined up with the Indian Army but had not been sent out of the country. As soon as he was demobilised, he took up his old work again. The children were rather vague as to what this was, but Sally guessed that it had something to do with forestry.

Now that the government of India had passed into other hands, his job had come to an end and he had sent his family on ahead of him and was following at the first possible moment. The children had never been in England before and everything was new and strange to them and, in a way that Sally could well understand, rather frightening.

"But surely you have some relations in this country?" she asked.

"Relations?" Nicholas queried the word.

"Aunts, uncles, grandmothers, cousins," Sally explained.

"We've never heard of any," Nicholas answered.

"You are quite certain you were not coming to stay with anyone in York?" Sally insisted.

"We were not going to stay in York," Nicholas said, "we were going out into the country. We were going to see…" he hesitated for the word and then remembered "…moors with heather on them. Mummy told us all about them."

"And why did you particularly want to see them?" Sally enquired.

"Because my Daddy lived here when he was a little boy," Prudence said, "and he told us all about them and the funny bird he used to shoot that went 'Clack, clack'."

"You mean a grouse," Sally smiled.

"That's right," Nicholas said. "Daddy said he would show us a grouse, lots of grouse,"

"And where did your Daddy live?" Sally asked.

But the children did not know.

She had been extremely grateful that Sir Guy had said nothing further about her having committed herself to look after Nicholas and Prue. She had been half afraid that he would have argued with her, but he seemed to have accepted her promise without question and had taken them out to the waiting car and seen efficiently to the disposing of all the luggage.

He had also remembered to get the name of the hospital where Mrs. Redford had gone and the telephone number, but when Sally had tried to thank him, he looked at her in that strange way and brushed her gratitude aside as if it were unnecessary.

The children had been thrilled at the sight of Bracken and he had made friends with them instantly, jumping up in an ecstasy of excitement when they patted him, wagging his stump of a tail and uttering little whining noises.

"He's a lovely dog, isn't he?" Nicholas said. "We've never had a dog, but Mummy has promised us we shall have one, one day, when Daddy comes home."

It seemed to Sally that everything was being postponed until Daddy came home and she guessed that much of this was due to a shortage of funds. Her first impression that there was not much money in the Redford family was borne out by their telling her that they had returned home on a slow and cheap ship, that they had stayed in an obscure boarding house in London, and that they intended to find a place in Yorkshire which, as Prue put it, "would not cost Mummy too many pennies".

And yet nothing, however poor, however meagre, could hide the beauty of the children or disguise their good breeding. They had perfect manners and the thinness of their intelligent faces only revealed the lovely bone construction of their jaws and the elegance with which their heads were joined by long necks to their graceful little bodies.

Even in her pain Mrs. Redford had been pretty, but somehow Sally guessed that much of their breeding came from their father. That they adored both their father and mother was very evident. They talked of them eagerly, as children will, of those they love and Sally realised with a sense of poignancy that they were both desperately anxious and afraid for their mother, even while their upbringing made them do their utmost to appear self-controlled before strangers.

After a little silence when nobody had spoken, Prue suddenly asked,

"When shall we see Mummy again?"

"I can't tell you that," Sally replied frankly, "but I am sure Sir Guy will telephone to the hospital as soon as we get to his home and will find out how she is."

"Poor Mummy! I expect she is lonely in a big hospital all by herself and without us."

"They will look after her very well," Sally reassured her, "and she will want to know that you are happy and not worrying too much."

The children made no reply to this for they were looking around them, staring out of the window at the countryside through which they were passing.

"There are the moors," Sally said, pointing to where in the distance they rose, rounded and beautiful, their tops clear against the blue sky.

"Where? *Where?*"

The children started up in their eagerness and Sally put out a restraining hand, to steady them as they stared in the direction to which she pointed. After a moment Prue looked disappointed.

"I thought they would be purple," she exclaimed.

"Not at this time of year," Sally said, "it is too early. Now they are green but wait until the autumn and they will be the loveliest purple you have ever seen in your life."

Nicholas did not say anything, but he looked at them for a long time and then, as he sat down beside Sally, he remarked,

"It's difficult to know what things are like by just looking at them, I want to feel them."

Sally flashed him a look of understanding. How well she knew what he meant! How difficult it was indeed to judge things by what appeared on the surface! And yet, she asked herself suddenly, wasn't that just what she had done?

For a moment her misery and loneliness swept over her once again in a darkening wave, then resolutely she tried to put her own unhappiness away from her. Almost like an answer to a prayer these children had been sent to her to take her mind off herself. They needed her attention and in administering to them she could, for the moment, forget her own aches and pains.

There was silence at the back of the car. Prue was definitely drowsy and Sally slipped her arm around the little girl and held her lightly, but while she hesitated to be so familiar with Nicholas, she felt his head against her arm and knew that he too was relaxed, if not asleep.

She thought at that moment how much she would like a child of her own. She had had very little to do with small children, for those who had come to the farm ware usually much older and in their teens. Nicholas was seven and Prue was six, but to Sally at that moment they seemed very tiny and very precious.

And now for the first time since they had left York Sir Guy spoke from the front seat.

"We are nearly there," he said, "the drive gate is at the end of this road."

Nicholas sat upright, interested and alert, but Prudence made no movement and Sally, rather than disturb her, could only look ahead without shifting her position. They had approached nearer to the moorland, which stretched away on one side of the road, wild and beautiful and without a sign of human habitation, but on the other side were a river, green fields and dark belts of verdant trees. In a few moments they turned in through a big iron gate with a small stone lodge at one side of it.

There was a long avenue of trees and at the end of it, Sally saw a house. Somehow she had expected something very pompous and impressive, something in keeping with the gravity and solemnity of Sir Guy himself. But she saw instead a long rambling building with irregular rooftops and chimneys of different periods pointing to a sunlit sky. There was a creeper growing over part of the house, but the rest was of mellowed red brick with windows of varying shapes, which gave the whole building an extraordinarily pleasant appearance. It was left to Nicholas to describe it most vividly,

"It is smiling at us," he cried.

"What is?" Prue remarked sleepily, wakening suddenly and moving in the shelter of Sally's arms.

"The house, of course," Nicholas answered. "Look at its face, look for yourself."

Prue sat up as they turned into a gravel sweep in front of the house. Staring out of the car she announced solemnly,

"Yes, it is smiling," and Sally guessed that this was a conversation they often had between themselves, with regard to houses.

As the car drew up, a grey-haired butler came down the front steps.

"How are you, Bateson?" Sir Guy asked.

"Much better, thank you, Sir Guy," the butler replied and opened the door of the car.

First Prue and then Sally climbed out, while Nicholas, swift as a little eel, opened the other door and ran round the car to join them.

"My legs were all squeezed up with sitting so long," he said. "Can we explore the garden? Please say yes."

Sally looked at Sir Guy, but he had not heard and she felt too shy to ask him the question herself.

"Come into the house first," she said to Nicholas in a low voice, "and then we will see if you and Prue can't stretch your legs."

Sir Guy had been speaking to the chauffeur, now he turned to them.

"Shall I lead the way?" he asked, and without waiting for Sally's reply he went up the steps and into the house.

Sally had the impression of polished floors, of oak-panelled walls and big family portraits in gilt frames as they passed through the hall and into a long, low room bright with sunshine, with tall French windows opening on to a garden. There were bowls of flowers everywhere and a small Cairn terrier flung himself forward yelping a welcome.

Then Sally was conscious that there were two women at the far end of the room, one with grey hair, who was coming towards Sir Guy with her lovely face alight with pleasure, while the other, a younger woman, was standing a little in the background.

Sir Guy bent to kiss his mother.

"This is Miss St. Vincent," he said. "You were expecting her, Mother?"

"Yes, dear, of course," Lady Thorne said in a sweet, soft voice.

She held out her hand to Sally and then looked in surprise at the two children.

"You didn't say you were bringing anyone else with you, Guy."

"I didn't know I was," Sir Guy said. "They are Nicholas and Prudence Redford. Their mother was taken ill on the train and was rushed off to hospital at York. The children had nowhere to go, so we brought them along."

"How lovely!" Lady Thorne said, smiling down tenderly at the children.

"Well, Nada, how are you?" Sir Guy asked and Sally saw his hands go out to greet the younger woman.

"I am glad you are back, Guy."

Her voice was low and deep, with a strange intonation that Sally, at the moment, could not place.

"Miss St. Vincent, my cousin, Nada Thorne," Sir Guy said.

Sally went forward and put out her hand, but with a sense of embarrassment she realised that the girl was bowing to her stiffly in the continental manner. Her hand dropped to her side and she had a sudden sense of being rebuffed.

Nada Thorne was good-looking, there was no mistake about that. Her hair was dark and was drawn back to reveal her square forehead and tiny ears. Strongly marked eyebrows were like wings over oval-shaped eyes. Her skin was white as magnolias and her whole appearance was so foreign that Sally knew why she had been surprised at the intonation of her voice. Her name might be Thorne, but she was definitely not English.

"The children can have the two little dressing rooms opposite the lilac room, where we have put Miss St. Vincent," Lady Thorne was saying. "Will you see to it, Nada?"

As she went, she looked at Sally with dark, unsmiling eyes and Sally felt that she resented not only her own coming but that of the children, too.

"And now, Guy, tell me all about everything," Lady Thorne commanded.

She sat down on the sofa and Sally thought that she had never seen anybody quite so exquisite. Her hair was dressed in an old-fashioned way on top of her head and she certainly made no effort to improve her beauty, even though it would have been difficult to do so. She was not made-up and her lips were natural in colour. She wore a dress of some dark silk material which owed nothing to any particular fashion. There was a chiffon scarf round her shoulders, while her neck was covered by a soft piece of tulle which tied in a bow at the back.

She was certainly not fashionable and certainly not smart, yet Sally knew by just looking at her that Lady Thorne was everything that anybody's mother should be and should look like. Her voice was perhaps the most charming thing about her. It was so soft, so gentle, and there was love and tenderness too in her eyes as she looked at her son and then down at the children.

"I expect you two want to have a run in the garden until it is tea-time," she smiled.

"Oh, please, may we?" Nicholas asked. "I didn't go to sleep in the car, but my feet did."

"I went to sleep all over," Prue added.

"Well, you must wake yourselves up with a good run on the lawns," Lady Thorne said. "You will find a swing under the big copper beech tree. But don't go too far away, for tea should be here in five minutes' time."

"We will listen in case someone calls for us," Nicholas assured her solemnly and then swiftly they were across the floor and the sound of their voices, high with excitement, could be heard as they rushed over the lawns.

"What sweet children!" Lady Thorne said. "Tell me about their poor mother."

Sir Guy told her what had happened in the train.

"But weren't they coming to stay with relations or friends?" she asked.

For the first time Sir Guy looked at Sally as if to include her in the conversation.

"They told me that they didn't know anyone in England," Sally said shyly. "They said they were coming here because their father used to live here as a boy."

"Redford," Lady Thorne said softly, then gave a little exclamation. "Guy, could it be old General Redford's son at Merton Grange?"

"But I thought he was disowned?" Sir Guy replied.

"Yes, don't you remember he made an unfortunate marriage. The girl was an actress or something of the sort and the old man was so furious that he cut him off with a shilling in the real Victorian style."

"Yes, I remember something about it," Sir Guy said, "but there is no reason to suppose that these are General Redford's grandchildren."

"Why not?" Lady Thorne asked.

"Well, I suppose it might be the Redford's we know," Sir Guy said, "but the children said they know no-one in England."

"What do you think, Miss St. Vincent?" Lady Thorne enquired.

"Mrs. Redford looked and seemed very nice," Sally said, "She was in terrible pain, but her one thought was for the children."

"I am not surprised. They are sweet children," Lady Thorne said. "It would be interesting if their father is the General's son."

"The General won't be interested, if you are," Sir Guy teased her.

"I wouldn't be too sure," his mother answered. "There they sit in that big, lonely house, a lonely, dull old couple with no interests and nothing to look forward to except an empty old age."

Sir Guy walked across the room to take a cigarette from a box by the fireplace.

"I can see, Mother, that you have already made up your mind to unite the General and his wife with a couple of children whom you have just seen for the first time. You would be wise to make certain of the facts first."

"Darling, as if I should do anything else," Lady Thorne said, then she turned to Sally with a sigh. "Guy is always the practical and sensible one in this family. It is Tony who is so impetuous…"

She stopped suddenly, arrested perhaps by the colour that flooded into Sally's cheeks. Then she looked up at Sir Guy a little uncertainly.

"Oh, but, darling, I had forgotten. You said on the telephone that you had something about Tony to tell me. He isn't ill, is he?"

"No, Mother, don't upset yourself," Sir Guy said quickly.

With a kind of horror Sally suddenly realised that Lady Thorne knew nothing about what had happened between Tony and herself. She was not aware even that she and Tony had been going to be married, because it had been kept secret until the very last moment and, though she had heard Tony tell Lynn that he had informed his family, she realised now that only his brother had known, while his mother was still in ignorance. Suddenly she felt that she could not bear it, could not sit and listen while Tony's act of desertion was recounted in front of her. She got to her feet.

"May I please go with the children?" she asked and before either Sir Guy or his mother could answer her, she went hurriedly through the open window into the garden.

She almost ran from the house across the lawn to where, under the wide-spreading branches of the great tree, she could see Nicholas pushing Prue on the swing and as she went, she told herself over and over again that she must get away, she must find something to do.

'I can't stay here,' she thought. The house, Lady Thorne's gracious loveliness, the sunlit gardens, in fact the whole atmosphere were harder to bear than if, as she had expected, there had been merely pompous grandeur.

It was because all this was so lovely and because it had been Tony's background as a child that she felt it to be unbearable. She had not visualised Tony's family and she had thought of him as being, like herself, without a home. He had never talked of his childhood and in all their conversations together Sally could hardly remember that he had ever mentioned his mother. Why he hadn't, she could not understand, but how gladly, how happily, would she have come here as Tony's bride. How she would have liked to know this house, had it welcomed her as one of the family.

She had only had a fleeting impression of everything, yet it was enough, and she saw not only her loss in losing Tony, but also all she had missed throughout her whole life and the barrenness of her relationship to Aunt Amy.

There were tears in her eyes as she reached the children and they stopped swinging and ran towards her.

"It is lovely here, really lovely," Nicholas said. "We had a swing in India, but it was not as good as this one and we had to be awfully careful in the garden there because of snakes."

"I'm afraid of snakes," Prue said, "aren't you?" She looked up at Sally as she spoke and added suddenly, "Why are you sad?"

"I am not really sad," Sally lied, blinking away the tears which would insist on filling her eyes.

"You look sad," Prue said, "but you have got to be brave, you know, however sad you are. That's what Mummy said to us when we wanted to cry at saying goodbye to Daddy."

Sally bent down and kissed her.

"I am being brave now," she said. "Shall I give you a swing?"

"Oh, please do," Nicholas begged. "I want to see if my feet can touch the leaves."

"Well, hold on tight then," Sally told him.

There were whoops of delight as she swung Nicholas up until his toes did just touch the leaves of the tree, and then it was Prue's turn. As she began to slow down, Sally saw Nada Thorne come out of the house and across the lawn towards them.

"Here is Miss Thorne," she said, "I expect she is coming to tell us that tea is ready."

She took hold of Prue's hand and drew her across the lawn, with Nicholas following behind.

"She is beautiful," Sally told herself and yet she thought there was something sullen and unsmiling about Nada's face, something that was definitely not attractive.

"Lady Thorne asks that you will come in to tea," Nada announced in her slow, deep voice as they met in the centre of the lawn.

"I thought that was what you were coming to tell us," Sally said. "I am sure the children are ready for theirs."

Nada made no reply, and anxious to be friendly, Sally added,

"I do hope we haven't given a lot of extra trouble."

"This is my cousin's house," Nada replied. "He can invite to it whom he pleases."

Sally felt as if her tentative effort at friendliness had been brushed aside with a hard hand.

Tea was laid in the morning room and Nada led them there, her dark head held high, her shoulders somehow expressing her dislike and disapproval as she entered the room ahead of them. Sally, subdued and a little humiliated, realised at once that Lady Thorne had been crying. She looked older and more transparent than she had when they arrived a short while ago and Sally was suddenly aware that she was an old woman. Getting on for seventy, she guessed, and she saw that her hands trembled as they moved among the crested silver tea things on the big silver tray.

"There is milk for the children," she said. "Do you like your tea strong or weak, Miss St. Vincent?"

She did not look at Sally as she spoke and Sally thought that the friendliness with which she had greeted her on her arrival, had vanished.

'I have made her unhappy,' she thought. 'Sir Guy disapproves, and Miss Thorne hates me. Why, why, why have I come here?'

She felt very forlorn as she ate her tea in silence while the children chattered gaily and as soon as the meal was over, she escaped once again with them into the garden. After a little while they tired of running about and she was sitting on a seat telling them a story, when she looked up to see Sir Guy standing beside them.

"I have just been telephoning to the hospital," he said. "I could not get through before as the lines were engaged.

Mrs, Redford has been operated on and the operation was quite successful. She has had a bad time but is going on as well as can be expected and they hope to have much better news of her progress, in the morning."

"What is he saying about Mummy?" Prue asked and Sally, putting her arms round the child, tried to explain.

"They have taken away that horrid pain that was hurting your Mummy and though she is feeling rather tired and sleepy now, they hope she will be feeling much better in the morning."

"Oh, good," Prue said. "Then will she come here to us?"

"Not tomorrow," Sally said, "but perhaps you will soon be able to go and see her."

She looked up at Sir Guy for confirmation of this and he nodded his head.

"Yes, as soon as your mother is well enough, I will take you both into York to see her."

"Oh, thank you," Nicholas exclaimed. "Do you think we may be able to go tomorrow?"

"I am not certain," Sir Guy answered, "I imagine it might be the next day or perhaps the day after that. Your mother has been very ill, and you have got to give her a chance to get strong and well again."

"I understand," Nicholas said, and then to Sally's surprise he slipped his hand confidently into Sir Guy's. "You see," he explained, "Daddy said I was to look after Mummy and even if Prue can't go, I ought to go and see her as I am looking after her."

"I want to see her, too," Prue said passionately.

"You shall both see her at the first possible moment," Sir Guy said and his calm voice was utterly convincing.

"My mother suggests, Miss St. Vincent," he said, "that the children should go to their beds early and have a light supper in their rooms. It is what we always had as children," he added unexpectedly.

"I will put them to bed," Sally said, "and after that could I speak to you?"

Sir Guy looked surprised and then he said,

"Of course, I shall be in the library. It is on the opposite side of the hall to the drawing room. I think you can find it quite easily."

"Thank you," Sally said. "Come on, children, I will race you to the house."

Sir Guy stood looking after them as they all three ran across the lawn and then slowly he followed them and went into the library, which was his own sitting room.

It was a big room lined with books almost from floor to ceiling and it had been used by generation after generation of Thornes until everything in the room, from the inkstand to the coal box, was traditional and in its own way part of the family. On the table by the fireplace were several photographs, among them a photograph of Tony in the uniform of the Grenadier Guards. Sir Guy stood looking at it for a moment.

He turned round to hear the door open. Nada stood in the doorway. For a moment she looked at him across the room and then she came slowly to his side.

"Guy," she said, "why have you brought that girl here? Aunt Mary is upset."

"There was nothing else I could do," Sir Guy replied. "Tony had behaved badly, extremely badly. I see my mother has told you the whole story, so there is no need for me to go into details."

"Yes, she has told me," Nada said, "but how could Tony have thought of getting married without letting Aunt Mary know? It would have broken her heart. And you, why didn't you stop it?"

"I did all I could," Sir Guy answered. "He rang me up the night before and asked me to go to the wedding. He told me that he was telling Mother himself in his own good time. I tried to argue with him, but he informed me there was nothing to be said. I don't flatter myself that any remarks I made to him changed his mind. There were other reasons, in particular, I imagine, the job in Paris that he had always wanted."

"But why bring the girl here?"

"She had nowhere else to go and I could not find her employment at twenty-four hours' notice. Quite frankly, Nada, I meant to offer her money, but when I saw her, I don't know why, the words stuck in my throat. It would have seemed so *damnably* insulting after what Tony had done."

Nada shrugged her shoulders.

"Men are all the same. They are so stupid. You are deceived by a pretty face."

"It is the first time you have ever accused me of anything so frivolous," Sir Guy said with a smile.

Nada looked up at him and her eyes softened. She waited as if expectantly for him to say something more, but he turned away and crossed the room to his desk.

"I see there is a lot of correspondence for me," he said, "I had better get to work."

Nada stood looking at him for a moment, an undecipherable expression on her face, before she walked towards the door. As she reached it, she said clearly,

"It would be best if you would concentrate on finding something for Miss St. Vincent. There must be work of some sort for her in York."

Sir Guy gave no indication that he had heard her, and after pausing for a second, she went out of the room and shut the door.

He was still opening his letters nearly half an hour later, when he heard a quiet voice ask,

"May I come in?"

He looked round to see Sally coming across the room.

"Of course," he said, getting to his feet and going towards her.

"The children are in bed," Sally said. "They are so tired that I think they will fall asleep right away."

She spoke quickly and from sheer nervousness, for somehow Sir Guy seemed very frightening in this big and impressive-looking room.

"You wanted to speak to me," he reminded her.

"Yes, I know," Sally said. "I came to ask you to help me to get away as soon as possible."

He raised his eyebrows.

"You don't like it here?"

"It is not that," Sally said. "I ought never to have come here in the first place. I have upset your mother and – your cousin doesn't like me."

"Has Nada said so?" Sir Guy asked, surprised.

"No, of course not, but I think one knows those things without being told in so many words. Your mother had been crying when we came into tea."

"She was a little upset," Sir Guy admitted. "She has always been very fond of my younger brother. Unfortunately, he has given her a great deal of worry and caused her much unhappiness during his life. He has always been wild and ever since he became infatuated with…"

He stopped suddenly. There was a pause and then he said, "as a matter of fact he has not been home for some years. It has hurt her very deeply."

"That is why Tony never spoke of his home," Sally said. "I wondered. You see, if I had a home like this, I should be so proud, so thrilled that I should never want to leave it."

She spoke almost passionately because she could not deny the hunger in her own heart for security such as this house offered.

"And yet you want to leave us at once?" Sir Guy questioned.

"Of course," Sally said. "Everything here is quiet and peaceful and lovely. Do you think I want to change that? Do you think I want to make people different and unhappy because I have come here unexpectedly?"

Sir Guy walked across the room.

"It is funny you should say that," he said. "I don't know whether you know it, but this house is called 'The Priory'. Hundreds of years ago it was a Monastery, but it was destroyed during the reign of Henry VIII. After that another house was built on the old site, but that was partially burnt down, and this present building, added to of course by every succeeding generation, grew up to be known still as 'The Priory'. It is a strange thing, but everyone who comes here speaks of the peace and the quiet. There is almost a healing quality about the house, something, I fancy, that has been left behind by the old monks."

Sally stared at Sir Guy in astonishment. It was the first time he had spoken to her without reserve and without that look of contempt in his eyes. She said nothing and after a moment Sir Guy went on,

"It often seems to me that things appear different when one comes back here. The house seems to put the problems of the outside world into their proper proportion. I am sorry for you. Miss St. Vincent. I was not so sorry for you before. I felt that you were almost as much to blame as my brother for what had occurred, but now I am not so certain. May I say that I would like you to stay on here in my home, at least until we can find something really suitable in the way of employment?"

He stood looking down at her, and because his kindness was so unexpected Sally found herself utterly bereft of words.

"Thank you," she managed to stammer after a moment, and then she added, "Please, will you tell your mother how desperately sorry I am."

"You at least are not responsible for my brother's behaviour towards his family," Sir Guy said and his voice was stern, but Sally was aware that his anger was not directed towards her.

Sally got to her feet, then she hesitated. Sir Guy looked at her and realised that some decision was being made in her mind He waited, and at last Sally said in a very low voice,

"You know – Tony's address, don't you?"

Sir Guy nodded.

"If you are writing to him," Sally went on, "would you please not mention that I am here, I-I would rather he did not know."

"I understand," Sir Guy said. "If I write to my brother, which I may have to do, I will not mention your name at all. I think he has forfeited the right to have anything more to do with you."

"It is not that," Sally said. "It is just that I-I would rather he did not know."

She looked up at Sir Guy shyly and without saying any more she went from the room. She went upstairs to change for dinner. She felt a sense of surprise that he had been so unexpectedly kind. Had the house really healing qualities? She hoped it was true, for she needed them desperately. She felt as if she had been bruised all over, that her pride had been humiliated beyond any hope of recovery and that never again in the whole of her life could she be certain of anything.

She went in to see the children. As she had expected they were both asleep. Nicholas' head was thrown back on the pillow, his arms above his head, the bedclothes kicked off. She stood staring down at him and she had a strong desire to pick him up in her arms and hold him close. Here was something she could love, who would not turn away from her simplicity. In the next room Prue was cuddled up under the clothes like a small dormouse. Only the tip of her nose was showing and her hair was rumpled over the pillow, so small and so sweet.

Sally thought how they trusted her and wished that in her turn she had someone in whom she could put her trust. Slowly she closed the children's doors and went to her own room. A housemaid had unpacked for her and lying on the bed was a dinner frock of aquamarine blue. It was very lovely, but the mere sight of it brought a sense of utter unhappiness. She had planned to wear it on the first night of her honeymoon, the first night when she and Tony would have been together as man and wife.

She crossed the room to the window seat, sat down and stared out of the window. Beyond the park and the gardens was a glimpse of the moors with the sinking sun casting strange shadows over them.

Sally looked for a moment, then she hid her face in her hands.

"Oh, heal me, *heal me,*" she cried to the house.

She felt that the pain of her loneliness was more than she could bear.

8

Sally was aroused by a knock at the door. She jumped up quickly, guiltily aware that she had let herself sink into a kind of stupor of despair.

"Come in," she said after rubbing her eyes, although there were no tears in them, and touching her hair with flurried fingers.

She expected to see a housemaid, but to her surprise Lady Thorne opened the door.

"May I come in?" she asked in her low, sweet voice.

"Of course," Sally answered and added nervously, "Am I late? I'm afraid I have no idea what the time is."

"Oh, no," Lady Thorne replied, "it is not yet seven o'clock and we do not dine until half past eight. I peeped in to see the children, but they are fast asleep. They have had a long and exhausting day. They must have been very tired, poor darlings."

"Yes, they were," Sally agreed. "That is why I put them to bed so early."

"Quite right," Lady Thorne said approvingly.

She walked across the room and sat down on the wide window seat where Sally had been crouching but a moment before.

"Come and sit near me, dear," she said, "I want to talk to you."

She patted the seat with its bright floral chintz with her hand as she spoke and Sally did as she was told, sitting down beside her hostess, but looking at her slightly apprehensively.

"I wanted to talk to you alone," Lady Thorne began, "and it is always a difficult thing to get anyone alone in this house. There always seems to be someone about, if it is not the household then it is people from the village. When my boys were little, they used to tease me about it, and if they wanted to tell me something, they would come and knock on the door and say, 'Madam, may I have a word with you?'"

Lady Thorne's voice was as tender as the smile on her lips.

"It makes me feel young again," she added, "to have those two sweet children here. But how thin they are! We must feed them up."

"I've always heard that living in India is hard for children," Sally added.

"So have I," Lady Thorne agreed, "and I have been wondering ever since you arrived whether they are General Redford's grandchildren or not. When their poor mother is well enough, we must try to find out."

"It is very kind of you to have them here," Sally said impulsively, "and even kinder of you – to have me."

"That is what I wanted to talk to you about," Lady Thorne answered – and Sally's heart sank, because inadvertently she had returned to the one subject which she wished to avoid.

"I have been thinking," Lady Thorne went on, "that we were not very welcoming in our manner to you. You must have been surprised. My son, Guy, merely telephoned from London to say that he was bringing a Miss St. Vincent to stay, who was a friend of Tony's and that he would explain everything when he got here."

"Oh!" Sally's cheeks were suddenly crimson. She could not help her embarrassment at Lady Thorne's words. "A friend of Tony's!"

Yes, that was what she had imagined she was – a very sweet friend – until yesterday.

"I was, of course, glad to offer hospitality to any friend of my younger son," Lady Thorne said, "but now that Guy has told me all that you have been through, I want to tell you how sorry I am. I cannot quite understand why or how my Tony behaved as he has, but he has been very strange lately, especially for the last two or three years since…"

Lady Thorne stopped abruptly as if she had suddenly remembered that she must check her words. She went on,

"He was such a loving and affectionate little boy and I used to think that we shared everything together, he and I, and that we had no secrets from each other. But once children grow up, they grow away from their homes and their mothers. One can do nothing but wait patiently and pray that sooner or later they will need us again – our love and our understanding – and will come back to us."

There was so much pain in Lady Thorne's voice that Sally put out her hand and touched hers.

"Oh, please," she said, "you must not be unhappy about Tony. I don't understand why he left me or why at the very last moment he did not want to marry me, but I can assure you that he has always been very kind and very nice to me. In fact, I can't imagine him being horrid or unkind to anyone. I was frightened of him at first and then he was so, so friendly that I grew to love him."

Sally's voice trembled on the last two words, but she forced herself to gaze steadfastly at Lady Thorne as if she willed her to believe her. Lady Thorne smiled, but there were tears in her eyes.

"Thank you, dear, for telling me that. I think, like you, that there must be some very good explanation, which perhaps one day we shall hear from Tony's own lips. In the meantime, I want to tell you that I am glad to have you here and that you must stay as long as you wish."

"Oh, thank you," Sally said softly, "but as soon as I can, I must get a job. I have no money, you see."

"My son, Guy, has gold me that," Lady Thorne said, "and please do not worry about it for the moment. This has all been a terrible shock for you and I know in a much milder degree it has been a shock for me, too, so we must just take things easily, you and I, until things smooth themselves out. They do, you know. Time simplifies everything, one finds that as one grows older."

"Thank you," Sally said again, for there seemed to her there was nothing else to say. She felt almost passionately grateful to Lady Thorne for her kindness. It was as if she laid a healing hand on a wound so raw that it was agony even to think of it and yet her very touch brought peace and healing.

'How could Tony neglect his mother?' Sally wondered, 'and how could he stay away from this wonderful home of his? How lucky, how very, very lucky he was to have them!'

As if she guessed what Sally was thinking, Lady Thorne said,

"My son tells me your parents are dead?"

For a mad second Sally wished she could tell Lady Thorne the truth and then, because she hated to lie to somebody so transparently honest and good, she answered.

"My father died at the beginning of the war."

"Poor child! You must miss him!"

"I do," Sally answered. "He was always immersed in his books, but still it was wonderful to know that he was there – that I belonged."

An expression of sadness came across Lady Thorne's face.

"Isn't that what we all ask of life," she said gently, "to belong to someone we love? My husband died when my boys were quite small, yet I don't think a day has passed that I have not missed his love and understanding, his strength and his unceasing care of me."

Sally felt a sudden lump in her throat. That was what she wanted from life. How beautifully and simply it expressed her yearning, all that she had prayed might come to her through her marriage with Tony. And now she was alone.

Lady Thorne reached out and took her hand in hers.

"Yes," she said, "we all want to belong to something or somebody and I want you to feel, dear child, that for the moment you belong here. We lead a quiet, uneventful life, but there always seems to be plenty to do, people to think about and to help."

Sally's fingers tightened on hers.

"Perhaps I could help a little," she said. "That is what I tried to do when I lived with my Aunt Amy in Wales – to help other people, but I don't think I was always successful."

"One can only do ones best," Lady Thorne replied, "first of all you can help those poor little children whose mother is so ill and then I feel sure you can help me, just as I feel I might be able to help you."

"Oh, I will try," Sally whispered.

"I am sure you will," Lady Thorne answered, "and now I must leave you to change for dinner. You will meet Captain Pawlovski at dinner. He is staying here while he conducts some very special and secret experiments on our private airfield."

There was an expression of surprise on Sally's face and Lady Thorne explained.

"Yes, we may live in an out-of-the way spot, but we are not entirely out of touch with progress. Guy had his own aeroplane before the war, but now that he has given up flying, the hangers and workshops have come in useful. Captain Pawlovski is a Pole and a friend of my niece, Nada. He has got special permission from the Government to conduct his experiments."

"How interesting!" Sally exclaimed.

"That is what we all think," Lady Thorne said, "but he won't tell us very much. He is not very communicative, poor man, for like my niece, he suffered much before he escaped to England,"

"Do you mean Miss – Miss Thorne?" Sally asked,

"Yes, Nada," Lady Thorne replied. "I expect, like everyone else, you wondered how she could have an English name and yet be so very un-English in herself. Well, my husband's second brother, who was in the Diplomatic Corps, never married until he retired. Then he married a Polish woman and went to live with her in Poland. We never saw him again, for he died soon after his marriage, but he left behind a daughter.

"I communicated occasionally with my sister-in-law, but it is always difficult to write to someone whom one has never met, especially when one lives in such entirely different environments. But we exchanged photographs of our respective children and through them I watched Nada grow from a pretty child, into an attractive young girl. Then came the war and silence for a very long time. We made all possible enquiries through the Red Cross only to learn eventually that my sister-in-law had been shot and that no-one knew what had happened to Nada.

"Then in the last year of the war Nada escaped and came to England. She came in search of us at once and we were glad to offer her a home after her terrible experiences. One day perhaps she herself will tell you about them, although it is best for her to forget them."

"So she is alone in the world," Sally said, feeling a bond of sympathy between herself and the orphaned Nada.

"Yes, poor child, except that she has us," Lady Thorne said, "and we try to make up to her for some of the things she has lost."

She looked up, as she finished speaking, at the clock on the mantelpiece.

"I must go," she said, "for we shall both be late for dinner and Guy hates being kept waiting. I tell him he is getting pompous, but he always was the conventional one of the family."

She walked across the room and then, as Sally held the door open for her, she bent down and kissed the girl's cheek.

"Bless you, dear," she said, "and try not to be too unhappy. There are so many lovely things in life lying ahead of you."

Her sweetness made it impossible for Sally to answer, but though there were tears in her eyes as she closed to door, she felt as if the black clouds which had pressed down upon her until she felt utterly lost and encompassed by their darkness had lightened a little. She had lost Tony, but she had found Tony's mother and, for the moment at least, even if it were only for a very short time, she belonged somewhere.

Quickly she changed into the blue dinner frock, arranging her hair as Lynn's *coiffeur* had taught her, and when she looked at herself finally in the glass, she knew that she looked both smart and attractive. But it was a very superficial veneer. Inside herself she was shy and hesitant, so unsure of herself that, like an animal which has been ill-treated, she could hardly distinguish clearly between friend and foe. She looked in at the children and wished she could, like them, be lost in consciousness, self-forgotten in a dreamless sleep. It was almost agony to force herself to go downstairs, to brave the household and sit through a conventional meal. She walked very slowly, dreading, the moment when she must enter the drawing room and face Sir Guy again.

Halfway down the stairs she heard footsteps and turned to see Nada behind her. The older girl was wearing a black velvet dress simply cut and obviously not an expensive gown, but it revealed the whiteness of her neck and arms and somehow accentuated rather than detracted from the darkness of her hair and eyes.

Sally waited for Nada and tried to smile but was conscious even as she did so of that same antagonism. It was unmistakable and it made her definitely uneasy. As Nada drew level with her, she said,

"There is no need, Miss St. Vincent, to dress so smartly here. We are very simple people."

Sally blushed.

"I am sorry," she answered, "but I have so few clothes and they are all new."

"But of course," Nada exclaimed, "they were doubtless chosen for your honeymoon – with the reluctant Tony."

The sneer in her voice was quite definite and Sally knew that she meant to be cruel. But she made no reply, only putting out her hand to hold on to the banister as she descended, feeling that the hard wood supported her in more ways than one.

She knew now for certain that her first impression of Nada Thorne was correct. The girl disliked her and resented her presence, though why Sally could not imagine. As they went into the drawing room Sally, standing back to let Nada precede her, thought that the Polish girl was not so young as she had at first appeared. It was difficult to judge, but Sally imagined that she must be about twenty-five. She would have been surprised if she had known how accurate a guess it was.

Lady Thorne was sitting on the sofa and Sir Guy was standing on the hearth smoking a cigarette. Both looked up as Nada and Sally entered, and Lady Thorne, smiling at Sally, said,

"How quick you have been, dear! I was afraid that I should make you late."

"Were with you Miss St. Vincent then, Aunt Mary?" Nada asked and to Sally there was a suspicious note in her voice.

"Yes, dear. We had a little talk," Lady Thorne said, "and she has had to be very quick in consequence. What a pretty dress, Sally, and how well it suits you!"

Sally smiled at Lady Thorne, but as she did so she was aware that Nada was looking at Sir Guy meaningly. Sally suddenly felt uncomfortable and an interloper, but she had no time to analyse her feelings for at that, moment a man came into the room. He was short and dark and would have been good-looking had it not been for a nervous scowl that drew his eyebrows together and gave him a look of permanent impatience.

"Oh, here you are, Ivor," Nada exclaimed, "I was beginning to think that you had forgotten the time."

"No, my stomach told me it was the hour for dinner," Captain Pawlovski answered, speaking with a strong accent, which made his words a little difficult to understand. He crossed the room to Lady Thorne's side.

"Will you forgive me, Madam, if I do not change tonight? I wish to make a flight after dinner."

"Oh, Ivor, you work too hard," Lady Thorne said. "Surely you can take a few hours' rest sometimes?"

"In my country we have a proverb, which roughly translated says, 'When things are going well, that is the time for work'."

"Then things are going well?" Nada questioned before Lady Thorne could speak.

Ivor Pawlovski looked at her.

"It is never safe to boast," he replied and the scowl on his face seemed intensified.

"Wait a minute, children, before you start talking technicalities," Lady Thorne said. "Ivor, we have a new guest. Sally, this is Captain Pawlovski who I told you is working on our airfield. Ivor – Miss St. Vincent.

They shook hands and Sally was acutely aware that Captain Pawlovski was no more pleased to see her than Nada had been.

"A glass of sherry, Ivor?" Sir Guy asked and the Pole walked across to the side table where the decanter and glasses stood on a silver tray.

"May I pour one for anyone else?" Captain Pawlovski asked.

All three women refused and Sir Guy already had one, so Captain Pawlovski helped himself and drank in silence.

Dinner was not the ordeal Sally had anticipated, because Lady Thorne talked almost incessantly of local affairs and interests and Sir Guy was more communicative than Sally had imagined he would be. Captain Pawlovski said little and gobbled up his food as if he were ravenously hungry but also impatient at the time he must spend eating. Nada ate very little and seemed to concentrate all her attention on Sir Guy.

Long before the meal was ended Sally felt desperately tired. She supposed it was reaction from all she had experienced and also from the hours she had lain sleepless the night before. Waves of exhaustion swept over her and when at last they rose from the table and went into the drawing room for coffee, she said to Lady Thorne,

"Would you mind if I went to bed?"

"Of course not, dear," Lady Thorne answered, "you must be very tired. It might have been kinder if we had suggested that you would like something light brought to you in bed."

"Oh, I wouldn't have wanted to cause any trouble. But I am terribly sleepy."

"Then go up to bed right away," Lady Thorne said. "And if there is anything you want, ring the bell or go along the passage to Nada's room. She sleeps at the far end of the corridor."

"I won't want anything," Sally said firmly, appalled at the idea that she might have to ask the assistance of Nada.

"Goodnight then, dear child."

Sally put out her hand, but Lady Thorne drew her face down to hers and kissed her gently on the cheek. Sally looked uncertainly at Nada.

"Goodnight, Miss Thorne."

"Goodnight."

Nada's reply was more in the nature of a curse than a blessing and thankfully Sally escaped from the drawing room and went upstairs. She hurried into bed, but with the perverseness of nature, once her head touched the pillow she was no longer sleepy. Her tired brain began to review the events of the past forty-eight hours.

Once more she experienced her agony at being turned away from the church by Mary, of thinking that Tony was dead, of being humiliated by the truth. Once again she felt her bitter disappointment at not being able to say 'goodbye' to Lynn, her sense of being abandoned and alone in the world and that utter despair, which had kept creeping over her all day to numb every other feeling, was now agonisingly inescapable.

She lay hour after hour wide-eyed in the darkness. She knew the time because far away in the depths of the house a clock struck the hours. Eleven o'clock – twelve o'clock – one o'clock.

'I'm being ridiculous,' Sally told herself angrily.

Suddenly she heard a sound. Instantly it occurred to her that one of the children had wakened up and was frightened at being in a strange room. She sat up in bed, switched on the bedside lamp and listened intently, but now she could hear nothing. Still unsatisfied, she got out of bed and slipped on her silk dressing gown. Quietly she opened her door and went across the corridor. Nicholas was fast asleep, his bedclothes kicked on to the floor. She pulled them over him once again, tucked him in and went into Prue. She, too, was asleep. Whatever the sound, it had obviously not been made by the children.

Sally turned out Prue's light and was just leaving the room when she heard a sound in the passage. Instinctively, without really intending to hide, she stepped back. A second later, as she stood in the darkness of the half-closed door, she felt someone pass along the corridor. It was someone who was walking very quietly and on tip-toe. The footsteps passed by and though Sally could not see who it was, she was certain in her own mind that it was Nada.

She had no desire to exchange words with her at such an hour of night and in consequence stood very still in the shadows until softly, so softly, that unless she had been specially listening for it the sound would never have been heard, Sally heard a door close.

She waited for a few seconds longer and then stepped from Prue's room, quietly pulled the door to behind her and groped her way across the passage back to her own room. She had closed the door when she left it, but now as she opened it again the light from her bedside lamp came flooding out and she saw something lying in the passage at her feet. Looking down, Sally wondered for one surprised second if it was a note laid outside her door. But when she picked up what lay there, she saw that it was an identity card. She opened it and read a name written inside it –

RICHARDSON, *William*

There was no entry in the space for the holder's address and no signature, only the name. Sally put it down on the table just inside the door of her room.

'I will give it to Nada in the morning,' she thought. 'It must belong to one of the maids.'

She took off her dressing gown and got into bed and now at last she felt drowsy.

Her next conscious thought was of the housemaid pulling her curtains. It was morning, and the night, with its tortured thoughts, seemed far away. There was certainly no time for introspection first thing in the morning. Sally got up hastily, glad of the hot cup of tea that the housemaid had brought to her bedside with a wafer-thin piece of bread-and-butter on a tiny plate of flowered china.

As soon as she was dressed, she hurried into Prue's room. The children were both there, chattering excitedly. Nicholas, leaning out of the window, was in imminent danger of falling out and breaking his neck, while Prue, more circumspect, was sitting up in bed looking at a book of pictures she had found on the chest of drawers.

"What about getting dressed?" Sally suggested.

"Oh, can we? At once?" Nicholas exclaimed. "I can see lots of places we didn't explore yesterday. This is a lovely, lovely place. I do hope Mummy will soon be better. She will love it."

"I am sure she will," Sally said, "and we must ask Sir Guy to telephone to the hospital and find out how she is."

The children were soon dressed and dragging Sally along in their impatience and they ran downstairs to the garden. Bracken greeted them enthusiastically and Nicholas and Prue raced him across the lawn, followed by Sally at a more sober pace. They disappeared into the trees at the end of the garden and Sally found they had gone ahead so quickly that she had only the distant sound of high-pitched, joyous voices to guide her.

The trees thickened and she was just wondering where they could have got to when suddenly the ground sloped down and she found herself standing at the top of a big sandpit, while the children below her were watching Bracken digging furiously in a rabbit hole.

"Look where Bracken has brought us! Isn't this an exciting place?" Prue called.

It was exciting, Sally thought, looking round her at the thick trunks of trees, the carpet of pine needles and fir cones, the bright moss and clumps of green bracken. The sandpit had cliff-like sides, which were partially covered with briars and wild roses – their fragrance attracting a few early bees.

"I bet there are lots of rabbits here," Nicholas cried, "but Bracken makes such a noise he would frighten even a tiger away."

"There are no tigers in England, stupid!" Prue said, "are there, Sally?"

"No, of course not," Sally answered, "and now you must climb up here again and come to breakfast. We will come back here afterwards if you like and Bracken can go on looking for his rabbits, although I doubt if that is the way to catch one."

The children, with almost surprising obedience, did as they were told. They scrambled up the sides, sinking into the soft sand, which filled their shoes and had to be emptied out when they reached the top. Nicholas managed for himself, but Prue found it difficult to tie her laces and Sally had to help her.

"Now we shall have to hurry back or we shall be late," Sally said, "we have come a long way from the house."

"It was not our fault." Prue said, "Bracken brought us, didn't you, Bracken?"

Bracken wagged his tail as if he agreed to take the responsibility. Then they were all four running through the wood.

They were late for breakfast as Sally had feared but Lady Thorne did not seem to mind. Only Nada said acidly that the cook was particular about everyone being punctual for meals.

"Oh, but Mrs. Harris hasn't seen the children yet," Lady Thorne said. "When she does, she won't mind how late they are. She always spoilt Tony abominably and I can't remember him being on time for anything."

"Mrs. Harris was not the only one," Sir Guy said from his place at the head of the table.

"I suppose you mean that I spoilt Tony," Lady Thorne answered. "Yes, darling, I did, but I spoilt you too – as much as you would let me."

"And look how badly I've turned out," Sir Guy said.

"That is quite untrue," Lady Thorne replied. "I am very proud of my sons."

She said the words half defiantly as if she expected someone to contradict her.

Sir Guy laughed and Sally thought that when he smiled or laughed, he looked much younger and showed an unexpected resemblance to Tony.

"I have got some good news for you children," Sir Guy said to Nicholas and Prue.

"About Mummy? Is she coming here today?" Prue cried.

"I am afraid that is asking too much," Sir Guy replied, "but she has had a good night. If the doctor agrees, I may be able to take you in to the hospital tomorrow, just to have a peep at her."

"Just a peep?" Prue said. "But when is she coming here? We've got lots and lots of things to show her. This is such a lovely house."

"I am so glad you think so," Lady Thorne said gently, "but you have both got to be very sensible and realise that your mother won't be able to join you for quite a little time."

"How long?" Nicholas insisted.

"I don't really know," Lady Thorne said. "How long do you think, Guy?"

"I am as much at a loss as you are," Sir Guy said, "but shall we say ten days or a fortnight at the very least?"

"Oh!"

There was no mistaking the disappointment on the two small faces.

"It is sad, but I am sure you can make the best of things," Lady Thorne said, "and Sally will be here to look after you."

"That's good," Prue smiled.

"What we wondered," Lady Thorne went on, "was whether you happen to know your father's address? We thought we ought to send him a cable telling him what has happened to your mother."

"I know the address of our home," Nicholas answered, "where we lived until we came away in the big ship."

"And you think your father might be there?" Sir Guy asked.

"I don't think so," Nicholas replied, wrinkling his brows as if with a great effort at memory. "I think Mummy said he had to go to a big city somewhere. I wish I could remember the name."

"I think perhaps we had better leave things as they are until we see Mrs. Redford," Sir Guy said. "What do you think Miss St. Vincent?"

Sally almost jumped because he had addressed her direct and because she was not expecting it, she stammered her reply.

"I-I think it would be best – as you say – to wait. After all, Major Redford cannot do very much and it would only worry him."

"Yes, I am sure you are right," Lady Thorne approved.

Nada got up suddenly from the breakfast table.

"If you will excuse me, Aunt Mary, I have a great many things to do."

She went from the room and Sally also rose.

"Could I perhaps help in the house by doing the children's rooms and my own?" she asked gently. "I am used to housework as I always did a lot at the farm."

"Thank you, dear," Lady Thorne answered. "It would be very kind. Gertrude is getting old and she finds making beds rather trying when her lumbago is bad."

"Then I will do ours," Sally said. "Shall I go and tell her so now?"

"Yes, please do," Lady Thorne agreed and, leaving the children still eating their breakfast, Sally went from the room and up the staircase towards the bedrooms. As she turned into the passage, she saw Nada just ahead of her, and suddenly remembering the card she had found on the floor during the night, she called out,

"Oh, Miss Thorne, I think I have something of yours."

Nada had almost reached the end of the passage. Now she turned round and came slowly towards Sally, who opened the door of her room and picked up the identity card from where she had laid it on the table, saying,

"I found this last night. I think you must have dropped it outside my door."

Nada stared at it for one moment and then, snatching it from Sally's hand, said furiously,

"Where did you find this? How did you get it? Spying on me?" Her tone was so ferocious that instinctively Sally recoiled a step or two.

"I'm sorry, but I don't know what you mean," she said. "I found the card outside my door and I thought you might have dropped it."

Nada's dark eyes were looking into hers, searchingly and suspiciously and then she said slowly,

"You found it outside your door?"

It was a question.

"Yes, last night," Sally repeated. "I went to see if the children were asleep and, as I came back to my room I picked it up."

She did not say that she had thought that Nada had passed her in the dark. Something was wrong, she could not understand what, and she was only too anxious to placate the anger that was all too apparent in Nada's face. Because she was nervous, Sally continued,

"I thought perhaps it belonged to one of the maids."

"Yes, that is right," Nada said with a curious lack of conviction, "it belongs to one of the maids. I had it in my possession because I do the housekeeping – you understand?"

"Yes, of course," Sally answered, "and I am sorry that my finding it should make you angry."

"No, it is not that," Nada said hastily. "I did not understand. I thought you had…But it is all right I dropped the card outside your room. That is all there is to it."

"Yes, of course," Sally repeated.

Without another word Nada turned and went down the passage. Sally stared after her and then went into her own room.

How very strange she was! Sally felt perturbed and uncomfortable, yet even now she was not sure what had happened. Why should Nada have been so angry? It must be only because she disliked her personally, because she resented her coming her and the children with her. Now, however, there was no time for further thoughts. Gertrude was coming down the passage, her footsteps slow and heavy. She was a big woman and nearly sixty.

Sally explained to her that she had arranged with Lady Thorne to do her own room and the children's and she was certain that Gertrude, though she was by no means effusive, was pleased.

"I don't want no one to put themselves about on my account miss," she said. "I've managed this house for nearly thirty years and I daresay I can manage for a few more."

Sally was, however, quite used to dealing with women like Gertrude. They were the type who came to the farm.

"And you will be managing it for at least another thirty," she said flatteringly, "but you must let me do some work here or I shall feel I am just being an encumbrance on our kind hostess. I expect I shall make lots of mistakes, but you must be kind enough to tell me what they are."

"You'll make mistakes all right," Gertrude said with what was almost a grim pleasure. "I don't suppose you've done much cleaning in those smart clothes."

Sally looked down at her morning frock of flowered crepe, which was Lynn's idea of a simple summer dress. She was half inclined to tell Gertrude just how much housework she had done in the past and then realised it was better to say nothing and give Gertrude the pleasure of patronising her. So instead of arguing she smiled and said,

"I'll make the beds and then perhaps you will show me where you keep the brushes and dusters. I will put them back when I'm finished."

"You'd better," Gertrude muttered. "People who leave things lying about are more trouble than they're worth. As I've said to her ladyship often enough, I'd rather manage on me own than have some of those half-witted village girls hanging about the place."

Sally was not afraid of Gertrude or her grumbles and as she brushed the carpet in Nicholas' room, she told herself that it was ridiculous to be afraid of Nada. But there was something sinister about such unprovoked antagonism. She tried to find one reasonable explanation for it and failed.

'Think of the devil and you'll see him,' Sally almost said out loud as she looked up to see Nada standing in the doorway. Being on her knees with her dress pinned up round her waist to keep it out of the way, Sally felt at a disadvantage.

As Nada did not speak, she straightened her back and brushed her hair from her forehead with the back of her hand.

"Did you want me?" she asked.

Nada came further into the room before she answered.

"Yes," she said at length. "I wanted to tell you that the children are not to go on the airfield. You quite understand? Captain Pawlovski will not have them there. Besides, it is dangerous and they might get hurt."

"I will tell them," Sally said, "though at the moment I have no idea where the airfield is."

"Well, when you find it, keep away," Nada said, "both you – and the children."

She was gone as silently and unexpectedly as she had come and Sally wondered how she could manage, without saying more than a few words, to disrupt the whole atmosphere.

'I suppose it is because of all she suffered in Poland,' she thought charitably. She was used to people being queer and strange because of their wartime experiences. Perhaps that was the explanation of Nada's anger when she gave her the identity card. She might have persecution mania and believe that everyone was against her.

Sally had known two women who had been like that. One had woken night after night in screaming hysterics to rush terrified into other people's bedrooms and beg them to save her from the enemy, the other had always listened at the door before entering because she believed that everyone was talking about her behind her back.

Sally wondered if Nada had seen a doctor and she remembered a brilliant specialist who had been a friend of Aunt Amy's and who specialised in just this particular branch of neurosis. Then she told herself that it was nothing to do with her personally and she certainly would not recommend Aunt Amy's friend to Nada. She finished brushing the carpet and started to dust. When she had done the rooms, she came downstairs and found the children waiting impatiently for her with Bracken beside them.

"Do come on, Sally! What a long time you've been!" Nicholas complained. "You know you promised to come with us to the sandpit."

"Why didn't you go alone?" Sally asked. "I don't suppose you would have come to much harm."

"We wanted you to come too," Prue said, slipping her hand into hers and Sally warmed to the compliment.

They went across the lawn and were soon lost among the trees.

When they came to the sandpit the children slid down the bank with shrieks of laughter while Sally descended more carefully. Bracken was already busy inspecting the rabbit holes, and the children looked round with that air of possession which children adopt so quickly when they find some place that they really like, and which has some strange and inexplicable attraction for them.

"This is a lovely place," Prue said approvingly and when Sally agreed, she took her by the hand and pulled her towards the lower part of the sandpit where there was an old ruin.

At first Sally thought it was only a heap of stones, then she imagined it might have been a summerhouse. But now, as she entered through what had once been a doorway, she saw that it was probably the remains of a chapel.

"It is very nice here," Prue said in a lowered voice and Sally, looking at a fragment of a Gothic window and the stump of a pillar, was sure that it had been a chapel.

Ivy had grown over some of the fallen stones, there was bright yellow and red lichen on others, and on one side of the door trailing sprays of golden honeysuckle seemed to scent the air like incense.

"Yes, it is nice," Sally repeated to herself, thinking how inadequate an adjective it was and feeling a sudden sense of happiness and contentment steal over her,

"I think a very good man once lived in this little house," Prue said, but when Sally, startled by the statement, asked her why she thought so, she became reserved and offhand, as children always do when questioned too closely about their instincts and she replied,

"I don't know."

Shouts from Nicholas brought Sally and Prue out of the enclosing walls of the ruined chapel.

"Oh, there you are!" he exclaimed. "Come and see what I've found."

He was standing high above them on the other side of the sandpit.

"What have you found?" Prue asked.

"Come up here and see for yourself," Nicholas replied.

The side of the pit was sheer and it took a great deal of scrambling on Sally's and Prue's part to join him, but at last they managed it. Here the trees were sparser and there was a great thickness of bracken and undergrowth.

"Look," Nicholas commanded and following the direction of his finger, Sally understood his excitement. A big hedge of brambles grew about a dozen yards ahead of them, but at the hedge the trees ended and beyond lay a big level field in the centre of which stood an aeroplane.

"An aeroplane!" Prue exclaimed. "Oh, Nicholas, let's go and look at it."

Quickly Sally put out a restraining hand, frightened that they would dash away before she could stop them.

"Listen, children," she said urgently. "You are not allowed in that field. Captain Pawlovski – you haven't met him yet, but he is staying at the Priory – is working on some very important experiments. I don't know what they are, but they are secret and he says no one, no one at all is to go on the airfield."

"But can't we just go and look at the aeroplane?" Nicholas asked, his eyes dark with disappointment.

~190~

"I am sorry," Sally answered, "but we have been told we mustn't go, none of us."

"Daddy has been in an aeroplane lots of time," Prue said, "but Nicholas and I have never seen one except in the sky."

"Perhaps your Daddy will be able to take you to see one when he comes home," Sally said, "but this one is forbidden. You do understand, don't you?"

They said they did, but Sally saw that they were both desperately disappointed. They peered across the hedge and it was obvious that the aeroplane exercised a tremendous fascination for them both.

Sally remembered her own childhood and how, when she had been denied things by Aunt Amy, they became all the more tempting because they were forbidden.

"Let us go back to the sandpit," she said. "Perhaps Bracken has found a rabbit."

But the sandpit had lost some of its excitement now that there was something even more thrilling beyond it. The children slid down obediently, but they wandered about rather half-heartedly, when before they had darted from place to place like streaks of lightning.

'Why was there so much mystery about the aeroplane?' Sally wondered. After all, however secret Captain Pawlovski's experiments were, they were not likely to be endangered by two children aged six and seven looking at his aeroplane. She resolved that she would appeal to him, if she could possibly get him alone and out of Nada's hearing, to allow Nicholas and Prue to visit the airfield just once.

The aeroplane was forgotten a few moments later when Bracken actually found a rabbit and followed it in full cry through the woods above the sandpit. Nicholas and Prue joined in the chase. Their quarry was lost near the kitchen gardens, but the children had the delight of exploring the greenhouse and even looking for early strawberries under their protecting nets.

All too soon it was time for luncheon and Sally announced that they must go back to the house. They were crossing the lawn when Sir Guy came out to meet them. As he walked towards them, Sally was suddenly conscious of her flushed cheeks and windswept hair. The children had been tugging at her arms, each one trying to drag her a different way and now, as Sir Guy approached, they seemed to sense her embarrassment and let her free.

"We have been playing in the garden," Sally said unnecessarily, feeling that some explanation was required of her.

"So I see," Sir Guy answered drily. "I came to tell you that they have just rung up from the hospital. Mrs. Redford is so anxious about the children that the doctor thinks it would be wise for her to see them – and possibly you – if only for a few minutes. I will drive you in this afternoon."

"But how wonderful for them!" Sally said, looking round for Nicholas and Prue, but finding that they had already run on ahead towards the house. "They will be thrilled. They love their mother very dearly."

"They seem well brought-up," Sir Guy said.

"Oh, but they are, indeed they are," Sally said quickly. "They have the most beautiful manners and they are both very obedient. I don't know a great deal about children, but I think Mrs. Redford must be an exceptional person in every way."

She spoke hotly in defence of Mrs. Redford because she well remembered that reference made inadvertently by Lady Thorne, to an actress or something of the sort.

Sir Guy's eyes were on her.

"Do you always champion those you like so fiercely?" he asked.

"Was I being fierce?" Sally asked. "I am sorry."

"I didn't ask you to be sorry," Sir Guy replied. "I like people who are positive in their opinions."

"Do you?" Sally said eagerly, surprisingly glad to find some point of human contact with Sir Guy.

But at her eagerness it seemed as if he drew away and the cynical lines on his face between nose and mouth deepened.

"Luncheon will be ready in about ten minutes," he said abruptly.

Sally felt herself dismissed, but she was not hurt. Once again she was aware of him in a double guise – detached and disapproving and as a knight in armour.

Her vision of him as the latter was there, insistently clear as it had been that day at the railway station and because the fantasy, if fantasy it was, was comforting and somehow happily familiar, she smiled at him before she turned and hurried towards the house.

9

Sally had been at the Priory more than a fortnight before she gradually began to be aware of Sir Guy as a personality rather than as a disapproving elder brother of Tony. Slowly, as the first numbed misery of her disillusionment passed from her, her old sensitiveness and interest in other people returned and while at first she was very conscious of the sweetness and gentleness of Lady Thorne, by degrees the stronger character of Sir Guy became evident so that Sally was increasingly aware of him whenever he entered a room or talked to the children in his quiet, grave manner.

She had not expected Nicholas and Prue to like him, but she soon realised that next to her, to whom they gave a wholehearted and flattering adoration, Sir Guy was their favourite. At his appearance their faces would light up and they would run to him, usually to ask some question about the countryside or the house and would hang almost breathlessly on his words.

Sally had not lived in the country without growing familiar with the old countryman's adage that the instinct of children and animals is seldom at fault where people are concerned. At first because of the children and later because of her own strangely mixed feelings, she began to watch Sir Guy and to accumulate small details of knowledge about him, which made up for the sparseness of his conversation to her and the way it seemed at times as if he deliberately avoided her.

It was Gertrude who told her most about him, for Sir Guy was her favourite of the whole family.

"He's a real good son," she said in her downright tone of voice that brooked no argument, "and it's a pity there's not more to appreciate him. Young Master Tony with his

~194~

coaxing ways and his flattering tongue would always get the best of everything, especially from his mother. But he couldn't twist me round his little finger. It was Master Guy for me every time."

Gertrude was so garrulous where the family were concerned that it would have been impossible to stop her talking even if Sally had wished to and soon the pain of hearing Tony's name vanished and she found that she, too, could speak of him quite easily.

"They must have been attractive children," she said to Gertrude.

"They were," Gertrude replied, "but it was Master Tony who always came first. He was never shy like his brother and with his fair hair and laughing eyes people would stop and say flattering things about him as if the child were deaf.

"'You'll turn the boy's head', I told them often enough, but who would listen? No, it was 'Master Tony this' and 'Master Tony that', until he began to think the world revolved round him, and 'deed it did – for his mother anyhow. Many's the time I've bitten back the words on my lips when I've seen how she's passed Master Guy by or made him take second place to his younger brother.

"'Tis not right', I've said to myself often enough, but who was I to speak?"

"But surely Sir Guy must have been very weak to let his mother have everything her own way?" Sally prompted.

"It wasn't weakness," Gertrude said scornfully, "it was good nature and as I've said often enough, it's the good-natured ones in this world as gets the hard knocks. Look what happened in Master Guy's case. Cruel hard I calls it."

"Oh, what happened?" Sally asked.

Gertrude looked over her shoulder, then she walked across the room and closed the bedroom door. She and Sally were making Nicholas' bed, but Sally invariably found that when Gertrude helped her things were much slower than when she managed by herself. Now Gertrude said ominously,

"You never know who might be listening. I ought not to be telling you them things, if it comes to that, but there, I'm glad to see you here, I am really. We need a bit of life and laughter in this house, getting old and stale we are!"

"But what about Miss Thorne?" Sally asked, merely for the joy of seeing Gertrude's face darken, and hear her snort,

"Oh, her!" she exclaimed and the pronoun contained a wealth of opinions unexpressed.

"Well, go on," Sally pleaded, "you were going to tell me about Sir Guy."

"So I was," Gertrude continued. "Well, he grew up into as nice a young man as ever you did see. There was no show or window dressing about him, he was gold through and through and a real gentleman if ever there was one. What's more, he was content to stay at home and look after the estate and do a bit of farming on his own. It was Master Tony who must be off to Paris and all the other places where there was fun to be had. It was Master Tony, too, who had to have all the money that could be spared. With my own ears I've heard Master Guy cancel an order for a new tractor or a farm cart because the money has had to be sent to his younger brother."

"It certainly doesn't seem fair," Sally interjected.

"It wasn't," Gertrude said, "and then to crown it all he goes and falls in love with Lady Beryl."

"Who was she?" Sally enquired.

"Lady Beryl Claveron was one of the prettiest young ladies I've ever seen in the whole of my life," Gertrude said. "Pretty as a picture she was and so sweet to talk to that there wasn't a man, woman or child in this country that wouldn't have done anything she asked of them. It was only to be expected that Sir Guy – for he was too old for me to be calling him Master then – should fall in love with her, and happy we were about it too. There was no one we'd rather have seen here as mistress than our own Lady Beryl whom we'd known since the moment she was born.

"Lord Claveron's estate was next to ours and she and Sir Guy had been boy and girl together, got to know each other in their prams as it were."

Gertrude paused for breath.

"Go on," Sally begged, "I am so interested."

"Well, we were all looking forward to the wedding, although there was no question of fixing the date because both Lady Beryl's parents and her Ladyship thought the young people were too young. Lady Beryl would come riding over here practically every morning of the week. I can see her now with her red hair streaming out in the wind and her face bright as the sunlight as she gallops up to the front door and calls out for Sir Guy. As nice a pair as you can imagine anywhere, as I've told you, but the Claverons are wild – I'd always heard tell there was bad blood in them right back from her great-grandfather. He'd been hanged, they say, for killing a man in a duel. I'm not doubting a word of it, for there was Sir Guy as much in love as any man should be with a pretty girl – when she ups and breaks his heart and ruins his life for him."

"Why? Whatever did she do" Sally asked.

"She ran away with – a gipsy," Gertrude said, lowering her voice as if she hardly dared speak the words.

"With a gipsy?" Sally repeated incredulously.

"Yes, that is what he was, sure enough. Oh, he had been in the films and got himself talked about and had his pictures in the paper, but for all that he was a gipsy by birth and a gipsy by nature. I'll say this for him, he had made no secret of his birth and when he was not play-acting he would move about the countryside in his caravan – a dolled-up, luxurious contraption, to be sure – but a caravan for all that. And that's how Lady Beryl meets him."

"But how?" Sally enquired.

"Oh, it's a great place round here for gipsies," Gertrude explained. "They come every summer and one of their camping grounds in those days was on the Claveron estate. We get to know some of them when they come year after year, though they keep themselves very much to themselves as a rule. But Lady Beryl, being young and like all young people curious, goes down to have chat with them and meets this film-star chap. The next thing we know is she has gone off with him – eloped without a word to anyone – and there's Sir Guy left with a broken heart if ever I've seen one."

"How terrible!" Sally cried. "Poor, poor Sir Guy!"

"That's what I've said often enough," Gertrude said, "and a couple of years after that happened along, comes the war. Sir Guy goes to it and when he comes back he seems quieter and graver and somehow, against things. I can't put it into words exactly what I means, but he seems to mistrust man and beast as the saying goes."

"Cynical," Sally suggested.

"Yes, maybe that's the word," Gertrude agreed, "and then we learns that Lady Beryl has died out in America or some such outlandish place where this man of hers had taken her – doubtless to escape the war, for he was that sort of chap."

"Does Sir Guy ever talk about her?" Sally asked.

"I've never heard him," Gertrude answered, "and her name is never mentioned in the house, so don't you go letting out what I've told you."

"But of course I won't," Sally promised.

"Sir Guy gave orders," Gertrude continued, "that the gipsies were always to be allowed on any land that he owned. That shows you the type of man he is – too good-natured by far to my way of thinking. So now they comes here every year."

What an extraordinary story it was, Sally thought later. It was somehow hard to imagine Sir Guy desperately in love. It was easier to think of Tony in love, to hear the laughter in his voice and see the flicker of light in his eyes. Would Sir Guy ever fall in love again? Sally wondered and she watched him, grave and courteous, as he listened to his mother or made a decision on some problem concerning the estate.

She suspected, although she could not discuss it with Gertrude, that Nada was in love with her cousin. There was something hungry about her lips and in the darkness of her eyes when she looked at him. But to everyone else Nada was utterly detached and indifferent to the point of rudeness. She was also in some indefinable way secretive. It was nothing one could explain, nothing one could put ones finger on and yet she moved in an aura of mystery.

When she came into a room, it was somehow surreptitiously, when one met her in a passage she gave the impression that she did not wish to be seen. Sally kept telling herself that she was being uncharitable, that however horrid Nada was to her she should try to be kind to one who had suffered so intensely. But it was impossible to be nice to someone who was so determinedly aggressive and gradually Sally got into the habit of keeping out of Nada's way and of coming directly in contact with her only at meal times.

The children were both a defence and a protection, for not only did she find it possible to absorb herself completely in their interests and needs, but she also made them an excuse to go out of a room when Nada came into it and even to escape from the confines of the house into the open air.

The weather was lovely and the children were already very different in appearance. They were still much too thin, but the pallor of their faces was gradually being replaced by a healthy tan, and whereas at first they had only pecked at their food, they now ate ravenously at every meal.

Mrs. Redford had been desperately ill, but every day reports of her progress were more and more encouraging. Sir Guy had cabled to tell Major Redford what had happened and he had replied that he was making every effort to return home as swiftly as possible. Everything having been done that could be done, Sally's only task was to keep the children happy and well, and in this she succeeded admirably.

But they had not been successful in finding out if the children were related to old General and Mrs. Redford. Lady Thorne had met the General at a Red Cross meeting and had come back rather shaken to tell Sir Guy and Sally what had occurred.

"You know what a funny reserved old man he is, Guy," she said in her soft voice. "He frightens me and always has, but I thought I really must make an effort and so when the meeting was over, I went up to him and asked how he was and if Mrs. Redford was well. Then, feeling rather nervous I said, 'Do tell me, General, about your son. I don't seem to have heard of Bobby for so many years'."

"Oh, how brave of you!" Sally interjected. "What did he say?"

"He just looked at me under those heavy eyebrows of his," Lady Thorne said, "then after a moment he said, very clearly and distinctly, as if I were some idiot on a parade ground, 'Madam, I have no son' and walked away."

"But how awful for you!" Sally sympathised.

"I really felt, as though I might sink into the ground," Lady Thorne said, "I would have given anything not to have mentioned it."

"Well, he could not have meant that Bobby was dead," Sir Guy reflected, "because we should have heard if he had been killed. I'm sure you are right, Mother, and Nicholas and Prue are the General's grandchildren, but I don't see that there is much we can do about it."

"Well, I certainly won't try to do anything again," Lady Thorne replied, "I still feel quite shaken by his behaviour."

After that nothing more was said about the children's ancestry because the mere mention of the General was likely to upset Lady Thorne. She was a strange person in some ways. Sally, thought, as she got to know her better. She was so fragile and feminine, so utterly sweet and yet so lacking in strength of character. Perhaps Sally had all her life known strong personalities – Aunt Amy, Lynn, women who for better or worse, made firm decisions and lived a life of action. But Lady Thorne drifted through in a kind of happy haze, being kind to people because it was impossible for her to be anything else and completely content to live, as Sally saw it, on the very surface of existence in a sunshine of her own making. Nothing seemed to touch her very deeply. When Sir Guy told her what had happened on the farms, she would smile at him and say, "How clever of you, dear, to arrange that!" or "I am sure you know best" and Sally had the impression that she listened with her ears only and that whatever Sir Guy had told her, her reaction would have been exactly the same.

Somehow Sally found it in her heart to pity Nada. If the girl had been through terrible horrors and privation, how difficult it must be for her to find in this calm, undisturbed backwater no understanding, no real appreciation of what she had suffered. And yet, even while she was sorry for her, Sally was aware that Nada did not want sympathy. She treated her aunt as one might treat a child or an invalid with soothing phrases and with an artificial pleasantry.

On the third Sunday of her stay at The Priory, a very strange thing happened. The first Sunday occurred only two days after her arrival and Lady Thorne had suggested that, as the children looked rather tired, it would be best not to take them to church. Sally had agreed and had sat reading to them in the garden until the others returned.

The next Sunday they all went to church, driving to Sally's surprise several miles to a rather ugly Victorian building where a sparse congregation was gathered for Morning Prayer. This Sunday when Sally brought the children downstairs dressed in their best clothes, Lady Thorne was waiting for her in the hall, but there was no car at the door.

"We can walk to church today," Lady Thorne said, and then, as Sally looked surprised, she explained, "This Sunday we go to our own church. It is only at the end of the park."

"Oh, now I understand," Sally exclaimed, "I wondered why the church was so far from the house."

"Unfortunately, our vicar has two parishes," Lady Thorne said. "We are not very fond of the other church, as the children always called it. Our own is so beautiful, it is very old and was built with stones from the original Priory, so for us it has a particular pride of possession. The Thornes have all been buried there and you will see their tombs. There is quite an amazing array of them."

Sir Guy joined them and they started to walk down the drive. "Isn't that a little chapel in the sandpit?" Sally asked somewhat shyly.

"Yes, it is," Sir Guy answered, "but that was not the original chapel belonging to The Priory. That was unfortunately destroyed at the same time as the main building. The one in the sandpit was a very small place as far as I can gather from the old records, more of a cell than a chapel, it was built by a very saintly monk, revered by all the community, who would often go into retreat there for long periods. He was a Franciscan and the chapel was, of course, dedicated to St. Francis, and that was why he built it in the woods so that he could commune with the birds and the wild animals."

"What a lovely idea!" Sally said.

"Oh, tell us more about him" Prue pleaded, slipping her hand into Sir Guy's.

"I wish I knew more," Sir Guy replied, "unfortunately when The Priory was destroyed the records were burnt with it. I am quoting now from the legends which have been handed down and from a few plans which were discovered years later, and which were able to show the general layout of The Priory grounds."

"Don't you know anything more about the saintly monk?" Nicholas asked.

"I don't even know his name," Sir Guy answered, "but there was supposed to be a secret passage from The Priory to his cell, though nobody has ever discovered it."

"A secret passage!" the children exclaimed almost in the same breath. "We'll look for it, won't we, Sally?"

"I am afraid that is only a legend too," Sir Guy smiled.

"We'll look all the same," Prue declared. "Nicholas and I often find things when other people can't find them."

"Yes, do you remember Mummy's scarf that the monkeys had stolen," Nicholas asked, "and Daddy's cufflinks which had fallen into a tiny crack in the boards"

"We found them," Prue explained to Sir Guy, "and we'll find your secret passage for you, you see if we don't."

"I shall be delighted if you do," Sir Guy said, "but don't be too disappointed if you fail and even if you discover the entrance, I'm afraid the passage itself will have fallen in centuries ago."

The children, however, would not be put off and could talk of nothing else until they reached the church. Here, as Lady Thorne had said, was a very different building from the church they had visited the week before. It was small and grey, and its lichgate and wide, nail-studded door seemed to welcome them in. The pews were all of carved oak and some of them, Lady Thorne told Sally in a whisper, had been salvaged from the old Priory Church. They were carved with birds and beasts and flowers and they were worn dark and smooth by successive generations of worshippers.

Lady Thorne led the way to the front pew on the left-hand side of the aisle. It was a big wide pew with a thick, red velvet seat and high hassocks of the same material. The children knelt to pray, but their eyes remained wide open, staring with delight at an ancient oak snake that ran along the front of their pew and at a squirrel which sat cracking a huge nut at the end of it.

Sally rose from her knees and helped Prue and Nicholas on to the seat, which was a little high for them. She felt the peace and loveliness of the old church encompass heir. Well might Lady Thorne call it 'their church', for everywhere around were tombs and memorials to the Thorne family. A marble memorial ornamented with weeping angels and a broken urn and a long poem had been erected on the wall just in front of the pew and, having studied it with interest, Sally looked across the aisle.

When she did so, she held her breath in sheer astonishment. For a moment she could only stare, bewildered and incredulous, at the huge tomb which lay directly in front of the pews on the right-hand side of the aisle.

It was the tomb of a Knight in armour and she could see his face quite distinctly – the closed eyes, clear-cut nose, firm mouth and broad forehead. The whole figure was in a surprisingly good state of preservation, only the Knight's sword lying beside him was broken, his hands, which seemed to have been clasped in prayer, had been severed at the wrists, while the dog that lay at his feet had lost its head. But his plumed helmet was intact, as was the tasselled pillow on which he slept.

But Sally stared only at the Knight's face and then she turned her eyes to Sir Guy who sat in profile to her at the end of the pew. His chin was a little raised as he looked towards the altar. Now at last she knew why, when she had first seen him and again at other times, she had thought of him as a knight in armour with a plumed helmet.

Gradually the jigsaw fitted into place. She had been very small, not as big as Prue, when she had sat in the pew on the other side of the aisle and stared at the tomb of the knight. She could see Nanny's hand, encased in a grey cotton glove, handing her a hymn book and pointing out the words of the hymn, although they were too difficult for her to read. She could see her feet sticking out in front of her, too short to reach the floor and the hem of her little red coat with the frill of her white muslin dress peeping beneath it. And there in front of her had been the Knight.

'Her Knight' she had called him to herself and she had made up stories about him not only in church but when she had been put to bed and it was dark and rather frightening in her bedroom. She had thought then that her Knight was beside her, scaring away the evil things that were waiting ready to pounce on children who could not go to sleep quickly. *Her Knight!* She remembered him for many years and then he slipped away into the limbo, of forgotten things only to come partially back to her memory when she had first seen Sir Guy.

Why, Sally asked herself, had she been here in this church? All through the service the question tantalised her. Automatically she knelt or rose to sing or sat to listen, but all the time she was trying to grope her way back into the past and recapture an incident of her childhood. How could she possibly have been here? And yet she knew she had sat in that pew, had stared at the tomb of the Knight and made him, for the time being at any rate, an intrinsic part of her life.

Sally looked at the pew now. It was empty, although the pews behind it were well filled with villagers, and it seemed to her that it must be left empty intentionally. She was sure it belonged to some special family, just as the pew in which she now sat so obviously belonged to the Thornes. There was a little box to hold their hymn books, which were all bound in red leather and embossed with the Thorne coat-of-arms, and there were the comfortable cushioned seats and high hassocks.

Sally craned her neck to see if the pew on the other side of the aisle was equally comfortably furnished, but the old-fashioned carved door of the pew blocked her view.

The service came to an end, and Sir Guy stood on one side to let Lady Thorne precede him down the aisle. Nada followed, while Sally and the children came behind. Outside in the sunshine Lady Thorne stopped to say a word to many of the villagers and then at last, after what seemed to Sally a long time because she was so impatient, they were all walking back up The Priory drive.

"What an excellent sermon the vicar preached today!" Lady Thorne said. "It is always a delight when he speaks of the countryside."

"Do tell me," Sally asked and her voice was breathless because she was so anxious to receive an answer, "do tell me, who does the pew belong to on the other side of the aisle?"

"Do you mean the front one?" Lady Thorne enquired. "It is the Redfords' family pew, but alas, they can seldom occupy it nowadays. They have so little petrol that they usually have to go to another church which is only half a mile away from Merton Grange, but this is their parish church."

The Redfords! Now that Sally knew the answer, she felt that she had expected it and the other pieces of the jigsaw began to fall into place.

~206~

There was an elderly man who had been Daddy's friend and a boy older than herself, who had rushed noisily about the house but had little to say to her. The Redfords! Of course it would be the Redfords! Was there nothing in life that did not link up some way or another? Was there any action that we did, unknowingly and unwittingly, but it was in reality part of the pattern, of the fore-ordained plan in which we all play our tiny but all-important parts?

Sally was very silent as they walked back to The Priory. She was fascinated and yet afraid of what she had experienced. It was all so strange – the strange feeling she had experienced on seeing Sir Guy on the wayside station, her first meeting with him on the doorstep of Nanny Bird's flats, the realisation that he was Tony's brother, and now the knight whom she had loved as a tiny child. Her memory, once released, kept presenting her with new pictures, flashes of the past, tantalising in their incompleteness, yet absorbing because they suggested so much more that she had forgotten.

She saw part of a room. It had white walls and there were blue curtains at the window through which she had looked down into a garden where there was a boy kicking a ball about. Had that boy been Nicholas and Prue's father? Was he called Bobby? Oh, why couldn't she remember?

She had a vague memory of a deep voice speaking of her father, of a woman, shadowy and rather indecisive, of a wide staircase and Nanny helping her up it, but they were all indistinct compared with the memory of her knight. She had seen him lying with closed eyes, recumbent on his tomb, but for her he was alive. He walked beside her, he guided and protected her. He shielded her from danger. She had called to him when she was afraid and his face had been the face of Sir Guy, only his eyes had in her imagination been gentle, they had soft and understanding, and she had thought that he loved her because she loved him so much.

After the Sunday luncheon, which was the traditional meal of roast beef and fruit tart, she took the children down to the sandpit. They were as impatient as Sally to get away from the house, but for a different reason. Nicholas and Prue wanted to search for the old passage.

"We will see if we can find where it came out," they kept saying, "and then later we will look in the house. The entrance is sure to be somewhere down in the cellars."

While Nicholas and Prue poked around the brambles and under briar bushes, Sally sat in the ruins of the little chapel. Long before she knew its history, she had known it was a chapel, for something within her told her all too clearly that it was a holy place. Now that her instinct had been confirmed she looked at it with new eyes. Surely the birds seemed to alight there more often than in any other part of the wood? Surely, although they scurried away at her approach, there was an extraordinary number of rabbits and squirrels nestling against its lichen-covered stones? There was always a rustle of wings and the small stirrings of unseen wild things, but the sounds only seemed to intensify the stillness.

As the children ran about shouting excitedly to each other, Sally sat and waited. Now she was sure that Sir Guy had been right when he said that The Priory was a place of healing. But there was more than a healing quality to be found in this tiny chapel, its very stones were impregnated with faith. She could feel a glow of warmth reaching out to her, possessing her whole being. For a moment she was lost to time and space – past and present, it was all hers and all immeasurably clear. She was no longer alone, but one with the whole universe.

Then suddenly as the moment had come, it was gone and she was conscious of the stillness and that she was listening. The sun filtered through the green leaves of the overhanging trees, the birds were singing. Sally was sure, quite sure that there was a message for her here in the peace and undisturbed loveliness of the wood. She waited, almost holding her breath in anticipation, then it came, and she knew what she must do.

She looked at her watch. It was only half past two. They had lunched early because the staff liked to have a long Sunday afternoon free. Sally called the children to her.

"I want to go for a walk," she said, "and I want you both to come with me. It will be quite a long walk. Do you mind?

"Oh, must we come?" Nicholas asked. "We want to find the secret passage."

"We will try to find that another day," Sally said quickly. "We have got something more exciting to do this afternoon."

"What it is?" Prue asked.

"We are going over to a house where I stayed when I was a little girl," Sally said. "It really is exciting. Come on."

When Lady Thorne had spoken of the Redfords, Sally had asked her where they lived and learned that their house, Merton Grange, was about two miles from The Priory by road. Sally had, however, learned a certain amount of the geography of the country in the last two weeks and she guessed that by going across the field to Merton Grange, they could cut off half a mile or so.

The children, although reluctant to leave their efforts at exploration, were obedient, as they always were. They climbed now to the top of the sandpit and striking through the wood, came to the meadows on the far side of it. It was a lovely walk and soon the children, forgetting any disappointment they might have had at being taken from the sandpit, were rushing here and there exclaiming with excitement as they disturbed a hare, or put up a brace of partridges.

They were not tired and the time passed quickly until they reached the gateway of Merton Grange. Only as they walked up the drive and Sally reached up her hand to pull the old-fashioned bell chain, did she feel suddenly a little unsure and half afraid. Suppose she, like Lady Thorne, failed, and yet what she had experienced in the ruined chapel made her confident.

A maid answered the door.

"If Mrs. Redford is in?" Sally said, hesitating a little, "would you ask her if she will see Miss St. Vincent who stayed here many years ago."

"I will ask, miss," the maid replied and invited Sally and the children into the hall.

Now she remembered it. There were the dark, oak-panelled walls and the wide staircase with heraldic newels on the banisters. The children were entranced by them.

"Look at the little lions," Prue said. "Aren't they sweet? What are they holding in their paws?"

"Shields," Sally answered.

"Look, there's a tiger," Prue shouted, pointing to a rug laid in front of the big fireplace. "Daddy shot one like that in India. Mummy was going to have it made into a rug, but the ants ate it up. Daddy said that we needn't be frightened of tigers if tiny little things like ants could eat them up."

"He only said that because you thought you heard one in the night and you were frightened," Nicholas said.

"I *did* hear one," Prue said, "and it was very frightening."

Sally felt her heart beating quickly and she longed to tell the children not to talk about India, but she thought it best to leave them alone. If she made them in any way self-conscious, her plan might not succeed.

The maid came back.

"Will you come this way, miss?"

They followed her into the drawing room, a big, formal room. A man and a woman rose as they entered. As soon

~210~

as she saw them Sally recognised the General and his wife. They were much, much older than she remembered, in fact the General, who had seemed to her when she was a child a big man, appeared now to have shrunk to half his size. Mrs. Redford, with her grey hair and rather sad smile, had changed too, but she remembered them quite vividly.

"Is it really Sally St. Vincent" Mrs. Redford asked, coming forward and holding out her hand.

"Yes, it is," Sally answered. "It is clever of you to remember me."

"Of course we remember you, dear. Why, funnily enough, I was only speaking of you to my husband the other day."

Sally shook hands with the General.

"It must be fourteen years since you stayed here," he said. "You were smaller than this young lady."

He looked down at Prue.

"This is Prudence and this is Nicholas," Sally said quickly. "They are staying with me at The Priory and as it was such a lovely day, we thought we would walk over and call on you."

"How nice of you!" Mrs. Redford said. "But you must be hot and tired after such a long walk. I am sure the children would like a lemonade."

"Thank you very much," Nicholas said.

"And what about you, Sally? We shall be having tea in a little while and hope you will stay for it."

"I am afraid we shall have to get back," Sally said, "and I don't want anything to drink at the moment, thank you."

"Well now, sit down and tell us all about yourself," Mrs. Redford said. "My husband was so upset to hear of your father's death. We read about it in the paper. It was very sad, you must miss him very much."

"I do," Sally answered.

"And how is Amy?" Mrs. Redford enquired.

"She is dead, too," Sally replied, and she told them how Aunt Amy had died and about the farm she had started in Wales.

"How like Amy!" Mrs. Redford exclaimed. "She always had marvellous ideas for helping people. We were at school together and even as a girl she was always altruistic."

The maid brought in lemonades for Nicholas and Prue. They drank them down and then, bored by grown-up conversation, wandered towards the windows. It was Prue who saw the fountain first. She gave a little cry and ran back to the General.

"You have got a fountain! I can see it from here. It is not a very big fountain, but please can we go and look at it?"

"Yes, of course you can," the General said and rose to open the French windows for them. They sped out, laughing and shouting, to where in the centre of a round ornamental fish pond a small fountain played and tinkled in the sunshine.

Mrs. Redford and Sally watched them from another window.

"All children love a fountain," Mrs. Redford said softly and, turning to her husband, she added, "Turn it on fuller, Lionel. They will like it when it goes up high."

"Yes, I will," he replied.

He followed the children out of the window and down the steps to the fountain side. Sally saw Prue run towards him. He took her hand and led her with Nicholas to the ball-cock that controlled the flow of water. He turned it on for them and Mrs. Redford and Sally heard their shrieks of joy as the fountain rose up some twelve feet into the air.

The sun was golden on the wind-blown spray and on the flushed and excited faces of the children as they ran round and round the little pond.

Sally was suddenly conscious that Mrs. Redford was wiping her eyes.

"Such pretty children," she said, "and such nice manners! Are they any relation of yours?"

"No," Sally replied, "I met them in the strangest way."

Without hinting that she herself was staying at The Priory in unusual circumstances, she told Mrs. Redford what had occurred on the train.

"Their mother is so pretty and though I have only met her once or twice when I have taken the children to the hospital, I feel that she must be a charming person in every way, for the children are so beautifully brought up. They have the right ideas about everything, they are so truthful and extremely obedient. Nicholas admires courage above all things and Prue is the most tender-hearted little person. She cannot bear that people or animals should suffer. It almost broke her heart when we found a dead bird on the lawn the other morning."

"It was very kind of Lady Thorne to take them in," Mrs. Redford said, "but how right she was."

"I think Lady Thorne loves having them there and she will be very sorry when they have to go."

"Perhaps…" Mrs. Redford hesitated, "you will bring them over here again. My husband and I are very lonely and it is nice to hear young voices about the place. Look at Lionel now, I have not seen him so energetic for years."

The children had found a ball and were throwing it to the General. When he caught it, he threw it high in the air, so high that it seemed almost to top some of the trees surrounding the lawn, and then as it came down the children rushed to catch it, missing it as often as not, and falling over each other with shrieks of delighted laughter.

"The General certainly seems to be enjoying himself," Sally smiled.

"You must stay to tea," Mrs. Redford said suddenly and there was almost a note of pleading in her voice. "I will ask Sarah to bring it at once. Do say yes?"

"I think we would love to," Sally replied, "if you are sure it will be no trouble. We don't have tea until late at The Priory, so they won't be worried about us."

"That will be lovely," Mrs. Redford exclaimed. "I will go and tell Sarah and see if there is something really nice for the children. Perhaps you would like to go and join them in the garden."

Sally went out into the garden, she sat down on the terrace, watching and listening to the children, but making no attempt to join them and the General. Soon they got tired of playing ball and went off to see the ferrets that the General kept for ratting. When Mrs. Redford came back, she found Sally alone.

"They have gone to look at the ferrets," Sally said.

"Oh, they are always an excitement," Mrs. Redford said. "I remember when my son was a boy he loved his ferrets, and he had two of his very own."

She spoke hesitatingly of her son. Sally guessed that it was a long time since she had been able to mention him, but the presence of the children having made it easier, she was glad of the excuse.

"Nicholas has quite a way with animals," Sally replied. "I have been brought up with them myself and I know it is either a thing you have, or you haven't got. He handles them absolutely fearlessly and they seem to trust him."

"My Bobby was just the same," Mrs. Redford said, "I remember when he was only four, I saw him taking a young rat out of a trap in which it had been imprisoned. He already had it in his hands when I reached him. I was in absolute terror that the thing would bite him, but it kept quite still while he released it with his funny little baby hands, then it jumped free and ran away without harming him in the slightest."

"How extraordinary!" Sally exclaimed with interest, "because rats are usually such ferocious animals!"

"We got quite used to Bobby and his animals," Mrs. Bedford said. "I think he had the strangest pets of any child I have ever known."

Sarah brought in tea and Sally saw there was a plate of chocolate biscuits and some special sandwiches which she was sure the children would like.

They came running in with the General from the garden, very excited and rather grubby.

"May I wash their hands?" Sally asked.

Mrs. Redford got to her feet.

"I will take you upstairs," she said.

Sally and the children followed her up the wide staircase, which Sally remembered climbing with Nanny's aid. Up they went and then turned right along the corridor, coming to Mrs. Redford's bedroom with its adjoining bathroom. Sally poured the water for the children and told them to wash their hands carefully. Mrs. Redford was looking in a drawer in her bedroom and Sally guessed, before she saw it in her hands, that she was looking for a photograph.

"This is a picture of my Bobby," Mrs. Redford said, "when he was about the same age as Nicholas."

There was no mistaking the likeness. Bobby had been bigger-boned and much plumper, but there were the same clear-cut, exquisitely moulded features, the same courageous carriage of the head. Was Mrs. Redford blind not to see it? Sally wondered, as with appropriate and conventional expressions of interest she handed the portrait back.

But Mrs. Redford's eyes were on Nicholas as they went downstairs. Prue ran at once to the General, who was sitting in a chair by the fireplace.

"I do like your lions," she said. "Have you got names for them?"

The General looked bewildered.

"She means the heraldic lions on the staircase," Sally explained.

"No, I'm afraid I haven't thought of giving them names," the General replied.

"Oh, but you must," Prue insisted. "Shall I think of names for you?"

"That is a very good idea," the General agreed with a smile. "You can think of them while you have your tea."

Mrs. Redford seated the children on small chairs at each side of the table. She poured out Sally's tea and passed the cup to her.

"Do you children have milk or tea?" she asked.

"We have milk," Nicholas answered, "with a very little tea in it, but they call it tea to make us feel we are grown up." Everyone laughed.

"I've just remembered something Daddy told me," Prue said suddenly. "When he was a little boy, there were two lions in his house and he called them Growler and Prowler."

Mrs. Redford turned very white. For a moment she seemed to hold on to the table as if for support. She looked across the table at her husband and their eyes met. Then she turned to the children.

"What are your n-names?" she asked, and her voice broke on the last word.

Sally drew in a deep breath, but Nicholas answered before she could speak,

"I'm Nicholas Redford and my sister is Prudence Redford."

There was an awful silence. Sally could not look either at the General or at his wife and then at last, in a voice so small that she could hardly recognise it as her own, she said lamely, "I-I wondered if by any chance they – they were relations – of yours."

10

Sally walked swiftly through the wood, for once not pausing to watch the antics of the red squirrels or to note the lovely contrast between sunshine and shade. She was anxious to reach the sanctuary of the little chapel where she could sit and think. Her hand, deep in the pocket of the blue cardigan which she wore over her cotton dress, was clutching a letter from Mary. She had only had time to glance at it at breakfast, but now at last she was alone and could read it slowly and ponder over it to her heart's content.

The children had been fetched by their grandmother a few minutes ago and had driven off to see their mother in hospital. Everything had worked so smoothly and happily since Sally, with what had seemed to Lady Thorne great daring, had gone to Merton Grange and confronted the General with his grandchildren.

The old man's defences and the anger that he had sustained for so many years had collapsed in a manner that was almost pitiful to see and he had reached out eagerly at the chance of a reconciliation.

Sally often wondered what had happened when he and Mrs. Redford went the very next day to the hospital to see the children's mother. She gathered from subsequent conversations that the General had uttered what for him must have been a very abject apology. Anyway, his and Mrs. Redford's joy at knowing that their son was on his way home and that, when he arrived, the children would be installed at Merton Grange was apparent to everyone.

Major Redford was due to arrive in two or three days' time and by then there was a chance that his wife would be allowed out of the hospital and, instead of her coming to The Priory, as had been originally intended, it was arranged that she was to go straight to Merton Grange. Sally's delight that things had turned out so well for Nicholas and Prue was tempered with the unhappiness of knowing that she would lose them.

Now she had got to think really seriously of her future. Reaching the ruins, she drew Mary's letter from her pocket and glanced once again at the cheque that was folded inside it. It was for twenty-five pounds and Sally was extremely glad to have it because she had been wondering for some time how she could purchase the clothes that she would need for a farm job, when she obtained one.

More than once she had looked helplessly at the lovely frocks and suits that had been part of her trousseau. In their glowing colours and delicate materials they were clothes that any girl would have been thrilled at flattered to own, but Sally could not see Madame Marguerite's delectable creations or the charming little hats that went with them being useful, when she milked the cows or helped with the harvesting.

'I have got to get a job,' she told herself now as she slipped the cheque into her pocket.

But for the moment her attention was concentrated to the exclusion of all else on Mary's news of Lynn. Lynn was married! Lynn was happy and was being a tremendous success in South America. But beyond this Mary's letter held little information and no details and Sally guessed that Lynn, who hated letter-writing, had sent her news by cable.

What she did not guess, as she read the bald sentences again and again, was that Lynn had also cabled to Mary the money to pay some of her bills and the cheque in her pocket had been secretly diverted from other and most importunate claimants. Lynn was too busy to remember her daughter's problems, but Mary had worried about Sally ever since she left Berkeley Square with her little chin held high and unshed tears in her eyes.

Sally put the letter down on her lap and sighed. Lynn was happy! How she wished, she could have seen her married! How beautiful she must have looked wearing her happiness as another woman might have worn a conventional wreath of orange blossom and a lace veil! Her eyes would have been dark and mysterious with strange lights in them when she looked at Erico. Sally remembered how she had intercepted burning, passionate glances between Lynn and Erico. She had been conscious of the vibrations between them, of a magnetism that made the very air they breathed seem electrically charged. She had been shy, embarrassed, fascinated, and they had not even remembered that she was there.

Yes, they would be happy together, she thought, with a happiness that she personally could not understand. Her love for Tony had been such a quiet, gentle feeling compared with those fierce, tumultuous emotions that vibrated from Lynn and Erico.

Sitting alone now in the atmosphere of peace and healing that she always seemed to find within the ruins of the little chapel, Sally wondered if such love would ever be hers. Would she ever hear in her own voice that note of breathless hunger that she had listened to in Lynn's? Would the almost savage light in a man's eyes part her lips and make her eyes shine as Lynn's shone when Erico looked at her?

'Perhaps I have never really known love,' Sally told herself and even as she formulated the words she knew that they were true. But she did not wish at this moment to be concerned with thoughts of Tony or of herself. It was Lynn who must absorb her whole, undivided interest, and yet even Lynn seemed now to belong to the past. Without meaning to be disloyal she found herself thinking of the children and of the joy that lay ahead of them. For them there was the prodigal's homecoming and the welcoming feast, even though they were too young to realise that they had been so long exiled from their heritage.

And yet Sally felt that, unformulated in words, the acute sensitiveness that she had noticed both in Nicholas and Prue must have reacted subconsciously to their father's longing for the home in which he had been brought up and to their mother's consciousness that so much had been sacrificed by her husband in his love for her.

But now all would go well. Sally wondered once again at the pattern of things that gradually and so surprisingly became apparent when one was bound up in them. How sweet the children were and how much they had meant to her! So much of her aching misery and the numb sense of shock had been forgotten or healed because she had been busy with Nicholas and Prue.

She could imagine nothing nicer than being allowed to look after them. She adored their serious, intense little way of talking, their directness, and the affection they lavished on everyone who was kind and understanding to them. Had they been children of less character they might well have become spoilt at The Priory, because Lady Thorne adored them and the maids tumbled over themselves to do things for them and to give them treats in the way of cakes or special dishes. Only Nada and Captain Pawlovski managed to keep aloof from them, but then they were both so strange and alien to everything and everybody, that Sally believed it was not so much their lack of interest in the children themselves as in the fact that they wished to remain unidentified with anything in their present surroundings.

She was well aware that Nada thought of herself not as a British subject, which she was, but as a Pole. It was perhaps understandable when one remembered that she had always lived in her mother's country and that England, although it had proved a haven of refuge, was unfamiliar and entirely different in every way from all she had ever known and loved.

Nicholas and Prue were still determinedly seeking for the hidden passage. Sir Guy, half alarmed at the enthusiasm he had aroused so unwittingly, told them over and over again that even if they found the entrance, the passage would have caved in and have become quite impassable by this time. But the children were not to be put off. To them a secret passage was something so thrilling and exciting that Sally began to realise what a sparse entertainment had been theirs in a small bungalow in India.

It made her increasingly glad to think that they would now at last begin to live the life that might have been theirs since their birth. There would be ponies to ride, gardens to play in, wide stretches of moor over which they could roam at will, but in the meantime until these things materialised, they were utterly absorbed in the finding of the secret passage. They had brought spades down to the sandpit and begun to dig in the bushes, hoping to find the opening and when this failed, they had gone clattering down the back stairs towards the cellars of The Priory.

Nada had come angrily in search of Sally.

"You will take these children out into the garden," she said sharply. "They are not to go tearing over the house like this, making a mess with their muddy shoes. It is not fair to the maids. You should look after them better."

"I am sorry," Sally said, uncomfortable because Nada was obviously so angry and not daring to argue that the servants minded very little what the children did and always had a welcome for them whatever room they invaded.

"It will be a good thing when they leave here," Nada stormed. "They are spoilt and opinionated, in my country children like that would get a good whipping."

Sally looked at her in surprise. She had not been aware until this moment that Nada actively disliked the children.

Now she knew that she was looking forward to their departure as much as she herself was looking forward to her own. Because she was, as usual, shy and uneasy, Sally moved quickly towards the door.

"I am sorry if they have upset you," she said. "I will tell them to go into the garden. They will go at once because they are good children and they always do as they are told."

She spoke quietly and un-aggressively, but she could not help making this small defence of the children she loved so well. But Nada was not appeased.

"Take them out at once and keep them out," she commanded, and because her tone was so peremptory and in its way, so rude, Sally felt the blood rushing to her cheeks.

'Why must she be so horrid?' she asked herself as she ran to call the children up from the cellars.

"Oh, but, Sally, there are lots of exciting rooms down here," Nicholas protested when she found them, "and I am sure in one of them there will be a secret door leading into the tunnel."

"I'm sorry, darlings," she said, hating to see the disappointment in their faces, "but Miss Thorne says you are not to come here and we must do as she says."

"Why?" Prue asked as she came obediently up the stairs.

"Well, for one reason because she belongs here and we are only guests."

The children digested this opinion until they were out in the garden, then Prue said decidedly,

"I *hate* Miss Thorne! She is horrid!"

"You mustn't hate anyone," Sally said quickly.

"I don't hate anyone else," Prue answered.

"Prue is right," Nicholas interjected. "She is horrid! And that Captain Pav – something – he is mean, too. I asked him very, very politely if Prue and I might just look at his aeroplane, but he would not let us. He shouted at me, 'No! No! No!' until I ran away. Why is he so mean, Sally?"

"I don't know," Sally answered helplessly, "He is making very secret experiments and I suppose he is frightened that you might guess what they are."

She smiled cynically to herself as she made the explanation to Nicholas. Really, the way Captain Pawlovski went on about his aeroplane was quite ridiculous, as if any of them were likely to guess his silly secrets. Sally had come to the conclusion that the mystery he made about his work was simply to cover up the fact that his experiments were not going very well. If they had been, she felt he would have been more excited, would look more pleased with life or at least be human enough to take them, into his confidence. As it was, he just drifted into the house at meal times, scowling fiercely and seldom speaking unless he was spoken to.

At night she would hear the engine humming as he went off on a flight, but once when she had asked him civilly if it had been cold the night before, he merely glared at her as if he considered her question impertinent and went on eating in silence.

She had often wondered what Sir Guy thought of Captain Pawlovski and why he tolerated his surly presence in the house. Lady Thorne seemed hardly to notice whether he was there or not, and Sally supposed it was because of their affection for Nada that they put up with anything the Captain did, rather than turn away a compatriot of hers. Well, Nada was strange, too, although she was pleasant enough to Sir Guy and Lady Thorne.

Sally sighed and wondered with surprise how her attention could have wandered so far from Mary's letter. She looked down at it, and even as she did so she heard Nada's voice. There was no mistaking that peculiar intonation. She was speaking, and now someone was answering her. That, too, was a strange voice, sharp, and raised as if in protestation.

Sally instinctively got to her feet. She could not bear that Nada should find her amongst the ruins of the little chapel. It. was so essentially her own place that she shrunk in horror from the idea that the peace and holiness she found there might be disturbed by Nada's baleful personality.

She came out into the sandpit. She could still hear the voices, but there was no sign of the speakers. Without considering what she did, she scrambled up the further side of the sandpit, which she and the children had climbed the very first day when Nicholas had looked over the briar hedge and seen the aeroplane. When she reached the top, she could see Nada and the person to whom she was speaking.

Hidden by the high briar hedge and in the shadows of the trees, Sally saw several things that surprised her. First of all there were gipsies in the field beside the airfield. There were five caravans and a number of horses were cropping the grass. A fire had been built in a little hollow and the children were playing round it, while on the bushes and scrub the women were hanging a strange assortment of coloured clothes and rags to dry. These were all together on the ground, which sloped down to the river, but inside the field where the aeroplane hangar was built, parked against the dividing hedge, was another caravan and beside it was Nada, loudly talking to a gipsy.

"You will clear out now, the lot of you," Nada was saying, and her voice was very angry.

"You have said that before, lady, but I tell you we will not go," the gipsy replied. "For many, many years have we come here. It is our right, and the master, he gives his permission."

"Well, you have not got his permission this time," Nada said sharply, "and once again I tell you, you are to get out now and at once."

It was obvious that the gipsy was nearly as angry as she was.

"And I tell you, lady, that my little girl is ill. I would not move my caravan from here, not if you offered me a thousand pounds. Here I will stay until she is better."

"You will take my orders in this," Nada retorted, "or I will fetch a policeman. You understand, a policeman. He will make you go away. This is private property and you are trespassing."

"The master, he always lets us come here. Last year we come and the year before that and for many years now. We do no harm, we rest here a few weeks and then we go on."

"A few weeks!" Nada almost screamed. "You will move out of here tonight or in the morning you will all find yourselves in prison!"

She stamped her foot in sheer rage, and suddenly Sally was aware that she was eavesdropping. This was none of her business and she had no right to be listening. She sat down quickly on the top of the sandpit, ready to jump down, and as she did so she heard Nada say,

"You quite understand? I shall fetch the police if you are here tomorrow morning."

Then there was the sound of her footsteps walking angrily through the top of the wood, the dry sticks snapping almost like pistol shots as she moved between the trees. Sally kept very still, for she had no desire for Nada to see her and realise that her conversation had been overheard.

Then while she waited, hearing Nada's footsteps recede into the distance as she skirted the top of the sandpit and went towards the path which led direct from the house to the airfield, Sally wondered whether Nada was exceeding her authority. Had she really the right to send the gipsies away? She remembered what Gertrude had told her – how, because of his love for Lady Beryl, Sir Guy had said the gipsies would always be welcome on his land. Would he have gone back on that invitation suddenly for no apparent reason? Sally was almost certain that in some way and for some reason of her own Nada was taking upon herself to turn the gipsies from The Priory estate.

It would, of course, be yet another part of her and Captain Pawlovski's fantastic desire for secrecy where the aeroplane was concerned. They might be frightened that the gipsies would look over the dividing hedge, but even the one caravan which was just inside the airfield was a long way from where the aeroplane usually stood when it was out of its hangar and Sally imagined that it was too far away to be in any way a danger.

How ridiculous they were! And suddenly she felt sorry for the gipsy with his sick child. On an impulse, driven partly by her sympathy for any child that was ill and partly because she thought Nada was once again being bossy and autocratic, as she had been about Nicholas and Prue exploring the cellars, Sally got to her feet and circumventing the briar hedge climbed into the field.

The gipsy was sitting on the steps of his caravan, smoking a pipe. He was tall and very thin, his skin was a golden bronze, his hair thick and dark, and it was difficult to guess his age. As Sally approached, he got to his feet with a sudden lithe grace and stood unsmiling and on the defensive.

Now that she was face to face with him Sally felt tongue-tied and wondered what she could say and why she had taken it upon herself to intervene.

"Your little girl is ill," she said at length.

The gipsy nodded. Sally noticed that his eyes were suspicious and wary like an animal who senses a trap.

"I heard you say so," she went on. "I-I'm afraid I was listening just now."

"I cannot go away."

The gipsy's voice was sullen.

"I think there is some mistake," Sally said, "because I know Sir Guy Thorne always lets you come here."

"That is true," the gipsy said passionately. "Always, always have we come here for many years. And now my little Zeela, she is unwell. She has the fever. She has been given the soothing herbs. She will sleep, yes, for perhaps two days she will sleep and then she will wake quite well. But we must keep still. The caravan must not bump over the ground or she would wake and it would go badly with her."

"I understand," Sally said. "Is that what the doctor ordered?"

"We have no doctor," the gipsy answered. "We have our own medicines – herbs – which we have used for centuries of time. But they must be given right, exactly as we are told, or it is not well with those that take them."

"How interesting!" Sally exclaimed, "and you really mean that your little girl will be quite well when she wakes up?"

The gipsy shrugged his shoulders.

"Quite well? That is a question! But the fever will have gone. It will pass from her in her sleep."

"Yes, I'm sure it will," Sally said, remembering how some of the old shepherds in Wales would never use the medicines recommended by the vet, but used to brew a strange concoction themselves from plants they picked on the hillside.

She felt a sudden faith in the gipsy, she was sure that he was telling her the truth, and she was certain, too, that his child mattered to him, more than anything else in the world.

"I tell you what I will do," she said slowly. "I will tell Sir Guy about your little girl and I am sure he will allow you to stay whatever anyone else says. Unfortunately, he is away from home this afternoon. He has gone into York, but when he returns, I will speak to him and ask him to come down here tonight and see you."

The man's eyes were smiling at her before she had finished speaking.

"Thank you, lady, you are very kind. Yes, you are good, too. I can see that. Not like that other." He looked darkly in the direction in which Nada had departed.

"She doesn't understand," Sally said quickly, feeling that she must defend Nada. "She is afraid that you are in danger here on this airfield, that you might get hurt. We are none of us allowed to go on to this field."

"Why does she wish to keep it so private?" the gipsy asked.

"Oh, I don't know," Sally replied uncomfortably, feeling that she must not give too much away to a gipsy. "Aeroplanes can be dangerous things, I believe, if the wind is not right for them when they land."

The gipsy nodded his head and then he said firmly,

"There is no danger here for us, only the danger of moving while my little one sleeps."

"Well, I hope we have not wakened her by so much talking," Sally said. "I will speak to Sir Guy and if he cannot come himself, I will come down tonight and tell you what he says."

"You are very kind, lady, and thank you."

Sally turned to go. As she did so there was a whimpering sound from beneath the caravan. She stopped.

"It is a dog," the gipsy explained. "We found him caught in a trap when we were coming here. I have not yet had time to see to him."

"Oh, poor thing," Sally exclaimed. "May I look at him?"

The gipsy bent down and crawling under the caravan brought out the dog, which was lying on a bundle of rags. It was a very small black and white terrier, thin and rather emaciated, and the flesh on his back leg, which had

~228~

obviously been caught in one of the old-fashioned gin traps, had been torn from the bone and the bone itself was fractured just below the joint.

"Look at his poor leg!" Sally exclaimed. "He must be in agony. We must set it at once. May I help you?"

The gipsy nodded and then without a word went through the hedge and down the field to one of the other caravans. Sally knelt beside the dog, talking to him, scratching his ears and neck and trying to make him feel that he was loved and cared for. He was licking her hand when the gipsy came back with a stick as a splint, a piece of clean rag and a jar of strange looking ointment.

"You hold him," he said to Sally.

"What is that?" Sally asked, looking at the ointment.

"More gipsy medicine," he replied, in a tone, as if he were laughing at her and then, apparently feeling that he owed her an explanation, he added, "It will make him well. It will make the wound heal very quickly."

He bent down, and from the deft way his long, thin brown fingers touched the dog's leg Sally trusted him. Every action was quick and swift and though he did up the leg in a manner she had never seen before, she was sure that it was well done and that he was right in saying that it would heal.

She held the dog still, talking to him, soothing him, and when the splint was firmly bandaged on his leg she lifted him gently in her arms.

"May I take him back and give him a good meal?" she asked, and then feeling that she had been unintentionally rude, she added, "I was only thinking that you might be too busy with your little girl to attend also to a sick dog."

"He is yours," the gipsy said, "I give him to you."

"Oh, but..." Sally hesitated, then understood it was his way of saying 'thank you'.

"I would love to have him," she said, "but are you quite sure you don't want him?"

"He is my gift to you," the gipsy repeated. "He likes you. You are a good lady and my little girl will think so too when she awakes."

"She won't want him herself?" Sally asked.

"She has not seen him," the gipsy replied. "She was ill when I found the dog and there is no ache for what a heart has not known."

"Well, then, thank you," Sally said, "I would love to have him and I will look after him and see that his leg is soon well again."

"You will be good to him and he will be good to you," the gipsy said and there was a look in his eyes as if he made a prophecy. Sally held out her hand.

"Thank you," she said again.

The gipsy took her hand in his. His fingers were as strong as steel, but the feel of them was rough and warm.

"Don't worry until you hear from Sir Guy," Sally said.

"I shall not move for all the angry ladies and all the policemen in the world," the gipsy replied and he laughed suddenly.

Sally laughed, too, and carrying the dog very carefully she went back through the wood, taking the easy path towards the house.

It was only as she neared The Priory that she wondered how she could explain yet another acquisition. She was certain that Lady Thorne would not mind another dog in the house. She adored animals and in addition to Bracken and the small Cairn terrier, there was an old retriever, which had attached himself to Bateson, the butler, and followed him round like a decrepit shadow.

There were also three cats in the kitchen, which seemed by tacit consent to belong to the cook, and a cage of canaries that the kitchen maid had won at a fair. Nada was the only person who would be likely to make trouble, especially if she knew that Sally had received the dog from the gipsy with whom she was so angry.

Surreptitiously, feeling for the first time that she, too, must be secretive, Sally crept into the house by the garden door near which was the back staircase leading to the corridor where she slept. She hurried upstairs and reached her room without meeting anyone. There she gave the dog a drink and, after making him as comfortable as she could in the armchair, she went downstairs in search of food for him. She met Gertrude in the passage leading to the kitchen. Sally stopped her.

"The gipsies have come, Gertrude," she announced. "Do you remember telling me that they were allowed to camp here?"

"Oh, they have arrived, have they?" Gertrude said. "Regular as clockwork they are. I was only saying to Mrs. Harris last night that it was about time we saw them about the place,"

"They are allowed here, aren't they?" Sally persisted. "Someone said something about their being forbidden since last year, but I was certain that it was a mistake because of what you told me."

"They're allowed here right enough," Gertrude replied, "and the only person who will be minding them coming is poor Mr. Booth, the keeper. He complains they ruin the game, but then, keepers are like farmers, never satisfied. There's always something wrong."

"How right you are, Gertrude!" Sally smiled and having found out what she wanted, she went into the kitchen and begged a meal of fresh meat and chopped-up vegetables for her dog.

The little terrier ate ravenously and when he had finished, settled himself as comfortably as his leg would allow and seemed prepared for sleep. Sally went along the corridor to Lady Thorne's room. She guessed she would be lying down, as she usually did after luncheon. She never slept but lay on the sofa in her room reading religious books and sometimes old letters which she kept in a big despatch case at her side.

Sally knocked at the door.

"Come in," Lady Thorne said and smiled when she saw who was there.

"Oh, it is *you,* Sally dear. Come and sit down and talk to me."

"I have come to ask you a favour," Sally explained.

"What is it?" Lady Thorne asked.

"I have been given a poor little black and white terrier that had caught its leg in a trap. I wonder if I may keep it. Would you mind?"

"But of course you can keep it," Lady Thorne said. "Poor little thing. Where is it?"

"It is in my bedroom," Sally said. "I have given him a good meal and he seems happier, and more comfortable already."

"Traps are such terrible things," Lady Thorne said in her gentle voice. "I can't bear to think of them catching rabbits or even vermin. Yes, Sally, of course you must keep your dog."

"It won't be for long," Sally said, "because now that the children are leaving, I must try and get a job. You don't know of one on a farm, do you?"

"You must talk to Guy, dear," Lady Thorne replied. "He looks after the farm and knows far more about it than I do."

"Oh, I didn't mean on your own farm," Sally exclaimed, feeling that she was presuming on Lady Thorne's kindness. "I meant somewhere about here. I don't want to be a nuisance to you."

"You could never be that, dear child," Lady Thorne said. "I have grown very fond of you since you have been here and I am only sorry that you are not my daughter-in-law."

Sally went crimson.

"Oh, what a sweet thing to say!" she exclaimed. "Thank you for telling me."

"Dear child!" Lady Thorne said, then sighed. "I do so wonder how Tony is getting on. I wish he would write to me. I used to get a letter every week until he got…"

She stopped suddenly.

"You were saying?" Sally prompted, but it seemed to her that Lady Thorne looked embarrassed.

"Nothing, dear, I was just reminiscing over the old times, as all mothers do. Oh, well, one day I expect Tony will surprise me. He will come rushing in when we least expect him, making us all happy just because he is here with us once again."

She smiled, but her eyes were sad. Sally felt there was nothing she could say, and after a moment she got to her feet, thanked Lady Thorne once again for permission to keep the dog and went back to her room.

When the children returned from York, Sally told them, as a secret, that there was a new dog in her bedroom and took them up to see it.

"Oh, poor little thing," Prue said with tears in her eyes. "Poor, poor little dog."

"He will soon be all right now," Sally promised her.

She felt a pride of possession in having something of her very own. When she went into the room the dog greeted her with little whines and barks of welcome and the wagging of his tail. He had evidently decided that she was his mistress, and he watched her moving about as if he feared to let her out of his sight.

Sally confided in the children the dog had been given to her by a gipsy but told them that they must not mention it to anyone else. She had not really meant to be so communicative but she felt suddenly childlike and excited at the whole episode and had an irresistible urge to tell someone.

"It is our very own secret," she warned them, "just among the three of us."

"We won't tell anyone," Nicholas said stoutly, and Sally knew that he meant what he said and never would give away a secret when once he had given his promise to keep it.

"What are you going to call him?" Prue asked.

"I don't know," Sally answered. "You are both good at names, what do you suggest?"

"What about Gip?" Nicholas suggested.,

"Gip is rather too like gipsy and people might guess our secret."

"Yes, that is right," Prue agreed.

"I know," Sally exclaimed. "Why not Rom, short for Romany.

"Oh, that is awfully good," Nicholas approved. "We'll know it is part of the secret, but no-one else will guess, will they?"

"No-one," Sally told him.

She left the children to stroke and pat the dog while she went downstairs in search of Sir Guy. She guessed that he would doubtless be back by now and sure enough she found him in the library. He was sitting at his desk writing, his head and broad shoulders silhouetted against the window. She stood for a moment looking at him before he was aware of her presence, then he turned round, half instinctively and rose when he saw who was there.

Sally closed the door behind her before she walked across the room. As always, she felt shy in his presence and now she was uncomfortably aware that what she was about to tell him, was almost like sneaking at school on another pupil. Nevertheless, she started the story briefly. She admitted to eavesdropping, and went on to explain how, worried about the little girl being ill, she had gone to speak to the gipsy after Nada had left him.

"I had heard that the gipsies are allowed to come here year after year," she faltered at length, "and I thought perhaps Miss Thorne did not know this and so I promised I would speak to you and ask if they could stay at any rate until the little girl is better."

"Of course they can stay!" Sir Guy's answer was sharp and abrupt.

"Will you tell them so?" Sally asked.

"I will speak to the man myself."

Sir Guy walked to the window and looked out as if he half-expected to see the gipsy caravans in the distance. Sally hesitated, not certain whether to stay or to go. Then at length, plucking up courage, she said,

"If it is possible, I would rather you did not tell Miss Thorne that I have interfered."

Sir Guy turned round.

"Are you afraid of Nada?" he asked.

"A little bit perhaps," Sally admitted and added as if to excuse Nada, "You see, she belongs here, and as a stranger it is really none of my business."

"You were right to tell me," Sir Guy said. "Don't worry. The gipsy and his sick child will not be turned away and I shall not mention to Nada how I found out that there was any question of their going."

"Oh, thank you."

Sally smiled at him suddenly and to her surprise he smiled back. She knew that for that moment they were united together against Nada, and then she was ashamed of herself for trying to make trouble.

"Thank you," she said again and turned towards the door, but Sir Guy's voice arrested her.

"Are you happy here?" he asked.

"I have been very happy," Sally replied. "I have wanted so often to tell you how grateful I am for all your kindness. It was so wonderful of you to take me in when – when…" she hesitated for the right word, "when things went wrong. I was talking to your mother just now and saying that as soon as the children go, I must get a job. I wonder if there is any chance of my getting work on a farm in this district?"

"What could you do?" Sir Guy questioned.

"Oh, everything and anything," Sally answered. "There is very little in the way of farm work that I have not attempted at one time or another. I can even shear sheep."

He looked at her – at the lovely delicacy of her face, at the soft transparency of her skin, which had lost its tan and which gave her somehow an appearance of fragility, at her long, finely moulded neck, above which her little chin was raised so proudly at times, at her sensitive lips and small straight nose.

"And yet you don't look…" Sir Guy began.

Sally's laugh interrupted him.

"You must not judge me by my clothes," she said. "In these I should look ridiculous on a farm, I'm well aware of that, but today I received some money, a cheque for twenty-five pounds from Lynn."

It seemed to her as if unexpectedly his face darkened. Hurriedly, while she had the courage, Sally went on,

"I was wondering if you would be very kind and cash it for me. I shall spend it all on proper working clothes, breeches, boots and a really good mackintosh."

"Give it to me."

Sir Guy's words were abrupt.

Sally pulled Mary's letter out of her cardigan pocket and took out the cheque. She held it out to him and he looked down at it.

"Have you endorsed it?" he asked.

"Oh, I'm sorry," Sally apologised, "I forgot."

Sir Guy put the cheque down on the blotter on his writing table, then pushed up the big leather-covered armchair in which he habitually sat. Sally looked in the pen tray.

"I must not use your pen."

"It won't matter," he replied.

She took it in her hand and dipped it in the ink. Only then did she glance up at him towering up above her, a strange, rather inscrutable expression on his face.

"Please find me a job soon," Sally pleaded. "You have been so kind to me here that I don't want to become an encumbrance."

"Do you think you could be that?" he enquired, and suddenly their eyes met. Sally was conscious of a very unusual sensation and her eyes dropped before his. She was not certain what had happened, she only felt a little breathless and as if her fingertips were quivering. Shyly she turned her face away from him and wrote her name on the back of the cheque.

"I will give you the money tomorrow," Sir Guy said.

"Oh, thank you," she answered, getting to her feet.

Accidentally, as she moved, her hand brushed against his. Again she was aware of some sensation that she could not explain even to herself and, because she felt strange and almost overwhelmingly shy, she went from the room without another word.

As she shut the library door behind her, she saw that Nada was standing in the hall. Sally instantly felt guilty, as if she had been actually caught out in some wrong-doing. She waited for Nada to speak and when she said nothing Sally turned and ran up the stairs, uncomfortably conscious of the dark eyes which were watching her.

When she reached the landing, she looked back. Nada was walking across the hall towards the library.

Sir Guy was standing where Sally had left him at the side of his desk. He was staring down at the cheque on which she had written her signature and as Nada entered, he folded it up and put it into the breast pocket of his coat.

"I want to talk to you, Guy," Nada said, coming across the room determinedly.

"Well, I am here," Sir Guy said somewhat uncompromisingly.

He turned round to face her, and she walked straight up to him until she was near enough to touch him. Then she flung back her head and looked up into his eyes.

"Send her away, Guy," she said softly.

He did not pretend to misunderstand her, instead he asked,

"Why? Does she worry you? She does no-one any harm."

"She disturbs me," Nada said. "Always she is lurking about the house, watching me, interfering."

"I think you exaggerate," Sir Guy said.

"But there is another reason," Nada said, "another and more important reason. Cannot you guess what it is?"

Her voice was very low and rather thrilling as it came from between her red lips. Sir Guy seemed for the moment as if he were penned between her and the desk.

"Well, what is the reason?" he asked at last.

"She comes between you and me," Guy."

Nada put out her hands suddenly and laid them against his chest. Quickly, even as she touched him, Sir Guy took her hands, put them down at her sides, and turning his shoulders so that he could pass by her, he walked across the room to stand with his back to the mantelpiece.

"Nada, my dear," he said. "You are making this very difficult for me, but I will tell you something that I ought to have told you a very long time ago and would have done if I had thought you would be interested. Once I was in love, once I was engaged to be married. Nothing came of it. The girl I loved married someone else and later she died. I shall never marry."

Nada moved across the room to stand beside him once again.

"I am not asking for marriage, Guy, but why should love pass you by? You are a young man and a handsome one. For a long time we were together in this house, alone, except for your mother. I was very happy then, because I felt that you and I understood each other. But now other people come and they spoil what lies between us."

"Nada, nothing lies between us," Sir Guy protested. "I have told you. I shall never love anyone again."

"If you believe that, you are a very stupid man," Nada retorted. "You are not yet dead, Guy. There is warm blood in your veins, your heart beats. You have only to relax a little, to let go of that perfect English self-control and then you would find how wonderful life can be when one loves and is loved."

Nada reached out her arms suddenly and put them round Guy's neck. She drew very close to him. He could feel the warmth of her body through the thin silk dress she wore, was aware of the strange exotic perfume which seemed to come from her hair. He was looking down at the darkness of her eyes and could feel against his cheek the breath coming softly from between her lips.

For a moment he was very still. For a moment it seemed as if she held him within her thrall, then very gently Sir Guy put out his hands and unlocked her arms from his neck.

"I am sorry, Nada," he said and there was a weariness in his voice that defeated her more utterly than anger would have done. "I am sorry," he repeated.

He walked to the window and stood looking out. A little pulse was beating quickly in his neck.

When he turned round again, the room was empty.

11

As Sally came down to breakfast with Nicholas and Prue, she heard voices and, looking through the drawing room door, saw Nada and Ivor Pawlovski talking together on the terrace. They were speaking in Polish and their voices were sharp and raised a little, as if in anger.

It was usual for Ivor to have his breakfast very early before the rest of the household came down and then to go straight to the airfield. Sally guessed that this morning he had been and come back, and that the reason for his return was to complain that the gipsies were still there.

Quickly she hurried the children into the dining room to find that Sir Guy and Lady Thorne were already down and helping themselves from the silver dishes that stood on the side table. When the children had said, 'Good morning' politely, Sally settled them at the table and put their bowls of porridge in front of them. She had just sat down herself when the door opened and Nada came in.

There was no doubt that she was extremely angry. She was followed by Ivor Pawlovski whose scowl was more apparent than ever, but he slipped rather nervously into the room as if he wished to be as self-effacing as possible. It was obvious that they had arranged who was to be spokesman, for Nada strode up to Sir Guy where he was seated at the head of the table and said in a clear, challenging voice,

"Guy, I wish to speak to you."

"Good morning, Nada," he parried.

"It is about the airfield," Nada continued, ignoring his greeting. "You know that Ivor has always said that no-one, no-one at all, must be allowed on the airfield and yet, unless the man lies, you have given permission for a gipsy caravan to remain there. It is not fair to Ivor and what is more, it is dangerous."

Nada was breathless as she finished speaking for her words had tumbled out one after another. As always when she was moved, her foreign intonation was accentuated.

"Now wait a minute, Nada," Sir Guy said. "Suppose we talk this over quietly – and by the way, I don't think you have said good morning to my mother."

There was a rebuke in his voice, but Nada was quite unabashed.

"Aunt Mary will understand," she answered impatiently. "There are more important things than saying good morning. Here is Ivor working night and day on his most secret experiments, which even the Government acknowledges are important, and you allow gipsies – yes, gipsies to camp, not only in the next field, but on the very airfield itself. And I know why you have done it, too. I told him he was to leave, to move his caravan at once, and what happens? He tells Ivor that a kind lady spoke to the Master for him. I can well guess who that 'kind lady' was!"

Nada flashed Sally a look of burning hatred and Sally, feeling as if she had been lashed with a whip, felt her face go crimson in response. The tension was relieved for a moment by Nicholas.

"Are there really gipsies on the airfield," he asked, "because if there are, can we go and look at the aeroplane, too? Oh, please let us!"

"There! You see!" Nada said, making a sweeping gesture with both her hands. "That is what happens when we allow one person to break a rule. Now the children want to look at the aeroplane, next it will be the staff and then the villagers. How can anything be kept secret under such circumstances?"

Sir Guy got to his feet. He pulled out an empty chair from the table and held it out to Nada.

"Sit down," he said quietly, but it was a word of command.

Surprisingly she obeyed him, and then he looked across the room at Ivor Pawlovski who was standing just inside the door and looking acutely uncomfortable.

"Suppose you shut the door and come and sit down, too, Ivor," Sir Guy said. "We can discuss this amicably while I, at any rate, finish my breakfast."

Captain Pawlovski also obeyed him, slouching a little as he came to the table with almost a hunted air so that Sally was certain that he had not wished to make trouble, but that Nada had insisted on it.

"Let me explain," Sir Guy said. "The gipsies have always had my permission to camp on The Priory estate for some years past. The field where they are at present, is the one they have always used because the river runs at the bottom of it. It also happens to be waste land and is therefore eminently suitable for the purpose. I have known this particular community for some time. You are suspicious of them, but I have found them very personable, in fact, as far as I know, they have not abused my hospitality beyond trapping an occasional rabbit which I am only too glad for them to have.

"The caravan of which you complain, so vehemently, Nada, belongs to the head of the community. He is a decent chap, for I have spoken with him before, and his wife died last year. He adores his child and I can well understand his feelings when she was taken ill. He told me, as he doubtless told you, that he had given her a certain gipsy medicine, which is effective only if the patient has a complete rest and quiet for forty-eight hours after it is taken. I do not think any order to move, even if it were given him by the highest authority in the land, would be obeyed at the moment and I should not attempt to ask anything so unfair or so unjust of him. You state that his position is dangerous. I have used

~242~

the airfield for many years before Ivor, and I know that there is no possible danger for the caravan where it is parked at the moment.

"In answer to your second point that the gipsies interfere with Ivor's experiments, I imagine they are not in the slightest interested in aeroplanes, having seen far too many of them. Anyway, they have given me their word that they will not venture on the airfield. When the child is better, the caravan will be removed into the other field where the rest of the gipsies are encamped. In the meantime, Ivor will, I assure you, not be inconvenienced in any way whatsoever."

While Sir Guy was making this speech Nada had sat staring at him with smouldering eyes, her fingers drumming restlessly on the tablecloth. Now she started to her feet so violently that her chair almost fell over backwards.

"You make it sound very plausible, my dear Guy," she said scornfully. "But you do not understand how much you have humiliated us. Yes, that is the right word – humiliated – both Ivor and myself. You give him the airfield, you promise him complete secrecy – that no-one shall go there and then you allow first a gipsy to disobey your orders and then Miss St. Vincent, who not only goes and intrigues with the gipsy but comes sneaking to you behind my back. What right has she, this stranger, this girl of whom we know nothing, to interfere between us – you and me – who are of the same blood? What do we know of her, save that your brother was wise enough not to marry her at the last."

"Nada, be quiet!"

Sir Guy thumped his fist angrily on the table.

"That is quite enough," he said sharply. "You are forgetting that Sally is a guest in this house, and I do not allow my guests to be insulted."

"No, it is your relations who can be insulted. It is I who must bear your rudeness and must apologise for it to my own countryman," Nada went on, spitting out the last words as if by identifying herself with Poland rather than with England, she threw back insult for insult at Sir Guy.

She turned on her heel and ran from the dining room, slamming the door behind her. There was a moment's silence, then Ivor Pawlovski got to his feet.

"I will go and find her," he said. "I must apologise for this." He looked at Lady Thorne and then at Sir Guy. "It is quite all right about the caravan," he said. "I understand."

Sally felt sorry for him as he hurried in an embarrassed manner after Nada, she wondered if she, too, ought to apologise for having been in part responsible for this most uncomfortable scene.

But Prue broke the silence.

"What is she so angry about?" she asked Lady Thorne, her eyes wide, her small face bewildered.

Lady Thorne smiled.

"Don't worry about it, dear. Grown-up people get angry at times just as you do."

"They are foreigners, aren't they?" Prue asked. "Foreigners get awfully excited. I know the Indians used to and we were not allowed to go out of the bungalow on Feast days, were we, Nicholas?"

"They used to shout and sing and sometimes roll on the ground," Nicholas said.

"I remember when I was in India many years ago…" Lady Thorne began and told them a long story about a Durbar she had witnessed, and this kept the children interested until breakfast was over.

Sally, feeling that it was impossible for her to eat or drink anything, sat in silence. She wished now that she had said nothing about the gipsy and had let things take their course. Yet she knew it would have been impossible for her to hold her tongue when she thought of the child suffering because of Nada's quite unnecessary fussiness. She dared not look at Sir Guy, she was so humiliated by Nada's reference to Tony.

Lady Thorne, the only person who seemed to remain unperturbed by Nada's outburst, interrupted her story to the children to say,

"Will you give me some more coffee, Sally?" and as Sally jumped to her feet she added, "Thank you, my dear child, you are such a help to me."

It was, Sally knew, Lady Thorne's way of comforting her and of apologising for Nada's cruelty, but the hurt remained.

When breakfast was finished, she hurried upstairs to do the rooms and was followed by Nicholas and Prue demanding forcibly that they should be taken to see the gipsies.

"All right," Sally promised recklessly, feeling that she had involved herself so much already that a little more did not matter.

It was quite clear, though, that she could not stay any longer under the same roof as Nada. It was only a question of days now until the children's mother came out of hospital and they went to their grandparents. She was free of responsibility where they were concerned, and with twenty-five pounds in her pocket, she could at least find lodgings somewhere until a job turned up.

The children plied her with questions about the gipsies and their caravans until at last she had finished their rooms and all three went down the back stairs towards the kitchen. Mrs. Harris, the cook, who, as Lady Thorne had predicted, had become the willing slave of both Nicholas and Prue, was all smiles as they entered the kitchen.

"Now I know what you've come for, m'ducks," she said, reaching for the tin where she kept her special biscuits and adding in an aside to Sally, "They're looking better, the little loves, but they still want feeding up. They neither of them eat enough to keep a mouse alive."

"Don't you believe it," Sally laughed. "They are eating heartily now, and if they stay here much longer, they will be eating Lady Thorne out of house and home."

"There's nothing we should like better," Mrs. Harris said, beaming as Nicholas and Prue dived into the special tin and drew out biscuits shaped like stars, and tiny iced cakes ornamented with crystallised cherries and green angelica.

"What we really came for, Mrs. Harris, was to beg a bowl of your special soup," Sally said. "One of the little gipsy girls is very ill and I know if anything would help her to get better, it would be some of your special bone soup."

"I'll get you some right away and welcome," Mrs. Harris replied. "It's lucky that I made some only yesterday. I'll put it in a basin and you tell them, all they've got to do is to heat it up when they wants it."

She got the basin ready, talking all the time, inviting the children to help themselves to another and yet another cake and when at last they were ready to leave she would not let them go until Nicholas and Prue had filled their pockets with some of her special sugar almonds.

"She's awfully kind, isn't she?" Prue said to Sally as they went across the lawn.

"She likes having children to spoil," Sally answered.

"That's lucky for us," Nicholas said gravely, "but I think, Sally, that I will give the little gipsy girl some of my sugar almonds. If she's been ill, I expect she would like them."

"She will love them," Sally told him.

But when they arrived at the caravan the door was still closed and the gipsy was sitting on the steps.

"My Zeela still sleeps," he told Sally, "but the fever is broken and she should wake sometime this evening."

"I will come down and see her then – or tomorrow morning," Sally promised.

She gave him the soup and instructed him how to use it. He listened attentively and then looked at her with a transparent gratitude in his strange, dark eyes.

"You have been very kind, lady."

"I was glad to be able to help you," Sally answered. "I could not bear to think of your little girl being so ill."

Unexpectedly he reached out and took her hand in his, turned it over and looked at the palm.

"Someday you will have children of your own," he said. "Three, perhaps four. They will be fine children and you will be fond of them. But first you will cross water, you will suffer darkness and much fear and you will find your happiness, where you least expect it."

He let go of her hand, but Sally stood still, looking down at her own palm.

"How can you tell all that by just looking at my lines?" she asked. "Do you really believe that is true?"

The gipsy smiled as if at the foolish questions of an ignorant child.

"One day you will know that I speak the truth," he said.

The children, who had been busy looking at the caravan from all sides, now came running back.

"Oh, please, may we see the other caravans? Please, *please*," Nicholas pleaded.

"Yes, come with me," the gipsy replied. "I will show them to you."

He led them away to the lower field, but Sally felt that, while the children might be acceptable to the gipsies, she would appear merely a curious interloper, so she sat down on the short grass to await their return. There was not much sun this morning and there were still the shadowy remnants of a dawn mist lying over the river. The sky was opalescent and the lines of the hills beyond were hard to define. It made the whole world seem a little unreal and Sally, hearing the gipsy's voice again, wondered whether the fortune he had told her had only been the figment of a dream.

Of course it would be ridiculous for her to believe in it. Every fortune teller said one crossed water, every fortune teller foretold that there would be happiness after difficulties and tribulations. The latter invariably came true and one could go on hoping for happiness to the very end of ones life.

Looking at the gipsies with their colourful caravans, brilliant, if tattered clothes, their swarthy skins and dark, flashing eyes, Sally wondered if with all their perception they found life any easier or less complex than she did. It was for everyone an adventure, which was made more complicated by the fact that it was impossible to anticipate what lay ahead. And yet life was often thrilling, always exciting, always worth living.

Sally was sure of that, sure of it now if she had not been sure of it before. When one was unhappy and encompassed about with despair, one lost that feeling of joy and anticipation, yet always it came back, always it was just round the corner waiting to revive within one's heart and whisper that the future would be better.

'I shall find happiness one day,' Sally told herself, looking on the little encampment and beyond it at the misty river. At that moment the sun came through the clouds. It was to Sally as if the heavens pledged themselves to honour her promise. She felt herself caught up into the golden glory of the sunbeams, part of them, one with them. She knew in that moment what happiness could mean and how it transfigured those who held it in their hearts.

All through the day she was conscious of that same sense of wonder and beauty that came to her at that moment. She was afraid of meeting Nada, embarrassed at the thought of Sir Guy, yet surprisingly neither of these things mattered as they had mattered before. She felt something new within herself, something she could not put into words but that, nevertheless, kept recurring again and again to her mind.

While she told the children stories or raced them round the garden or joked with them in the sandpit, it was there, a little fire or hope lit by the sun.

Nada did not appear for luncheon, which Sally thought was a great relief to everyone. Then in the afternoon she went with the children for such a long walk over the moors, that they got in late for tea and everyone had finished. She had meant to go down and see the little gipsy girl before dinner, but what with coming in so late and then getting Nicholas and Prue to bed early, she had no time.

Dinner was a difficult meal because both Nada and Ivor Pawlovski were there and Nada was now indulging in an icy sullenness. She would not speak unless spoken to but sat very proudly and disdainfully at the table. Lady Thorne and Sir Guy both pretended that they saw nothing unusual in her manner and Sally noticed that Ivor Pawlovski made an effort to speak more than usual as if he wished to make amends for Nada's rudeness. She could not help thinking to herself that temperamental people were a bore. They made things so uncomfortable for everyone else, or rather for most people. It was obvious that Sir Guy was not in any way perturbed by Nada's behaviour.

Sally, sure that Nada loved him, thought how stupid she was to try such methods where he was concerned, and then humbly she told herself that she had no right to criticise when she had been unable either to attract, or hold the man she loved. For a moment she longed for Tony, for his good humour and laughter, for his smile and the way he managed to keep the conversation going however shy and embarrassed anyone might be. Then she realised surprisingly that it was the first time she had missed him for some days.

There had been so many things to occupy her mind and while she had often felt lonely and afraid, she had not missed Tony as an individual.

'I am getting over my unhappiness,' she told herself and felt her heart sing again because of it. Then, looking across the table, she met Nada's eyes and felt herself shiver. How the older girl hated her!

But it was no use worrying, Sally thought. Soon she would be gone and Nada would have the place to herself and could bully Lady Thorne and Sir Guy into having things exactly as she wanted them. Yet Sally was unable, by words or reason, to dispel the depressing effect of Nada's hatred and silent enmity. When dinner ended, she knew she could not remain in the room with her any longer and as the women walked towards the drawing room she asked Lady Thorne if she would mind if she retired to bed.

Lady Thorne seemed to understand.

"No, of course not, dear. Run along."

"May I go at once?" Sally enquired. "I don't want any coffee."

"Yes, dear. Goodnight."

Lady Thorne bent and kissed her cheek and Sally, without a backward glance at Nada, hurried up the front stairs. When she reached the first floor, she went in to see if Nicholas was asleep and found that he was still awake.

"Oh, Sally, come and tell me a story," he begged.

"I shall do nothing of the sort," Sally answered. "You ought to have been asleep hours ago."

"I can't help it if my mind won't go to sleep," he said plaintively. "It keeps thinking all by itself and I can't stop it."

Sally laughed. How well she knew that feeling! Wasn't it something that everyone experienced at some time or another? Because she loved spoiling him, she started a story about a miller who had three sons, and long before the third son had made his fortune Nicholas's eyelids were dropping and he was too drowsy to realise it when the story came to an abrupt end.

Sally crept away and closed the door softly behind her. Prue was asleep and now there was nothing to do but to go to her own bedroom. It was not yet half past nine, she felt very wakeful and thought resentfully of Nada who had driven her away from the drawing room where she could have stayed for another hour talking to Lady Thorne or listening while Sir Guy and his mother discussed the affairs of the estate.

She loved the evenings at The Priory. They were usually so peaceful and homelike and somehow she often longed to be there in the winter, when she pictured them all sitting round a big log fire with the curtains drawn and the snow lying white over the gardens. How secure and homelike The Priory would seem then – a refuge and a security against the world, something she had always wanted, something she had longed for all her life. But now her time was almost at an end. She would always be grateful for the peace and healing The Priory had given her, but she could no longer nestle within its sheltering arms.

On an impulse Sally suddenly slipped down the back stairs and out through the door which led into the garden. She would not waste one of these last precious hours. She would walk in the gardens and look at the house under the evening sky. She would go through the woods and visit the gipsy and would ask him how his little girl was and perhaps, if she were brave enough, question him once again about her future.

"I am getting like those silly women who are always consulting fortune tellers," she teased herself, yet she found an excuse for her foolishness because for her the future was so very, very problematical.

The moon was just rising over the house and the garden was bathed in its light. It was so lovely that for a moment Sally could only stand still and hold her breath, as if afraid that the wonder of it might vanish before she could take it all in. Roofs and chimneys, silhouetted against the sky, held a mystery which was not apparent in the daytime. Great trees flanking the lawns were secret in their shadows, and the path to the woods was like a silver ribbon.

She moved slowly across the grass, lost in a magic spell – a feeling that only deepened as she came to the trees and saw how the moonlight sent strange shafts of light through the boughs, illuminating here a twisted tree trunk and there a heap of stones, transforming them into strange patterns and designs, so that the wood itself seemed enchanted and Sally walked as if she were part of a fairy story.

She came at length to the caravan. Lights were on and she guessed that the child was awake, yet for some moments she could not bring herself to climb the steps and knock upon the little door. Instead, she could only stand looking towards the rest of the encampment. The gipsies sat around a great fire, the flames leaping high, red and orange. Someone was singing softly, a strange song almost like a chant, while beyond in the shadowy darkness, lay the river.

'It is like a dream,' Sally whispered to herself. Then, as if she were afraid of so much beauty, she ran quickly up the steps of the caravan.

She knocked on the door. Almost instantly it opened and the gipsy stood there.

"Oh, it is you," he exclaimed. "Come in, lady."

Bending her head, Sally stepped in. The child was sitting up in her bunk, a red shawl over her shoulders and the bowl of soup in her hands.

"She is better," the gipsy said before Sally could speak. "My Zeela is better."

"I am well," the child said, and Sally saw that she had a dark pointed face like a little elf, her straight hair braided in half a dozen plaits which reached to her shoulders.

The caravan was airless, but it smelt of herbs. An oil lamp hanging from the centre beam cast strange shadows and Sally could see that the caravan was crowded with things of all shapes and sizes stacked on the floor and on shelves that ran along the sides. She had only time, however, for a fleeting impression before the gipsy brought her a chair and set it for her beside the child's bunk.

"Sit down, lady," he said and then to Zeela, "This is the kind lady who brought you the soup."

"Thank you, lady."

Zeela lowered her head a little and looked at Sally under her eyelashes. She was obviously shy.

"I am so glad you are better," Sally said gently. "We have all tried to be very quiet in case we should wake you up. I brought a little boy and girl here to see you today. Their names are Nicholas and Prue, but they could not see you because you were fast asleep."

Sally was talking to the child to gain her confidence and now Zeela looked up.

"Are they here now?" she asked.

"No," Sally said, "they are both in bed asleep. It is late."

"I have been up much later than this," Zeela boasted.

"I expect you have," Sally answered, "but Nicholas and Prue have to go to bed early. They are not so lucky as you and do not live in a caravan. They live in a house."

"Did they always live in a house?" Zeela asked.

"Yes, always," Sally answered, "but eat your soup while it is hot."

"Yes, that is right," the gipsy said. "Eat your soup while it is hot. It will do you good."

The child obediently took a few more mouthfuls, then she held out the bowl.

"No more, no more."

"Oh, a little more, to please Daddy."

"No, but I will have an apple."

He took one from the shelf, rubbing it on the seat of his trousers before handing it to her. She sank her strong white teeth into it, watching Sally all the time as she did so.

The gipsy looked at Sally as if for approval.

"She will sleep again tonight and tomorrow she will be well."

"I am glad, so glad," Sally smiled, "and now I must go."

She got up, realising that it would be impossible to talk to the gipsy again about herself, for he had eyes and ears only for his child. He opened the door for her and when she reached the bottom of the stairs she turned back to tell him in a whisper, so that Zeela should not hear,

"The little dog is much better. I changed the bandage tonight and the leg is healing in a wonderful way. I don't know what you put on it, but it must be magic."

The gipsy laughed.

"Yes, that is right. It is gipsy magic. We have it, you know."

"I shall always believe in it after seeing Zeela and the dog," Sally said, and then she turned to go. "Goodnight. I will come and see Zeela tomorrow and bring the children."

"Goodnight, lady."

He waved to her and she waved back.

She started her return journey through the woods, but she did not hurry. Once again in the moonlight she felt akin to all the wildness and mystery of the night. She liked to feel the springing softness of the pine needles under her feet, to hear the rustle of the dry leaves as the hem of her frock swept over them. She thought imaginatively that she must look like a ghost herself, for she was wearing a dinner frock of soft white chiffon cut low to leave her arms and neck bare.

She had passed the top of the sandpit and was nearing the edge of the garden when she was aware of someone coming towards her. It was a dark figure walking quickly. For a moment she thought it was Ivor Pawlovski on his way to the airfield and she shrank from the thought of seeing him, feeling that, although he was not as antagonistic towards her as Nada was, he was indeed no friend of hers.

Then she saw that it was not Ivor but Sir Guy. She stood still in the shadow of the trees, not attempting to hide, not going forward to meet him, not frightened but yet a little uncertain as to why he was coming, or whether he expected to find her there. He reached the beginning of the wood, moved on and saw her standing, the moonlight behind her haloing her fair hair as she waited for him. He came towards her and now she could see his face. She noticed in surprise that he was very pale, the lines between nose and mouth deeply etched, his eyes surprisingly dark.

He did not speak but came right up to her and drew a deep breath as if he were breathless. He stood looking down at her searching her face. Then at length in a voice which she hardly recognised for his he asked,

"Where have you been?"

"I have been to see the gipsy," she answered wonderingly.

"I thought you had. I saw you go," he said, and then astonishingly, so unexpectedly that she could not believe it was true, his hands went out and grasped her shoulders.

"Do you need a man so badly that you must go after a gipsy?" he cried and his voice was raw with anger. "You told me that you had had no experience with men except with Tony. I should have thought you had learned your lesson with him. You little fool, can nothing stop you from hurting yourself?"

His hands were like a vice and Sally, listening, felt that he must have gone mad. Then before she could speak or before she could move, his arms were round her and he took her into his embrace.

"If we must seek disillusionment, why don't we seek it together?" he asked – and he kissed her.

His mouth was hard and cruel. As if in a dream she felt his lips bruise hers. She wanted to cry out, wanted to struggle against him, yet she was powerless and utterly helpless against his strength. He kissed her again and yet again – burning, passionate kisses that seemed to sap her strength and her resistance. It was as if he conquered her, making her utterly subservient to his will so that she had no power left of her own.

Suddenly he was speaking again. His head was thrown back in the moonlight, his eyes aflame with passion.

"What are we waiting for?" he asked. "There is no truth, no innocence, no real beauty in anything. There is only hunger and greed and the desire of man for woman and woman for man. Once I thought differently, once I had faith in God and – in woman, but now I have learned my mistake. Why do we worry about it? Why not let us take, you and I, what we need of life and enjoy it till it grows sour and stale? Come!"

He kissed her again and now his lips were even more possessive, moving from her mouth to her cheeks, from her cheeks to the whiteness of her neck and to the blue veins that ran down to her breasts. Then at last with a desperate effort Sally threw off the inertia that paralysed her. Now she knew that Sir Guy was mad.

"Please! *Please!*" she heard her voice, very weak, pleading with him and then, as if he would check even that ineffective cry, his mouth was on hers again and as he kissed her, he raised her in his arms. He lifted her high against his heart and she realised for the first time how strong he was. He turned and she knew that he was about to carry her into the depths of the wood.

It was then at last that her strength came flooding back to her.

"Let me go," she cried. "Sir Guy, are you mad? *Let me go!*"

She fought him with all her strength and found how ineffective it was. She felt a moment of sheer panic and cried out again. It seemed as if her cry reached him. As suddenly as he had picked her up, he put her down on the ground. He stood her on her feet and drew back. They had come to a little clearing and die moonlight illuminated them both.

"Well," he said, and now his lips were twisted more cynically than she had ever seen them. "So you want to argue? Well, say it. All women must protest before they surrender."

"I don't know what you are talking about," Sally whispered.

Now that he had freed her she felt a sudden weakness as if she might faint. She put her hand out as if to hold on to something and, finding nothing, her hands crept over her breasts and her dishevelled dress.

"You know well enough," Sir Guy said.

"But I don't," Sally protested. "Oh, please, I want to go back to the house."

"You are sure you have had enough love-making? The night is still young."

There was something ominous in his voice and Sally was suddenly aware that he had not really freed her. He was there, ready to grasp her, ready to hold her to him. And now she was afraid, so afraid that she could only stand still and look up at him, trembling a little, her eyes suddenly filling with tears.

"What have I done?" she asked suddenly, and her voice was very small and very childish. "You seem to hate me, and yet – and yet you have kissed me. I don't understand. Oh, please, please, *let me go!*"

He put out his hands and drew her into his arms. She shivered but made no attempt to struggle with him because she knew it was utterly useless. He did not kiss her, instead he put his hand under her chin and tipped back her head against his arm. The moonlight was full on her face. He looked long and deeply into her eyes and she made no attempt to resist him, only looking up at him, her lips quivering, her eyes searching his, trying to understand, trying to find some explanation. His mouth was very near to hers and she thought that he would kiss her again. But suddenly he muttered,

"My God, if I should be wrong!"

He let her go. She stood looking at him, the tears wet on her cheeks, her hair tumbled about her shoulders. Then harshly and so loud that his voice made her jump, he said,

"Go on then, go, if that is what you wish."

Blinded by tears so that she could hardly find her way back through the woods, Sally ran towards the house.

12

Sally opened her eyes, shut them, then opened them again. It was a dream, she thought, as she had thought not once but a thousand times since she left the shores of England.

The drumming of the aeroplane engines was in her ears and the Atlantic stretched beneath her. The grey sky joined the grey sea at some misty, indefinable point, so that the whole world appeared to consist only of the aeroplane with its passengers and its interminable throbbing.

No, it could not be true and yet it was. She was here – she, Sally St. Vincent, halfway across the Atlantic, flying to New York. But most surprising of all, was the fact that sitting beside her was Sir Guy. Never in the wildest flights of her imagination had Sally visualised such a situation as she found herself in at the moment and a puckish sense of humour tried to make her smile, but her anxiety and her fear for Lynn thrust everything from her, save her desperate desire to hurry quicker and quicker towards her destination.

It seemed now ages since she had awoken early yesterday morning determined to leave The Priory and find a job. She had been utterly bewildered by Sir Guy's behaviour to her in the woods. She could not understand why he was so bitterly angry, why he had suddenly been transformed from his grave, indifferent self, into a monster of fire and temper who had bruised and hurt her both mentally and physically and who also – and this she hardly dared to put into words even to herself – had humiliatingly insulted her.

When, the evening before, she reached her own room, she had thrown herself face downwards on her bed to lie panting and exhausted but tearless with her heart thumping, her eyes wide in the darkness. She told herself that she must run away at once. She must leave The Priory. But like the tortures of some ghostly inquisition questions to which she could find no answers pressed in upon her.

What had happened? What had she done? She had only visited the gipsy! Then she remembered Gertrude's story and understood that Sir Guy had suspected her of behaving as Lady Beryl had behaved. Her cheeks burned in the darkness and she felt degraded. Slowly a sympathy and an understanding came to her.

What he must have suffered to imagine such things! She thought of his horror on learning that the girl he loved had run away. Lady Beryl's gipsy lover had been of the same community as Zeela's father. Somehow it was almost impossible to think of the latter in terms of love. In this Sally could identify herself with Sir Guy and appreciate his horror and his disgust. But after that she was left bewildered. Where Lady Beryl was concerned it was understandable, but where she was concerned it was a different matter. Sir Guy had loved Lady Beryl, therefore he was jealous. He would indeed have been jealous of any man she loved.

But Sally reasoned that in her case it was different. Sir Guy and she had no connection, one with the other, save that she was a guest in his house. Perhaps it was because of what he had suffered that he had a horror of any young woman, any girl of his acquaintance becoming attracted by a gipsy man. That must be it, Sally thought, and she tried to make her sound common-sense assert itself and bring her beating heart and trembling limbs back to normal.

She sat up and looked across the room to where Rom, vainly trying to attract her attention, was wagging his tail and whining. Because she was so much in need of comfort Sally went across to him, gathered him in her arms and held him close to her breast.

"Oh, Rom, Rom," she whispered, "if only you could explain things to me. I don't understand. It is all too difficult. I must be a very stupid person."

Ever since Aunt Amy had died people had behaved in the most unexpected fashion. First Miss Mawson turning her out of the farm, then Lynn wanting her to get married before she went to South America, then Tony vanishing on the very day of her wedding and now Sir Guy becoming, without any warning at all, entirely different from what she had imagined him to be.

"I am a fool," she told Rom. "I don't know anything."

He snuggled his wet nose against her neck and she kissed the top of his head and fondled his ears.

She might have expected Erico to behave savagely, she thought, but not Sir Guy. She could still feel the hard pressure of his arms and her mouth was bruised and tender because of the brutality of his lips. Why, why had he been so angry with her? And what had he meant when he had looked deep into her eyes and said, as if speaking to himself, "My God, if I should be wrong!"

Sally gave up trying to find any answers to her questions. She only knew that Sir Guy had increased her shyness a thousandfold, that her one desire now was to get away, to escape from The Priory and to start again somewhere else.

'It must be my fault,' she told herself miserably. 'Wherever I go, I upset people. Perhaps it would be best if I went back to Wales and found myself a job high up on the mountains where there would be nobody except the old farmer and his wife.'

For a long time she sat with Rom in her arms and then, at length, though she thought it was impossible for her to sleep, she went to bed. Surprisingly, however, she did sleep and more surprising still was the fact that she dreamed of her Knight as she had dreamed of him when she was a child.

It was a vague, indecisive dream, but he was there with his plumed helmet, and she was happy.

She woke to hear a clock strike six and lay for some time letting the events of yesterday gradually superimpose themselves upon the feeling of happiness with which she had awakened. Gradually she remembered everything as she got up, dressed, and tiptoed along the corridor to the box room where her suitcases had been stored. She brought them back to her bedroom and began to pack.

'I won't be inconveniencing anyone,' she thought, 'because the children will be leaving in a day or two and if they can't stay here, Mrs. Redford will be only too pleased to have them.'

Sally knew that Mrs. Redford was simply longing for the moment when her grandchildren would move to Merton Grange. She would have had them there before now if she had not felt it would be rather rude to Lady Thorne, who had been so kind to take them in when they were homeless.

Sally packed all the lovely clothes that Lynn had given her, thinking as she placed them between layers of tissue paper, how useless they were likely to prove in the future. This was Cinderella in reverse. Now she must go back to work and forget the weeks in which silks and satins had been the background to a newly discovered life.

All the time she was packing Rom watched her with his shrewd black eyes, his head on one side. The first thing Sally had done on waking was to bathe and bandage his leg. It was extraordinary how much better it was. Already he could hobble on three legs and it looked as if, by the end of the week, he would be almost himself again.

"I will take you out in the garden as soon as I have finished, my pet," she said, speaking aloud to him, and he wagged his tail as if he understood what she was saying.

It was half past seven by the time she had finished. She took him out and came back to waken the children. She had nearly finished washing and dressing them, for once listening to their chatter a little absent-mindedly as she wondered how she was to tell Lady Thorne that she was leaving immediately after breakfast, when Gertrude came panting along the corridor.

"You are wanted on the telephone, miss," she said, "a trunk-call from London."

"From London?" Sally exclaimed, and she knew at once it must be Mary and that something must have happened to Lynn. She ran down the front stairs three at a time.

"I have taken it in the pantry," Gertrude shouted after her.

Sally sped down the corridor that led past the dining room and through the baize door into the pantry. The telephone was the old-fashioned wall sort. She picked up the receiver, put it to her ear, then leant forward to speak into the mouthpiece which was fixed to the wall.

"Hullo!"

As she had anticipated, it was Mary's voice that answered her.

"Hullo, Sally,"

"Oh, Mary, is it Lynn?"

"Yes, dear, it is."

"Oh, what has happened?"

"Listen, Sally, Lynn is in trouble and I want you to help."

"But I will, of course I will," Sally answered.

"I knew you would," Mary said. "You see, Sally, the most idiotic thing happened to me yesterday. I fell downstairs and broke my ankle and I can't move from my bed for three weeks."

"Oh, I am sorry."

"Lynn telephoned me last night and told me to come to New York at once and I had to tell her it was impossible. She was furious with me, but even her anger would not mend my bones."

Mary gave a little laugh that was somehow lacking in humour.

"It was a very bad line and anyway Lynn would pot tell me much, but, Sally, she is in trouble, real trouble. It is Erico and something else that she was too frightened to say on the telephone, so I suggested that you go out to her. You were the only person I could trust."

"Oh, thank you," Sally said.

"I don't know whether you will thank me eventually," Mary said with a touch of asperity in her voice. "Lynn sounded almost hysterical. She is not an easy person when she is like that. Oh, I wish I could go, I wish I hadn't to bother you. You are too young. But I am tied to my bed and Lynn says she can't leave New York. I can't understand what it is all about and she wouldn't tell me."

"Don't worry, Mary," Sally said. "I'll manage everything."

"I can't think what has happened," Mary went on, ignoring Sally's interruption. "It must be something to do with Erico, of course, but why she has left South America at this moment I can't think. Anyway, Sally, the only thing we can possibly do is to get you out there just as quickly as possible and find out what all the mystery is about. Lynn is staying at the *Ritz Carlton* and for some reason best known to herself, she is registered under the name of Mrs. Donavan. She was most insistent that no-one should know that she is in New York."

"But – but how shall I get there?" Sally asked.

"You must come to London today, at once," Mary said. "If you catch the ten o'clock train from York, there is an afternoon plane, which will get you to New York tomorrow morning if there is a vacant berth on it. Luckily, I have got your passport here and I have a friend in the American Embassy who will see to your visa. When you get to

London, come straight here to pick it up and I'll have some money ready for you."

"Yes, Mary."

"I won't keep you talking," Mary said. "The most important thing is for you not to miss the train at York. You won't do that, will you?"

"No, of course not," Sally said. "Goodbye, Mary. I will see you this afternoon."

"Goodbye, Sally."

Sally replaced the telephone receiver and took a deep breath. Lynn was in trouble. That was all her heart told her.

She hurried down the corridor towards the hall and ran full tilt into Sir Guy. She forgot everything at that moment except that she must catch the ten o'clock train at York.

"Oh, please," she said, her hand on his arm, her eyes pleading with him, her words tumbling over themselves in her eagerness. "Could you, please, take me to York to catch the ten o'clock train I have got to go to London. It is very, very urgent."

"But why? What is the hurry? he asked.

She hesitated for a moment and then realised that the only possible course was to tell him the truth.

"I have got to go to New York on the afternoon plane."

"To New York?"

There was no mistaking the surprise in his voice.

Sally nodded.

"Mary Stubbs has just telephoned me."

Even as she said Mary's name, Sally realised that Sir Guy had guessed and she was half alarmed that she had given away some of Lynn's secret, but she told herself there was nothing to be afraid of where Sir Guy was concerned.

He stood looking down at her, frowning a little.

"But how can you go to New York alone…" he asked, "*if* you are going alone?"

"Yes I have got to go," Sally said. "Mary has broken her ankle. It is very, very urgent and there is no-one else to go. Mary is seeing to my passport and the money. I shall be all right, but please, I have got to catch that train at York. Could somebody take me?"

"I will take you," Sir Guy said.

"Oh, thank you, thank you so much."

Sally smiled at him, forgetting for one moment all her shyness and embarrassment of what had happened the night before. The only thing that mattered now was that she should get to New York and help Lynn. Lynn was more important than anyone else.

She looked down at her wristwatch.

"I wonder what the correct time is," she asked, "I make it nearly eight o'clock."

"It is one minute to," Sir Guy said gravely.

"I will go and bring the children down to breakfast," Sally said. "What time ought we to start?"

"About half-past," Sir Guy said.

"Well, luckily I am packed," Sally said and then she remembered why she had packed and felt herself flush with embarrassment.

Half afraid that he might ask her for an explanation, she ran away from him to find the children. When she got to the dining room, it was to find the whole household gathered round the breakfast table and in the midst of the excitement and explanations over her journey, Sally did not miss the expression of satisfaction on Nada's face.

Sir Guy left the table almost as soon as Sally and the children came down, so that he did not hear Nada ask,

"Will you be returning here?"

"If Lady Thorne will allow me to," Sally replied, "I shall come back to pick up my dog. I have left Rom with Mrs. Harris who has promised to look after him."

"Your dog?" Nada asked and Sally had the satisfaction of replying,

"Yes. He has had an injured leg and I have kept him in my room. That is why you have not seen him."

"You need not worry about him with Mrs. Harris," Lady Thorne said, "except that he will get so dreadfully fat. Mrs. Harris adores animals, but she overfeeds them so much that the poor things can hardly walk. I always tell her that her cats are quite useless as mousers."

"When you come back you will come and see us, won't you?" Nicholas asked.

"Of course I will," Sally answered.

"Perhaps by that time we shall have found the secret passage," Prue said. "We are going to look very hard for it before we leave The Priory. It would be a pity if we have to go to Grandpa's before we find it."

"Yes, it would be a pity," Lady Thorne said, "but you can always come over for the day and bring your spades with you to dig in the sandpit."

"Yes, we could do that," Nicholas said, "but perhaps we will find it today and that would save a lot of trouble."

"Yes, a lot," Lady Thorne agreed gravely.

Sally finished her coffee and ran upstairs to change and to say goodbye to Gertrude. When she came down again, her travelling coat over her arm, she heard the car come round to the front door. The children were waiting in the hall to see her off and Sir Guy came out of the library. To her surprise he took Lady Thorne on one side. They had a conversation which no-one could overhear, and as they were talking, Bateson, the butler, came through the hall carrying a large leather suitcase. He put it into the back of the car and, just as Sally was getting impatient in case she should miss the train, she heard Lady Thorne say in her soft voice,

"I'm sure you are right, Guy dear, you always know best."

Then she reached up and kissed her son and crossed the hall to kiss Sally.

"Goodbye, dear Sally," she said. "We shall miss you very much. Please write to us and comp back as soon as you can."

"Goodbye, Sally. Write to us from New York," the children shouted. "Goodbye! *Goodbye!*"

They hurried after her to the front doorstep. Sally noticed with satisfaction that Nada was missing.

She got into the car and Sir Guy took the wheel. Only then did she think for a fleeting second that she had a long drive ahead of her alone with him, but with a sense of relief she saw the chauffeur get in behind. There was a final waving of hands and they were off. Sally settled down in her seat with a little sigh of relief. She had been so afraid something would prevent her from starting. It would have been awful not to have caught the train, to have disappointed Mary and to have failed Lynn.

She glanced at Sir Guy. He was looking at the road ahead, his profile stern. She wondered what he was thinking about and felt that the events of the night before had been only a wild nightmare.

There was absolutely nothing she could think of to say and as Sir Guy did not speak, they drove the whole way to York in silence. When they got to the station, a porter came forward to take their luggage. Sally's cases were put on the barrow and she saw that Sir Guy's suitcase was added to them.

"I will get your ticket," Sir Guy said, the first words he had spoken since they had left The Priory.

"I will give you the money," Sally suggested and started to open her bag, but he shook his head and walked away to the ticket office.

When he came back, he made no effort to hand her her ticket, but merely said,

"The train is on Platform Six."

He led the way through the crowds and she followed him, feeling thankful that there was someone to take charge of her even for this stage of the journey. There were people pushing and shoving in every direction, queues at platform barriers, porters hurrying about with luggage. It was all bewildering to a girl who had been brought up in the peace of the Welsh mountains.

'I have got to grow up and learn to look after myself,' Sally thought to herself.

She knew it was experience she wanted, and she wondered with a sudden sinking of her heart how she would fare on this long and unknown journey that lay ahead of her.

Sir Guy led the way down the train to where their porter was waiting outside a first-class carriage.

"I've got you two corner seats, sir," he said.

Sir Guy tipped him.

Sally got into the carriage and to her, surprise Sir Guy got in after her. He pulled the door to and shut it. There was no-one else in the carriage.

"Are – are you – coming to London?" Sally asked.

"If you are going alone, I am coming with you to New York," he said.

Her eyes widened.

"Oh, but – but – you can't!"

"Why not?" The question was sharp and when she did not answer, he added, "You told me you were going alone."

"Yes, I am – but you needn't – I mean, why should you go on my account? That is, if you are…"

Sally was almost incoherent. Sir Guy looked at her gravely.

"I think you are too inexperienced to make the journey alone and at such short notice."

Sally looked up into his eyes.

"You don't mind coming?"

She was not sure why she asked the question.

"I intend to come,"

His reply was final, almost brusque in its determination. She dropped her eyes before his. There was something in his expression she dared not question. But she was conscious that her feeling was not so much one of astonishment as of relief. It was a sense of relief that persisted all through the journey. Their train was late in getting to London and when they drove to Mary's flat, they found that they had to rush off to the American Embassy to get the necessary visa on Sally's passport. This took time and they only just got to the aerodrome in time to catch the plane.

Sally was breathless with fear and apprehension of missing it altogether, but Sir Guy was calm, getting her through the Customs with the minimum amount of time and seeming to command attention by his very presence. More than once it was on the tip of her tongue to thank him for being there, but somehow she could not say it. The day before yesterday it would have been easy to say thank you, but after what had occurred in the wood this was not the Sir Guy she knew, but a stranger, a man who had kissed her, who had held her close and believed strange things about her. And yet, she asked herself now, had he believed it of her or had he merely in a moment of madness identified her with another woman? It was all so bewildering. Sally tried to sort out her thoughts but mixed with the throb and rumble of the engine they were too chaotic.

What had happened to Lynn? That was the question she asked herself over and over again and she told herself that she had no right to worry with her own concerns, when

Lynn was in trouble. Lynn needed her. More than once she wondered how she was to explain Sir Guy away when she got to New York. She had not told him in so many words that she was going to Lynn, and he had not asked her, but she knew he guessed.

Mary had said nothing when she told her that Sir Guy was going with her. If she disapproved, she had not voiced that disapproval as Sally had thought she would.

What a tangle and mess-up it all was! But then her life had been growing more and more complicated day by day, week by week, in fact ever since she had left the Welsh mountains to come to London.

'Is this growing up?' she asked herself, with a wry smile and wondered if it was possible to remain a simple child for ever. Yet somehow, now deep in her heart, she was conscious of a sense of adventure. Perhaps it was the novelty of flying, or maybe it was just the strangeness of being up here high in the air beside Sir Guy. Whatever it was, she felt strangely excited and keyed up within herself.

Things were happening. At least she was no longer crushed with that numbness and despair which had cast her down into an abyss of misery after Tony had left her. Now she came to think of it, she had not felt like that the night before last when Sir Guy had kissed her. She had felt surprised, astonished and she had been frightened, but she had not been desperate, she had not been cast down and annihilated as she had been before.

That was what she dreaded most. That awful feeling of being flattened out, of hardly daring to raise her head from the ground. No, life was dancing in her veins. She was young, she was alive! She felt courage and strength seep through her, as if she could face anything, even the most terrible reverses. What was the point of being so shy, she asked herself. And leaning forward, she said to Sir Guy,

"Shall we be arriving soon?"

~271~

"In about half an hour," he replied.

"Oh, good."

Sally felt her heart quicken. To be in America, to have crossed the Atlantic, that was something in itself, but to know that she was about to see Lynn, whom she loved – that was even more wonderful. She felt it was necessary to explain a little to Sir Guy.

"You know," she said, choosing her words with care, "that I have got to see a Mrs. Donavan. That is what I have come for and she is at the *Ritz Carlton*."

Sir Guy nodded.

"Mrs. Donavan," he said. "I will remember."

He was not deceived, and somehow Sally was grateful to him for asking no further explanation. It was like him, she thought suddenly, to make things so easy for her. Other people might have asked questions, have forced her to lie or prevaricate.

She found herself relying on him once more when they arrived at the airport. There were customs formalities to be gone through over again and then, in what seemed to Sally an extraordinarily short time, they were speeding through the streets towards the *Ritz Carlton*.

It was terribly hot. Sally had expected heat, but not this dry, airless heat, which seemed to sap her strength and burn through her until her very skin felt tight and dry. In the Central Park people were lying under the shade of the trees on the grass, too hot to move or even to think.

They arrived at the *Ritz Carlton*. Inside the hotel it was cool. Sally went to the desk.

"Is Mrs. Donavan here?" she asked and her voice trembled as she said it.

She did not know why, but she seemed to have come such a long way that anything might have happened to Lynn in the meantime.

"Miss St. Vincent?" the clerk enquired with a nasal twang. "Mrs. Donavan is expecting you. Will you go right up? Suite 82."

Sally looked at Sir Guy.

"Will you telephone me later when you know what you are going to do?" he asked.

"You will be staying here?" Sally asked and was more relieved than she could say.

"Yes, here," he reassured her.

"Thank you."

She went to the lift, got out on the eighth floor and walked along the corridor to find a door numbered '802'. She rang the bell and waited a moment until it was opened. Rose stood there.

"Oh, Rose!" Sally exclaimed.

"It is nice to see you, miss," Rose said. "Did you have a good crossing? Madam is in the far room."

It was a big suite, Sally noticed vaguely as she half-ran towards the room at the far end. The door was ajar and she went in. The blinds were half drawn, the room was dim and she was acutely conscious of Lynn lying on the bed propped up with pillows.

"Lynn!" she said, and her voice broke on the word.

"Oh, Sally, my dear."

Lynn held out her hand and Sally ran towards her. She would have kissed her but as she drew near the bedside, she saw to her horror that Lynn's neck and the lower half of her face were swathed in bandages. Lynn's eyes, very large in a white face, were staring up at her, and she looked ill – very ill.

"Oh, Lynn darling, what is the matter?" Sally asked.

"I'm glad you have come," Lynn said, "so glad, Sally. I had to have somebody."

Her grip tightened for a moment on Sally's hand and then in quite her old voice she said irritably.

"It is so tiresome of Mary to have broken her ankle just at this moment when I wanted her."

"Please tell me what has happened?" Sally asked.

She felt emotional and very near to tears.

"I don't know where to begin," Lynn said. "There is so much to tell you. Besides, you had better shut the door. One never knows who might be listening."

Sally got up to obey, but at that moment Rose came in.

"Would Miss Sally like to take off her hat, and shall I bring her a drink?" she said, "it is very hot."

"Oh, I would love a drink," Sally exclaimed. "Thank you, Rose."

As she spoke she pulled her hat from her head and held it out to the maid. She was only wearing a thin flannel skirt and a silk blouse, having long ago discarded the coat, but she felt hot and sticky as though she were dressed in furs.

"You can have a bath later," Lynn said. "Shut the door, Rose."

Rose did as she was told and Lynn and Sally were alone. Sally, forgetting everything but Lynn, went back to the bed.

"What have you done to yourself, darling?" she said. "Why have you got bandages round your neck and your face? What has happened?"

For a moment there were tears in Lynn's eyes.

"My neck, Sally, my neck!" she said, "the marks will be there forever."

"What marks?" Sally asked.

Lynn swallowed and then she answered,

"Perhaps it will be all right. I've seen the best surgeon in New York. He says there is every chance that they will heal nicely, but even clean scars take time. But no-one must know, no-one, you understand."

"Know what?" Sally asked, bewildered. "Oh, Lynn, do tell me from the beginning."

"Yes, I will," Lynn said. "I will tell you from the very beginning, Sally."

The door opened and Rose came in with a tall glass full of a cool drink on which floated tinkling ice.

"For Heaven's sake," Lynn said, "go away, Rose, and shut the door. We don't want to be disturbed."

"It is only a drink for Miss Sally," Rose said soothingly. "Now don't upset yourself! You know what the doctor said."

"Yes, I know what he said," Lynn answered.

Rose went out again and Sally took a long drink before putting the glass down.

"Tell me," she said.

She felt half ashamed that she personally should have any physical needs when there was Lynn to be considered. Lynn began, and her voice was very low,

"Erico and I got married the morning we arrived in Buenos Aires," she said. "No-one knew anything about it. Erico made all the arrangements and it was kept completely secret from everyone except the necessary officials. I made my appearance, in the city as Lynn Lystell. I expected to be a success, Sally, but not the amazing success that I was. It was just one triumph after another. It was quite fantastic and very exciting. Everywhere I went people made a great fuss of me and Erico began to get jealous. I suppose I was stupid to insist on us still keeping secret that we had been married. I blame myself now, but at the time I thought it seemed the sensible thing to do, for the same reason that, as you know, I was always half afraid before of someone finding out that I had been married.

"To be perfectly honest, I was afraid to do anything that might change my luck or damp down the fire of the public's enthusiasm. Darling, the flowers, the presents – if you could have seen them – the cheers when I appeared! the curtain calls, twenty or thirty every night! and people waiting for days on the off-chance of a seat in the theatre!

"I planned, that as soon as we left Buenos Aires, I would announce that we had been married, not saying the actual date or when or where. It was deviating a little from our original ideas, but Erico and I were together some of the time and, as we were staying in the same villa with friends of his, I thought he should be content. But he was not satisfied with what he called 'a hole in the corner affair'. He got more and more angry with me and more and more jealous. I was stupid, Sally, I see that now, but it rather pleased me to have so much power over him. After all, I was his wife and I told myself it would do him good to be thwarted, he had always had the world at his feet because he was so rich, so many women had loved him and he had always had his own way with them.

"I forgot that South Americans are very fiery people. One night there was a dance. There was another man there who had been paying me a great deal of attention. He was a charming person, a Chilean. I liked him and because it amused me to inflame Erico, I flirted with him and danced with him perhaps more often than was wise. Towards the end of the evening we went together into the garden. It was a wonderful night and we were wandering among the flowers when suddenly Erico came upon us. I saw at once that he was in a violent rage. He flew at my companion and I am ashamed to say that instead of standing his ground, my Chilean admirer ran away. Erico was much the bigger man, so perhaps he had some excuse, but at any rate he was fainthearted, for he turned and ran. Then Erico went for me. He said something about ensuring that I would belong to him forever and that no other man would look at me and before I was aware what he was doing I felt a violent pain in my neck and on my face.

"I screamed and fell backwards into a flower bed. I think my falling saved me from worse injuries, anyway I fell down and the stiletto, or whatever it was Erico had in his hand, instead of cutting straight down my face only grazed the corner of my chin and cut into my neck. My screams brought Rose to my side. She had been looking for me because she thought it was too late for me to be out in the garden without a wrap. When he saw her coming and thinking perhaps he had killed me, Erico disappeared. Luckily he just missed the artery or he *would* have killed me. Rose took me back to the house. When she saw what had been done to my face and neck, she was wise enough to realise, that not only would it do me irreparable harm for the world to know that my beauty was damaged, but also that the scandal to my reputation would be even more ghastly – a secret marriage and then to be attacked by my own husband! Can you imagine anything worse?

"Rose got hold of the manager of my company. We let him into the secret because there was nothing else that we could do. He chartered a private plane and before daybreak I was on my way here to New York. No one knew I had left – no one knew where I had gone. I am here as Mrs. Donavan and I am in the hands of the finest plastic surgeon in this country. The wounds will heal and the surgeon hopes the scars will not be too utterly disfiguring, but it is going to take time and there are bound to be scars, I'm afraid. That – is my story, Sally."

"Oh, Lynn, *Lynn!*"

The tears were running down Sally's cheeks. There was something in the matter-of-fact and quiet way in which Lynn had told her story which made it all the more moving.

"I was a fool," Lynn whispered and closed her eyes.

"But Erico?" Sally asked. "Didn't you let him know where you had gone? What will he do?"

"What *can* he do?" Lynn asked.

She spoke the words wearily as if she was utterly disheartened and Sally had not the heart to question her further. Lynn lay against her pillows with closed eyes. Now that she had grown used to the dimness, Sally could see that Lynn had aged remarkably. She was still beautiful, but she was much thinner – there were deep, dark lines beneath her eyes and many little wrinkles that had not been there before. Also, that attractive sparkle which had made her so radiant when she was in London, had given place to a listlessness that made Sally feel that Erico had killed her spirit when he tried to destroy her beauty.

Sally longed to ask Lynn if she missed Erico, but she felt it was too intimate a question and that Lynn might think it an impertinence.

"How can I help you?" she asked at length, bending forward and taking Lynn's hand in hers.

"Just by being here," Lynn replied. "I can't bear being alone and I can't see anyone. Who does Mrs. Donavan know in New York?" she asked with a sudden flash of her old humour.

"Won't there be a hue and cry for you in South America?" Sally asked.

"I can trust my manager to see to that. He will say I have taken to religion or gone to stay with friends in the country. He is a very clever young man and being Irish, extremely inventive. The only thing we need worry about, Sally, is getting my beauty back. What use am I if I am not beautiful?"

Now at last Sally dared to ask it.

"And Erico?" she asked, "for after all you are married to him."

Lynn's lips tightened.

"Look what he has done to me."

Again Sally dared to say what she thought.

"Because he loved you."

~278~

"A strange sort of love," Lynn answered.

Sally could say no more. It was no use. She felt that, badly as he had behaved, Erico must be feeling desperate at Lynn's disappearance.

She released Lynn's hand and bent forward to take another sip of the iced drink. As she did so, Lynn suddenly spoke again.

"I am so unhappy, Sally," she said. "I hate my life. I hate everything to do with it. I wish Erico had killed me. I don't want to stay here. I don't know what I do want. I certainly don't want to be ugly and marked. I thought I had everything in the world, but instead I have got a hotel bedroom in New York, where nobody wants me, and months of waiting, waiting, while my scars heal."

"Oh, poor, poor Lynn," Sally said again.

Lynn looked up at her.

"It was nice of you to come, Sally," she said slowly, "Mary ought not to have asked it of you. I know really that I am being paid out for all the bad things I have done in my life and I have behaved particularly badly to you, if it comes to that,"

"Oh, Lynn darling! What rubbish! You have always been wonderful to me," Sally protested.

"Wonderful?" Lynn questioned. "Dear little Sally. You have always been so trusting and I have treated you abominably. Tony was right. You were too good, too decent, that is what was wrong with you,"

"I-I don't know what you mean," Sally said in a bewildered tone.

Lynn looked up at her, and there was real pity in her eyes.

"Haven't you wondered, Sally, why Tony did not marry you at the last moment? Yes, of course you have! Why do I ask such a stupid question? Of course you have wondered and being you, because you are too decent, you would not find the answer. I will tell you now. I will tell you so that you will see what a rotten woman your mother is and how she deserves everything that has happened to her, deserves that and a great deal more. Tony was in love with *me*, Sally dear, in love with me for years, and I made him promise to marry you, even when he did not want to do so, because you had money."

"Oh, Lynn, Lynn, what are you saying?" Sally cried.

"I'm telling you the truth," Lynn said, "and now that you know it, you had better go back to England and leave me alone. I deserve to be left alone, I deserve that and everything else that has happened to me. Go on, Sally, go away and leave me."

Lynn's voice broke on the words and the tears started to pour down her face.

13

Sally was horrified by Lynn's tears.

"Don't, darling, *please don't,*" she pleaded, feeling as if the whole world had fallen in pieces at the sight of Lynn, the beautiful, sophisticated Lynn, broken and suffering by her own humility. But Lynn, once she had started, was determined to drink her cup of bitterness to the very dregs. She stretched out and took Sally's hands in both of hers.

"I have got to tell you," she whispered. "I have got to. While I was lying here waiting for you to arrive, I've been thinking, and Sally, I've realised for the first time in my life how few real friends I have, how few, piteously few, people love me for myself."

"But, Lynn, we all adore you," Sally protested.

"We all?" Lynn questioned with a break in her voice. "Who are they? Mary – yes, Mary loves me, though Heaven knows why – and you do, too, dear little Sally, whom I have treated so badly."

"But you haven't Lynn," Sally cried loyally.

"You can still say that?" Lynn questioned, "after what I have told you – after the way I behaved about Tony?"

Sally dropped on her knees beside the bed.

"Listen, Lynn," she said earnestly, "I was hurt, desperately hurt when Tony left me, because I didn't understand, but one thing I do know now is that I didn't really love him. I don't think I have ever known real love. I was flattered, pleased and very excited that such an attractive young man should take an interest in me and when he left me in that strange way, I was miserable because I thought there was something wrong with me, something revolting or horrid that I didn't understand. But if I hadn't been so blind and stupid, I would have known it was you he loved, and who could help loving you when you are so beautiful?"

"Oh, Sally!"

For a moment Lynn's tears choked her and she could not speak. Then, as she let go of Sally's hands to wipe her eyes, she said,

"You make me ashamed! Your love is something I don't deserve, for I've been such a beast all my life, I see that now. Always I have wanted to take everything and give nothing. I was cruel to Tony, too, poor Tony. Once I thought I loved him just a little, but even then I was greedy. I wanted not only his love but that his whole life should be dedicated to me. I took him away from his family – yes, Sally, I deliberately tried to destroy the love and affection he had for his home and for his mother. I knew that he respected his brother's opinion and I worked on his feelings until he became afraid of Sir Guy and kept away from him as much as possible. Tony was only one of the many people in my life to whom I did exactly the same thing. I never let myself become a part of their circle and their environment. I took them into mine and possessed them utterly and completely possessed them just because I was beautiful."

There was so much misery and pain in Lynn's voice as she spoke the last word that Sally could only cry out once again,

"Don't Lynn, don't torture yourself. It is not true! You are saying this because you are unhappy and hurt, but it is not true."

"I wish I could think that," Lynn said, and now, as if all she had said had cost her a tremendous effort, she lay back against her pillows, her face very white, her eyes tired.

"It is no use, Sally," she said weakly. "I have been awake night after night going over it all and for the first time in my life, I have realised that my beauty, of which I thought so much, has brought me none of the things that matter. With the exception of you and Mary there is no-one in the world who will care about me now."

Sally got to her feet and walked across the room. She felt an infinite pity for Lynn and it was sheer physical agony to listen to her. She wanted to help her and yet it seemed as if there were not enough words in the world to help or to heal her misery. Her feelings must have shown on her face, for suddenly Lynn stretched out her hands and said,

"Come here, darling. Once again I'm being selfish. I'm putting my burdens on you."

"Oh, Lynn, I can't let you talk like this, but what can I say?" Sally asked desperately.

"Nothing," Lynn answered. "This is my punishment, I know that, and Sally, I know too, that if Erico had not injured me, I should be carrying on in my old triumphant, selfish manner without a thought of all this or you or anyone else."

"You are determined to paint yourself in the blackest colours," Sally said.

She tried to smile, for she knew that this misery and introspection was very bad for Lynn at the moment.

"Oh, darling," Lynn exclaimed. "How sweet you are!"

Sally bent down and kissed her cheek very gently,

"Don't worry," she said. "There are so many lovely things for you to do, so many people left in the world who will adore you."

Lynn tried to smile.

"How angry Mary would be with me if she were here," she said, "and yet at the same time she would know that I am telling the truth. In her own forthright way, she has tried to warn me over and over again of the harm I was doing, of the un-kindnesses that I was committing, but I wouldn't listen."

"If Mary were here now," Sally said, "she would tell you to stop crying and make us laugh at ourselves."

"I believe she would," Lynn said. "Dear Mary! Will you telephone her tonight and tell her that we are thinking of her."

"Yes, of course I will," Sally said. "And now, Lynn, we've got to make plans if I'm to look after you until Mary can come out here."

"Plans?" Lynn echoed. "What plans can I make? I have just got to lie here, for weeks, perhaps months, until my neck heals. The surgeon has done all he can and only time can do the rest. He won't even tell me whether I shall be terribly scarred or not. If I am, I suppose even my career is finished."

"Now that is nonsense," Sally said with good sound common-sense. "Your position on the stage, Lynn, doesn't owe everything to your beauty. Because you are glamorous and lovely, some people come just to look at you, but you can act, and I don't believe for one moment that, even if your face were badly damaged, which it isn't, the public wouldn't flock to see you just the same."

"My face *is* damaged." Lynn said obstinately. "I shall always have a scar on my left cheek."

She raised her hand to where the bottom part of her jaw was swathed in bandages and touched it gently with her long thin fingers.

"I'm sure it won't show," Sally said. "When you think of all the wonderful plastic surgery that has been done in the war, I do believe, Lynn, that you will not be scarred half as badly as you think. You are merely making the worst of it and torturing yourself unnecessarily."

"Perhaps I am," Lynn admitted, and then she said, "Oh, Sally, I'm so unhappy."

"Is it only because of your face?" Sally prompted feeling quite certain, there was another reason.

"No," Lynn replied, "but I can't talk of it."

Sally did not press her, instead she said,

"Now I'm going to take everything off your shoulders that I can, but first of all I must tell Sir Guy that I am staying here and thank him for bringing me over."

Lynn looked surprised.

"Sir Guy Thorne? Tony's brother? Did he come with you?"

Sally nodded.

"When Mary telephoned and I had to leave for London immediately, to my surprise he came with me. It was kind of him, but only typical of the kindness that both he and Lady Thorne have shown me ever since I went to The Priory."

"But to come all the way to New York with you!" Lynn ex-claimed – and then she looked searchingly at Sally. "Is he in love with you?"

"No, of course not," Sally said quickly, then she remembered that strange encounter in the woods and her cheeks flushed guiltily.

"Then he is!" Lynn insisted.

Sally shook her head and her eyes were troubled.

"No, really, he isn't," she answered. "I always thought he hated me until – well, until the night before last and then he was strange, very strange, but before I understood what it was all about, I was on my way here and he was with me."

Sally was obviously agitated at having to make any explanation and with unexpected kindness Lynn forbore to question her further. Instead she said,

"Does he know whom you have come to see?"

"I didn't tell him," Sally replied in a troubled voice, "but he knew that I was coming in Mary's place, so I think that he may have guessed."

"Well, what does it matter?" Lynn said with a little shrug of her shoulders. "Once I should have minded so terribly, but now I no longer care. I don't think I care about anything."

"That is only because you have been ill," Sally said soothingly. "Soon you will want to be out in the world again, Lynn, and all this unhappiness will have passed away."

"Never!" Lynn replied, and then quickly she added, "Don't let's talk about me anymore. I am sick of myself. Go and tell your kind Sir Guy that you are staying here to nurse an old, fractious and disillusioned woman and if he wants to take you out to dinner, you must accept."

"Oh, but, Lynn, I wouldn't think of leaving you alone," Sally exclaimed.

"Rubbish!" Lynn replied. "I have got to learn to try and be unselfish. Don't spoil my one valiant effort in that direction."

She smiled and Sally laughed a little shakily. Somehow it was infinitely pathetic to see Lynn trying to be courageous and yet brought so low that her pride was in the dust.

"I will go and telephone him in the other room," Sally said. "I won't be long."

"Be kind to him," Lynn said. "He deserves it because I have done everything to make Tony's family hate me."

Sally left her in the bedroom and crossed the corridor to the sitting room of the suite. Alone, she stood amongst the stiff, formal furniture, trying to collect herself and her thoughts She could hardly realise all that had happened to Lynn. Paramount in her mind at the moment was the last sentence Lynn had spoken. "I have done everything to make Tony's family hate me."

Now at last she understood so many things. The references to Tony by his mother, which were so often broken off sharply, the way his home-life, like his letters, had ceased two or three years ago when he had first become infatuated with Lynn. No wonder Lady Thorne had spoken disparagingly of actresses, no wonder Sir Guy had looked badly at any girl who had come from the house of the woman who had taken Tony so completely away from them.

Sally's head throbbed as so much knowledge pressed upon her. So many puzzles and problems were answered by the realisation that it was Lynn whom Tony had always loved and never herself.

'Oh, why couldn't they have told me?' she asked herself and felt humiliated in knowing how gullible she had been, how completely and easily she had been taken in. She had believed so confidently that Tony loved her, but she had not even begun to understand the meaning of the word. She had thought herself in love with him and it had been just the vanity and easily aroused affection of an unsophisticated country bumpkin.

If Lynn in her confession had humiliated and reproached herself, she yet had the satisfaction of having played a major part in what had happened. She might indeed have been wicked, but wickedness, Sally felt, was infinitely preferable to sheer, unadulterated stupidity.

"What a fool I have been!" she said, and for a moment she felt the hot tears of shame and self-pity burn in her eyes. She forced herself to control them. There was really no time, she told herself, to think of all this now. There was so much she had to do, and there was Lynn whom she had to look after, Lynn to whom she must give new hope and fresh courage. She had got to try and make herself as efficient as Mary would have been in the same circumstances and she knew that Mary would have let no personal problems interfere with her care of Lynn.

Sally walked across to the writing table and picked up the telephone. She asked to be connected with the Reception desk. They gave her Sir Guy's room number and it was only a moment or two before she heard his voice.

"Hullo," he said, "is that Sally?"

"Yes."

"Is everything all right?"

"I think so," she answered doubtfully, "I would like to see you."

"I was hoping you would be able to. Will you come to my sitting room or shall I come up to you?"

Oh, I will come to you," Sally said quickly.

"Very well! Room 789. It is one floor down and you turn to the left when you get out of the lift."

"Thank you," Sally answered. "I will come to you right away."

She put down the receiver, thinking as she did so that it would be much easier to tell Sir Guy anything on the telephone than to say it to him personally. There was something in his eyes that disconcerted her, something in the way he looked at her, and in his height and the breadth of his shoulders. He was so strong, she thought, and then shivered because she could remember his strength only too well.

What had happened that night in the wood? Had a strange madness possessed him? Or had there been more to it than that? For the first time since the journey started, she thought again of his wild words. What had he meant? Why indeed had he chosen to express to her in such a way his disillusionment and what indeed must be his desperate unhappiness? Always she had thought of him as being cynical, now she knew that that word hardly expressed the burning fire of misery which lay within him.

Did he indeed miss Lady Beryl so much or was it something more than that? What had he meant by saying that everything failed him? Why had he lost faith in God and his faith in woman?

'I'm sure I am being stupid once again,' Sally told herself and it seemed to her there was no answer to all those questions and that she would never dare to ask them of Sir Guy himself,

From the moment they had started on their journey he had been circumspect, aloof, almost as indifferent as he had always been in the past and now, she felt that she must have dreamed the whole episode in the woods. Anyway, this was the end, she told herself, for she was unlikely to see much of him in the future. He would go home and she would stay with Lynn until she no longer required her. It might be weeks, it might be months, as Lynn had said, anyway she would be here until Mary could take her place.

She felt a sudden pang, almost one of homesickness, at the thought of never seeing The Priory again. How she loved it! Loved the gracious dignity of its walls, the atmosphere of peace and healing, the beauty of the polished furniture, of the ancient gilt mirrors and hangings mellowed with age. It was a home such as she would love to have called her own.

But what was the point of thinking of all this? Sally asked herself and she realised that some minutes had passed since she had telephoned Sir Guy. She jumped to her feet, looked at her reflection in the mirror over the mantelpiece. She tidied her hair, thinking as she did so that she looked absurdly young,

"When I grow older," she said aloud, "I expect everything will seem much simpler."

As she left the sitting room, she saw that another door in the suite was open. She peeped in and found Rose ironing.

"I won't be more than a few minutes," Sally told her. "I'm just going to see someone."

"That's all right, miss," Rose, answered, "I'll go and see if Madam wants anything."

Sally almost ran down the long corridor towards the lift. She must not be long, she told herself, in case Lynn might want her. What was more, if Sir Guy did ask her out this evening, which was most unlikely, she had no intention of accepting his invitation. It was wonderful of Lynn to be so unselfish, but it was obviously bad for her to be alone, to lie in bed with nothing to do, but think.

Sally rang for the lift and it took her to the next floor. She thanked the attendant, then turned along the corridor to the left as Sir Guy had told her to do. As she did so, a man came out of a room a little ahead. He slammed the door and put the key in his pocket, then turned and came face to face with Sally. She hardly glanced at him as she was looking at the numbers of the doors on the other side of the corridor, then she heard him give an exclamation and cry,

"Sally! Surely it is Sally?"

She turned round and recognised him at once.

"Erico!"

"Sally! You, here in New York! Then Lynn is here, too! I was certain of it! That was why I came! Oh, Sally, where is she? You must tell me at once."

In his agitation he put out his hands and gripped her by the shoulders.

"But Erico, I don't know what to say."

"There is nothing for you to say," Erico replied. "You just take me to Lynn at once, do you hear?"

His words were commanding, but his eyes pleaded with her.

"But – I can't," Sally stammered. "I must ask Lynn first."

"Then she is here in this hotel! Oh, Sally, if you only knew what I have been through. I have been searching New York, I have been walking the streets, going to hotel after hotel. Always they have told me there is no-one staying there who even looked like Lynn. Oh, Sally, let me see her!"

"I must ask Lynn," Sally said, bewildered and distressed at this strange encounter.

"Oh, please make her see me," Erico said. "I have been crazy with anxiety. I have not known what to do or where to go."

Suddenly his voice changed and he asked,

"She is ill?"

Sally nodded her head.

"Yes, Erico."

"It is I who have made her ill. Is it bad?"

Sally drew a deep breath.

"They don't know yet how much disfigured she will be."

Erico put his hands lip to his eyes, and Sally, watching him, knew that he was not acting. He was suffering, suffering as she had never seen anyone suffer before. When he looked at her again, his face was stricken.

"Will she ever forgive me?"

Sally made a little gesture.

"I don't know! Honestly, I don't know."

"Sally, I swear to you I would have given my right hand for this not to have happened. I was mad! She drove me mad with her beauty, with her desire for secrecy, and I thought – Oh, God knows what I thought – but it was sufficient to make me want to kill the one person I have really loved in the whole of my life. What am I to do? Tell me what I am to do."

It was a cry for help such as Sally had never heard in the whole of her life before. She had thought that she must hate Erico for what he had done to Lynn, but now she was pitying him, being unreservedly sorry for him. Love had driven him into desperate straits but love also had made him suffer. He looked older, she thought, and realised that his face was haggard and drawn. She was certain that what he had told her was true, that he had searched desperately for Lynn.

She hesitated, and then at last she said,

"Listen, Erico, as you have seen me, you know that Lynn is here in this hotel. I am not going to pretend she isn't and I will take you up to her room now, but if she refuses to see you, will you promise me not to make a scene, to go away and wait until she says she will – if she ever does agree to seeing you again."

"Oh, thank you! Yes, yes, I promise."

He spoke so humbly and so gratefully that Sally felt a little smile tremble on her lips. What a dashing buccaneer Erico had seemed when she last saw him! The world had been at his feet because Lynn wore his engagement ring. And now all his fire and spirit had vanished and he was just a man lost and miserable because his temper had got out of control.

"Come along," she said.

She took him back to the lift and they went together to the eighth floor. When they reached Lynn's suite, Sally hesitated. Suppose she was doing something which was utterly wrong, suppose Lynn was angry with her? She looked up at Erico,

"You promise me to go away if she says she won't see you?" she insisted.

Her face was so earnest and worried that he smiled and touched her cheek with his hand.

"Dear little Sally," he said, "do not be afraid! I have learned my lesson – but plead for me. Beg my Lynn to see me if only for a moment. I will come to her on my knees if she allows it."

"Wait here then," Sally said.

She opened the door of the suite and led him into the narrow hall, then she went to Lynn's room. She knocked and entered at the same time. Lynn was lying as she had left her, her face very pale against the pillows, her hands lying listlessly on the bedspread.

"Back so quickly, Sally?" she asked as Sally entered.

Sally closed the door behind her.

"Lynn," she said, "when I went downstairs, I met someone."

"I thought you went to see Sir Guy?" Lynn questioned.

"Before I got to his room I met someone else," Sally said, "someone who wants to see you, Lynn."

Sally's tone said more than her words. Lynn looked across the room at her, her eyes wide,

"Not – not…"

She could hardly bring herself to say the word.

"Yes, Erico," Sally finished for her. "Oh, Lynn, he is so sorry. He has been searching for you, looking everywhere, in every hotel in New York. He is terribly unhappy and he wants your forgiveness."

"Erico!"

Lynn said the word to herself, and then suddenly to Sally's astonished eyes it seemed as if life and energy returned to her. Slowly the colour came into her cheeks, her eyes brightened, her fingers quivered for a moment, then raised themselves to her bandages round her neck, her lips parted.

"Oh, Sally," she said. "I have wanted him so much. Where is he? Bring him to me!"

There was such longing, such hunger in her voice that Sally felt the tears well up into her eyes. She could not speak, she could only open the door.

Erico was standing outside. He stepped forward, stood very still for a moment looking at Lynn, his eyes seeking hers. Lynn was trembling, her face strained and white, but her eyes were shining. It was a moment so tense, so poignant that Sally could almost hear their hearts beating in unison. With a cry that was half of triumph and half a sob Erico moved across the room and fell on his knees at Lynn's bedside. Then his cheek was against hers, her arms round his neck and their voices, broken with passion and tears, mingled together.

Sally closed the door and left them alone. There were tears on her cheeks, too. As she paused to wipe them away, she saw that Rose had come out of her room and was standing looking at her.

"Rose!" she exclaimed and Rose smiled at her.

"He has come at last," she said. "I wondered how long we were going to wait. That is good! Now Madam will get well very quickly, you will see."

"Oh, I hope so," Sally said. "Rose, is her neck very bad?"

Rose made a little face.

"It is bad enough," she said, "and for Madam, you will understand, it was a tragedy that anything could happen to her face and neck. The damage was deeper than the wound, you understand?"

"Yes, of course I understand," Sally said, "her beauty was perfection until now."

Rose smiled.

"When she is happy, she is always beautiful," she said. "I am glad that he has come."

She went towards her room, then paused.

"But poor Miss Sally, you have come all this way for nothing. Never mind, if you have not been to New York before, it is an interesting place, but give me London every time."

She closed the door of her room and Sally stood for a moment looking after her.

So she had come all this way for nothing! Yes, of course she had. Now that Erico and Lynn were re-united, she would not be wanted. Now she was uncertain what she should tell Sir Guy, but at least she ought to go down and see him. He would think she had lost her way between two floors.

This time she found her way without incident to the door of his sitting room. She knocked and he opened it immediately.

"I am sorry to have been so long," she said as she entered the room.

"I was afraid you might have lost your way," Sir Guy said.

"No," Sally answered, "but – but something happened".

It was going to be difficult, Sally thought, to explain anything to Sir Guy, knowing that she must keep Lynn's identity a secret.

"Won't you sit down?" he asked.

He indicated an armchair covered in grey velvet and Sally, looking around the sitting room, which was decorated in grey and silver, thought how out-of-place he looked. The background she always imagined for Sir Guy was either the moors stretching away to the horizon, or his big library lined with books and hung with portraits of bygone ancestors. But this little room with its delicate furnishings seemed to confine him as if it were an ornamental birdcage."

"Well, haven't you anything to tell me?" Sir Guy asked.

With a start Sally realised that he was waiting for her to speak.

"I-I had," she began lamely, "but now something happened on my way here that has rather complicated things and I am not quite certain whether I shall be staying here or whether I shall be returning to England. Not…" she added hastily, sensing the construction that he might put on her words, "that that will affect you one way or the other. First of all, I want to thank you so very, very much for bringing me here."

"It is not a difficult journey," Sir Guy said. "I daresay I was being unnecessarily fussy and that you could have managed the trip on your own."

"But I couldn't," Sally said, "and I am grateful, so very, very grateful. It is difficult to know how to say 'thank you' adequately for all you've done."

"Then don't try," Sir Guy suggested. "All I want to know is if you are all right?"

"Yes, I'm quite all right," Sally said with a confidence she did not entirely feel.

Sir Guy bent forward in his chair.

"Listen, Sally," he said. "Don't we know each other well enough now to be frank? I don't know what promises you have given as to secrecy, but I am not entirely blind, I am not entirely an imbecile and without straining my imagination very far I know you have come here to see Miss Lystell."

Sally looked at him in fright.

"I didn't say so," she said.

"No, you have told me nothing," Sir Guy said, "but let us just take it for granted that I know for a fact that Miss Lystell, or Mrs. Donavan as she calls herself, is ill or in trouble and Miss Stubbs could not come to her, so you came instead. All I want to know is, does she want you to stay on, or shall I take you back to England with me?"

Sally looked at him rather helplessly.

"The awful thing is that I can't answer that question. Ten minutes ago I was on my way down to tell you that I was to stay here for weeks, perhaps months, but now I don't know."

"When are you likely to know?" Sir Guy asked her gently.

"Perhaps later this evening," Sally answered, "or at any rate I suppose by tomorrow morning."

"Then what I suggest," Sir Guy said, "is that you come out and dine with me tonight. I would like to show you New York."

"Do you know it well then?" Sally asked in surprise.

"Fairly well," he replied. "I was here about six months ago and I was here for nearly a year during the war. I was on a special army mission at that time. I came back last winter to renew my acquaintance with several friends I made in this country."

It was rude to be surprised and yet Sally had somehow not expected Sir Guy to be travelled or to be acquainted with other countries save his own. It brought home to her once again how little she knew about him, this man who had come into her life in such a strange way and who was, whatever he did, indivisibly connected in her thoughts with the Knight she had loved as a child.

Because she was shy and because she did not know what to say to him, she got to her feet and walked to the window. She looked out at the high buildings and the traffic surging up and down the streets. It was still very hot and the sun was sinking, making everything golden, glittering on the windows and the roofs, gilding everything so that Sally's eyes were dazzled.

"I would like to show you New York," Sir Guy repeated behind her.

Suddenly, on an impulse, Sally turned to him.

"There is something I want to say to you," she said and her voice was very low and serious.

"What is it?" Sir Guy asked.

"It is about your kindness to me," she said, "after – after Tony left me. I didn't know until today the reason why he acted as he did, but now that I know, I understand his point of view very dearly. What I can't understand was your kindness – yours and your mother's. You knew that he loved Lynn, you knew that she had taken him away from you all, and yet you were kind to me, to a girl who…"

She hesitated for a choice of words, but Sir Guy supplied them for her.

" Who is Lynn Lystell's daughter."

Sally gave a little cry.

"Who told you that?"

"No-one," he said, "again I guessed it."

Sally looked frightened.

"Even if you think such things, you must not say them."

"Why not," he asked, "if I only say them to you? Must we have so many secrets between us Sally?"

"You will only say it to me, won't you" Sally begged.

"Only to you," he promised and then he added, "you have learned something of the past today, perhaps it has upset you. I have a feeling that it has, but I have something to suggest as regards the past – your past and mine. Sally, let us forget it, let us start from today, from the present, and get to know each other a little better. Shall we?"

There was a note in his voice that she had never heard before. She felt herself respond to it, wanting in that moment to agree with him, to promise him whatever he asked, but some shyness held her back.

"Can we ever forget the past?" she asked hesitatingly, not quite certain what she meant, but feeling that there was so much on which to turn her back.

To her surprise Sir Guy turned away wearily and it seemed as if his face, which had lightened for a moment, settled once again into its familiar lines of cynicism.

"Perhaps it would be impossible," he said. "Experiments of that sort are seldom successful."

She looked at him, uncertain of herself and a little bewildered, then she said quickly,

"The future is certainly more important to me than the past. It seems as if once again I am to be nobody's child – looking for a job."

"Does it?" he said, "then somehow we must plan what to do with you. Poor little Sally! The world is not very kind, is it?"

"You have been kind," she answered.

~298~

"Don't be too sure of that!"

He turned his back on her for a moment as he took a cigarette from the box on the table beside him. She looked at his bent head and wished she knew what he was thinking, wished she could understand him better. Then he turned to face her again.

"About this evening," he said and his voice was casual, "unless you telephone me that you cannot come, I will be waiting for you in the hall at eight o'clock."

Their interview was at an end. As if he had said it in so many words, Sally knew that he had terminated it.

As she went back to Lynn's room, she wondered why she had failed. For one moment she had felt as if they were close to each other, then he had gone away from her again and there was that same, strange barrier between them of which she had been aware ever since they had first met. What was it? she wondered. Suddenly she knew that she wanted Sir Guy's friendship more than she had ever wanted anything in her life before. And yet, was it really friendship she sought? She asked herself the question but was afraid of the answer.

14

Sir Guy looked at his watch.

"We should reach York in a quarter of an hour," he said.

Sally picked up her bag and gloves.

"Then I think we ought to get back to the carriage," she said. "Don't you?"

"Perhaps we had better," Sir Guy agreed and rose from the tea table.

Sally got up, too. The train was travelling fast and the dining car was at the end of the train. As she got to her feet and stepped into the aisle between the tables, she swayed with the movement and would have stumbled if it had not been for Sir Guy who put out his hand to steady her. She looked up at him and smiled.

"Thank you."

Her eyes met his and she looked away again, but in that moment she knew that she was in love. Walking along the crowded corridors, waiting for people to get out of her way, climbing over suitcases and parcels, steadying herself through every communicating coach, Sally was conscious only of her quickly beating heart.

She knew now that she had loved Sir Guy for a long while, so long that it seemed as if there had been no interval between the time when he had ceased to be the Knight with the plumed helmet and had become the grave, disapproving brother of Tony. Always she had loved him, and yet she had never known it until now – now in this rocking, overcrowded train carrying them home.

She felt her mind clutch at the word 'home'. For that indeed was what The Priory meant to her and she had known it should mean that from the very first moment she saw it, when the children said it smiled at them. Sir Guy's home! If only it could be hers too!

She wanted to sigh, but nothing could still the glory within her, the joy beating in every vein in her body. She was in love. She loved Sir Guy and had become aware of it in that split second when he put out his hand to steady her. There were so many and better occasions when she might have discovered it. In New York's most glamorous nightclub, *El Morocco*, for instance, where Sir Guy had taken her to dine, but amused by its blue walls and ceiling of twinkling stars, she had listened to the band rather than to her own heart. She might have discovered it at the top of the Empire State Building, or when they had walked together in Central Park because, as he told her, every American would talk to her sentimentally of Central Park. She might have learned it on Fifth Avenue, or as their aeroplane took off and they had their last glimpse of those strangely beautiful skyscrapers that are the hallmark of modern civilisation.

But at none of those times, glamorous, exciting, interesting as they had been, had she realised that she was in love. No, it was now in a prosaic, hurrying English train that the knowledge must come to her with a sudden and overwhelming shock.

Sally reached their carriage and, picking up her coat, which she had left to mark her seat, sat down. A moment later Sir Guy came in and sat opposite her. There were two other people in the compartment, both immersed in their newspapers. Sally looked out of the window. She saw nothing of the sun-drenched countryside, she was conscious only of Sir Guy. How blind she had been not to know sooner, how stupid not to realise, days if not weeks ago, that her thoughts and indeed her entire consciousness were vitally and acutely aware of him!

"I love him," she whispered to herself, but found the rapture within her heart checked by the recollection that he did not love her. And yet somehow, she could not believe that he was altogether indifferent. Apart from his strange, inexplicable impulse to come to America, which she might attribute to chivalry, she would not have been a woman if she had not known that on more than one occasion he had warmed towards her.

She had known that he was interested in her, known that he was watching her and then inevitably something, some word, some movement that she could not explain even to herself, would cause the barrier between them to rise again and he would withdraw into his icy indifference.

'What is it?' she asked herself now. 'What is it which makes him draw back even at the very moment when he seems most likely to be expansive, most ready to be friendly?'

She puzzled her head, but somehow coherent thinking was too hard, she only knew that she loved him.

The very wheels of the train were throbbing out the refrain, 'I love him, I love him, I love him'. They said it over and over again and she was half afraid to look in his direction, lest he should read her feelings in her eyes. How right she had been when she had realised that she had never loved Tony. She had, like many other people, mistaken friendship for love, affection for something deeper.

This was love, this breathless passion that seemed to consume her whole body, which beat in her veins and in every heartthrob, which made the most ordinary and commonplace words difficult to say lest they should sound too endearing.

"We are nearly there now."

Sir Guy's voice was almost a shock because it broke in on her thoughts.

"Yes," she answered. "Will anyone be meeting us?"

"My mother will have sent a car," he said, "I wired her the time of our arrival."

What a commonplace conversation! And yet Sally felt as if she were crying out, for all the world to hear, her love and adoration for the man opposite her. Then the cold hand of caution made her pause. She must be careful! She loved him, but she was not so infatuated that she was unaware of the barrier that lay between them. What it was she did not know, but perhaps love would reveal it.

"Oh, please, God, let me find but what it is," Sally whispered to herself and as she prayed, the train drew into York Station,

The chauffeur was waiting with the car. It was not the car they usually used. This was a larger one with a partition between the driver and the passengers.

"I am afraid the Humber is laid up, Sir Guy," the chauffeur explained. "I have had to give her a thorough overhaul. She will be all right in a day or two, I am sorry I could not bring her, for I know you like her best."

"That's all right, Groves – you drive," Sir Guy answered and he got in the back beside Sally.

Sally was not certain whether she was glad or sorry. When Sir Guy was driving she could sit beside him and not be obliged to talk but now, for the next hour, they would be together and she was half afraid, half fascinated, by the idea of their being in such close proximity with nothing to distract their attention from each other.

Now at last she began to understand how completely love could possess one. Never before had she really understood what Lynn and Erico must have suffered, both in their love and in their quarrel. For a moment Sally envied them more than she had ever envied anybody in her whole life before. She thought of them at this moment – wildly, ecstatically happy – flying towards California where Lynn was to convalesce with the help of the best possible medical attention.

From the moment of his return into Lynn's life, Erico had swept all before him like a driving storm. Nothing could stand in his way, nothing and nobody.

"You are mine, *mine,*" Sally heard him tell Lynn, "and I will look after you. I will do everything for you. You are not to think and if you wish for anything, you have only to tell me and it is yours."

It was not even possible to laugh at his impetuosity, because he was so utterly sincere, because he had, too, an almost magical way of getting things done. From the moment of his arrival the whole place had become exciting and glamorous. It was the right background for the Lynn whom Sally had known and loved – not the broken, penitent Lynn she had found on her arrival in New York. And yet, though the tempo rose, though the rooms were so stacked with flowers and presents that one could hardly get into them, and though Lynn, with shining eyes and smiling lips, looked twenty years younger, Sally was conscious that she had altered a little from the old Lynn. There was something deeper, something more loving in her now than had been there before.

Thinking about it, Sally understood that change even better than she had understood in New York. It was because Lynn herself was in love, it was because Lynn at last was giving as well as taking.

'Perhaps I, too, shall alter and grow more sensible,' Sally thought and she smiled at her own thoughts.

"Something amusing you?" Sir Guy asked and she started because engrossed in her thoughts of Lynn, she had almost forgotten that he was there, for they had driven for a long time without speaking.

"I was thinking how happy Lynn and Erico are," she replied, turning a little towards him.

He nodded, and Sally thought how surprising it was that they had got on so well, the four of them. Lynn had liked Sir Guy and, most astonishing of all, he had seemed to like Lynn. She had been afraid when Lynn had insisted on seeing him, that they would clash terribly, for she could not forget how often he had showed his distaste when she was mentioned.

"But of course, I must thank him for bringing you here, you stupid child," Lynn said when Sally had protested that there was no reason for her to trouble herself over the matter.

Then Sir Guy had gone in to see Lynn alone. What they had talked of, what had passed between them, Sally had no idea, but when he came out, they were friends, she was sure of that.

Now, remembering Lynn's beauty – even more vivid after Erico's return – she thought that it would have been hard for anyone, even the grave Sir Guy, to resist her. The scars would heal, but even if they remained on her neck and on her jaw, who would notice them when they looked into Lynn's eyes? Who would worry about them when they could see the enticing curve of Lynn's mouth? Quite unreasonably Sally was suddenly jealous of Lynn. She had so much, she was so lovely.

"What are you thinking about?" Sir Guy asked.

"Shall I tell you the truth?" Sally asked.

"I hope you will always do that," he replied.

"Very well then, I will," Sally answered, trying to laugh at herself. "I was wishing that I looked like Lynn. I was wishing that I was beautiful."

There was a moment's silence. Sally was certain that he had heard her and because she expected him to say something, she turned her head swiftly and looked at him. He was looking down at her and there was an expression on his face that she had not expected to find there, one of tenderness and of pity. At last he spoke,

"But don't you know that you are lovely?" he asked.

Sally's heart gave a startled leap and almost as if she were afraid that it would burst out of her body, she put up both her hands to her breasts and her eyes widened, her lips parted. It was somehow the last thing she had ever expected to hear Sir Guy say.

"You – you are teasing me."

"I'm not," Sir Guy replied. "You stupid child, your Lynn is very lovely of a type, but you – you are different."

"Oh, *oh!*" Sally breathed the words a little breathlessly, and then she looked away and out through the window, afraid of the excitement aroused within her.

Sir Guy suddenly stretched out his legs and leaned back a little in the car.

"But then, of course, you have been told that before."

"I haven't," Sally answered.

"Really? I think you must have forgotten that you said you would tell the truth."

"But I am telling the truth," Sally answered.

"Then it is nice for me to be able to tell you something that you did not know," Sir Guy said. "Shall I put it a little clearer still? I think you are very lovely and very attractive."

There was something in the way he said the last word which arrested Sally's attention. She turned her head and looked at him and saw the expression in his eyes. She did not know why, but almost immediately the memory of that night in the woods returned to her. She had forgotten it in these last days in New York, she had forgotten it while they were flying back across the Atlantic, she had forgotten it in the joy of knowing that she loved him, but now it resurrected itself to stand there a spectre, frightening her, haunting her.

She looked at him, her eyes held by him, and her lips trembled. Quite suddenly, without a word being spoken, she felt as ravaged as if he had kissed her once again in the moonlight. She turned her eyes from his and felt the blood creeping up her cheeks in a crimson flood.

"Must you pretend to be so shy?" There was a sharp note in Sir Guy's voice, which lashed her as if he had used a whip and then, before she could speak, she heard him mutter beneath his breath, "or so innocent".

Now once again she felt that same bewilderment creep over her, felt it hold her tense and numb as she had been after that night in the woods. What did he believe of her? Was he confusing her with Lady Beryl? What did it mean? Even while she puzzled, bewildered and at the same time afraid, she looked up to see with a sense of relief that she recognised the country through which they were passing and she knew that in a few minutes they would turn in at the lodge of The Priory.

Now some of the joy that she had felt on returning home had gone, and she was aware that she was confusing in her mind the Sir Guy she loved, with the Sir Guy as he was – a grim reality who suspected her and who still remained an enigma.

They passed the lodge and because Sally was in love and because, desperately above all things, she hated to feel that Sir Guy had withdrawn himself from her, she turned to him, trying hard to be ordinary and at ease.

"It is lovely to be coming back. I am looking forward so much to seeing Rom and I know who will want to see you."

"I suppose you mean Bracken?" he said and she noticed with a sense of relief that he, too, was trying to be congenial.

"Yes, Bracken," she answered, "and I ought really to like him more than all the rest of the Thorne family, because he was my first friend. Do you realise that?"

"No," Sir Guy answered, not really listening, for he was bending down to pick up a coat that had fallen on the floor.

"Well, he spoke to me first on that little wayside station," Sally said, her eyes looking ahead for the first glimpse of The Priory as they went up the drive. "I remember feeling so lonely and wondering what lay ahead of me when I got to London, when I felt a cold nose, and it was Bracken."

"Whatever are you talking about?"

There was almost a note of irritation in Sir Guy's voice now and Sally laughed.

"Oh, I am sorry," she said. "I forgot, I was never able to tell you about it before, because of course, I couldn't mention Nanny Bird until you knew about Lynn, but I have often, wondered why you never said anything about meeting me at Hill Street that morning. The train got in after all hours before your car and I went first of all to Covent Garden where I found out Nanny's address. Isn't it funny? Mrs. Bird, who looks after you at your flat, was my old Nanny, so I went to see her and then, as I was leaving, I ran into you and Bracken again."

They were nearing the house, but Sally's attention was suddenly diverted by Sir Guy's behaviour. He turned round in his seat, put his hands on her shoulders and turned her round roughly to face him.

"What are you talking about, Sally?" he asked, and his voice was loud and it seemed to her almost wild.

She looked up at him and saw that he was frowning, his eyes dark.

"I was trying to tell you about Nanny Bird," she answered. "It is a long story and I shouldn't have started it now."

"Tell me, you have got to tell me," he commanded. "Where had you been that night, the night when we met on the doorstep at six o'clock in the morning?"

"But I have just told you! I was on the same train as you coming from Wales. I suppose you didn't notice me, but Bracken did. You went off with your friend to get a car, while I went on with the train. Funnily enough the train arrived in London first…"

Her voice trailed away and she thought for a moment that Sir Guy was going to faint. His face went very white and the pressure on her shoulders tightened, then he said almost beneath his breath in a voice that she hardly recognised,

"Oh, my God!"

"What is the matter?" Sally began.

At that moment a voice said,

"Good evening, Sir Guy. Good evening, Miss Sally. I'm glad to welcome you home."

Sally turned to find Bateson holding open the car door. They had drawn up at The Priory while they were still talking. She got out and instantly there was a sound of barking and yelping as the dogs came running out of the hall to welcome them. Bracken sprang up at Sir Guy and Sally's arms were round Rom – Rom fat and well-looking and able to walk on his four legs.

"Oh, Rom, *Rom,* I am so pleased to see you!" she exclaimed, feeling him wriggle in her arms and his tongue on her hands. She looked up to see Lady Thorne on the doorstep.

"Here you are, dear," she said. "Come along in. And, Guy, I am so glad you are back, my dear."

Lady Thorne kissed them both and drew them into the hall and as she went, she said softly in her gentle voice,

"We have a very special visitor, who I think will be a surprise and I hope a pleasant one."

Sally looked across the hall and there, standing in the drawing room doorway, was Tony. Just for a moment she felt breathless, and then, as he smiled at her and his hands went out, she found herself running towards him.

"Oh, Tony! How lovely to see you! When did you get here?"

It was surprisingly easy to be friendly and natural, in fact she was really glad to see Tony again. It was impossible not to be. He was just the same – good-natured, friendly, smiling, his laugh ringing out and seeming to echo through the whole house.

"Sally, you are the last person I expected to find staying here! And Guy, what are you doing running about to the pleasure-spots of the world? I thought they were my prerogative."

No! No-one could be angry with Tony. They all settled down over a glass of sherry to tell him about the trip, how hot it had been in New York, and to ask innumerable questions about Paris. Sally had not realised it would be possible to see Tony again and not feel embarrassed. But he spoke of his job in Paris as if it were the most natural thing on earth for him to be working there, and without any effort at all they both avoided any mention of Lynn.

There was so much to talk about that they were all late in going up to dress for dinner. It was only as Sally was hurrying upstairs that she met Nada coming down. She had almost forgotten her existence, but now that she saw the older girl, she held out her hand in a friendly way.

"Hullo, Nada, how are you?"

"So you're back!" Nada spoke slowly.

"Yes, I am back," Sally answered. "Are you surprised to see us so soon?"

"I am seldom surprised," Nada answered. "It always leaves one at a disadvantage."

She made this somewhat cryptic remark in ominous tones and walked downstairs. Sally could not help laughing. Poor Nada, she thought as she went along to her room. She

~310~

would insist in being dramatic. Well, if Tony stayed long enough, he ought to cure her of that.

He certainly did his best at dinner, and Sally watched him with amusement doing his best to flirt with Nada, who responded somewhat obviously, with many a side glance at Sir Guy to see if he was noticing.

"'I suppose she is jealous of me,' Sally thought and then sighed because she wished there was some reason for Nada to be jealous.

Seeing the two brothers together, she wondered how, even for a moment, she could have thought herself in love with Tony. He was fun, he was amusing, and he was extremely good-looking, but there was a lack of stability about him. With Sir Guy it was so very different. Compared with his younger brother he was like a rock and the impression of his strength was given not only by the feeling of his complete reliability, but also by the sense of power that emanated from him. There was no doubt about it that, if there was one commanding personality in that room at dinner, it was Sir Guy's.

'We are all pigmies compared with him,' Sally thought and she felt her love rushing from her because she was so proud.

More than once she thought that Sir Guy looked at her in a strange way, but there was no chance of their having a word together and when Lady Thorne led the way into the drawing room, Nada said,

"I want to have a word with you, Guy, about something that has occurred while you have been away."

"Can't it wait until tomorrow?" Sir Guy asked impatiently, but when Nada insisted, he followed her into the library.

As Lady Thorne was looking for her knitting, Tony whispered in Sally's ear,

"Come on to the terrace."

She obeyed him quickly, and when they got outside, he said,

"This is my only opportunity to get you alone. I had to see you, Sally, to ask about Lynn. How is she?"

"She's all right," Sally replied.

"I guessed that you went to America to see her. But Guy? Why did Guy go?"

"He very chivalrously felt that I was too young and inexperienced to go alone."

Tony put back his head and laughed.

"How like Guy! And disapproving of the whole scheme, I suppose?"

"He didn't know, until we got there, whom I was going to see, but I think he guessed, so after that I had to tell him. But your mother doesn't know."

"No, I gathered that, and we won't distress her by telling her."

"No, of course not," Sally agreed.

"But Lynn, tell me about Lynn!"

His voice softened and Sally understood just how much he loved her.

"She is married to Erico and they are very, very happy. They had a quarrel, that is why I went to New York, but they have patched it up and have gone to California. Erico has bought a house there and they are going to have a long, quiet honeymoon together. I think that is what Lynn needs, Tony, to be quiet for a long time. She has been working hard for a great many years and has never really taken a rest. She is going to be in California for perhaps four or five months and then after that they are going to plan the future together."

For a moment there was a cloud on Tony's face and then he smiled.

"I have got to be glad, Sally, for Lynn's sake, haven't I?"

"Yes, Tony," Sally said. "Erico is the right person for her. If I was not certain of that at first, I am now. He will look after her and bully her a little. Lynn needs that, you know."

Tony nodded.

"You are right! I was too much of a doormat, but, Sally, I loved her."

"Yes, I know you did, Tony."

Sally's voice was soft.

"And knowing that, do you forgive me?"

"Of course!"

"You understand, I couldn't marry you, Sally, loving Lynn as I did. When it came to the point, it seemed a cad's trick, but one day you will find the right man and he will love you too."

"Oh, I hope so, Tony."

Sally's reply was half a prayer. Tony looked down at her.

"Dear little Sally! You are so sweet – such a lovable person. It is nice to think we can be friends."

"Yes, friends, Tony."

She raised her face and he kissed her on the cheek, and hand in hand they walked back to the drawing room. They sat talking and laughing with Lady Thorne until it was quite late. Sir Guy joined them eventually and Sally noticed that he was very quiet and she wondered more than once what was wrong with him.

His eyes always seemed to be upon her and she had the feeling that he wanted to speak to her, but she dismissed it as being ridiculous. Anyway, it was not possible, for Nada was with them and so was Lady Thorne, until they all went upstairs to bed.

As they said goodnight, Lady Thorne said to Nada,

"What about. Ivor, Nada dear?"

"Oh, he is out on a flight," Nada replied. "I don't know what time he will be back, but I have told them to leave some food for him in the dining room."

"It is so bad for him to miss his dinner," Lady Thorne sighed.

"Oh, don't worry about Ivor, he is used to eating at odd hours."

"Very bad for the digestion," Lady Thorne said. She turned to kiss her two sons, "Goodnight, Guy, Goodnight, Tony. It's lovely to have you both home again."

"I can't tell you what fun it is being here," Tony answered.

He kissed his mother on both cheeks and then bent and kissed Sally.

"Goodnight, Sally, I think I am entitled to that as an ex-fiancé."

"Tony, really!" his mother said in shocked tones, but Sally laughed.

"He's incorrigible, isn't he, Lady Thorne?"

"I have said so for years," Lady Thorne replied, "but it doesn't seem to do any good."

Sally ran up the first flight of stairs and then looked down into the hall. Sir Guy was looking up at her. She didn't know why, but she felt there was an appeal in his eyes.

"Goodnight, Sir Guy," she said.

"Goodnight, Sally."

She had an idea there was something he was going to add, but if there was, he checked the words and walked into the library. For one moment she hesitated. She had a wild desire to run after him and say, as Nada had said, that she had something to talk to him about, yet she knew that when she got there, she would be shy and tongue-tied and would probably only be hurt by the things he would say to her.

She went slowly up the stairs. On the landing she kissed Lady Thorne goodnight and went to her own room.

Rom was waiting for her. She kissed and hugged him and then put him to bed in his basket. It was nice to think that something belonged to her, even if it was only a small black and white mongrel dog. She sat for a moment on the floor beside him, talking to him, making a fuss of him, and then at last she undressed and got into bed. She was tired and fell asleep almost immediately. She was awakened out of a deep slumber by a small whining noise and for a moment could not think what it was. Then, as consciousness returned to her, she sat up in bed and realised that Rom wanted to go out. He was scratching at the door.

"Wait a minute," she said, and putting on her bedside lamp, she got up and looked for her dressing gown. It was three o'clock and very dark.

Rom was waiting for her, his head on one side, his whole body alert, as if he begged her to hurry.

"All right," she told him, "I'm coming."

Sally opened the door and they went together down the back stairs, which were nearest the garden door. She tried to remember where the lights were in the passage but she could not find them, so she felt her way to the door and turned the handle. To her surprise it was unlocked.

Rom, with a little yelp of delight sped out into the garden. Sally stood for a moment in the doorway trying to watch where he went, but the night was very dark and there was a cold wind, so that after a while she felt chilled and closed the door. She stood just inside the passage leaning against the wall, her eyes closed and half asleep, her mind still bemused with her dreams.

How long she stood there she did not know, but suddenly she heard a noise and pulled herself up with a little jerk thinking it was Rom returning. Even as she did so, the door opened and someone put on the light. It was one of very small power but it was sufficient to illuminate the passage and the people coming in at the door. First there

~315~

was Nada, then to Sally's astonishment there were three strangers – two men and a woman – and finally Ivor. Nada came to a sudden halt, and the others stopped behind her.

"What are you doing here?"

There was no mistaking her astonishment or indeed her consternation.

"I am letting my dog out," Sally answered.

Nada looked at her, then she glanced at the three people who followed her. The men were middle-aged, but the woman was young and rather good-looking. Nada said something in Polish to Ivor and he answered in the same language, then without a word Nada led the way down the corridor, the others following her. Sally watched them go. Only as they disappeared at the turn of the stairs, did Ivor turn back and look at her. There was something in his glance that made her afraid.

She went to the door and called for Rom. He was there a second later and she picked him up in her arms, shut the door and went to her own room. She put him back in his basket, took off her dressing gown and got into bed, but she did not turn off the light. For a moment she wanted to think. Who were these people? Why was Nada bringing them to the house? She looked at her clock. It was nearly a quarter past three.

Slowly she began to understand – Ivor's flights – the identification card that was dropped outside her door on the first night she came – the secrecy about the airfield – Nada's insistence that the children should not explore the cellars. That was where these people must have gone now – the cellars. There had been plenty of talk of people being smuggled into the country, of people being rescued from behind the Iron Curtain that Russia had imposed between Eastern and Western Europe.

What Ivor did was now very obvious and Sally wondered why no-one else had guessed it before, and yet, she asked herself, did no-one else know? Had Sir Guy no inkling? But even as she asked the question, she was certain that he had none, for above all things he was honourable, and she was certain that he would never associate himself with anything that contravened the laws of the land.

Now she understood Nada's suspicions of anyone else coming to The Priory – why she wanted to keep everyone away, why she had been so antagonistic from the moment of her arrival. Everything and everybody who came spelt danger, danger for her, danger for Ivor, danger for the project to which they had pledged themselves. Sally, though she felt it was reprehensible, could not help admiring their pluck and she realised how skilful and clever, or lucky, they had been until then.

There was no doubt at all that Ivor had got experimental facilities from the Government. They were doubtless easy to get and, as he was allowed a private aerodrome and hangar, no-one was likely to worry about him or make too many searching enquiries as to what he was doing. A report every so often would keep the authorities quiet and in the meantime, he flew when he liked. He would go out in the evening and come back in the very early hours of the morning with passengers who, once they were brought into the country were easily concealed after they landed. For one thing he could fly them to other parts of the British Isles, or Nada doubtless had various ways of getting them to York and thence by train to other friends and relations who had been rescued in a similar manner.

Oh, it was clever, very clever! And no-one would have discovered what was going on had not Rom whined at her door and wakened her from her sleep.

Suddenly Sally was rigid. Now she understood something else.

Of course Nada wanted to marry Sir Guy! That would make things doubly sure. As his wife she would have even better facilities for helping her countrymen, and if later on something were discovered, it would be difficult for him to give her away. Besides, she could well understand that Nada loved Sir Guy for himself. Didn't she feel the same way about him?

Sally put her hands up to her face. What was she going to do about all this? For the first time she realised that now she was personally involved. She knew their secret. Nada had always hated her, now that hatred would be even more intensified. What was more, she was Sir Guy's cousin. Were she to be discovered, were other people to come upon the secret, as she, Sally, had done, what a scandal there would be! And Sir Guy himself might be involved – Sir Guy, Lady Thorne and Tony. Who would believe that this had been going on in this quiet, respectable household without anyone having any idea of it? There would be prosecutions and disgrace.

Sally shivered. What ought she to do? She listened. She had expected Nada to come to her room to speak to her but there was no sound of anyone moving about. She thought that the little party must have gone to the cellars to stay there. Perhaps they were discussing what to do, what to tell her. Would they throw themselves on her mercy?

She yawned suddenly. Whatever Nada's decisions, one thing she was certain of at the moment was that she was tired, terribly tired.

She turned out the light and cuddled down under the bedclothes. So many strange secrets had been revealed to her today, but the most important of all, in fact the only one that really mattered, was her love for Sir Guy.

How much she loved him!

15

Sally had been awake for a few minutes when she heard the door open.

"Who is there?" she asked in surprise.

Although she had been listening to the birds outside in the garden, she knew that it was very early and not nearly time yet for Gertrude to call her. In answer someone entered the room, closed the door and crossed to the window. A hand went up to draw back the curtains and then the light came flooding in, that very early pale light that follows the dawn.

Sally sat up in bed in surprise. Nada was in the room. Nada dressed as she had been her the night before, her face grey with fatigue and with deep lines of sleeplessness under her eyes.

"What is it?" Sally asked – and now she was very wide awake, remembering all that had happened last night – and on her guard.

To her surprise Nada smiled.

"I am sorry to wake you so early, Sally," she said, "but I have got so much to tell you and please, I want your help."

"My help?" Sally repeated a little stupidly.

This was somehow the last thing she had expected Nada to ask of her.

Nada nodded.

"Won't you help me?" she asked softly.

"But of course," Sally answered. "What can I do?"

"You are kind," Nada said. "I was sure that you would not refuse and so was Ivor. Will you get up, Sally, because there is no time to be lost?"

In answer Sally threw back the bedclothes and got out of bed.

"What is it?" she asked. "Is someone hurt? One of those people you brought here last night?"

She lowered her voice instinctively as she spoke and Nada replied in lowered tones.

"I will tell you everything later, but please hurry. Do hurry!"

Sally poured some cold water into the old-fashioned, flowered basin in the corner of her room. She washed her face and hands, then quickly slipped into the blouse and skirt in which she had travelled and that she had lain on the chair when she had undressed.

"On the top of my suitcase," she said to Nada, as she turned to the dressing table, "you will find a cardigan. It is just on the top because I wore it in the aeroplane. Will you get it out for me, please? I feel a little chilly."

Nada did as she was asked. Sally had only unpacked a few necessary things the night before and her suitcases were lying open in the corner of the room. Having combed her hair and put some powder on her nose, Sally slipped her arms into the cardigan that Nada held out for her.

"Now I am ready," she said.

"Good!" Nada exclaimed. "You have been quick! Now come with me!"

But suddenly Sally was doubtful.

"One minute, Nada," she said, as the older girl turned towards the door. "If you are in trouble, real trouble, am I the right person to ask? What about Sir Guy? After all, this is his house."

Nada turned and put her hand on Sally's arm.

"Please, Sally," she said. "No-one can do this except you. That is why I have asked you. Later you will understand. Please let me explain in my own way and time."

There was definitely a note of pleading in Nada's voice and Sally capitulated immediately. It was, at least, something that the old antagonism had gone, at any rate for the moment.

She had expected Nada to be angry, had expected fury, temper and a demand for secrecy, but not this, not this appeal for help, this quiet, heavy-eyed Nada who seemed very different from the one she had so often encountered in the past.

"I will do what you want," Sally said and was rewarded by another of Nada's unexpected smiles.

They went down the back stairs. The house was still quiet, the maids had not yet come down to start the day's work. When they reached the ground floor Nada led the way down the large stone steps that led to the cellars of The Priory. Down they went in semi-darkness and came to the labyrinth of small rooms that had so intrigued Nicholas and Prue. They passed through a room filled with lumber and came to a door, which Nada unlocked.

At a first glance there seemed to be no way out of this room, but at the far end were a number of crates, which appeared to have been moved on one side leaving the centre of the wall bare. When Sally followed Nada across the room she thought at first they were facing a blank wall, then she saw the faint outline of a door that must have been concealed for years by being papered and whitewashed by many successive generations. Nada lifted a loose piece of paper carefully and revealed a lock into which she fitted a key that she took from her pocket. She opened the door. It was pitch-dark for a moment. Then Nada switched on a light.

Sally saw that now they were in a passage. At the end of this they came to another door also locked and this, too, Nada opened. Here, for the first time, Sally saw signs of something unusual. There was a trestle table in the middle of the room and on it were the remains of a meal. There was a loaf of bread, a plate, which had contained butter, a few fragments of cold meat and some glasses. Some old, rather dilapidated chairs were arranged round the table.

There was no-one to be seen and now it seemed to Sally that Nada relaxed a little and was not in such a hurry as when she had come to her bedroom. She locked the door behind her, putting the key in her pocket.

"This is where you entertain your visitors?" Sally said, feeling that some comment was required of her.

Nada nodded.

"My countrymen!" she said proudly. "The ones you saw last night, Sally, have suffered greatly. They were very, very happy to reach safety."

"And where are they now?" Sally asked, looking to see if there was another room behind this where they were likely to be.

"Oh, they have already gone," Nada replied. "Ivor has taken them some fifty miles north of here to a place where we have friends. He will make a forced landing – a technical difficulty with his aeroplane, you understand – and while he is seeing to it, his passengers will disappear. It is all very easy."

Sally almost said aloud that that was what she herself had thought must happen but she imagined such a remark might be tactless, so instead she said,

"It is a dangerous job for Ivor and you."

"Very dangerous," Nada admitted, "especially when he is picking up those we wish to save. On this side it would mean prison, but over there it would mean certain death."

"But, Nada, aren't you afraid both for yourself and for him?"

"Sometimes," Nada admitted. "Yes, sometimes I am very afraid, but I have known so much fear. For so many years I have been afraid, perhaps I have grown used to it."

"But – if your visitors have gone," Sally asked suddenly, "how can I help you?"

"Wait," Nada said. "We have further to go."

She went across the room to open yet another door and Sally saw that this, too, had been concealed by packing cases. As Nada moved one of them out of the way, she said,

"When we are not here, everything has to be put back and no traces left in case anyone should by any chance find their way into these quarters. This morning you see us at a disadvantage and you must not be critical."

"It is the last thing I am likely to be," Sally said. "I admire your courage, Nada, but I think it is wrong of you to do it here. If it was found out, it would cause a fearful scandal, which would involve both Lady Thorne and Sir Guy. After all, you bear their name."

Nada had opened the door. She turned and made an expressive little gesture with her hands.

"I am not interested in my English blood. Haven't you realised that by this time?"

Sally felt there was nothing she could say, so she followed Nada through the door and then she gave an exclamation, for here the whole character of the room was changed. The roof, low as it was, was supported on arches. The stones were grey and cold, yet mellow with old age and full of that lovely colour which only comes after centuries of use. The floor was cobbled and light came from tiny, arrow-slit windows, which must have been hardly visible from the outside.

"Yes, the old crypt," Nada said, seeing the astonishment on Sally's face. "This is all that remains of the original Priory and of its chapel. It is lovely, isn't it?"

"It is beautiful," Sally exclaimed. "Does Sir Guy know it is here? Why has he never mentioned it?"

"I don't think anyone knows of it except Ivor and me. I found it by chance when I was searching the cellars for a convenient hiding place. The locks in the doors were rusty and we had the greatest difficulty in forcing them open. Ivor managed that and put in the electric light and we told no-one of what we had found."

"But it is too beautiful to keep to yourself!" Sally exclaimed.

"Well, you have seen it now," Nada said, "but come, this is what I want to show you."

"To show me?" Sally said a little puzzled. "I thought you wanted me to help you."

"To help me too," Nada said. "Come!"

She led the way through the crypt, coming at the end to what seemed to Sally a blank wall. Nada put out her hand and drew a loose stone from the wall. Sally could see nothing but a hole where the brick had been.

"What is there?" Sally sked.

"Look into it and see," Nada suggested.

Sally looked but could still see nothing. Nada smiled.

"Now for a surprise! Stand back!"

Sally did as she was told.

Nada put her hand into the hole and pulled an iron lever, which Sally had not been able to see, at the back of the cavity. There was a queer grinding noise and then a section of the wall swung forward, disclosing a large dark opening.

Sally gave a cry.

"Oh, Nada, I know what it is. It is the secret passage!"

"Yes," Nada said. "It is found! Ivor found it!"

"Oh, how thrilled the children will be!" Sally exclaimed. "Is it possible to use it?"

"I am afraid not," Nada said. "After a very short way the walls have collapsed. Go and look."

Sally stepped forward into the darkness of the hole, put out her hands and touched the sides. They were solid rock. She could just see her way for a yard or so, but immediately ahead of her was a large heap of stones.

Even as she stared at them, the grinding noise was repeated and she was in darkness. She turned round. The door in the wall had closed behind her.

"Nada!" she called. "The door has closed!"

There was only the faint light coming through the hole where the loose stone had been.

"Nada!" she called again. "I can't see! Open the door!"

"I am afraid I can't do that," Nada answered through the aperture.

"What do you mean?" Sally asked, suddenly frightened.

She started to grope her way towards the door. It was only a few feet, but the passageway was uneven and she was afraid of tripping.

"What I say, Sally," Nada said. "You said you would help me and you can help me best by remaining where you are."

"Remaining here?" Sally questioned. "But for how long? I don't understand.

There was a moment's pause as if Nada considered her words, then she said ,

"You are very stupid, Sally. I always thought you were. Surely you didn't imagine for one instant, that Ivor and I, having risked our lives not once but a thousand times, would let our secret be jeopardised because one stupid girl happened on it by mistake. But perhaps it wasn't by mistake! From the moment you came to The Priory you spied on me, you watched me, you pried about the passages."

"Nada, it isn't true!" Sally cried. "Let me out and we will discuss this sensibly."

"No, Sally you have got to remain there," Nada answered.

"You are crazy!" Sally said. "You don't suppose that I won't be missed. People will search for me."

"I don't think they will search very hard," Nada answered. "You see, Sally, I am used to intrigue. I take trouble over what I plan. Already I have written a letter to Guy, saying that, having seen Tony again, you felt you could not remain any longer under the same roof with him. When Gertrude goes to call you, she will find that note on your pillow in the traditional style."

"Nada! It is ridiculous! And there are my clothes! How will you account for them?"

"They will come in very useful for my poor countrywomen," Nada answered. "Some of them have had no new clothes for nine years. Think of it, Sally, nine years, without a new dress, and yours are so pretty."

There was something horrid in Nada's voice now, something that reminded Sally of a cat torturing a mouse before it kills it. Suddenly she was frightened as she had never been frightened before. Putting out her hands straight ahead of her, she stumbled to the door of the passage.

"Listen, Nada," she cried, "let me out of here. You can't mean this as anything but a joke. I will keep your secret if you ask me to but let me out of here. You are frightening me."

"I am sorry for that, Sally," Nada answered, "but I, too, have been frightened. I am sorry in some ways that this had to happen, but you would interfere."

"I didn't, not intentionally," Sally answered, and her voice was desperate, for she knew now that she was pleading for her life. "You can't do this, Nada. Sir Guy will find out."

"You can leave Guy to me," Nada said softly.

"But – it is murder. If you leave me here, I shall die."

"So many of my countrymen and women have died," Nada replied. "I have seen death so often that it no longer shocks me. We thought of other ways, Sally, but this is really the kindest. Goodbye!"

"But, Nada, you can't mean it! *Nada…* "

Sally's voice choked into silence. Nada had suddenly replaced the stone in the hole through which she had been speaking – and there was darkness, complete darkness and a silence that was the more terrifying because the only thing Sally could hear was her own breathing.

"Nada! *Nada!*" she called loudly – and then she screamed.

But even as she did so, she realised how useless it was. The stone walls enclosing her sent her own voice back to her. There was no echo, nothing, only the disturbed silence and the knowledge that no-one in the house would ever hear her.

Sally felt her knees give way under her and she sat down on the stone floor, her back against the door. For a moment she could only think that the whole thing was crazy – not a nightmare, but a kind of waking dream that could exist only in some madman's imagination. Then she remembered it was happening to her.

She sat very still, trying to find some flaw in Nada's plan, trying vainly to see some hope that her story would not be believed, that someone, for some reason would start to search for her, yet even if they did, why should they search for her here? If Sir Guy did not know of the crypt yesterday, it was unlikely that today of all days he would find it. And Nada would be there, ready to put him off, to put every obstacle in his way, to cover her tracks more carefully than she had ever done before.

How clever it was! Sally thought. There was no prospect that anyone would discover the way to reach these unknown rooms and passages. Nada or Ivor must have found the secret by accident. What a perfect hiding place for the visitors who came in Ivor's aeroplane! They could be spirited away as soon as they had been reclothed and given identification cards and ration books and anything else they needed that could be bought illegally and quite easily by those who knew how to go about it.

Yes, Nada was clever, so clever that Sally had no doubt that Sir Guy would believe the ingenious little note, which Gertrude would find on her pillow, and her suitcases would have vanished from her room, as Nada had said. Someone, very likely Nada herself, would have some suggestion that Sally had left The Priory in a hired car or by getting a lift at the drive gate. Anyway, everything would have been thought of, and it might be months before Lynn or Mary would begin to get worried and to ask what had happened to her.

Sally put her hands up to her face. Panic was beginning to creep over her, superseding her reasoning. It might be months, while she lay here dead, with no-one to know, no-one to discover how she had been tricked and murdered by a girl who hated her. And Sir Guy. She thought of him – and now for the first time there were tears of self-pity in Sally's eyes.

"You can leave Guy to me," Nada had said and Sally knew only too well what that meant. Nada was determined to become his wife and mistress of The Priory. Doubtless she would succeed in this as she had succeeded so successfully in other things. Ruthless people usually got what they wanted and Sir Guy would never know, as he walked about the house he loved, that the bones of someone who had loved him lay unburied beneath his feet.

"Oh, Guy, Guy, *save me!*"

Sally said his name aloud, then, as her own words seemed to come back to her, she got up suddenly and beat her hands against the stone.

"Guy! *Guy!*" she called. "Come to me! *Come to me!*"

She called his name until her voice was hoarse. Finally in a passion of weeping she sank down where she stood. She did not know how long she lay there, she only knew at the end that she was exhausted with her weeping and her shouting.

She half lay and half sat on the stone floor, conscious of nothing save her own misery. It seemed to her hours had passed, and yet it might have been only a short while. She sat up, aware that she was hungry.

'I am going to get out of here,' she thought. 'Why should I let Nada do this to me? Why should I just calmly lie down and die?'

Nada had said that the passage had collapsed, but perhaps she was lying as she had lied about other things. With her hands outstretched in front of her Sally groped her way forward. For a few feet she was all right, then she felt in front of her fallen stones. Even as she did so, she struck her head against the roof.

For a moment she was stunned, then putting up her fingers she felt an open cut and blood trickling down on to her cheek. Patiently, she wiped it away and began to feel the stones ahead of her. They were firmly wedged, and their roughness merely broke her nails and hurt the tips of her fingers.

"Oh, what am I to do?" she asked herself out loud – and then she heard her own voice scream and scream again.

'I am going mad,' she thought and was terrified at the very thought. It was bad enough to die, but worse still to be mad before one died.

For a moment desperation was on her. With arms outstretched she felt round and round her prison only to knock her head again and again on the low roof, though not so hard as before, for she was careful now to move slowly. She dropped to her knees. There was nothing she could do, *nothing!*

She must die bravely. Here was the moment when she must be worthy of every fine thought and noble impulse that had ever been hers. This was her moment – her enchanted moment – when she must rise above all self-interest and even above hatred. She threw up her chin proudly, she would try not to be afraid of death even though the pain of dying was hard to bear.

'Perhaps Nada is only frightening me after all,' she thought. 'Perhaps she means to come back and get me to promise that I will never tell what I have seen and this is her way of ensuring that I shall keep silent.'

But she knew that she was only teasing herself with a hope that had no substantial root in reason. Nada would not come back. She must have sat up with Ivor laying her plans very carefully. Sally could imagine them thinking of many different ways of disposing of her, perhaps contemplating the idea of taking her out to sea in the aeroplane and dropping her out, but that might have been dangerous. No, this was the perfect plan, Nada's plan, and there was no escape.

Sally thought of Nada talking to Sir Guy, having breakfast with him, perhaps luncheon by this time. She would be looking up into his eyes, trying to entice him with that strange dark beauty of hers. And Tony would be laughing too, talking to his mother and perhaps saying how silly he thought it was of Sally to run away.

"She seemed quite friendly last night," he would say.

Nada would smooth over their suspicions, if suspicions there were, and gradually they would forget all about her. She would become 'that girl who stayed here for a short time', 'that girl who looked after the children'. They might even forget her name. Sally – what was her name – the girl you took to America, Guy?

And yet would Sir Guy forget her so easily? Sally thought of the strange expression on his face last night. There was something he wanted to say to her, she was certain of that, but now the opportunity was gone for ever.

She would have cried again, wept for her lost life, for the love she might have known, for the happiness that she might have found, but somehow her eyes were dry. Now she was cold, her fingers were numb and her whole body was chilled by the surrounding stone.

She got to her feet, very carefully this time because of her bruised and injured head. But as she moved to ease her cramped limbs, she wondered why she bothered. The quicker she died the better. It was the only thing which she could pray for now, a quick death and one in which she would not suffer much. She sat down again. She wondered how long one could keep alive, for now she felt dreadfully hungry. She had been told that after a day or two of starvation one ceased to want to eat. A day or two! That was horrifying! Perhaps by now it was nearly afternoon. She was not sure. Perhaps only a few hours had gone by since Nada had left her. If she was to linger for days like this…

"Oh, Guy!" she cried to herself.

She thought of how he had looked after her on the aeroplane. He had thought she was too inexperienced to go to New York alone, but surely she was too inexperienced to die in the dark alone like this. Just for once, before she died, she wished she could have felt his arms around her again and known his lips on hers, not in anger and brutality, but in love. She closed her eyes and leaned back against the wall. At least she could pretend to herself that she was in Sir Guy's arms, pretend that his face was close to hers. She had only to move her lips to kiss him.

"Oh, my love, my dear love," she whispered.

She was conscious once again of the terrible cold. She wondered if one died quicker when one was cold or when one was hot. Cold was supposed to preserve bodies. She felt another wave of fear come sweeping over her, blinding her to everything save the desire to cry out, to beat her hands unavailingly against the wall.

"Guy! *Guy!*" she called, "Help! Help! *Save me!*"

It was hopeless and yet she had to do it, but even as she finished calling, she sank down once again on the ground exhausted by the tempest of her own feelings. As she lay there, she was conscious of another sound, a sound she had not heard before. It was a kind of scrambling and scratching sound and in a horror more intense than anything she had ever known previously Sally whispered to herself,

"Rats!"

She was terrified of rats, had always been even as a child, and now the idea that in the darkness they were to be her only companions was almost more than she could bear.

"Rats!" she whispered again.

Still she heard the scrambling sound and screamed a wordless, ghastly scream of sheer terror. Then there came an answer, an answer she had least expected. There was a bark and a whine. For a moment she could hardly believe her ears, then it came again, the little sharp bark of a dog that demands attention.

"*Rom!*"

Sally cried his name and in a moment there was a pushing and a scrambling, a sudden shower of stones and Rom was upon her, his body, warm and excited, was twisting and wriggling in her arms, while his tongue was licking her face and he was uttering the shrill and excited noises that a dog makes when his Mistress has come home.

"Oh, Rom! *Rom!*"

The relief was more than Sally could bear. The tears poured down her cheeks and she laid her face against his short fur and sobbed aloud.

"How did you get here? *Oh, Rom!*"

He licked her face in answer. And now at last the full significance of his appearance made her start up with a little cry.

"Rom, if you can get here, we can get out! You have got to show me the way! The passage is passable! Oh, Rom, show me the way."

He barked as if he understood what she said and then, pulling herself together, Sally said,

"Home, Rom! Take me home!"

He seemed to understand. She heard him run a few feet and then wait for her.

She groped her way to the pile of stones that she had vainly tried to move.

"How did you get through, Rom?" she asked.

She heard him scrambling and then, while she still sought for him blindly, he was on the other side.

"Rom! Rom! *Come back!* I don't know how you got through."

It was as if he understood, for he came back to her – and this time she caught him by the collar and found a small hole halfway up the pile of stones, on the side nearest the solid walk. It was wide enough for Rom, but not nearly wide enough for her. She pushed him through and started to move the stones. It was a laborious job. Stone by stone she pulled them away, more than once dislodging others and once an avalanche of them tumbled forward, grazing her knee and almost crushing one of her feet.

At last she could squeeze and crawl her way through, tearing her skirt and her cardigan as she did so. But she was on the other side! She had learned caution now, for as she walked, she put up her hands to feel the height of the passage, thus saving her head from further blows.

They went a little way and came to what felt like another untraversable wall of fallen stones. The same process was repeated.

When she managed to get through, she was so exhausted that she lay down on the floor of the passage.

"It's no use, Rom," she said. "I can't go any further."

~333~

Her fingers were bleeding and so were her legs. One knee hurt her terribly where the stones had fallen on it and her head was cut and bruised in several places.

In answer Rom licked her face.

"It's no good," Sally said. "You go, Rom! I shall never get through, never."

She heard him patter away a few steps, then she gave a sudden cry,

"Rom!"

Was he literally obeying her and leaving her alone? To her relief she heard him drinking and found a little trickle of water seeping down one side of the passage. Sally collected a little in the palm of her hand and drank it. It had a strange taste, earthy and rather brackish, but it revived her and she was ready to go on again.

The rests she had to take after moving each fresh pile of stones grew longer. Once she lay in a stupor and slept for a while. She woke to find Rom curled up beside her, his warm body against her breasts.

At one part of the passage the air was terribly bad. It was hard to breathe and even Rom moved slowly and, it seemed to Sally, with some difficulty. She could hardly gasp her way through it, but after that she felt that she and Rom were no longer alone. There was somebody else there, a man in a brown habit with a beard and a kindly face. He seemed to understand, to be helping her, to be forcing her forward, awakening her when she wished to lie down and sleep.

"I am so tired," she told him. "I can't go on any further."

But he made her go on and now there was someone else. It was a Knight, the Knight she had known as a child. She called him Sir Guy, though she knew it was not the Guy she loved, but another and older edition of him. He too was helping her. Sometimes it seemed to her that even the stones that she moved with her bleeding hands rolled the more easily because of the two men who assisted her. But all the while she argued with them.

"Let me be! Let me rest – a little while! I will go on tomorrow! I am so cold – and it is so difficult to work when one is cold – tomorrow I shall feel better – I know the air is bad here – but I don't need so much of it when I am sleeping and – Rom can sleep beside me. Oh, let me rest! I am so – tired, so terribly – terribly – tired."

But they would not! They forced her on. Sometimes they seemed to vanish and there was only Rom, whining and barking, running a few steps, then running back to her, licking her face when she fell, recalling her to consciousness.

"I am coming! *I am coming!*" she would say, feeling angry at his very impatience, yet knowing that she must keep on because he desired it of her.

She was growing so exhausted now that she would even try to squeeze herself without moving any stones through the holes that Rom negotiated. Her skirt was in ribbons, her shoulders were bare, bleeding and scarred and she had scraped the skin off both her elbows, but she didn't care. She knew that she had to keep going on until she found the way out.

She passed one more obstacle, fell on the far side of it, and lay there bruised and shattered.

"I can't go – any further," she gasped. "I can't…"

It was then that she saw them very clearly, the monk with his kind eyes and the Knight with his plumed helmet. They were smiling – and she knew that she had won. Yet, bemused, she was not certain what she had won – life or death. She heard Rom bark.

"It's no use, Rom," she tried to tell him, "I am too – tired."

"I can't go any further – I can't…"

But she did crawl forward a few more feet, uncertain whether her eyes were open or shut, for she was used to moving in the darkness. Suddenly she felt herself slipping and then falling forward. She struggled to save herself, was conscious that she clutched at a bush, was blinded by a light and knew with a sudden intake of breath that she was in the open air.

She was in the sandpit! She knew that as she struck the ground and felt sand on her face. Then darkness, merciful and delivering, crept over her and she knew nothing more.

16

Sleep – dreamless, all embracing, all possessing – sleep that left one desiring only sleep and yet again more sleep.

Sally was occasionally conscious of quiet voices, of a firm hand on her wrist, of sudden pains, which were stilled by the prick of a needle in her arm or which vanished in a darkness like sleep, only deeper…

Sometimes she would half wake and know the security and warmth of her bed, the shadowy outlines of the room and the rustle of someone whom instinctively she trusted, before she slept again. In her conscious moments she deliberately sought oblivion, wanting nothing more than the rest for which, it seemed, her whole mind and body ached. And then suddenly and surprisingly she was awake.

She lay with closed eyes, aware that she felt different, knowing, as consciousness returned to her, that there was much she must think about, much she must know, yet savouring deliciously those first moments between sleeping and waking.

There was someone in the room. She could hear movements, soft, gentle movements that nevertheless proclaimed somebody's presence. Very slowly she opened her eyes. The curtains were drawn and the blinds were lowered so that only a very little sunshine and light came into the room, making it dim, shadowy and very cool.

At the furthest window she could see a nurse. She knew now who had ministered to her, whose hands had moved her and who it was whom she had trusted even in her sleep. Sally turned against her pillows so that she might see the nurse's face more clearly, but instantly the woman moved and came across the room to the bed. Sally looked up at her.

It was a sweet face, kind and understanding, with greying hair showing beneath the white cap.

"I thought you might wake this morning," the nurse said, smiling. "Would you like something to eat?"

"Is it morning," Sally asked.

The nurse nodded.

"About ten o'clock – aren't you hungry?"

"I believe I am," Sally said.

She thought for a moment and then smiled.

"I think I should like an egg and a cup of tea, if it isn't too much trouble."

As she spoke, there was an excited noise from the floor. The nurse looked down.

"It's your dog," she said. "He has heard you speak. He has been as good as gold all the time you've been ill, but we couldn't keep him out of the room."

"Oh, can I see him?" Sally asked.

She put out her hands, then stared at them in dismay. Every finger was shrouded in bandages, which reached to her wrist. She was conscious then that there were bandages round her head and found her legs too. The nurse seemed to understand her look of consternation.

"You are much, much better," she said consolingly, "and the bandages will be off very soon. But, before you start asking questions, let me get you some food."

She picked up Rom and put him on the bed.

"Don't let him worry you," she admonished and went from the room.

Rom squirmed against his Mistress in an ecstasy of excitement.

"Rom, dear Rom," Sally murmured, and now everything came flooding back to her mind.

She remembered those awful hours in the darkness of the passage, the way Rom had rescued her, and she remembered struggling with stones, forcing herself through each new obstacle, fighting against the cold and the urgent desire to lie down and drift into unconsciousness. It was difficult to remember what had happened after that. It just seemed endless, the misery and pain of moving the stones, of squeezing through the places where Rom led her.

"Rom, my precious, you saved me!" Sally said out loud.

He wagged his tail as if he understood,

The door opened very cautiously and Gertrude's head appeared. Sally gave a little cry.

"Gertrude! Oh, it is nice to see you!"

"You are better? Glory be to God!" Gertrude exclaimed and came into the room.

"Yes, I'm better," Sally replied. "Have I been ill long?"

"Long enough," Gertrude answered. "When we were all afraid we were going to lose you."

"Gracious! Was it as bad as that?"

Gertrude nodded and Sally pushed herself up a little on the pillows.

"Gertrude," she said, "tell me quickly before Nurse comes back. What has happened?"

Gertrude made no pretence of not understanding Sally's question. She came nearer the bed.

"You're quite certain you're well enough to hear?" she asked. "no-one has been allowed in this room – doctor's orders. He said you were to have absolute quiet and get over the shock."

"I'm feeling fine," Sally said, "and I must know everything – otherwise I shall go mad with curiosity."

"I can understand right enough," Gertrude said.

She leaned against the end of the bed and began to speak quickly.

"It was the gipsy who found you. He heard Rom barking his head off and went to see what was the matter. He picked you up in his arms and brought you straight to the house. It was just before dinner and everyone was in the drawing room. He walks across the lawn with you and in through the French windows. You can't imagine what you looked like, Miss Sally. Half-naked you were and bleeding from every pore. Your clothes were in ribbons and your very shoes torn off your feet.

"I believe her Ladyship was near to fainting at the sight of you, but Sir Guy takes you from the gipsy and carries you upstairs and I meets him in the passage. I got the shock of my life, I'll tell you that. He comes in here and lays you down on the bed, then he just looks at me and says, 'Gertrude, is she dead?'

"I wasn't certain how to answer him, for you were blue with cold and what with the blood and all, if you weren't dead you looked to me as if you weren't far from it. I gets blankets and hot bottles and wraps you up and Sir Guy helps me. While we were doing this, Mr. Tony telephones for the doctor. He tells him what has happened and the doctor comes along here as quick as his car can bring him. As soon as he sees you, he sends a car to fetch a nurse and though I don't hold with them as a rule, she's as nice a woman as one would care to meet. I'll say that for her."

Gertrude paused for a moment, but it was Sally who was breathless.

"Yes, yes, Gertrude, go on! Tell me what happened after that. What did they think had happened to me? How did they think I'd got into such a state?"

Gertrude's story, as she told it to Sally, was a very factual outline of what had occurred, because not only had Lady Thorne, Sir Guy and Bateson talked to her, but she had been long enough in the house to sense when things happened that concerned the family and although it was some time after this before Sally learned all the details, the tale as Gertrude told it that morning, was essentially correct in all that mattered.

After the doctor had seen Sally and done everything possible to revive her and had left nurse in charge, he turned to Sir Guy for some explanation of her extraordinary condition. It had not been easy for Sir Guy or Lady Thorne to explain that Sally, who had been a guest in their house for some time, was supposed by them to have left early that morning and that they had no idea where she had been, or why she should be in such a condition.

Nada was not present during this interview, which took place upstairs after the doctor had left Sally's bedroom. Sir Guy went downstairs and calling Tony from the drawing room where he was sitting with Nada, he suggested to him that they should go to see the gipsy and examine the place where Sally had been found.

Tony agreed, and after suggesting to Lady Thorne that she and Nada should have dinner and not wait for them, Sir Guy and Tony set off through the wood. They found the gipsy in his caravan and went to the sandpit with him. It was still light enough to see the actual spot where Sally had fallen and they realised that she had tumbled down the bank and through the briars which had covered the opening of the passage.

It was then that Sir Guy understood clearly that here was the exit of the hidden passage for which the children had been searching so diligently. The question was why, having found the passage, Sally had hidden herself in it. Discussing every possible reason Sally could have had for this strange behaviour besides the one she had given in her letter, the two men returned to The Priory, had their dinner and then joined Lady Thorne in the drawing room. She was alone because, she explained, Nada was tired and had retired to bed. They told her what they had found.

"Well, then, Sally must, have entered the passage from the house," Lady Thorne exclaimed.

Sir Guy and Tony had already thought of that and they rang the bell for Bateson. When he came, they asked him for the keys of the cellars.

"I have the key to the wine cellar, Sir Guy," he answered, "but Miss Thorne has the other keys."

"What other keys?" Sir Guy enquired,

"The keys of the other rooms, Sir Guy. Miss Thorne insists that they must be kept locked and that no-one must enter them but herself," Bateson replied somewhat sourly, showing that this had obviously been a bone of contention since Nada's arrival at The Priory.

"I will go and ask her for them," Lady Thorne said rising, but Sir Guy put out his hand and stopped her.

"Don't worry, mother, I will get them."

He went upstairs and knocked on Nada's door. When she said, 'Come in', he entered and found her still dressed and sitting at her desk. She looked up in surprise at seeing him.

"I am sorry to bother you, Nada, but I want the keys of the cellars."

He was watching her face as he spoke and just for a moment he saw a flicker of fear in her eyes.

"The keys of the cellars?" she asked slowly, "But Bateson has them."

"Bateson has the key to the wine cellar," Sir Guy replied, "I mean the keys to the other rooms."

Nada was already mistress of herself.

"Oh, you mean the key to the lumber room," she said. "I believe I have got it here somewhere."

She looked round and her eyes fell on the dress that she had worn that day and which was thrown over the back of a chair. It had big patch pockets and she knew that the keys were in it. The key to each room was a different shape and Nada had no need to look at them to know which was which. The difficulty now would be to take the correct one from her pocket without Sir Guy knowing that there were other keys there as well. She looked round the room.

"I think I must have left the key downstairs," she said, "I will go and find it."

"1 think they are here," Sir Guy said quietly.

"What makes you think that?"

"Shall I just say that I have 'a feeling'," he asked.

Nada hesitated, then she was angry.

"Don't be ridiculous, Guy. Why should I say the key is downstairs if it is here?"

"I am quite certain the keys are in this room, Nada," he replied. "Shall I help you to look?"

"I think you are being stupid and rather insulting, Guy. I don't know why."

He seemed very big and very imperturbable as he stood in the doorway. Very patiently he said,

"I suggest you begin looking. I think that is the dress you wore today and I have an idea you used those keys when you were wearing it."

Defeated for the moment, Nada walked across to the dress and put her hand in her pocket. She pulled out the key to what she called the lumber room and handed it to Sir Guy, but unfortunately as she took it from her pocket, it clinked against the others and his ear caught the sound. He took the key from her and then said,

"And the others, please."

"What others?"

"The other keys you have in that pocket."

"They are not the keys of the cellars."

"I think they are," Sir Guy said. "Anyway, I would like them."

"Guy, don't be ridiculous, they are the keys of – well, the keys of the box room – the storeroom beside the kitchen – and…"

"I would like them."

"But why should you want them?"

"Is there any reason why I should not have the keys to my own house."

"None, if you put it like that, but they are quite useless if you want to go into the cellars."

"That remains to be seen," Sir Guy said. "Let me have them, please."

With an ill-grace Nada took the other keys from the pocket of her dress and held them out to him. He put them into his own pocket, then turned and held wide the door.

"I would like you to accompany me."

"But why – and where are you going?"

"To look for the opening of the secret passage," Sir Guy answered.

Nada laughed and it was not a pleasant sound.

"That fairy tale! I thought you were too old to believe in nonsense of that sort."

"Nevertheless, I would like you to accompany me, Nada."

"Oh, very well."

Nada tossed her head and preceded him downstairs.

Tony and Bateson were waiting at the top of the cellar steps.

"I've got a couple of torches," Tony said. "Bateson says there is no electric light in some of the rooms."

"Then we shall certainly need the torches," Sir Guy approved. "Better give me one of them."

He took one from his brother. It was an exceptionally powerful torch of the type that was issued in the war to the Home Guard.

They went down the steps to the cellar. Very carefully they inspected several small rooms which contained old wine cases, ancient trunks and dilapidated and broken furniture. They came eventually to the lumber room.

"This is locked," Tony said as he reached the door at the far end.

"I think I have the key," Sir Guy answered. "Which one is it, Nada?"

He held the three keys out to her. She touched the right one disdainfully without speaking. Sir Guy opened the door and they looked round at the big, low, whitewashed room and at the pile of empty packing cases at the far end.

"There doesn't seem much here," Tony said.

But Sir Guy was watching Nada's face and saw the quickly suppressed expression of relief on her face at Tony's words.

"I think we will just move those packing cases, one never knows," he said quietly.

Bateson and Tony pulled them aside.

"Nothing here," said Tony.

"I wonder," Sir Guy replied, and he began a very careful scrutiny of the wall, using his torch to supplement the somewhat faint light from the electric lamp.

After a moment or two he exclaimed,

"Tony, can you see anything peculiar here?" and he ran the beam of his torch up and down the wall.

Tony looked closely.

"Is that a crack?" he asked, "or the outline of a door?"

"A door, I think," his brother replied, "How do we open it, Nada?"

"How should I know?" Nada snapped, but her voice held a strange note of fear.

Sir Guy started to tear the paper thick with dust and dirt from the wall and after a minute's work the keyhole was revealed. The three men stared at it in silence, which was more expressive than words. Then Sir Guy tried first one key and then the other. The second one fitted and the door swung open. After that it was not difficult to find their way through the passage to the room where Sally had seen the trestle table holding the remains of the meal.

Here things began to happen. Nada had boasted to Sally that everything was always tidied away and the remains of the food had certainly gone, but the plates were there, because in talking to Sally she had cut things rather fine and she consequently had not had time to put them away in a packing case as she usually did. The cups had been left on the table and also the knives and forks. These were surprising, but even more surprising still were Sally's suitcases standing in a corner of the room.

Sir Guy looked at them for a moment without speaking, then he turned to the old butler.

"I think we shall not need you any longer, Bateson," he said.

Bateson turned on his heel almost like a soldier.

"Very good, Sir Guy."

He knew, without it being explained to him, that what was going to happen now was entirely a family affair.

Alone with her conscience, Nada began to break down and it was only a question of time before voluntarily she led them into the beautiful crypt and showed them the movable stone, the iron lever and the ancient door that led into the secret passage. For the second time that day, and now without bravado or a note of triumph, she told of how she and Ivor had rescued his countrymen and brought them to the safety and security of England.

While she was talking, Sir Guy and Tony listened gravely and when she had finished making a clean breast of the whole story they were silent.

"Well?" she asked at length. "What are you going to do with me?"

But they could not answer her, for they did not know themselves.

When they finally went upstairs, it was late. Lady Thorne had gone to bed and they did not disturb her. Sir Guy sent Nada to bed while he and Tony sat up till the early hours of the morning talking and arguing, trying to find a way out of the hideous tangle in which Nada had involved them all.

When at last wearily they climbed the stairs to their own bedrooms, they had found no solution and had only come to the conclusion that they must talk it over with Ivor in the morning. But by the morning Nada had taken things into her own hands. She and Ivor were gone before the household was awake. She left a letter for Sir Guy in which she said that she intended to marry Ivor and would therefore forfeit her British nationality and become what she had always believed herself to be – a Pole. They were going to live in Eire and they would continue to work for their own country in every way that remained open for them. They would not trouble the Thorne family again and she added shrewdly that she thought it unlikely that the Thorne family would wish to trouble them. In connection with that she mentioned that she had taken with her, as a wedding present, the balance of the housekeeping money which amounted to a little over fifty pounds, and she was certain that Sir Guy would not begrudge her that. She had also taken as many of her own belongings as it was possible to get into the aeroplane and, if possible, she would send for the others at a later date.

Sir Guy read the letter and laughed. It was so like Nada, and he could not help admiring her courage in making the best of what was really a very bad situation. In other words, as he said to Tony, she had got away with it.

They decided that they would tell Lady Thorne nothing about the strange visitors who had been brought to The Priory from another land and would merely say that Nada had shut Sally in the crypt because she was jealous, meaning to let her out some time later, but that Sally had been clever enough to escape through the secret passage.

She had escaped and that was all there was to it. It was best not to contemplate what would have happened otherwise. Both Tony and Sir Guy agreed on this point and it only remained for Sally to be generous over the agonies she had suffered and the injuries she had sustained.

*

Gertrude had just reached the end of her story when she heard the nurse coming down the passage.

"She'll scrag me if she knows I've been talking all this time," Gertrude said hastily. "Shut your eyes, Miss Sally, and I hopes to goodness I haven't tired you."

"You haven't," Sally answered in a whisper.

She closed her eyes obediently, while Gertrude hurried to the washstand and was busy emptying a basin as Nurse came into the room. She brought a tray to the bedside. Sally opened her eyes and looked up.

"Oh, what a lovely breakfast," she exclaimed. "I shall eat it all."

She did – and then, unaccountably, she felt tired again and slept through the morning and well into the afternoon. But after tea she was fresh enough to lie thinking over what Gertrude had told her, wondering about many things and feeling most of all a sense of relief and satisfaction at the thought that Nada had gone for ever. She had not forgotten the pain she had known when Nada had told her through the grille that she could leave Sir Guy to her.

"Oh, Guy, *Guy*," Sally whispered to herself – and she knew now that she must get well quickly because she wanted so much to see him again.

Yet she had to learn patience in the days that followed. Lady Thorne came to see her every day, but there was no suggestion that Sir Guy might visit her. Tony had gone back to Paris, she learned, but he wrote to her and even sent her a postcard with a ridiculous picture of a *Can-Can* dancer on it, which Lady Thorne was certain must have shocked the local Post Office.

At every knock on her door and every time nurse said, "Would you like to see a visitor?" Sally's heart leapt, but Sir Guy never came.

The bandages were taken from her fingers, her nails were still very short, but they were growing again and the cuts had practically disappeared. Those on her forehead were better too. One of them was crimson against her white skin, but the others were hidden by her hair and could not be seen. The injuries to her knees were the worst, but as the doctor said jokingly,

"You won't notice the marks even through an expensive pair of nylons! And now," he added, "what about getting up?"

"Oh, may I?" Sally asked. "I'm tired of staying in bed."

"My job is finished," he told her. "You are convalescent now and I am taking Nurse away from you tomorrow. All you have to do is to eat a lot, get as much fresh air as you can and do exactly as you like. That's what the doctor orders."

Sally laughed.

"What a perfect prescription!"

"I thought you would think so," he said. "Well, get up this afternoon, but don't blame me if your legs feel like cotton-wool. You had better go back to bed for dinner, and you will want to, I promise you that."

"It will be lovely to be up," Sally cried.

Nurse helped her to dress after luncheon and chose her prettiest frock of white crepe with a pattern of pink-and-blue flowers on it, which had been part of her trousseau.

"I don't want you to go downstairs the first day," she said, "I want you to sit in the window and enjoy the sunshine."

"That will be lovely," Sally agreed.

As the doctor had said, her legs did feel like cotton-wool, but otherwise she felt very bright and clearheaded. It was lovely to look down on the garden, to see the roses in full bloom, to look across the lawns to where the woods lay green and verdant and to see beyond them the moors climbing upwards towards the sky.

Nurse had gone from the room and she was alone when there came a knock at the door.

"Come in," she said, expecting Lady Thorne, but when she turned with a smile to welcome her hostess, she saw Sir Guy standing in the doorway.

Her heart gave a little frightened leap and then, as he closed the door behind him and came towards her, she felt it beating almost agonisingly quickly beneath her breast. She had forgotten how tall and broad-shouldered he was, and how grey his eyes. He said nothing until he was standing close beside her, then in a voice strangely gentle he asked,

"You are better?"

Sally nodded her head. Somehow for the moment she dated not trust her voice.

"I'm glad. We have all been very anxious about you."

"Have you?"

Unconsciously she made the question a personal one – and then having asked it, was surprised at her own courage.

Sir Guy answered her gravely.

"I have worried about you all the time, Sally."

She felt herself blushing and, afraid of her own weakness, sank down upon the cushioned seat. He too sat down nearer than she expected and then unexpectedly reached out and took her hand in his. He opened her fingers and she saw that he was looking at the scars on them. At his touch she felt her whole body tingle, the same strange sensation that she had known once before in the library making her quiver and tremble – and yet it was not with fear.

"Poor little hands!" Sir Guy spoke very softly – and then he said suddenly in a voice deep and hoarse, "Sally, I have got a great deal to say to you. Are you strong enough to hear it?"

"Strong enough?"

She looked up at him and saw something in his eyes that held her spellbound. Her lips parted, her breath came a little quicker.

"Yes, strong enough," he repeated. "I can wait if you would rather I did not talk to you now, but, Sally, I have waited a long time."

She was shivering now, shivering with some delicious excitement that seemed to run through her veins like fire. Instinctively her fingers tightened on his and she held on to them as a child might hold on to someone older and able to protect her.

"Oh, please," she said, "please tell me now."

"May I?" he asked. "Oh, my darling, I love you so much."

The words seemed to burst from his lips and then, as Sally gave a little gasp, he said,

"But before I say anything I must ask your forgiveness and, Sally, you must try to understand, for only by understanding could you ever forgive me."

"Forgive you?" Sally asked, bewildered.

"Let me explain!" Sir Guy said – and though he still held her hand, it seemed to Sally that the lines on his face deepened and he looked as she had so often seen him look – detached and cynical.

"When I was young," he began, "I fell in love with someone very beautiful. I thought she was in love with me

– at least for a time we were very happy together. Then she grew strange, moody and restless and I could not understand what the matter was until one night, as we walked in the garden after dinner, she told me what was wrong. She loved me, as she always had, with a deep affection and a friendship that had been ours since childhood but she was madly, crazily attracted physically by someone else – a man – with whom she had nothing else in common."

Sally drew in a deep breath, for she knew she was hearing the real story of Lady Beryl.

"I argued with her," Sir Guy went on, "I pleaded with her and begged her to be sensible for her own sake if not for mine. She was very frank with me, she told me she could no more give up this man and the passion he aroused in her, than a drunkard could give up drink. That night she ran away with him."

Sir Guy paused and Sally gave a little exclamation of sympathy.

"How awful – for you!"

Sir Guy did not look at Sally, but his fingers tightened on hers until his grip was almost painful.

"That was enough to make me wary and suspicious of women and shortly afterwards I was forced to help Tony out of a very unsavoury mess in which he had involved himself. There is no reason for me to go into details, sufficient to say that the girl was the wrong sort – beautiful to look at and rotten to the core. She was unfortunately one of many. Tony seemed to have a genius for landing women whose bodies were the only beautiful things about them. I began to think that all women were alike, to believe that a pretty face was only a mask to hide the hideousness of lust."

"Oh!" Sally breathed.

"I don't want to shock you," Sir Guy said, "but I do want you to understand my feelings and why I thought what I did when I saw you first on the doorstep in Hill Street at six o'clock in the morning."

Sally took her hand from his and raised it to her cheeks.

"You mean…" she faltered, "that you thought – that Tony and I…"

"Yes," Sir Guy answered, "I thought that, and although I had never seen you before, it hurt me to think such things, because you were so lovely and so very young."

"How could you?" Sally asked, the colour flaming into her cheeks, then ebbing away to leave her curiously pale.

"I've asked myself that same question a thousand times since I knew the truth," Sir Guy said, and his voice was raw. "I've lain awake night after night since you've been ill, cursing myself for the fool I was – but the poison had gone deep. I should have known that innocence in your face could never be assumed. I should have known that lost 'very young' look that came into your eyes when I was rude and cruel was the true you, the real, perfect, untouched Sally that only my brain refused to acknowledge – for my heart knew the truth."

Sir Guy bent forward and very gently drew Sally's hands from her face and took them in his again.

"Listen to me," he said, and then, as her long eyelashes veiled her downcast eyes, he added,

"Look at me, Sally."

For a moment she did not obey him. Then, as if some magnetism compelled her against her will, her eyes were slowly drawn to his and were held spellbound by the expression on his face.

"My heart told me the truth," he said again very softly. "I fell in love with you, Sally, when I saw you sitting disconsolate and bewildered in your wedding dress. I loved you when I brought you back here, when I watched you with the children, when I saw your affection for my home and for my mother. But I fought against my convictions,

~353~

trying to persuade myself that the evidence of my own eyes proved that you were like all the others, weak and vulnerable where your desires were concerned. Yet all the time, in spite of what I tried to make myself believe, I loved you, Sally, as I love you now, as I will love you all my life and for all time."

It seemed to Sally that the sound of Sir Guy's voice saying the words she had most longed to hear was too much to be borne. She felt the glory and the wonder of it blind her and she shut her eyes and turned away her head while the world rocked dizzily around her.

Sir Guy's voice died away. Sally made no movement. Suddenly he got to his feet, his face white, his eyes very dark.

"Perhaps I have spoken too soon," he said. "I have loved you so much and suffered so deeply these last few days that I had forgotten how badly I have treated you in the past. I must give you time to think, to get to know me. Perhaps then, if I am lucky, you will learn to care for me a little."

He walked across the short length to the window and stood looking out, his back to Sally.

"Do you think…" he began, and there was a note of pleading in his voice that Sally had never heard there before. "Do you think you could ever learn to love me?"

She could resist him no longer. A little unsteadily Sally stood up. At the slight movement he turned. She had been going to him, but he met her halfway. He looked at her wide and shining eyes, at her parted lips, and he put his arms round her. For a long moment neither of them spoke. At last, hoarsely, and in a voice broken with emotion, Sir Guy said,

"Answer me, Sally! Oh, my darling, *answer me!*"

"I – love – you, Guy. *I – love – you.*"

Sally's voice was hardly more than a breath between her lips, but he heard her.

At last she knew his kisses once again, kisses such as had been hers once before, but with such a difference. Fierce, burning, passionate, they utterly possessed her and yet the fire in them was divine, for it joined them in a unity which made them one – a man and woman who loved each other to the exclusion of all else and all the world.

"Oh, Sally, *Sally,*" Sir Guy cried – and his lips were buried in the softness of her neck as he lifted her high in his arms.

Printed in Great Britain
by Amazon